SHADOW
OF THE CROSS

David S. Britton

New Generation Publishing

This novel is dedicated to the memory of the **Rev. Professor Charles Kingsley Barrett** (1917 to 2011), my Theology Tutor at the University of Durham, who introduced me to the Gospel according to St. Mark and taught me to think for myself when it came to theological ideas and beliefs. May his soul rest in peace.

Control of the Church passed to the apostles, together with the Lord's brother James, whom everyone from the Lord's time till our own has called the Righteous, he drank no wine or intoxicating liquor and ate no animal food; no razor came near his head; he did not smear himself with oil, and took no baths. He alone was permitted to enter the Holy Place, for his garments were not of wool but of linen. He used to enter the Sanctuary alone beseeching forgiveness for the people, so that his knees grew hard like a camel's from his continually bending them in worship of God and beseeching forgiveness for the people. Because of his unsurpassable righteousness he was called the Righteous and the Bulwark of the People.

Eusebius: **The History of the Church**: 23.11

Acknowledgements

Sources used, consciously or unconsciously.

ALLEGRO, John: The Dead Sea Scrolls.

BAIGENT, Michael, LEIGH, Richard and LINCOLN, Henry: The Holy Blood and the Holy Grail.

BARRETT, C.K.: Mark.

ERIKSON, Steven: The Malazan Books of the Fallen. *(series)*

EUSEBIUS: The History of the Christian Church.

FULLER, Reginald H.: The Parables of Jesus. *(As well as other books on the Parables and Miracles of Jesus by a number of different authors.)*

GOLDMAN, James: The Lion in Winter. *(film)*

HAMPSON, Frank: The Road of Courage *(Eagle Comic serial)*

JOHN: The Gospel According to St. John.

JOSEPHUS, Flavius: The Wars of the Jews.

LLOYD-WEBER, Andrew: Jesus Christ, Superstar *(rock opera and film)*

LUKE: The Acts of the Apostles.

LUKE: The Gospel According to St. Luke.

MARK, John: The Gospel According to St. Mark.

MATTHEW: The Gospel According to St. Matthew.

MORISON, Frank: Who Moved The Stone?

PAUL: Letters to St. Timothy (1 & 2) and St. Titus.

POTTER, Dennis: The Son of Man. *(play)*

RYAN, Cornelius: The Longest Day. *(film)*

TURNER, H.E.W.: Jesus, Master and Lord.

WALLACE, Lew: Ben Hur. *(film)*

Contents

PART ONE: BAR MITZVAH

PART TWO: THE NORTHERN CAMPAIGN

PART THREE: SEVEN DAYS IN APRIL

PART FOUR: EPILOGUE

List of main characters

(Biblical versions of names, where different, in Italics)

The family of Yeshua

Yeshua *(Jesus of Nazareth)*, (also called Yeshua Bar Yusuf, Yeshua Bar Abraham and Yeshua the Nazirite): The central character of the story.

Abraham Bar Jochanan (also called Abraham Bar Abbas): Yeshua's birth father.

Mariam *(Mary)*: Yeshua's mother.

Yusuf *(Joseph)*: Yeshua's stepfather, Mariam's second husband.

Jacob *(James)*: Yeshua's oldest brother. (Yeshua's other siblings were Simeon, Judah and Mariam.)

Mariam *(Mary)*, **Martha, and Lazarus**: Cousins of Mariam, living at Bethany.

Mariam *(Mary)*: the wife of Yeshua.

Jochanan *(John)*: Yeshua's older son. He was, traditionally, the source of the Fourth Gospel in the New Testament.

Jacob *(James)*: Yeshua's younger son.

Jochanan *(John the Baptist)*: Yeshua's cousin, son of Elizabeth and Zechariah the priest.

(Note that **Mariam** *(Mary)* was a very common name among Jewish females in first century Palestine. You will come across a number of different bearers of the name in the book.)

The other disciples
The former followers of Jochanan
Thomas
Philip
Judah Ish Kerioth *(Judas Iscariot)* Ish Kerioth

means Man of Kerioth.

Simeon the Rebel *(Simon the Zealot)* The Zealots were the Jewish Resistance.

Thaddeus

Chosen by Yeshua

Simeon the Fisherman *(Simon Peter)*: (also known as Simeon Bar Zebediah and later as Cephas)

Andreas *(Andrew)*: Simeon's brother.

Matthaus *(Matthew)* – the former tax gatherer and traditionally the writer of the First Gospel in the New Testament.

Bartholomew (also known as the Son of Ptolemy)

Judas

Other followers of Yeshua

Marcus *(John Mark)* - See the note at the end of the Novel, page 419.

Julia: his sister

Salome: a former member of Herod's court.

Members of the Resistance

Judah the Galilean

Judas Bar Micah (also known as Judas Bar Abbas)

Hezekiah

Gaius

Enos

Members of the Jewish Sanhedrin

Annas: the former High Priest

Yusuf Caiaphas: the High Priest, son in law of Annas.

Gamaliel: leader of the Pharisees

Hosea: leader of the Sadducees

Zechariah: Sadducee, member of Caiaphas' cabinet.

Amos: Sadducee, member of Caiaphas' cabinet

Yusuf: Pharisee, sent to spy on Yeshua

Moshe: Pharisee, sent to spy on Yeshua

Nicodemus: Pharisee, secret supporter of Yeshua

Yusuf of Aramathea *(Joseph of Aramathea)*: Pharisee, secret supporter of Yeshua.

The Herodians

Herod Antipas: Tetrarch of Galilee and Peraea (Trans Jordan)

Aretas: King of Arabia Felix, Antipas' first father in law

Herod Philip: Tetrarch of Gaulitis (the northern lands), brother of Antipas

Herodias: divorced wife of Philip married to Antipas.

Salome: daughter of Philip and Herodias, stepdaughter and niece of Antipas

Archelaus: the original Tetrarch of Judaea and Samaria

The Romans

Tiberius: the Roman Emperor (called Gaius by Pilate)

Pontius Pilate: (also known as Publius – to Tiberius; and Gaius – to Antipas) the Procurator of Judaea and Samaria

Julia: Pilate's wife, related to the Roman Empress.

Marcus Antonius: Tribune in command at Caesarea.

Lucius Trebonius: Tribune in command at Jerusalem

Julius (1): Pilate's slave master.

Julius (2): Centurion in command at the Crucifixion.

Quintus: Senior Jailor at the Antonia in Jerusalem.

Frontiers of Herod the Great's Kingdom.
Lands of the Tetrarchs.

Antipas

Archaelaus – later Roman

Philip

Palestine in
30 AD

13

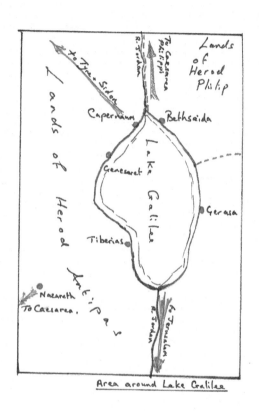

Area around Lake Galilee

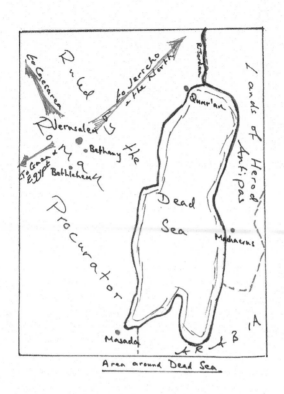

Area around Dead Sea

PART ONE

BAR MITZVAH

Child, why have you treated us like this? Look, your father and I have been searching for you in great anxiety.

Gospel according to St. Luke, chapter 2, verse 48

Chapter 1

Bar Mitzvah

Jerusalem, 7AD

"Mother, what is a bastard?"

Mariam was surprised by the quietly delivered question, but thought she knew why Yeshua asked it. In what she hoped was a stern voice, she said,

"Your father called you a bastard, Yeshua, because he was very angry about your behaviour and frightened by what might have befallen you."

"I know that," the boy responded stolidly.

Small, slim and agile, he was neatly dressed in a white tunic, and his short-cut black hair was combed back smartly.

"I was wrong and I'm sorry for what I did, I was interested in what the priests were saying and I asked questions, that's all. I completely forgot about both of you. Yusuf was right to punish me."

And here Yeshua shuddered as he relived that painful moment of chastisement, not long delivered, for going missing from his parents' side for quite some time.

"I wish he hadn't publicly shamed me though."

Early in the day, both Mariam and her husband still held misgivings about bringing Yeshua to the Temple of King Herod for his Bar Mitzvah, for they knew how unpredictable their twelve year old could be. But despite their justified reservations, Yusuf had concluded the journey from Bethlehem to Jerusalem should be made, as this was a very important day in the lad's life.

Said Yusuf, in his no nonsense voice,

"It is right Yeshua should become a man at the Temple. He is your first born."

This as ever, peeved Mariam, even if she did not remonstrate with Yusuf over it.

Yeshua had younger brothers and a sister, all fathered by her first husband, whose name was Abraham, who was presumed dead following his disappearance in the Judaean wilderness seven years ago; for no person survives in that place for long, being prey to dehydration, exhaustion, wild animals, or even the devils Mariam believed haunt the desert.

Yet, when, for the sake of her children, she had taken distant cousin, Yusuf, for her spouse three years after Abraham's disappearance, she had expected he would embrace her offspring. He hadn't. Plainly it was all a bit much for him presently, and she had to live with that. That and the fact that she and Yusuf were not in love with each other: and she, in her heart, still doubted Abraham was dead and so still loved him, and did not mourn him.

But, as things were, Mariam had now to obey Yusuf. That was why she, he and Yeshua were in Jerusalem today, while the younger children had been left with Mariam's cousin, also called Mariam, who lived with her sister, Martha, and her widowed brother, Lazarus, at nearby Bethany, not far from the Mount of Olives.

Mariam was feeling particularly tired and dusty from travelling, and the heat. The still young looking woman shook out her shoulder length raven hair, and ran her hands down her ankle length, pale blue dress (attire befitting a thirty years old married woman) in readiness for the final stage of the journey, the climb up the Sacred Mount.

"There's quite a crowd, but, once through them, we

shall be at the Temple," Yusuf told Mariam and Yeshua, perhaps a little unnecessarily. "Let's move!"

And he acted on his words. Soon they were at the imposing gates of King Herod's Temple, dominated by its golden eagle, the symbol of Roman power.

"That eagle cost so much Jewish blood, not twenty years back, when the old king crushed the rebellion that its presence caused," Yusuf dared whisper to Yeshua as they passed under it, into the great courtyard. Here Jews and foreigners met and traders sold animals for sacrifice (converting Roman coins into Jewish ones for the purpose and being cheated in the process; so much protesting at every exchange).

Above all this, on the steps of the Roman fortress which overlooked the Temple, Roman soldiers were on guard, ready to quell with spear and shield should noisy chaos descend into riot and revolt against Rome. Yusuf, an orthodox Jew, inwardly balked at the sight of these Pagan, Roman soldiers supervising Jewish worship; evidence of Roman political power and their control of his, and God's country.

At first everything was all right for Yusuf and his family. They bought two doves as offerings and presented them as sacrifices to the priest on duty. Yeshua read well a section of the Torah and answered one or two simple questions about Jewish history correctly. Everyone looking on clapped and congratulated the new adult, and Yeshua graciously received their best wishes.

They had then to set smartly about getting to their overnight stay in Bethany.

As on the way in, the tall burly figure of Yusuf, whose size practically dwarfed his wife, now concentrated to cleave a passage through the sea of people, like a battleship, pushing the water before it.

While he and Mariam instinctively walked apart

(looking more like friends than husband and wife). Yeshua followed behind them, as was right and proper.

His bright, brown eyes shone as he glanced this way and that, taking in the many sights and sounds with much interest.

In the course of turning round, he saw a group of boys sitting around a rabbi under a colonnade set to one side of the courtyard; and without saying anything to Mariam or Yusuf, he strolled over and joined the class, led by his curiosity.

When he remembered his parents, he swung about to spot them, but they were gone. He sought them for a bit, without any luck. Frightened now, he went back to the group gathered about the rabbi and this time he seated himself right with them. He reasoned his parents would return for him, and meantime he felt himself safe from harm. Eventually, he forgot why he was sitting there and became absorbed in the conversation, asking questions and impressing the old man with his understanding, exceptional in one so young.

Needless to say, Yusuf and Mariam did not notice Yeshua peel off; neither had thought to look back from time to time to check their child was following them. They simply assumed he was, because he normally did.

It was only when they had passed the city gates and Yusuf thought to point out to Yeshua that these gates were known as the Eye of a Needle because of its small size, that they became aware he was missing. And they were afraid - Jerusalem really was no place for a small country boy to be on his own.

"You should have been watching your son's movements; you know his wilful nature," a fretting Yusuf scolded his wife.

Mariam retorted, "Yusuf, as the man who expects to be thought of as the head of the family you should have been keeping an eye out for him too. It's time you did act like the head."

"Us arguing over who is to blame for his going missing isn't going to find him," replied Yusuf stiffly. "We have to retrace our steps and find him if we can."

Everyone knew how, thousands of years before, a boy named Yusuf had been sold by his brothers as a slave and taken to Egypt; and Rome is much further away than Egypt!

In gathering alarm, they began backtracking, stopping and asking passers-by if they had seen a small boy, obviously lost and on his own. Alarm was replaced by panic as the answer was always 'no'. They called on shops, visited side alleys, and even checked the hotels.

"No Madam," "Sorry Madam," "Twelve years old you say? No, can't say I have." "I'm sorry; I haven't seen him."

Mariam never realised there were so many different ways of saying "No".

Some did wish them luck. Others showed in their look what they thought of two parents who could leave their son behind in such circumstances.

Mariam began to weep.

Yusuf, who had no time for such unhelpful weakness, eventually growled, "I've had enough of this."

"Don't say it's my problem and you're going to leave me on my own to look for my precious son?"

That comment startled Yusuf.

"No Mariam, I would never do that. I mean, we'll have to go back to the Temple and ask the priests to help organize a search across the city."

In a state of heightened anxiety they duly arrived at the Temple, and once through the gates began to scan the scene for a priest to approach for help.

Yusuf's eye first caught sight of those Roman

guards, and, in turning away, so as not to look any longer at them, suddenly he saw Yeshua sat contentedly, cross-legged under a colonnade, talking with a rabbi.

"Mariam," he called to her, for she was looking in the opposite direction.

Mariam followed Yusuf's pointing finger and saw her son. She ran towards him, her arms outstretched, smiling widely as she went, in utter relief.

Yusuf responded very differently. He strode furiously over to the errant boy, and hauled him to his feet.

"I apologize for my child's behaviour," he said fiercely to the rabbi.

"He should not be here. We did not know where he was. Thank you for caring for him."

Then, right in front of all, he bent Yeshua over his knee, bared the boy's behind, and gave him a sound spanking.

"Don't you dare do that again you little bastard – wandering off!"

He synchronized his rebuke with each slap.

Mariam's motherly side wanted the punishment to cease but understood Yusuf was being head of the house for once, in disciplining a transgressor. With pride, she noted that her son did not cry, although he came near to doing so. She thought the humiliation of his near nakedness hurt him more than the blows he was receiving: as Yusuf intended, she realised.

Once back on the dusty road, away from the temple, Yusuf was quiet, a man in serious thought. He understood he was failing as a husband and a father, and for that he felt guilt and shame; though unwilling to admit that even to himself. The truth was that he did care about the children but he could not find love for them; nor bear to make love to Mariam – Abraham's

24

shadow lay between them.

Abraham was Yusuf's dearest friend, and he was feeling it curiously difficult to accept his being dead – which, of course, is something he shared with Mariam, did he but know it – for the man had always seemed larger than life. And it was out of loyalty to his late, lamented companion that Yusuf had married Mariam. He had also had to suffer the passing of his own beloved spouse.

Right now, on the road, Yusuf felt a compulsion to speak to Yeshua who was walking behind him, with his mother, whose brown, still youthful, face displayed both puzzlement and relief; the love between them was obvious. An enviable state of being between the two of them, if very disconcerting for Yusuf, who was rapidly concluding he ought to tell Yeshua that he did love him and had hated what he had done to him - easier thought than done, though.

"I know it's shameful for a man to be seen naked," he told Yeshua, whose full, as yet maturing face was stubbornly defiant, and still silently complaining of his punishment, causing Yusuf to be more gentle in his manner.

"But, you must understand, if we had not found you, you would have been stripped naked by strangers for all to see and displayed for sale in the slave market, and possibly sent to a distant land."

Satisfied Yeshua had taken in his words, he found he could say no more, and promptly turned around to continue to lead the tiny procession out of the city, on the road to Bethany.

Yeshua was used to being hurt emotionally by Yusuf because he admired him for being so strong, but Yusuf seemed not to care for him at all. Now Yeshua showed emotion and reacted by merely returning to speaking with his mother on the matter that actually bothered him more.

"It's not what Yusuf said to me, mother, when beating me. It's more that all the boys in Bethlehem, and many of the adults, call me a bastard. What does the word mean? And why do they call me that? After all, I haven't angered them in the way I did you and Yusuf."

"Oh, I wish you would call Yusuf 'father'. It's not right to call him Yusuf."

Mariam was trying to avoid answering Yeshua: she really did not want this conversation; one that she had dreaded for ages.

"Why should I call him father? I do not feel I am his son," Yeshua came back heavily.

"He does not call me his son. He always says I'm your son. I want to know what a bastard is, mother. Please tell me."

Mariam sighed in resignation.

"A bastard, Yeshua, is someone who does not have a father."

Yeshua laughed.

"That's ridiculous mother. Everyone has a mother and a father!"

"That's true, son. You do have a real father, like everyone else."

Mariam stopped and lovingly put her arms around Yeshua, to have him face her.

"The point is, Yeshua, not everyone knows who their birth father actually is. That might be because the father was not married to the child's mother. Or......," and here she paused, feeling ashamed even to mention such a possibility, "......Or the mother has slept with so many men that she does not know which one had fathered the child."

"Did you do that?" Yeshua asked, innocently.

Mariam blushed. She'd more than half expected that

question, for many men in Bethlehem had suggested the same thing to Yusuf when he agreed to marry her.

"No, son," she answered calmly "And don't let anyone tell you that is what happened."

With that said, she released Yeshua from her grasp, and the two ran to catch up with Yusuf.

"What did happen then, mother?"

Yeshua persisted with his questioning, when they were again walking behind Yusuf.

"The other boys are not called bastards – only me. Why am I different?"

Mariam didn't answer.

"Mother, why am I different? Did you not hear my question?"

Mariam still did not respond; she was thinking. For years she had rehearsed what she would say. Only she had not expected it to happen this soon, unaware of the insults her son had to endure.

"Mother?"

"This is not the time and place for this conversation, Yeshua. Ask me another time. When we're alone – you, me and your father."

The crowd in the street was jostling against the three of them, surrounding them with the reek of bodies in the heat of the sultry sun

Yusuf continued to use his stout frame to force their way through the narrow streets, and some of the horde, in a babble of different tongues, complained to him for doing this. The streets suddenly seemed full of menace, particularly to Mariam. Most of the people around her were going about their lawful business, of course, but some might have been otherwise; you could never be sure in Jerusalem.

Then the family were through the throng, and beyond the city gates and the border guards. But if

Yusuf, for one, was hoping for fewer folk about he was in for a surprise: the road was not clear ahead, not today.

"This is ridiculous!" he mumbled to himself, as he strained his eyes over the heads of others to see the cause of this unwelcomed blockage.

About 100 yards ahead a small unit of Roman soldiers was escorting a man who was bent double by the weight of a wooden beam slung across his shoulders, to which his wrists had been tied. Being a carpenter by trade, Yusuf knew just how heavy such a cross beam was to bear.

"You poor sod," he thought, "I wander what you've done to deserve this treatment."

And he caught his breath as the man stumbled and there came the crack of the whip as it was brought down upon the prisoner's back.

"What is going on, Yusuf?" asked Mariam.

"There's a crucifixion party ahead."

"Oh, my! Can't we go back and leave by another gate, for the sake of Yeshua?"

"No. The crowd behind us is too great. There's nothing for it. We must move on. The boy is going to have to witness it.......become a man today in more ways than one."

They continued to plod along, moving ever closer to the execution site, not that far ahead, Yusuf could see

The mood of the crowd was sombre and angry. Some amongst them shouted in protest. And Yusuf overheard someone say the convicted man was a well-known political activist, a nationalist, who in some way had offended both the Roman Governor and the High Priest. None dare to try to save the prisoner, recognizing Roman justice was brutal, abrupt, arbitrary, allowing itself to show no weakness in the face of opposition, though the guards did permit muted protest

- words hurt no one, it seemed.

Within thirty minutes the execution site was reached, a small hill beside the road; and the guards made the following crowd stop to watch what would happen next.

The convicted man was stripped naked and exposed to the crowd, who gasped in anger at the sight of the criss-cross of bloody lines on the wretch's back. Lashing whips had torn at the skin.

"Why do they do that?" asked an appalled Yeshua.

"The Romans first flog those they are about to crucify," Yusuf told him.

"Why is he naked?" Yeshua asked.

"Crucifixion is intended to be a lesson as well as a punishment. Crucifixion is supposed to humiliate before it kills."

"Like you humiliated me today?"

"Exactly," Yusuf replied. "In future honour and obey your father and mother, like it says in the Torah, or you may end up like this man."

Yeshua shuddered at the prospect, and, for once, resisted the temptation to say, "But you're not my father".

A Jewish woman approached the convict, who was standing helpless alone, and the guards allowed him the drink she offered him; even permitting the condemned man to be with her for a few minutes. Then she went back into the crowd.

"What was that about?" said Yeshua, addressing Yusuf.

"That would have been wine that was drugged, to enable the man to take the pain of the nailing and suspension, shortly."

"I don't know what that means."

"You will. Wait and see."

The prisoner was forced to lie on the ground. Next

29

the heavy wooden beam he had borne along the highway was set down flat so that his wrists might be tied to the wooden beam, one at each end. Then a kneeling soldier took hammer in hand, to drive a thick nail through each wrist, and set the pin deep into the timber. The man's hands were flexed with the action, but there was no other reaction from the prisoner.

"The drugs have numbed him," Yusuf explained to Yeshua, who was surprised there was so little blood.

An olive tree was behind the soldiers, and with their charge held fast to the beam, four of them, with some difficulty lifted the man and the beam, to hoist them both up the tree, and fix the beam horizontally to the sturdy trunk, using yet more nails and rope; some of which they employed to give extra support to the prisoner's arms, while he dangled, some six inches above the ground – a man on a cross now.

His ankles were ready to receive nails that once pierced flesh then deep into the tree.

Finally, a small ladder was leant against the convict's body, and a soldier climbed its rungs to nail a small piece of board to the tree above the drugged man's head. There was wording on the wood in Latin, Greek and Aramaic. "Traitor."

"That is the man's crime, the Romans have decided," Yusuf said in cold anger.

With their duty done, the soldiers sat themselves down in front of the cross and began to throw dice.

"They are playing for the prisoner's clothes and other possessions."

Yusuf could see that Yeshua was puzzled.

"There is nothing else to see. The action is over. The man will die eventually. And once you've watched one person die by crucifixion, you have watched them all ......unless it's a woman or a child, for instance, there is nothing to make you stay. We'll be on our way."

30

Freed to do so, they got themselves away from the sad scene and soon were gone from the throng; the three of them together, Yusuf one pace in front.

Yeshua seized the moment

"Well, mother. We're alone now, the three of us. You promised to explain what this word bastard has to do with me."

Mariam hadn't meant today with her words but, realising that Yeshua would not relent, she sighed heavily, and launched into her long rehearsed explanation. She spoke rapidly and without emotion.

"As I've said already, a bastard is someone whose father is not publicly acknowledged; it is as though he has no father. Of course, as you said, there has to have been a father. I could not have managed to produce you by myself! However, there are times when the father of a child does not want to be recognised as the birth father. For instance, if your father had been the Roman Governor, he certainly would not want his people to know a child of his was by a Jewish woman. Such a thing often happens with great and powerful men, – though it's not what happened to you. And don't let anyone tell you otherwise."

Mariam stopped talking for a moment, as a pondering Yeshua thought of something.

"What about the story of Hannah in the Bible, Mother?"

"What about her?"

"Well, doesn't the Bible say God blessed her and she became pregnant? Did that happen to you?"

Mariam laughed lightly.

"No! My cousin Elizabeth claimed that's what happened to her. Her son Jochanan was born when she was in her forties. You don't think me that old, do you?"

"You're only twenty-one Mother," Yeshua replied

31

gallantly.

"Of course, son. I'm twenty-one for the eighth time! I was only seventeen when I had you, so what happened to Hannah didn't happen to me. You're perfectly normal – just like Jacob, Simeon, Mariam and Judah all were."

"So, I'm not the son of a Roman Governor then?"

"No, son," Mariam said laughing. You're the son of my first husband, whom I married when I was very young – only sixteen."

"So is there another reason why a child's father is not acknowledged?"

"There is, son. That is when it would not be safe for the child's father to be known.... and that is the case with you. I know full well who your father was – well, I was married to him. He was potentially a very important man, and was certainly a danger to the people who govern this country – just like the man who was crucified today."

"Oh!"

"You've been in the Temple and you know that it's run by the priests. You do not become a priest; you have to be born one. They all come from the tribe of Levi. The man at the top.....,"

"The High Priest?"

"Yes. He is supposed to be a blood descendent from Aaron, the brother of Moses, who was from the tribe of Levi. Eleazer, the present High Priest, is not a descendent of Aaron. The Roman Governor appointed him to do his bidding. And the man you saw being crucified probably objected to this....... a dangerous thing to do!"

"I can see that!" Yeshua gave a nervous giggle.

"Your father, Abraham, was a direct descendent of Aaron. He should have been the High Priest, not the present man."

"Gosh!"

"Furthermore, our father was descended from the last Jewish kings and I am descended from the oldest Jewish king, David. So, Abraham should also have been king. Not Herod. The Authorities knew the truth of this, and that is why he disappeared. Even now I don't know whether he disappeared voluntarily or whether he was murdered."

"Oh, no! So you don't know whether he is alive or dead?"

"I only know that I have not seen him for seven years. And many people think you're not Abraham's son because you were born earlier than we expected. While others certainly know you aren't Yusuf's birth son. None of this is your fault and I have done nothing wrong. But that is why people call you a bastard - people can be horrible."

"Now I understand, Mother."

"It's good that you do. You just have to dismiss the torment and get on with your life. You were lucky that Yusuf married me and kindly took care of us. But this means you are no longer the son of a priest: you are the son of a carpenter and you will have to learn your father's trade, like every Jewish boy, now you're a man."

"That's right, boy."

Yusuf had been listening all the time, having sharp ears, from a pace ahead, and now invited himself into the conversation; pausing in their journey.

"The lessons of the trade start when we get home. And there'll be no more wandering off to sit with priests."

Yeshua nodded. "I promise."

"I may be getting on, but my hand is still strong!"

"I do know that.............father!"

Father! The unexpected word coming from

Yeshua's lips startled Yusuf, and, for a moment, he was flustered. Then he dropped to his knee, to embrace his son with genuine affection.

"Indeed you do ..... son! Indeed you do!"

Yeshua's response was at first rather stiff, before he dared relax, and throw his arms around the older man, who he now recognized was, at last, giving him love, the real love he had wanted him to show before. And needed.

"Right, this won't do," blustered Yusuf, standing up and composing himself.

"There's the rest of our family waiting for us in Bethany, and we are late for our evening meal."

As they moved onwards into the darkening evening, Mariam's soft smile was in recognition of an achievement – for the first time, they were walking in companionable silence. As a family. Perhaps there would be children from the union after all.

PART TWO

THE NORTHERN CAMPAIGN

"Who do people say that I am?" And they answered him, "John the Baptist; and others, Elijah; and still others, one of the prophets." He asked them, "But who do you say that I am?" Peter answered him, "You are the Messiah." And he sternly ordered them not to tell anyone about him.

Gospel according to St. Mark, chapter 8, verses 28 to 30

Chapter 2

The Prophet

Palestine 30 AD

Time passed. The boy became a man. He worked in the shop with the man he now called his father, and who accepted him as his son. He became a skilful carpenter and learned more of his religion and history – of more interest to him now since he knew his real background. He played with his brothers and sister, including his much younger half brothers and half sisters, the children of Mariam and Yusuf, and shared what he learned with them.

He married at sixteen; the normal age for marriage. Yusuf found him an attractive local girl, also called Mariam. Their wedding, as befitted a peasant couple, was simple but lively, marked by singing and dancing and a great deal of local wine mixed with water.*

When Yeshua moved into the house Yusuf bought for him, his eldest brother, took over his role in the family. Jacob kept an eye on the younger children and helped his mother. He also worked, with Yusuf and Yeshua, in the shop. The two young men became close, and, when Jacob's turn came to marry, shortly after Yusuf's death, Yeshua was his chief supporter and the chief marriage negotiator. He took over the family business, with Jacob as his assistant. Yeshua was a respected member of the Bethlehem community, an

---

* *Jews never drank wine neat. They always added water. This is because it was considered unseemly for a Jewish man or woman to become intoxicated.*

37

elected elder of the local Synagogue. When he became, in due time, the father of two boys – whom he named Jochanan and Jacob, his status and future seemed secure.

Yeshua Bar Yusuf seemed destined to live a quiet, contented, prosperous and, probably, happy life as a respected tradesman in a small town in a remote province of the mighty Roman Empire. Such people usually live long, often happy, and obscure lives. Yeshua Bar Abraham was dead, Yeshua Bar Yusuf lived. It seemed destined to be like this until he died in his bed, full of years, surrounded by his grieving family.

**

Far away in Rome, the capital of the world, the Emperor Tiberius was worried. He ruled an empire, which stretched right across Europe, from the English Channel to Romania, and which spread right around the Mediterranean Sea. He ruled it all. His rule was absolute and apparently unchallenged. However, not everywhere was as secure as he felt he was in Rome. Not even Rome was really secure. Rome, the great capital of the world, lived on a knife-edge. The problem was that the city was too big. It could not feed itself. The people depended on Egypt, which was the granary of the Empire.

Provided Rome held Egypt, everything was fine. However, Roman Egypt was like a valuable jewel on a thin necklace. The weakest link in the necklace was Palestine. That thin strip of land linked Roman Egypt with Roman Syria. A native ruler – Herod Antipas, ruled part of Palestine. Recently he had angered his neighbour and father-in-law, the normally friendly king of Arabia, Aretas. Herod had developed, in the eyes of

Tiberius, an unhealthy liking for Herodias, his brother Philip's wife. He won Herodias away from his brother, married her, and divorced the daughter of Aretas. This proved unwise. Aretas was a powerful king, with an effective army. He invaded Herod's territory and it needed Roman diplomacy, backed by the threat of Roman force and the liberal use of Roman money to persuade Aretas to leave. Tiberius forced a reluctant Herod to refund the Roman treasury, with a substantial sum charged in interest. Tiberius saw it as an alarm call. He decided he needed a reliable man in charge in Judaea and Samaria.

Tiberius called on a cousin of his wife, a Senator, Gaius Publius Pontius Pilatus, commonly known as Pilate. Pilate was every inch the Roman nobleman. He was tall, physically fit, with an arrogant but cruel look, which, Tiberius thought, accurately revealed his character. His face resembled a hawk. Pilate had gone through the normal training of a Roman aristocrat, joined the Senate, and served as a tribune to a Roman general in Spain. He had not got far up the Cursus Honorum, the normal road of progression for Roman noblemen. However, he had handled the junior posts he had held in Rome, successfully. He was married and had teenaged children. In his forties, he was due to be made a Consul, before going on to govern a province and make his fortune. That was the normal route for a Roman nobleman.

Tiberius was aware that his in-law had flaws in his character, but he knew that Pilate was decisive. Tiberius knew that, despite his personal weaknesses, Pilate was a firm administrator who was not afraid to use force when necessary. Far from it, in fact. Tiberius knew that Pilate often had to be pulled back from the excessive use of force. This was a pity because Tiberius also knew him to be an able diplomat, loyal to the

Imperial family. Tiberius expected that, with this combination of abilities, Pilate would be able to keep: the restless Jewish population down; the complicated relationships with the various local Jewish authorities stable; and Judaea firmly in Roman control. He was an ideal choice.

The only problem was that he did not want to go!

"Look Gaius," Pilate said drily, "I appreciate your trust in me – but why Palestine?"

"What's wrong with Palestine, Publius?" Tiberius asked.

"Well it's scarcely Spain, is it! I was looking forward to a real province. Palestine has only sun and sand and is full of dirty quarrelling barbarians, who don't bath, don't have a real god, and certainly have little money. There's no possibility of financial gain for me in Palestine. I won't even be able to raise my salary."

"I know all that, Publius. I know Palestine's not a real province. However, there's no part of the Empire as strategically important as Palestine and also so fragile. I need a person there I can trust and whose ability I know. You are that man. Sort out the problems, crush the risings, and keep the territory safe and I promise you that you will be able to choose any province you wish when you return. I will also move your sons up the magisterial ladder for you."

Pilate thought for a moment. When his in-law wanted something, he could charm the birds from the trees. He knew the Emperor would reward him. He also knew Tiberius would not accept refusal. Relative or not, refusal could mean exile from Rome or even death. He felt he had no choice. However, Pilate still wanted to feel he had won from the exchange. He spoke firmly and decisively, because he knew Tiberius respected that.

"All right, Gaius. I'll agree – but on two conditions."

"What conditions Publius?"

"First, my wife comes with me."

"No problem – we trust you. We don't need her here to keep you loyal. And the second?"

"You don't expect me to live in Jerusalem."

Tiberius laughed. He stood up and walked around to where his wife's cousin sat. He put his arm around Pilate's shoulder.

"You and I would both go mad in Jerusalem Publius. It's a terrible place from all accounts – the home of Jewish fanatics who hate us, led by a High Priest, who treats us with contempt, and probably plots against us. No, of course, you don't have to live there. The old king, called Herod, a great man, felt the same way about his capital as we do, and built a new one, a Roman city, patriotically called Caesarea, on the coast. You will live there, but remember to leave a strong garrison under an experienced commander in Jerusalem, and be sure to be there when they celebrate one of their festivals. That's when there's likely to be trouble. If trouble breaks out, crush it instantly – don't let it spread. A squad armed with shield, sword and spear can do wanders in a riot situation."

Tiberius paused, before adding, "And be careful how much confidence you put in the local Jewish authorities. You can probably trust the Tetrarch, Herod Antipas, but I'm not so sure about the High Priest, Annas, even though we appointed him."

Pilate nodded confidently.

"You know that I won't tolerate disorder, Gaius. I will follow your advice. How long do I have to stay there?"

"I don't know, Publius. It's not length of years, but stability that's the issue. I want you to make the country

41

safe for Rome. Bring the local rulers into line. Remove them if necessary. I will back your decisions. Crush any rebellion. Show no mercy to troublemakers. I don't care how many you crucify. If you run out of trees, I'll send you wood from Rome! Just make the country safe, and then you can come home and go to Spain or wherever else you want, with my blessing."

**

And so, Pontius Pilate and his wife came to Caesarea, and the country began to feel the iron grip of Rome. He was just in time. Rumours began to circulate in Caesarea about a wild man who had suddenly appeared from the desert, preaching fire and brimstone. The agitated local population flocked to the Jordan Valley to see him. Pilate tried to seize him. However, whenever he sent a squad of soldiers to capture him, the man always faded away into the desert. Pilate realised he would need to be more subtle. The problem was his men stood out like sore thumbs among the Jewish population, even when they dressed in local clothing. He decided to wait until his first visit to Jerusalem, when he could consult the two local rulers – Annas and Herod.

**

The rumours were right. The wild-eyed prophet who suddenly appeared in the Jordan Valley was Jochanan, the son of Mariam's cousin, Elizabeth and her priestly husband, Zechariah. He had disappeared, like Yeshua's father, into the Judaean Desert as a young man, after the death of Zechariah. His return, dressed and acting like the great prophet Elijah, as described in the Bible, acted like a thunderbolt on a people groaning under foreign oppression. Pilate might think of Herod as Jewish, but the people knew he was an Edomite, the ancient enemies of the Jews, and they hated him. They yearned for freedom from both the Herod family and their Roman allies. They were prepared to fight for freedom, as they did when the Jewish priest kings led them against the Greeks. They needed a leader, the Messiah, who would gather an army, and drive out the foreigners once and for all. They expected the great Elijah to return to announce him. Jochanan fuelled the fire of messianic expectation to white heat.

The strange thing was that Jochanan did not say anything new. His sermons were actually quite boring! The people who came out to see him heard such things every Sabbath in the synagogues.

"Don't cheat or lie," he told them. "Don't overcharge others. Don't take by force what is not offered to you freely. Be content with your lot and your pay." He told soldiers to obey their officers and officers to obey the Government. He urged moderation in drink and food. He never touched wine. He ate only locusts and wild honey and drank only water. He never cut his hair or shaved. He wore animal skins rather than proper clothing. His eyes were wild.

Jochanan hated the Priestly establishment – the Pharisees and Sadducees, although only the Pharisees came to see him. He knew they came to watch and report to their High Priestly master. When he saw a Pharisee with his little box, with the law in it, tied to his forehead, Jochanan always gave him a special welcome.

"What are you doing here?" he would ask. "Who warned you to escape the anger to come?"

The Pharisees grew to expect it, and wisely did not reply. They were not there to engage in dialogue, but to listen and report.

Jochanan never directly attacked the Romans, because that was much too dangerous. He did, however, suggest, obliquely, that they should not be there.

"The country is dirty," Jochanan said in one sermon, noted by a Roman agent. "It's like a public latrine which stinks and needs cleaning. God is going to clean it out soon."

**

When Pilate heard of that remark, he sent soldiers to seize Jochanan. They were spotted. Jochanan crossed the river into Herod's lands (where Roman soldiers could not go without permission) and then into the desert (where no soldier could safely go) and which Jochanan knew only too well. The soldiers waited, for a day or two, for Jochanan to return. Jochanan's immediate entourage watched them. When they gave up and left to report their failure to Pilate, Jochanan returned.

**

Like all religious Jews, including the Priestly Establishment, Jochanan hated the Herod family. The Jews endured the rule of the old King, because he was an effective ruler, and ruled the country well. However, the Herodians were too Roman for them, and copied many Greek and Roman ideas, which offended the Jews. Jochanan was especially critical of the new gymnasia, where male athletes performed naked. The Bible said that God cursed a man, who was seen naked. Jews accepted that the pagan Greeks were cursed by God, but were scandalised when their own young men also took part in the Games. They were shocked when the young men removed the marks of circumcision, which had caused the Greeks to mock them. Good Jews never attended the Games.

Jochanan, therefore, had plenty of reasons to dislike the son of Herod the Great, and Herod Antipas knew it. Like Annas and Pilate, he sent his own men to listen to Jochanan, and to wait for a mistake. Unlike the Romans, these men were Jews. Unlike the Pharisees, these men were civilians. They merged with the crowds, and no one knew they were there. Like snakes lurking in the long grass or under the stones, they were very dangerous. Jochanan always assumed they were there and took care not to stray too far in his attacks on Herod and Herodias.

On one occasion, however, Jochanan made a mistake. He was working a reasonably sized crowd. He gave his standard sermon and asked, as he always did, for questions.

"What should I do to avoid judgement?" asked a tax gatherer.

"You work for Rome," Jochanan said, to general laughter, "So you're probably doomed anyway!"

"But I have to live, Prophet. So how can I earn enough to feed my family and still please God?"

"Don't take more than the right tax from anyone," Jochanan replied.

"But that's not possible," the tax gatherer complained. "I have to take my salary from what I collect."

"Perhaps you should consider a career change," the prophet suggested.

The tax collector turned away, disappointed.

"What about me?" asked one of Herod's soldiers, off duty and enjoying the day out, "How can I be saved if I kill Jewish patriots?"

"Obey the orders of your officers, even if it is to

execute Jewish patriots. The Messiah hasn't come yet – so anyone who says he is Messiah is a liar, and cursed by God."

A voice from the crowd called out, "What about that bastard Herod?"

"What about Herod?" Jochanan replied.

"Should we pay taxes to him?"

"Why not?" Jochanan responded. "He provides some security, and his soldiers need to be paid. That's our duty. We must perform it."

"But Herod's an Edomite!" the voice persisted.

"And, Pilate's a Roman," Jochanan replied. "However, God still tells us to obey them, unless they break His laws, of course."

"But Herod has broken the Torah," the voice continued. "He is married to his brother's wife while his brother is still alive."

Jochanan paused. He realised this was dangerous ground.

"Perhaps Edomites see things differently from us," Jochanan temporised.

"Rubbish!" said another voice. "God's law applies to everyone. Herod isn't special. If we have to obey it, so does he."

"You're right, of course," said Jochanan reluctantly. "Herod has broken God's law, and, like all law breakers, will have to face God's judgement one day. However, we must still obey his lawful commands."

Another voice called out from the back of the crowd, "Are you the Messiah, or are we waiting for someone else?"

Jochanan looked around to see who had asked the question. Finally he spotted him, an ordinary man dressed in a grey tunic under a brown topcoat, and with a white kaffiyah on his head. He smiled at him.

"No, I'm not," he replied. "I am the one who has

come to announce his coming. He will come soon. You will know him when he comes because he will be so much more powerful than me that I will not even be worthy to be his personal servant."

The questions came to an end, and, after he had baptised those who wished it, the crowd left. Jochanan hoped that he had avoided the Herodian trap, but his lieutenants were not so sure. Thomas, a fellow graduate from Qumr'an urged him to be careful.

"Don't sleep in Herod's territories," he urged, "and, from now on, stick to the Roman side of the Jordan."

"I'll do my best, Thomas," Jochanan promised.

**

Pilate, in Caesarea, became increasingly concerned. He and his wife had scarcely unpacked before he received a warning from the third local ruler of the old King's realm – Herod Philip, who ruled in the far north. He was the one whose wife was stolen by his brother, Herod Antipas. He wrote that a man called Judah had raised an army in Galilee and claimed to be Messiah. He urged Pilate to take this rising seriously.

"Galilee is a hotbed of sedition and treason," Philip wrote.

"My brother rules there, but, when he stole Herodias, my former wife, the people turned against him. Part of his army joined the rebels, and the rest ran away to his fortress palace by the Dead Sea. The country is at the mercy of the rebels. Once established there, they will sweep south towards Jerusalem. Then you will have trouble! That's how the Syrian king, Antiochus, was defeated."

Pilate took the warning seriously. He sent half the garrison of Caesarea, under the Tribune Marcus Antonius, a capable commander, north. His men moved swiftly, caught the rebels by surprise out in the open, and smashed them before they could draw up their men in line of battle.

The Tribune split his prisoners up. He crucified half of them on the trees of Galilee. He handed over the other half to the Roman Navy to work as galley slaves. He brought the leader back to Caesarea, to face Pilate.

Pilate was in his office, working, when there was a knock on the door. In response to his invitation to enter, Tribune Antonius entered the room. Two soldiers accompanied him. They escorted a burly man, dressed only in a loincloth, manacled and chained. Pilate studied the prisoner, whose powerful body was covered in dust and bruises and streaked with dry blood. He stood up and walked around the prisoner, whose back bore the scars of beatings, both old and new.

"Who is my guest Marcus?" he asked the Tribune.

"This was the rebel leader, Excellency. I thought he might amuse you, so I brought him back as a prize for you."

"I see," Pilate mused.

He returned to his seat behind his desk, poured wine for himself and gave a glass to the Tribune, who also sat and sipped slowly. The prisoner glowered at him.

"It's very considerate of you Marcus, to allow me to share your fun. What happened in Galilee?"

"There were only about 3000 rebels, Excellency," the Tribune began. "They were poorly armed and poorly led, even the former soldiers. We took them by surprise, out in the open. We gave them no time to organise themselves before we attacked them. They fell apart under the javelins of our troops. The legionaries scarcely had even to draw their swords. We killed about 200 on the battlefield, and about 800 managed to escape. We let them go, since there was little point chasing them. They were no threat to anyone, and had even thrown away their weapons.

"We captured about 2000 rebels. These we stripped and tied hand and foot, before we questioned them. About half were former soldiers. We kept them with us. The rest were just peasants and fishermen. They are now at the naval base, where they will each pull an oar. They might as well serve the Empire until they die.

"The others we marched south, but like Crassus, we had fun with them. We would stop every 100 paces, select two prisoners, free them, throw them a sword each, and force them to fight, but not to the death. We crucified the loser, and made the winner fight another challenger at the next stop. In that way, we reduced the number to this fellow here – who was made to watch each fight. He expected he would fight the last battle – but we denied him the pleasure. And now he's yours, Excellency, to do with as you like."

"Thank you, Tribune, for a very succinct report, a model of its kind."

Pilate turned to the prisoner. He studied him intently from behind the desk.

"What's your name fellow?"

The prisoner said nothing. However, he straightened his back, and assumed a defiant air. One of his guards struck him across the face.

"Answer the Governor, fellow."

The defiant attitude collapsed.

"My name's Judah," he mumbled.

"So Judah, why did you lead an army against us?" Pilate adopted a kinder tone.

"I didn't lead an army against you, Governor. I led an army against the God-cursed Herod, the man who has stolen his brother's wife."

"The Tetrarch is an ally of the Roman people. When you attack him, you attack us. So, I repeat my question, Judah, if that's your real name, why did you attack us?"

"Because you're pagan, foreign bastards, oppressing the people of God and robbing God of what is rightfully His."

The answer was spat out defiantly.

Pilate smiled. It was the cold, humourless smile his opponents in the Senate knew well.

"I may be a 'pagan, foreign bastard', but I'm the 'pagan, foreign bastard' who rules this province for His Imperial Majesty, the Divine Gaius Julius Tiberius Caesar Augustus, to whom you owe allegiance. I'm also the 'pagan, foreign bastard' who is going to decide whether you live or die. I suggest you be careful how you talk to me."

Judah looked at the Procurator with thinly disguised hatred, cloaked in disdain and contempt.

"You have no control over my life, Governor. Only God has that, and, if I die on one of your crosses, or in one of your arenas, He will welcome me into His Kingdom, as one of His martyrs."

Pilate smiled his cruel, cold smile again.

"Is that your hope? You hope for a relatively quick death, like your deluded companions?"

There was no answer.

Pilate allowed the silence to continue for a while, before adding, "You're such a strong fellow, it would be a pity to deny the Emperor the fruits of your labour."

He turned to Marcus.

"Tribune, take this fellow away. Keep him in custody until you find a ship heading for Patmos. Put him on the first such ship, under guard, and send him to the mines there. Tell the local Commander that he is not to leave the mines alive. There should be no manumission."

Marcus raised his clenched fist across his chest in salute.

"Yes Excellency."

The Prisoner was marched out. Pilate called Marcus back.

"Thank you, again, Marcus, for a job well done. I will review the troops involved tomorrow. Let me know who needs rewarding."

**

News of the new prophet spread throughout the country. Eventually it reached the sleepy town of Bethlehem. Jacob discussed the news with his brother, Yeshua, who was as excited as everyone else about the strange phenomenon. There had not been a real Prophet for over 500 years. Everyone wanted to see him. However, no one seemed willing to lead the party. It was one thing to want to go, but they all had work to do, families to support and money to earn. The idea was discussed among the men and women of the town.

The women knew they could not go, but, as Yeshua's wife, Mariam, said, "We can experience the prophet through you men. When you come back you can tell us what he said, what he did, and what he looks like. Then it will be as though we were there too."

Nothing happened for a long time. Finally, after one Sabbath service in the Synagogue, one of the men asked the Rabbi if he would lead a group up to the Jordan.

"I don't know," the Rabbi said. "It's a good week's journey there and another week back. I'm not sure I can spare the time."

Yeshua, who had read the lesson that day and felt this visit was important for him, responded.

"Reverend Sir," he said calmly and politely. "I, too, have a full workload and two boys to bring up, but I feel we should make the time to see this Prophet. Mariam agrees with me, as do most of the men here. It is as if God is calling us. If that's what God wants, then we should leave the town in His care. Surely He can be trusted to look after our families, homes and businesses for two weeks?"

A stranger, a man from the Judaean city of Kerioth, who had been visiting Mariam's family, spoke in support of Yeshua.

"I agree with the carpenter," he said. "You're the Rabbi, and it's your duty to lead your people. If God is calling them to go to hear the Prophet, then he's also calling you to lead them."

"The stranger is right, Rabbi," one of the men said. It's your duty to lead us." He looked around. "Does everyone agree with me?"

There was a general murmur of agreement. The Rabbi looked at them all before replying, reluctantly.

"Very well! Since you all insist, I will lead you, but only after Passover has finished."

With this, they had to be content.

**

That Passover was also important for the rulers of Palestine. Pilate took half the garrison of Caesarea with him, leaving the other half under the command of Marcus. He left his wife behind in Caesarea for this first visit to a city he knew little about. He entered Jerusalem, on horseback, surrounded by cavalry. Conscious of Jewish hostility, Pilate ordered his infantry to march in battle formation, shields uncovered and spears at the ready, eagle standards proudly carried at the front of each regiment.

They marched through noisy crowds. These grew steadily larger and increasingly hostile. Eventually, a youth threw a stone at the troops. It bounced off a soldier's shield. No one was hurt. The first stone was followed by others. Some men began to seize pieces of wood to use as clubs and attacked the horses. These, frightened, reared and kicked out. Pilate halted his column. He ordered the infantry to turn to face the crowds on both sides of the road, draw their swords and attack. Twenty men and boys died under the Roman swords. Another dozen were captured, including the boy who threw the first stone. The rest fled, screaming, into the side streets.

Pilate never found out how many Jews were wounded. It was not important. They were only colonials without any rights. What was important to him was that none of his men were hurt. Pilate ordered the march to continue through the now empty streets, and for the prisoners to be brought to the Palace.

The Procurator's Palace was a fortress, the Antonia, in the middle of the city, with steps leading down to the big outer court of the Temple, where the sacrificial animals were bought and money was changed from Roman coins to the Jewish coins (which were the only ones allowed in the Temple). This was where trouble was most likely to break out. The Antonia had been built by the old King to enable him to intervene quickly in case of trouble. It had three purposes – Palace and office for the Procurator; fortress for his troops; and prison for those who offended him. The twelve prisoners were thrown into the cells until after the festival when they would be dealt with.

On the day after his arrival, Pilate invited Annas, the High Priest, and Herod Antipas, the Tetrarch, to a conference at the Fortress to discuss the situation. Annas refused to come, citing the Passover and Jewish law as the reason. Herod, however, did come.

Pilate greeted the Tetrarch and apologised for the High Priest's absence. Herod grinned.

"You obviously don't understand the Jews,

Excellency. They have some peculiar customs. They don't like any of us foreigners. As far as they are concerned there is no difference between you and me. They call us Gentiles and think they will be polluted if they come to our houses or we go to theirs."

"Does the High Priest actually expect me, a representative and relative of the Divine Emperor, to visit him?" asked an incredulous Pilate.

"No, Excellency. He's not that stupid! But, over the years, there has grown up a custom whereby the High Priest meets the Procurator on neutral ground. You will find the former Procurator had a second office, not within the main fortress, where the High Priest could be persuaded it was not a Gentile house, and the Procurator maintained his honour as the Emperor's representative."

"Are they all so prickly?"

"Absolutely, Excellency."

"Except you, Tetrarch."

"Ah, but I'm not Jewish!" Herod answered with a smile.

"I can see that I'm going to have to be very careful in future," Pilate observed cautiously. He stood up and walked over to the window. Herod rose and stood beside him. They looked down at the crowds moving noisily around the city.

"You will need to be a lot more careful than you were yesterday Excellency," Herod commented. "You caused that riot by your own mistakes."

"How so?"

Pilate showed his sudden anger in his voice. Herod answered calmly.

"You should have ordered the soldiers to cover their shields and standards. The other Procurators always did that."

"Why?"

"The thunder bolt on the shield is a sign of Jupiter and the eagle is a graven image. Both are against Jewish law. Remember, Excellency, this is their holy city. The Jews believe their God cannot be shown as a statue. They even rebelled against my father when he had a statue of an eagle built over the entrance to the Temple. They saw it as a graven image. No one lightly rebelled against Herod the Great! Hundreds died when his troops put down the riot. They still hate that eagle."

Herod paused.

"You should also not have ridden into the city. You, and all your cavalry, should have dismounted and led your horses through the gate."

"Why?" Pilate asked.

"Only the King of Israel can ride into the City. Only a <u>Jewish</u> King of Israel can do so. Not even I dare ride into the city!"

Pilate thought about this and, eventually, conceded that Herod was speaking sense. They returned to their seats. Pilate told Herod about events in Galilee and what Marcus had done about them. Herod thanked him. Then he added, "It's all that Prophet's fault, you know."

Pilate was surprised.

"I thought he didn't engage in politics. My agents found no evidence of treason against Rome."

"That's because he always sees them coming, and ensures he keeps on the right side of the law. It's different when there are no Romans present. He's more honest then."

"What do you mean?" Pilate asked.

Herod paused for thought.

"I will give you an example Excellency. General Pompey, when he marched into Jerusalem, caused a scandal by entering the Sanctuary in the Temple. (I warn you, Excellency, don't ever do that! The Jews will kill you, Governor or no Governor)."

Herod paused.

"Any way, Pompey saw that he could not order the Jews to sacrifice to an image of the spirit of Rome, like other subject people do, as a sign of loyalty. Instead, he ordered that a special tax be paid to Rome as evidence of continued loyal obedience. The Divine Julius and his successors Marcus Antonius and the Divine Augustus Caesar confirmed that arrangement. When Jochanan is asked about tax he says that it is wrong to pay the produce of the land of God to Caesar."

"What does he mean by that?"

"He says it's against the Torah to pay the Roman tax. As a result, tax revenues have begun to drop."

"So, you're saying that's treason, Tetrarch, even though he did not actually say 'Don't pay'?"

"He didn't have to use the words, Excellency. The meaning is clear enough in his native Aramaic. Your spies would have missed it, even if they had been present."

"In that case, I will have to stop him Tetrarch."

A slave brought in a bottle of wine and two goblets. The two men filled their goblets. Pilate noticed the corpulent and cheerful-looking Herod did not water his wine as the Jews did. He liked that. They walked over to the windows, which overlooked the parade ground. They watched the guards being changed. Herod resumed the conversation.

"You will never capture him by yourself, Excellency. Your troops stand out too much. We'll have to work together."

"What do you suggest?"

"We should both send troops to opposite sides of the river. He will see your men coming and cross the river as he usually does, and my men will seize him. I promise you will not see him again! Herodias is very anxious to have a conversation with him. Remember the old adage – Hell has no fury like that of a woman scorned! She has not forgotten his description of her as 'the Edomite Whore'. She will certainly make him regret it."

The two men spent time working out the details of this plan, before Herod turned to go. Pilate thanked him for the useful conference and bade him farewell.

However, before leaving, Herod turned back.

"Incidentally, Excellency, a final piece of advice. Remove Annas as High Priest. He could have met you in the outer office. His refusal suggests he is trying you out. He secretly resents Roman rule. I suspect he quietly encourages all these rebellions. He has a more amenable son-in-law, a man called Yusuf Caiaphas; I suggest you appoint him in his place."

**

Once the festival was over, and before he left for Caesarea, Pilate dismissed Annas and appointed Caiaphas High Priest. Pilate made Caiaphas watch as he decided the fate of the twelve rioters. He made the original offender stand aside, while the remainder drew lots. He sentenced the five losers to be crucified and sent them down for scourging. He walked to the front of the six winners and spoke to them, adopting a mockingly friendly tone.

"Congratulations, you have avoided a painful death ----"

The prisoners looked hopeful. Pilate smiled cruelly, before continuing.

"… for the moment. My tribune invited the men he captured in Galilee to duel for the honour of entertaining his troops by being crucified on the way back to Caesarea. You six are going to entertain my men and me in Caesarea in the same way. You will pair off and each pair will fight naked in the arena. The winner will go to the galleys and the loser to the crosses. It should be fun! Take them away. Have them ready to march with the troops in one hour's time."

The six prisoners were hustled out, chained together in a line, and made to wait, barefoot, and naked except for a loincloth, in the heat on the parade ground. There they watched as their five former companions, dressed as they were, but with their backs cut to pieces, were each forced to lift a cross beam and were marched out of the fortress under escort.

Pilate turned to Caiaphas, who stood, seething in helpless anger, knowing he dare not question the actions of the Procurator.

"Thank you for staying, Lord Caiaphas. Remember what you have seen and urge your fellow countrymen not to challenge the might of Rome in future. I will not tolerate disorder in Judaea or Jerusalem."

Caiaphas bowed stiffly.

"As you say, Excellency, I have seen how you dispense Roman justice. I will not forget."

Pilate smiled.

"That's what I hoped, Lord Caiaphas. Congratulations on your new appointment. I will look forward to meeting you during Pentecost."

Pilate offered Caiaphas his hand. The new High priest shook it, and then left. Once back in the Temple, he called for water, and washed the hand that had touched Pilate's hand.

Pilate now turned to his final prisoner. He had been stripped and chained like the rest, and was dirty and smelt like a latrine. Pilate looked him over and grimaced at the smell. He picked up a perfumed handkerchief from the table and held it to his nose. He turned to the two remaining guards.

"Take him out, scrub him down. Throw away that filthy loincloth. Then bring him back here."

"Do you want us to cloth him Excellency?"

"Don't bother. The little wretch doesn't deserve clothing."

"As you command. Excellency", the guard said, saluting. He shoved the boy in the back. "Move, you little bastard!" He ordered.

The boy stumbled out.

Pilate filled a glass with wine, and drank slowly, as he waited for the boy to be brought back. Fifteen minutes later, the naked boy, still chained, but now clean and dripping wet, was brought in. Pilate studied him closely. He was about fifteen. His body was young and hard, with long black hair down to his shoulders. He was beginning to grow a beard. His body was the sort certain men, including Pilate, found very attractive. Pilate felt he could turn a profit on him one day.

"Thank you soldier. Leave him with me. Find Julius and ask him to come in if you would."

"Certainly Excellency."

The two soldiers left. The boy looked at him without fear.

"Are you going to have me crucified?" he asked.

"Certainly not!" Pilate snapped. "It would be a waste."

"So, I'm going to the galleys then?"

Pilate smiled the familiar cold smile.

"Come here, boy."

The boy walked hesitantly forward, his movements hampered by the chains on his ankles. He stood in front of the Governor, who had left his seat and moved in front of his desk.

"Put your hands on your head."

The boy obeyed. Pilate inspected the boy. He opened the boy's mouth, checking his teeth. Then he ran his hands down the boy's body, back and front. Pilate did this slowly and expertly, becoming more animated as he did so. His cold smile became friendlier. The boy felt excited by Pilate's touch, and, to his shame, gained an erection.

"Not now, my sweet. You'll keep until tonight,"

Pilate smiled affectionately. He kissed the boy on the lips. The boy could not contain himself, dripping liquid from his member. He felt both shamed and excited. Pilate stepped back, watching him, fighting his own erection. He fought hard to control his breathing. Now was not the time. He decided he would keep him and not sell him.

At this moment Julius, Pilate's slave master, entered the office. He took in the scene at once.

"Do you want me to process this slave, Excellency?"

"If you would, Julius. Brand him with my mark on his arse. Give him a mild flogging to teach him honesty and bring him to my tent. Keep him chained and throw him in the wagon. Keep him from the other prisoners."

"What about clothing?"

"We'll find some later. He doesn't need any today. But get rid of the evidence of circumcision. Make him look more like a proper civilised man. Shave him, and cut his hair short, no more than chin length. Make him look like a Greek boy – not a Jewish one."

"I'll sort out the hair and do the flogging myself. I'll also give him a practical lesson in his duties as your pleasure slave."

Julius smiled suggestively.

"You know I enjoy that part of my work, Excellency! However, I suggest you leave the branding and the circumcision removal until we reach Caesarea. I'll do that in the slave cells there. Both operations would spoil your pleasures on the march, because his cock and arse will both be very sore. I know you like inflicting pain on your slave partners, Excellency, but I think this would be a little too much – and your enjoyment would be marred by his groans. Also he would not be as responsive as you would like."

"That's why I employ you Julius. You always think of my comforts. I accept your advice. But perfume him properly. I want him to smell like the whore he's going to become."

"Yes, Excellency. Does he have a name?"

"I neither know nor care Julius. Call him 'Boy'".

"Yes, Excellency."

Julius fastened a slave collar around the neck of the slave boy who stood, frozen in horror as he realised his fate. Using the chain attached to the collar, he pulled the unresisting slave away.

"Come along boy," Julius said. "The Governor has work to do, and so have we."

The slave was removed, and Pilate turned to more important matters. It was lucky, he thought, that few here knew of his other side. Homosexuality was growing among the Roman aristocracy, but it was still not generally approved by Roman society. Tiberius knew, of course, but then he was openly bisexual, especially when he escaped from the confines of Rome to the seclusion of his summer palace on an isolated island off Capri. Here he was free to do as he liked – and what Tiberius liked would have shocked Roman society, as corrupt as it was. He realised that when he returned to Rome he would have to lend this new, delicious, slave to the Emperor.

"Droit de Seigneur", he thought sadly.

**

61

Yeshua and Jacob joined the party of men leaving Bethlehem for the Jordan. There were about twenty in the party, led by the Rabbi. They walked slowly from the town, waved off by their wives and friends. They left at first light and made good progress during the day. They skirted around the outside of Jerusalem, to avoid the festival crowds leaving the city. They followed tracks known only to the natives, up and down hills and along the beds of dry rivers. When it rained, the land was green and the valleys were living streams. Now it was dry and dusty and the valleys were dry roads. They made good time, and so, by mid afternoon, reached the Roman road that linked Jerusalem with Caesarea and the coast. Here they had to stop, since a column of Roman troops was about to pass by and they knew it was forbidden to halt a Roman column, even for the five minutes it took to cross the road. They knew that, in exchange for those five minutes they would have to wait for an hour or more until the troops passed. Any other action could result in their sudden and violent deaths.

They stood by the side of the road, stifling their resentment, and watched as the troops drew level. They were led by men on horseback, at the head of whom was a man dressed as a Roman general. He was in full armour, with crested bronze helmet, and a red cloak that blew backwards in the wind, the fabric twisting idly. Behind marched the Roman infantry, carrying their packs and shouldering their spears, shields on arms. The air echoed with the clip clop of horses' hooves, the neighing of the horses, the clatter of the armour and the tramp of booted feet on the stones of the Roman Road. The soldiers were singing a marching song in Latin. They did not understand the words, but guessed that they were not the sort they would want their wives, daughters or mothers to hear.

Pilate was preoccupied that afternoon. As he was about to leave the Palace in Jerusalem, the Commander of the garrison spoke to him.

"Your Excellency," he began.

Then he stopped.

"Yes Tribune Trebonius," asked Pilate encouragingly.

"Your Excellency, do you remember the youth who began the riot by stoning our troops?"

"Of course," said Pilate impatiently. "I dealt with him and his friends this morning. Five of them are already decorating the road to Caesarea."

"With due respect, Excellency, you haven't."

"I haven't what Tribune?"

"Dealt with the boy's family adequately. It is the custom to seize all the possessions of such criminals: buildings, chattels and persons. You sell off the property, close up or destroy the buildings, and enslave the rest of the family. The adult males go to the galleys, the mines or the arena, while the women and children go to the slave markets."

"Fine. Arrange it Tribune – and send the best of the young slave girls to me as a present for my wife."

Pilate was still thinking of this conversation as he came face to face with a small party of men. They stood in a row by the road, watching them pass, as was appropriate. Pilate counted them. There were twenty-one in all. He pulled his horse round, halting the column behind him, and studied the men. He was particularly struck by one of them, who seemed to be the leader of the group. He called him over. He thought he was in his mid thirties, tall and handsome, with neatly trimmed black beard and the usual long black hair, tied in a ponytail, behind his back. He was wearing a long Jewish tunic, white in colour, worn under a brown cloth topcoat, open at the front, but tied with a sash around his waist. A white cloth covered his head and protected him from the sun and dust. He had intelligent brown eyes. He was carrying a wooden staff. He suspected the ladies would love him.

Yeshua saw a lean, tall man, with cold, cruel eyes, and a nose like a hawk's beak, lean down from his horse and speak to him. Yeshua sensed the Roman was cloaking his true nature. Pilate sensed there was a real, although indefinable, power in the man he saw. He was curious. He decided to speak to him. He leaned over from his saddle and addressed Yeshua.

"What's your name?"

"Yeshua Bar Yusuf, Your Excellency."

Pilate thought that the man's voice was quiet and confident. He was plainly not afraid of him.

"Where are you all from?"

"We've come from Bethlehem, Your Excellency."

"Where are you going?"

"The Jordan – to see the Prophet Jochanan."

"I see," said Pilate drily. "Well, we won't detain you. You can cross the road in front of us. For once, the Roman Procurator will wait for some of his subjects."

"Thank you, Your Excellency," said a surprised Yeshua. He led the party quickly across the road, and off in the direction of the Jordan.

Pilate, after a halt of five minutes, moved on. That evening, his men made camp in the Judaean hills, digging ditches and throwing up an earthen bank around it, as they always did. While he was reclining at dinner, a small troop of cavalry from the Jerusalem garrison rode into the camp. The Decurion in charge rode with a twelve-year old Jewish girl, with long black hair, across his saddle. Her hands and feet were tied with rope, and she was also gagged to stop her shouting and trying to bite him. On arrival in the camp, he dismounted, pulled the girl down, threw her over his shoulder, and entered the Procurator's tent. He threw her down on the grass at the Procurator's feet. Pilate stood up at the interruption. He looked down at the girl at his feet, puzzled.

"What's this about Decurion?'

"She's a present, Excellency, from Tribune Lucius Trebonius. He said you'd know what she was."

The girl lay face downward. Pilate used his foot to roll her over. She looked up at him, hate showing in her pretty brown eyes.

"Thank you Decurion. What happened to the rest of the family?"

"Four men have been sent down to the port, Excellency. Two adult women, seven younger children - three girls and four boys - have been sent to the prison in Jerusalem, to await your decision. This one is a present for your wife, as you requested."

"Thank the Tribune Lucius Trebonius for me and congratulate him on his zeal and efficiency, Decurion. Find accommodation for your men and return to Jerusalem tomorrow."

"Thank you, Excellency."

The Decurion saluted and left. Pilate acknowledged the salute before continuing to eat his meal, as he planned the entertainments he intended to inflict on his new slave that night. He decided he would name him Marcus, after the conqueror of the Galilean rebels. Pilate forgot the girl and left her lying on the floor. Eventually, Julius found her, took her away, and fed her. Pilate did not refer to her again. It was Julius who eventually handed her over to Pilate's wife, telling her that the Procurator had bought the girl as a present for her while he was in Jerusalem. She named her Julia, after her own name.

**

Yeshua and his party continued on their way towards the spot on the Jordan where Jochanan was baptizing people, which they reached five days later. Here they joined a much larger party, which had already assembled there, waiting impatiently for the prophet to appear. They waited all morning, wondering.

Jochanan did not appear. He was close by, on the other side of the river, receiving conflicting advice from his lieutenants. Thomas, a cautious northerner, was convinced that he had seen Roman troops, disguised as civilians among the crowd at the baptism site. Philip, also from the north, was equally certain that Thomas was wrong. A third lieutenant, the Judaean, Judah, felt that the situation was far from clear. The other two, Simeon and Thaddeus, two Galileans, agreed with Judah. Eventually, it was instinct that made Jochanan decide. He felt that day was special, and that he had to go, whatever the danger.

Once decided, he wasted no time, and walked briskly to the crossing point and splashed through the river, accompanied by his five lieutenants, towering above them all. Jochanan was a big, powerful man, made more fearsome by his choice of animal skins for his clothing, his dishevelled hair and beard, and his fierce, staring eyes, which burned with anger. Beside him, Thomas, Philip and Judah, all tall and powerful men in their own right, looked small. He called the people forward and began to speak to them, projecting his strong voice across the valley.

About sixty people were there, and no obvious spies. Jochanan guessed a Herodian or two might be among them, but he neither knew nor cared that much. It was not Herod he feared. His chief fear was that either Annas or Pilate would have him arrested. He saw no sign of that, and relaxed. He gave his usual sermon about honesty and love and obedience and then asked if there were any questions. There was only one, and that was from a man he learned was the Rabbi at Bethlehem.

"Who gave you the authority to do and say what you do?" he asked timidly.

"God, of course," Jochanan replied, to laughter and applause. "Who else would it be?"

There were no other questions, so the men stripped and came into the water, one by one, to be baptised. Jochanan meet them in midstream, and pushed each one totally under.

Finally, only two men stood on the bank. One was dressed, while the other was stripped. The one who had removed his clothing seemed younger than the reluctant one, and was arguing with him. Eventually the older man slowly began to remove his clothes, while the younger came forward to be baptised. As he came out of the water, he said to Jochanan, "That's Yeshua, my older brother. Be gentle with him!"

Jochanan promised, and the younger man went back to the bank to dry himself and get dressed.

The man called Yeshua splashed slowly and hesitatingly towards Jochanan. Finally, he stood in front of the prophet.

"What do you want me to do for you?" Jochanan asked formally, as he asked each man in turn.

"I wish to be baptised."

"Will you commit yourself to honest obedience to the Torah and to Messiah when he comes?"

"I will."

Jochanan turned Yeshua round, placed his hands on both his shoulders and pushed him under the water. The world seemed to go dark for a moment, and Jochanan felt he was falling. Jochanan was afraid. He had never experienced such power. Yeshua emerged from the water, streaming like a waterfall. He made to return to the riverbank, but Jochanan stopped him.

"That is no longer your way, Yeshua Bar Abraham. Tell your brother to bring your clothes and come with me to the other side of the river. We have to talk. Your friends can go back to Bethlehem without you."

Yeshua looked surprised but called out to Jacob to bring his clothes for him and to cross the river to join him. He asked Jacob to tell the Rabbi they were staying with the prophet for a while. He promised they would return later.

That night, as Pilate was entering Caesarea, Caiaphas was trying to explain to his first Council meeting why Annas had been deposed and Herod was explaining, for the apparently millionth time, to Herodias why Jochanan was still free, Yeshua was sitting by a camp fire, eating roast locusts and wild honey, and drinking river water. Jacob had gone to sleep, as had most of the camp, but Jochanan and Yeshua continued to talk. The flickering light from the flames lit their faces in the darkness. They spoke quietly together.

"I saw the surprise in your eyes when I called you Yeshua Bar Abraham," Jochanan said. "However, that is who you are, isn't it?"

"It is, but no one has named me that for years," Yeshua answered.

"I know, and I know why. I know who you are and what you are. I also know what you should be."

"But you do not know my mind. I have no wish to be other than what I am, the carpenter, son of Yusuf, of Bethlehem."

"It's not your choice, Yeshua. Remember the story of David. God chooses for us. We respond. I did not want to be a prophet. God chose me. He has chosen you. I know this. I saw it today."

"What do you mean Jochanan? I know who you are and that we are cousins. I know the story of your birth, and so, I guess I know why you feel God called you. But why is God calling me, and how do you know?"

"When you were under the water, I felt power flow into my hands. I thought a dark cloud surrounded me and I heard a roaring sound and saw light, as though it was a dove descending. God has chosen you for something and chosen me to help you and prepare for your coming."

"If you know so much of God's mind, Jochanan, what does He want me to do?"

"Tomorrow, you should leave here. My work is over and I will be arrested soon. You must not be here. I will send two of my most trusted men with you – Thomas and Philip. They know the Judaean desert and they will take you to the monastery at Qumr'an. Take your brother with you, for extra company and protection on the way. It's dangerous in the Judaean desert. There are wild animals, snakes and scorpions, and little water, unless you know where to find it."

Yeshua interrupted.

"The desert is the home of devils and demons. My father died there. I have no wish to go there, and Jacob will be terrified. Why must I go to Qumr'an anyway?'

"There are no devils in the desert, Yeshua. You, of all people, should know that! The dangers are purely physical and not spiritual. Thomas and Philip know the desert and its ways. They will protect you. You have to go to Qumr'an. It is at Qumr'an that you will find the answers to all your questions."

"What about my family? My father disappeared in the Desert. My second father has died. My mother, my wife and my children, not to mention Jacob's wife and children, will be distraught if we disappear in the desert too."

"Don't worry Yeshua. I have a third person I trust more than anyone else, Judah; he knows your mother, and knew your father. He will travel to Bethlehem to reassure your families, and then make his way to you at Qumr'an, so you can feel peace of mind."

Yeshua had no answer to this, and, wisely, fell silent. Eventually, the two men, with nothing more to say to each other, turned their backs on each other, rolled themselves in blankets, and slept.

Next morning, Yeshua and Jacob, accompanied by Thomas and Philip and four donkeys loaded with food and water, set out to cross the desert to Qumr'an, while Judah set out for Bethlehem. Yeshua took Judah apart before they left and spoke urgently to him, giving him a message to take to his wife and children.

**

One week later, Jochanan was chased across the river by soldiers belonging to Pilate, straight into the hands of soldiers belonging to Herod. Jochanan, and the two of his followers who remained with him were chained, placed on horses, and taken across the desert to Herod's fortress palace of Macchaerus in the far south, where he was imprisoned, to await his fate. His companions were freed, but chose to stay with the Prophet, caring for his needs and acting as his messengers. For the moment, Jochanan was safe, since Herod often came down to Jochanan's dungeon to talk with him and seek his advice.

Chapter 3

The Desert

Judaea, 30AD

The Judaean Desert is a tough and dangerous place.
Dry and sandy, it is marked by low hills and
treacherous gullies. There are the valleys of seasonal
streams, for when it receives its rare rain showers. Then
the desert turns green and the streams whisper down
their tracks to the Dead Sea, which receives their water
and turns it to salt. Once the water dies; so does the
brief flowering of the plants. They, greedy for life, but
knowing how brief it will be, grow quickly, flower, and
die, all within two weeks, and then wait, patiently,
seeds sown, for the next shower, to do it all again.

Through this sleeping land, four men marched, each
leading a laden donkey, for five days, deeper and
deeper into the desert. Their heads and faces were
muffled in kaffiyahs, Arab headdresses that shielded
them from the sun and dust. Despite this, in the intense
heat, they sweated, and had to stop every hour to drink.
Thomas and Philip knew the desert, having taken this
route several times on behalf of Jochanan. They
ensured they had enough water. To save energy, the
men did not talk on the way. Instead, they concentrated
on the route, watching for snakes and scorpions. They
kicked away the sand that clogged their sandals, and
tried not to be blinded by the glare of the sun.
Fortunately, the donkeys were docile. They too knew
the route, and, more importantly, they knew and trusted
Philip and Thomas. Yeshua had an inbuilt sympathy for
animals, which his donkey instinctively felt. Jacob had

71

to work harder to gain the trust of his animal, but, by the end of the first day, donkey and man had apparently gelled.

They followed the same routine every day. Rise early, wash, pray and eat. Walk for eight hours. Eat, wash, pray, sit around the campfire, talk, before sleeping under the stars. It was as cold at night as it was hot during the day, but they wrapped themselves up in their blankets, stayed close to the dying fire, for warmth and protection from wild animals, and survived.

Thomas and Philip used the evening discussions to answer the questions Yeshua and Jacob put to them, and to explain about Qumr'an, about which the two brothers knew nothing.

"Qumr'an," explained Thomas, poking the fire with a stick and causing it to flare up in a mass of sparks, "is a monastic community. About 100 men live there, on the northern shore of the Dead Sea, in an area where there is a natural spring. They study the Scriptures and prepare for the coming of Messiah."

"I've never heard of it, or them," said Jacob, shaking his head. "Who are they, and why are they there?"

"They call themselves Essenes," Thomas answered. "They are there because of an historical accident."

"I've never heard of them, nor of their monastery," Yeshua said, supporting his brother. "Why are they so secretive?"

"Security," Philip said briefly. "They do not want to attract the attention of Annas, Herod or Pilate.

"So they're enemies of the state," commented Jacob in a disappointed tone.

"No," said Thomas fiercely. "They are defenders of the Holy Land of Israel. They believe that Herod and Annas are false leaders, and the Romans have no right to be in God's land."

Jacob looked at the fire, watching a stick catch alight as a small flame flared at one end. He felt cold, rubbed his hands and moved closer to the fire. He looked at Thomas, whose face was a flickering mask of red and grey.

"Are they part of the terrorist network which has been causing us so much trouble recently?" he asked.

"Only partly," Thomas replied patiently, like Jacob rubbing his hands for warmth. The night was turning colder and the fire was dying. "From time to time they send people out to remind the public and our enemies and oppressors that the time for liberation is drawing near. Then they take the name Zealot. You also know them as the knife men, the Sicarii, because they often assassinate enemy leaders with their knives. Those men are usually martyrs for the cause. They seldom return from their missions. Unless you knife someone secretly, you are likely to be captured, tortured and killed. They know this, and undertake their missions knowing they probably will not return."

A lion grunted in the distance, its voice making all four men stare uneasily into the darkness. Further away a wolf howled. They drew closer to the dying fire for protection as well as warmth.

"They're Freedom Fighters then?" Yeshua commented. "Why, if they are working for God's power, do they not trust in God to convince people to follow His will?"

"God has always needed help from human beings," Philip commented drily, "and there are always human beings willing to give it."

There seemed nothing to add to that, and the four men sat in silent contemplation of the flames, unconsciously listening for the lion to speak again. Eventually Yeshua broke the silence.

"You said, Thomas, that Qumr'an was a monastic

community. When was it founded and by whom?"

"We don't know the names," Thomas answered, "but we do know the circumstances. About seventy years ago, King Herod's father seized power from the last of the priest kings, the descendants of Judas Maccabeus, the man who drove out the Greeks and gave us back our freedom. He deposed the last priest king, John Hyrcanus, first as king, and then as High Priest. He, followed by his son, Herod, declared himself to be king, and appointed his own minion as High Priest.

"Those who followed the Hasmonean priest kings fled into the desert and created a temporary camp by the Dead Sea, as far away from Herod as they could get. Their men watched the passes, and, as it became clear that Herod did not know, or did not care, about them, they turned their camp into a permanent structure. Others came to join them, and they began to create an alternative government, ready to replace the Herodians when the dynasty fell, as they expected it to do. When it did not fall, they began to plan a military campaign to destroy and remove it.

"When Herod died, they thought the time had finally come, but, instead, the Romans arrived and took over Judaea and Samaria. So now we have three enemies – the false king and false High Priest, instead of the true Hasmonean leader, who is both High Priest and King; and the Roman oppressor - the false friend who has turned into a ravening wolf."

"Wolf is an appropriate image for them," Philip commented drily.

"They believe they are descended from wolves. They certainly seem to behave like their claimed ancestors."

Jacob agreed with Philip. Yeshua did not like the way the conversation was turning.

"Not all Romans are the same," he said. "You saw how courteous the Governor was towards us the other day. That was not wolf-like!"

"You cannot trust an unbeliever," Thomas said vehemently. "They will present you with a fair face when they wish to do so, in order to trick you into a false sense of security. Then they will strike and kill you."

"I agree," Philip concurred, "the only good Roman is a dead Roman – but make sure he is dead before you leave his body. The best principle is to kill him twice!"

"That's crude, but simple advice," Jacob said enthusiastically. "I agree with you absolutely, Philip."

"I don't!" Yeshua said forcefully. "If we behave that way we are no better than our enemies. Surely we should show our values by the way we treat others?"

"You're wrong, Yeshua, although your error does you credit," Philip responded patiently. "Remember the Torah says 'Love your friends and hate your enemies'."

"How different would it be if we loved our enemies?" Yeshua mused, apparently to himself.

"So different, you would be dead rather than them," Philip responded forcefully, punching the air to make his point.

"And, on that note, I think we should all turn in. It's another long day tomorrow," Thomas said firmly.

The second day unwound in much the same way as the first. They had left the lush Jordan Valley, climbed up the dangerous road from Jericho towards Jerusalem, protected from the robbers who haunted the road by the swords carried prominently by the two followers of Jochanan, the obvious strength of Yeshua and Jacob, and the fact that they plainly were not worth the effort of robbing, and had entered the Judaean desert, passing to the east of Jerusalem, between the city and the Dead Sea. Then the party disappeared, as they struck out into the desert proper.

Jacob complained about the heat. He rubbed his face with his head cloth, rubbing the sweat out of his eyes.

"This heat. It makes you hungry and thirsty. It's a long time until we stop again."

"I wish sand were food," Yeshua answered, kicking the dust away from his feet savagely. "There's more than enough of it here for all of us."

Thomas overheard this conversation and laughed. He picked up a flat stone and showed it to Yeshua.

"See this stone, Yeshua. Look how flat it is; it looks just like one of our loaves doesn't it?"

Yeshua agreed. Thomas tossed it to him.

"Try to eat it!"

"You must be joking Thomas!"

"True – but if I was one of the devils who are said to live here I would tell you to turn it into bread. You could then feed our army."

"It's an interesting idea Thomas, but would God allow it? Surely God provided us with enough food to eat? We shouldn't try to force him to give us more."

Thomas smiled and turned to Jacob.

"Is your brother always as serious as this Jacob?"

"Pretty much," Jacob replied. "He hates Satan and all demons. He hates jokes about Satan. If Satan were to take him to the top of a mountain and offer him the rule of the whole world, he would refuse to accept it."

"That's good," said Philip. "We need men of such firm convictions." He turned to Yeshua. "Would you jump off the Temple if you were dared?"

"Certainly not!" Yeshua answered. "Do you think I'm a fool, Philip?"

"No, Yeshua," Philip said hastily, "but, if you trusted in God, surely He would send an angel to catch you?"

"I doubt it very much," Yeshua said. "I'm not sure

about angels and I don't think God would bother with someone so stupid as to jump off a high wall in order to impress others."

"I expect you're right, Yeshua," Philip conceded, but it would be fun wouldn't it if you could do it. Just imagine how people would react when you landed safely and walked away unhurt!"

"It would be fun if pigs could fly too," Yeshua remarked drily, "but I still would not eat pork!"

That night, around the fire, the talk turned to the war against the Greeks. Thomas asked the two brothers how much they knew about the history of Israel. They confessed that they knew little of events since the Return from Babylon.

"Have you heard of the Greek king, Alexander?" Thomas asked.

"I know the name," Jacob replied for them both. "Who doesn't? But I don't know much about him."

"I'm not surprised," Thomas commented, "The rabbis ignore him because he ignored Judaea. However, he was important because he destroyed Persia. If you remember, it was the Persian king, Cyrus, who let our ancestors return from Babylon."

Yeshua and Jacob nodded.

"Well, Alexander conquered the world, but he could not conquer himself. He died, still young, in Babylon, leaving a child to succeed him. Rumour had it that one of his generals poisoned him, tired of the endless campaigning. I think he died of exhaustion and excess of alcohol and rich food."

"Kings often do that sort of thing," Yeshua agreed.

"Absolutely, Yeshua," Thomas continued. He tossed another stick into the fire, which flared up briefly. "Alexander's generals did not allow his baby son to rule. I believe he was murdered, together with his mother, Roxanne, a Persian princess. The Greeks did that sort of thing. His three generals divided the empire between them. However, two of them, had a border dispute. One, called Ptolemy, ruled Egypt, and the other, called Antiochus, ruled Syria. They both wanted us.

"First Ptolemy ruled us, and then Antiochus took us over. He wanted us to obey him, so he made himself into a god. He put his statue in the Temple, and ordered us to worship it. The father of Judas Maccabeus refused, and organised a revolt. The Greeks sent a large army against us. Judas lured it into the desert here, and destroyed it among the hills. Then he captured Jerusalem, an event we still remember at Purim.

"When he had Jerusalem, he cleaned the Temple, but there was no High Priest, because the Greeks had killed him. The Maccabees were a priestly family, so Judas became High priest as well as king. His sons restored much of the Empire of David, but they continued as priest-kings."

"Until Herod overthrew them," Jacob added, taking a sip from his water bottle.

"Absolutely," Thomas said.

"So, why didn't Herod become High Priest?" asked Jacob.

"Because he wasn't Jewish," Philip said in a tone which suggested that Jacob had really not been listening. "Herod's father allowed the last Hasmonean king to remain as High Priest until he had a candidate to replace him. Then he had the man murdered. He would probably have murdered his family too, but the Essenes had managed to smuggle them out of Jerusalem, and they were safe in Qumr'an. Herod tried to find them, using the excuse that he was looking for someone to replace the last High Priest, but no one believed him, and they were kept hidden. Eventually, Herod appointed his own man – and things have gone on from there."

The conversation flagged. The men sat, listening to the silence of the desert night, which hung around them, black and menacing, lit only by the bright diamonds of the stars and the sliver of the crescent moon, held at bay by the feeble and flickering light of the fire. A snake slithered away into the darkness, frightened off by the heat of the fire and the shadowy figures sitting around it.

Yeshua broke the silence with a question.

"How did the Romans get involved?"

"Judas Maccabeus made an alliance with them against the Greeks," Thomas explained. "They were not seen as a threat then. Later, they destroyed the Greek kingdoms, and forced Herod to become a client king. He had to do as they told him. He was clever though. There were several civil wars between the Roman leaders, and you never knew from one day to the next who was in and who was out. Making a mistake in those circumstances and backing the wrong man, or backing the right man for too long, or too early, could be literally fatal for a local ruler. Herod never made any mistake, and survived. He was still there when the Emperor Augustus ended the civil wars, and was treated as a valuable ally by him. It was Augustus who decided to split his kingdom into three, and Augustus who removed Archelaus, the ruler of Judaea and Samaria, when he proved incompetent."

"So we invited them in," Yeshua mused. "We were the creators of our own misfortune. Why didn't Judas Maccabeus trust God, like King Hezekiah did when the Assyrians threatened Jerusalem?"

"Possibly because of what happened when King Nebuchadnezzar of Babylon surrounded Jerusalem," Philip answered. "Remember your history Yeshua. Divine protection appeared very uncertain at best. God helped Gideon, but not Saul. He defended Jerusalem against Sennacherib, but not against Nebuchadnezzar. He refused to defend Samson against the Philistines, but helped David against Goliath. I sometimes wander if He did anything at all!"

"Hush Philip," Thomas cautioned. "Such thoughts are dangerous. The Jewish leaders would stone you if they heard you utter them, even though they act as though they share them."

"That's because they're really politicians," Philip said truculently. "They use religion as a cover for political purposes, and religious teaching as a cover for keeping the poor suppressed. They oppress the poor in order to retain power. We need a revolution to sweep them all away, and start again."

"That's why we have Qumr'an," Thomas reminded him. "That is where the Revolution is being planned, the fighters are being trained, the philosophy and policy is being hammered out, and the right time and right people are being waited for. Don't be so impatient, and don't speak publicly too soon. A mistake could be fatal. We know we are surrounded by enemies and by our enemies' spies. Pilate, Annas and Herod seem to know what we think almost before we've thought it! Be careful, Philip, one slip could destroy us all."

Thomas turned to Yeshua and Jacob.

"And that is why, when you leave Qumr'an, you must never mention its existence. As far as your families and those who become your followers are concerned, you spent several months meditating in the desert, however implausible that is. Some will think you're very holy. Others will think you're very brave. Yet others will think you're stupid. But they will all think they know what you did – whether they consider it holy, brave or stupid, and they will not ask any questions."

In this way they continued their journey. In all they travelled for five days, until they saw the blue waters of the Dead Sea glittering below them. They turned along its shore, following the white, salt lined, beaches northwards. Thomas explained that the sea, or lake, was so salty that they could walk across it, but advised them not to try it when Jacob wanted to test his new knowledge out. They followed the shore for a day before turning back into the hills, and there they came across what looked like an encampment. The area was enclosed by a wall made of wooden stakes, and contained a large number of wood and thatch huts. From one, larger one, smoke rose and the smell of cooking came. In the centre was a large open area. Here a sergeant was drilling a group of young men, while others were practising with sword, shield and spear. Two men came and took their donkeys, leading them away to stables within the compound. The four men walked across the central square towards the hut from which the smoke was rising.

Yeshua expressed surprise.

"I thought you said this was a <u>permanent</u> camp," he said to Thomas.

"It is," Thomas replied. "The most important structures are underground, where, over the years, the brothers have hollowed out and extended the natural caves. These buildings are temporary. If an enemy is spotted coming this way, we can have the whole settlement down within a day, and no evidence will remain that we exist. How else do you think we have evaded detection over the years?"

"I never saw any watchers," Jacob objected.

"Perhaps not," Philip answered, but they saw us, and they know us. That's why we were not challenged. The sentries are scouts. They see and report. They are not expected to challenge or halt strangers."

"There's a contradiction there," Yeshua pointed out. "You said, Philip, that we would have been challenged had we not been with you, yet said the sentries do not challenge newcomers. Which is true?"

"Both. The sentries would see you and report. Later, a couple of harmless herders would have "found" you, asked where you were going, told you there was no such place as Qumr'an and led you away, if you were co-operative, putting you on the road to Jerusalem, and ensuring you had enough water to get there."

"And if we didn't co-operate?" Jacob asked.

"They would have cut your throats while you slept and left you for the wild animals to eat. You would have been seen as just another two fools who wandered into the desert and died there."

Thomas ended the conversation, and took them to the food hut, where he asked the cook to feed his three companions, while he left them to report to the Camp Commander. The three men ate, answering the cook's questions about their journey and about Jochanan. The cook was especially concerned for the Prophet's safety.

"Jochanan sent Thomas and me to bring these two here," Philip said, "and he sent Judah to Bethlehem to reassure their families, and then come on here to reassure them. However, he kept Simeon and Thaddeus with him, so he should be all right."

"Let's hope so," the Cook said, sounding unconvinced. "Our enemies are very determined, and Jochanan has frightened them, especially Herod. He's very vulnerable out there. The Commander has tried to recall him, but he has refused to come back."

"Don't worry," Philip said, "Jochanan may look like a fanatic, but he's got his head screwed on right. He won't be taken easily."

Thomas returned with an older man, grey haired, standing upright, and exuding authority. He wore civilian clothing like everyone else in the camp, despite his military air. Yeshua estimated that he was about sixty years old, which was a good age for any adult to reach. He bowed his head in respect when Thomas introduced him.

"This is Abraham Bar Abbas," Thomas explained. "He is the Commander here."

"You have a strange name," Yeshua commented. "Abbas is father – so you are the Son of the Father. Is that your real name?"

"You're shrewd, young Yeshua. Of course that's not my real name. I will tell you that by and by. It is my title as leader here. I am Abraham. I am also the Son of the Father – or the military and religious commander. If you like, I am the real King and High Priest of Israel. Our local area leaders are also called Son of the Father. For instance, our leader in Jerusalem is Judas Bar Abbas. If you want to find him, go to the main gate of the Temple and say to one of the men on the gate 'Where is the Son of the Father?' He will tell you to wait, and someone will eventually come and take you to Judas. That's the way we work."

The newcomer sat down and studied the two brothers as they ate and drank. Eventually, apparently satisfied, he turned to Thomas and Philip.

"Thank you for bringing them. I would send you back to try to persuade Jochanan to return here, but it would not work. I very much fear he has been taken. I heard that Pilate and Herod planned some sort of trap over Passover. Go and rest. Leave these two with me, but send Judah to me when he arrives."

Once Yeshua and Jacob had finished their meal, Bar Abbas took them away. He showed them around the compound on the surface, introducing them to some of the Brotherhood, before leading them down a long flight of steps underground. Here he had his own suite of rooms, and it was here that he plainly intended that the two bothers should stay. He promised to show them around the underground chambers later, but urged them to rest after their long and arduous journey. Then he left them to sleep.

When they woke, the Commander ensured his two guests were given water to wash off the dust of their journey, food to eat, and wine to drink. After they had washed and eaten he took them around the underground part of the monastery, which was lit by blazing torches, each fitted on sconces secured by bolts to the walls. In the uncertain light, the area looked huge. Yeshua and Jacob were astonished at the size and complexity of the underground workings at Qumr'an. There were small sleeping chambers, carved out of the sides of a central meeting chamber. There were water cisterns, tapping the natural spring at the heart of the complex. There were storerooms for food and weapons and places where the Brothers could write out the books, which were stored in the library. All this, the Commander explained, had been carved out of the already existing cave system, which had been expanded and adapted for use.

After the tour, the three men returned to the Commander's suite, which lay on the side of the central hall farthest from the entrance, and which was guarded by two men, each armed with shield, sword and spear, and wearing a breastplate and helmet. Here, in much brighter light, partly provided by a window cut through the rock overlooking the distant placid waters of the Dead Sea, twinkling far below them, the Commander provided them with watered wine, and made them sit on seats carved out of the rock, before he began to talk.

"I understand Yeshua that you already know the history of this place."

"Thomas and Philip told us a great deal on our way

here."

"That's what I hoped. It saves a great deal of time."

Bar Abbas paused.

"What do you know of us?"

"We learnt that you are descended from the Maccabees and fled here from the Herods. As far as I can understand, you are at war with both the Herods, the High Priests and the Romans."

Jacob said this with considerable force, laying heavy emphasis on each of the Order's perceived enemies.

"That's more or less true, young Jacob. I would not actually put it the way you have, but you're not far from reality."

"Did Jochanan come from here?" Yeshua asked.

"He came here as a sixteen year old. Instead of marrying a woman, he married the Order. He became a lifetime Nazirite and went out to spread the word and prepare the way for He Who Comes."

Yeshua corrected him.

"You mean the Messiah,"

"I mean 'He Who Comes', as I said. Whether he is also Messiah is another matter."

"What's the difference?" Jacob asked.

"We Jews have thought and written a great deal about Messiah, much of it speculative and in error. We think of him as a great soldier, like King David, but forget that David did not fight most of his wars. His great general, Joab fought most of them for him. We don't use the term here because it has so many connotations. It is almost impossible for us to use. 'He Who Comes' is different. That title is our own. It describes the Priest – King who will rescue the faith and restore the freedom of the country, in that order. He will first reform the religion, and bring the people back to God. Once he has done that, he will lead them against the foreign oppressors and rescue the country.

It's that way round, not the other – as the people want. The great Judas did it that way. He liberated Jerusalem from the Greeks, cleaned up and restored the Temple, and then drove the Greeks out of the rest of David's kingdom."

They sipped their wine meditatively, until Yeshua spoke for them both.

"Who is He Who Comes?"

"He is the legitimate High Priest who will also be the political leader of our people. He will be of the House of Aaron and a descendent of Judas Maccabaeus. He will replace both Herod and, as I understand it, Caiaphas, since Pilate has, wisely I think, deposed the corrupt and unworthy Annas. Having united both roles, he will lead the people to victory against Rome."

Yeshua studied his hands and then looked searchingly across at Bar Abbas.

"I can see there is much I need to learn about what you do here and what you believe. I feel I need to study and decide who I am, what I am, and what I believe."

"I know exactly who and what you are, Yeshua. However, I am not so sure as to what you are going to do. Only you can decide that. I agree that you should study here. I think your brother should do the same, since I feel he is more important than he realises at the moment. When you think you know enough, return to me and we will discuss what you are going to do."

They stood up to go, but Yeshua seemed irresolute. He turned back at the door of the suite, to speak to the Commander.

"I have another question, before we go, Commander," said Yeshua.

"What question is that, Yeshua?"

"Did you know Abraham our father, and did he ever come here?"

"The answer is yes to both questions. Yes, I know Abraham your father, and I know what happened to him. Yes, he came and settled here."

"Will you tell us what happened to him, whether he is still alive, and, if he is, where he is?" asked Yeshua, studying the Commander intently.

"All in good time young Yeshua. Go and study, and later you will be able to tell me the answers to your questions. I will send Judah to you when he arrives here from Bethlehem."

"A final question Commander," Jacob added.

"I seem to be set to answer questions all day!" Bar Abbas commented. What's your question, young Jacob?"

"How do you know what is going on in the country if you never leave this place?"

"I never said I never leave. You are making assumptions, Jacob. However, I know what I know because I maintain a network of agents throughout the country. I am certain that Jochanan has been arrested and I know that Annas has been replaced. I know, too, that Pilate recently crushed a revolt in Galilee and a riot in Jerusalem. He has enslaved one of the leading noble families in the city, giving the youngest daughter to his wife as a slave, and keeping a son as a catamite. I can tell you too that he will soon have to deal with another revolt, arising from the arrest of Jochanan."

The Commander smiled.

"The only thing I don't know is when the Governor goes to relieve himself! It is necessary to keep up to date with the news. To be reliably informed is to be forearmed. Now," with a smile, "go and find the Librarian, and begin your studies."

Chapter 4

The North

Galilee, 30AD

The news of the arrest of Jochanan hit the community at Qumr'an like a lightening bolt. The first reaction among the Brothers was one of stunned disbelief. They had been convinced that, since the Prophet was doing God's will, he would be safe from any of their three enemies. Thomas was sent to find the truth. He returned two weeks later with confirmation.

Following this, Bar Abbas sent a small group, carrying wine from the cellars at Qumr'an to the garrison at Machaerus. They sailed across the lake and down the eastern shore, before travelling inland to Herod's fortress-like palace on its hill. They met and talked with the guards, who confirmed that Jochanan was being held in Herod's dungeons. They were reassured when they learnt that Herod spent much of his time talking with Jochanan, seeking his advice.

Some of the wilder Brothers urged a raid on the Fortress to rescue the prophet. Bar Abbas stopped such talk, and the wiser military heads pointed out that they lacked the means to storm the place. The news brought by Bar Abbas's envoys about how Jochanan was being treated calmed them, and they decided to leave issues about the Prophet's fate to God. As one of the Brothers said, "If God wants to save him, He will save him."

Judah returned from Bethlehem, bringing reassuring messages for Yeshua and Jacob from their families. Thus heartened, the two brothers spent their time in the library, studying the practices and beliefs of the Essene

Brotherhood. They learnt about the Messianic figure the Essenes were expecting to come. They read the scrolls outlining the military organisation with which they intended to challenge the might of Rome. (This military organisation, based on the ancient structure of the Israelite Army, did not impress Yeshua, who had seen the disciplined Roman Army. He began to wander whether the Essenes actually had any answer to the issues they all faced.)

He did not feel able to speak openly of his growing doubts within the compound, so he asked Jacob to accompany him to the shores of the lake. Jacob agreed, so they left the monastery and climbed down to the salt covered beach that fringed the Dead Sea. They sat on the sand with their backs to the rocks scattered across the beach, watching the quiet waters. Here Yeshua felt it was possible to talk freely.

"I don't like what I've seen of the plans of this group," he began.

Jacob was surprised.

"I haven't seen anything that surprised me. What is it that concerns you so much Yeshua?"

Yeshua idly threw a stone into the water. He watched as it bounced on the surface, skimming its way across, until it ran out of force, and sank.

"You've seen the Romans Jacob. Their discipline is strong, and their tactics, I have heard, are the best in the world."

"I agree they're strong, Yeshua. But remember, the Greeks were strong too – however, Judas still beat them. They're only men, not gods. They can make mistakes, and we can use the country against them."

"I know all that, Jacob, but it's more than that. I wander whether their approach is actually right."

"What do you mean Yeshua?"

Jacob was confused. He stared at Yeshua, before

turning away to look across the Lake, as though the Lake could answer his question. Yeshua stood up and walked to the edge of the water. He kicked off his sandals and let the water splash over his feet, washing off the dust. He turned and faced his brother, standing there on the edge of the lake, his hands clasped before him as though he were praying.

"You don't fight a spiritual enemy with physical weapons."

Jacob looked sharply at his brother. He picked up a stone and studied it intently, running his finger over its smooth surface, trying to see how flat it was. He looked up at his brother.

"Do you mean the Romans and Satan are the same?"

"Certainly not!" Yeshua exploded. "The Romans are men, whereas Satan is a supernatural being. The Romans are both good and bad."

Yeshua raised his hand to silence the objections he knew Jacob was about to make.

"They are, like all men, a mixture of good and bad, and of worthy and unworthy motives. Satan, on the other hand, is totally evil. He is out only to rule and enslave human beings. You can't beat him with an army."

Jacob laughed.

"Why not, Yeshua? Just imagine leading an army down into Hell, to liberate the prisoners there. What a story that would make!"

Yeshua was annoyed, and showed it.

"Be serious for once, Jacob! I am trying to make you see that there is more to this role than fighting. You need spiritual weapons to defeat a spiritual enemy."

"Driving the Romans and the Herods out would be a good start though, Yeshua," said Jacob, finally standing up and pulling his hand back to send his stone skimming over the water, just past his brother. He walked down the short strip of sand to stand by Yeshua, who kicked water over Jacob's feet, before answering him.

"Driving the Romans out and dethroning the Herodians would not solve anything, Jacob, even if we could do it, which I doubt. The problem would still remain. Our history shows that. Kick out one set of conquerors, and we simply get another. Our ancestors drove out the Greeks from Egypt, only to get the Greeks from Syria. They drove them out, only to get the Romans. If we drive the Romans out, who will rule us then? And exactly who do you think will replace the Herods? Will they be any better?"

Jacob kicked the sand, his hands behind his back.

"I don't know," he sighed eventually. "They may be better or worse, who can tell? And can we not end the cycle of foreign domination?"

"Only God knows the answer to that one, Jacob, and I don't feel we should try to force Him to tell us."

"We wouldn't succeed anyway, Yeshua," Jacob said ruefully. "So what, exactly are you proposing?"

"I don't know," admitted Yeshua. "I only know I think the Essenes are wrong. I don't think that violence is the answer."

"You're back to your 'Love your enemies' theme aren't you, Yeshua?"

"I suppose I am. I wish I knew. Perhaps I will one day."

"All I can suggest is that you pray about it. Perhaps God will tell you what He wants."

"Have you read your Bible recently, Jacob? It does not encourage one to expect clear Divine guidance when one really needs it, does it?"

Yeshua walked away from his brother, head down, his hands still clasped, shuffling through the water. He said nothing. Jacob watched him go, quietly sympathising with a struggle he did not understand. It all seemed so simple to him. But nothing was simple for Yeshua. Jacob stood and watched, kicking the water, using his toes to move the stones around. Finally, he selected six of the roundest and smoothest. He threw them, one after the other, watching how far each of them would go.

Yeshua paced slowly through the gently breaking waves, hands clasped behind his back, head down, deep in thought.

What am I going to do, and where am I going to do it?

He remembered the conversations they had had in the desert with Thomas and Philip.

I understand what they told me much better now – but what does it all mean for me? It's like my conversation with mother at my Bar Mitzvah. Then I had to push and push to get an answer. I feel the same way now.

His mind reverted to the conversation with Abraham.

"I can see there is much I need to learn about what you do here and what you believe. I feel I need to study and decide who I am, what I am, and what I believe."

"I know exactly who and what you are, Yeshua. However, I am not so sure as to what you are going to do. Only you can decide that. I agree that you should study here. I think your brother should do the same, since I feel he is more important than he realises at the moment. When you think you know enough, return to me and we will discuss what you are going to do."

"I have another question, before we go, Commander."

"What question is that, Yeshua?"

"Did you know Abraham our father, and did he ever come here?"

"The answer is yes to both questions. Yes, I know Abraham your father, and I know what happened to him. Yes, he came and settled here."

"Will you tell us what happened to him, whether he is still alive, and, if he is, where he is?"

"All in good time young Yeshua. Go and study, and later you will be able to tell me the answers to your questions."

That's what Abraham told me, and it's true – I have answered most of the questions – except that last one. What happened to Abraham, my father?

Yeshua bent down and picked up a pebble. He studied it, shrugged his shoulders, and threw it idly across the lake, watching it strike the water, bounce twice, and finally sink below the surface. As he turned, he saw Jacob, some way along the beach, doing the same thing. The Sun shone brightly in Yeshua's eyes, and he saw Jacob only as a dark profile – and suddenly he knew the answer to his question.

What a fool I am! The answer was there all the time – Abraham Bar Abbas is our father. He is the Abraham who is also son of Jochanan, and descendent of Aaron.

Then who and what am I?

You are my servant, my chosen one. I have called you, just as I called Jochanan Bar Zechariah. His work is over. Yours is about to begin. Will you answer my call?

The voice within him came suddenly, unexpectedly, and unbidden.

I cannot be another Jochanan. His austerity is not mine. He may have been a lifelong Nazirite, but I am different. I have a wife and children. I love people and love life. I cannot be another Jochanan.

I don't need another Jochanan. I need a Yeshua. I have called you for what you are. Be true to yourself. You love people – but how much do you love them?

There is no greater love than that of the person who dies for his friends or those who will become his friends. Can you do that Yeshua Bar Abraham?

I can love, but how much I do not know yet. I will find out in time – but where do I start?

Judaea is too close to the Priestly establishment to be safe. I need to distance myself and build a base of support before challenging them. I will go north. Thomas comes from Galilee – from Capernaum. I will start there.

Yeshua turned, to begin the walk back along the beach to his brother, still standing where he had left him.

He is not yet ready for this mission. He needs to learn much more and to look after our family, while I do God's work. He must go back to Bethlehem.

Yeshua walked purposefully now that he had made his decision, back to his brother.

"You must go back to Bethlehem Jacob. I want you to look after the family. Go with Judah, who knows the trails, and then ask Judah to bring Mariam and the two boys to me. I am going to travel to Capernaum in Galilee. I will take Thomas and Philip with me. Judah should bring my family to me there."

Jacob was surprised. He had been so engrossed in his stone throwing that he had not seen his brother walk briskly back up the beach and stand behind him. He turned round to face his brother. Yeshua no longer seemed uncertain or irresolute. His face was set hard and his eyes shone. He had plainly made a decision.

"What are you going to do?"

"I am going to talk to Abraham, our father…..."

Yeshua ignored the startled look on Jacob's face.

"….and then I am going to travel north. That's where I feel I should start. Once there, I will decide what I have to do."

He paused, smiled at his confused brother.

"Come on, it's getting cold. Let's go back and find him."

Jacob looked at the setting sun, shivered as a cold gust caught his coat, and followed his brother up the beach.

Abraham Bar Abbas was surprised by the suddenness of Yeshua's decision to leave the Monastery.

"I'm sure you both realise, by now, that I am your father."

They both nodded.

"I don't think you're ready, Yeshua," he said. "However, I am prepared to accept that you know your own mind better than I do."

"I am certain this is right, father," Yeshua responded. "There is little more I can learn here, and the sooner I start work, the better."

"In that case, son, all I can do is give you both my blessing. Take care and remember to trust God and yourselves, in that order."

Yeshua thanked Abraham, and was to remember his father's final words to him throughout his ministry. They were spoken as Abraham stood at the door of his suite, before embracing both his oldest sons.

"I don't know what you are going to do, or even what you should do. You and I know that you, Yeshua, are the rightful High Priest and Ruler of this country. The decisions have to be yours, but so will be the price of success or failure. We will give you what help we can, but, as Jochanan found out, there are limits to what we can do. You must follow your own path. Don't let others decide it for you. You must feel sure what you are doing is right. If it feels right, it is right. Do not allow yourself to be turned aside by others, however well meaning their advice.

"As for you, Jacob, your time is yet to come. When it is right for you to begin your work, return here. I, or my successor, will always welcome you. But again, as with your brother, only you will know when that time is. But, remember, both of you, you are always welcome here."

They left next day. Thomas and Philip said goodbye to Jacob and Judah, and they followed different routes across the desert. Judah and Jacob went west, whereas Thomas, Philip and Yeshua travelled north. It took them two weeks travelling from Qumr'an to Capernaum, taking the dangerous road past Jerusalem and down to Jericho, along the sub tropical Jordan Valley, with its palm trees, its sweltering heat, and its wild animals, before climbing back into the hills and following the edge of Lake Galilee, to the port city of Capernaum. Here, using funds provided by Bar Abbas, they bought a house to act as a head quarters and waited for Judah to return with Mariam and the boys.

**

Four weeks after leaving Qumr'an, Yeshua was standing alone on the beach at Capernaum. The water in Lake Galilee twinkled in the sunshine, much as the water had in the Dead Sea. He idly watched a fishing boat, crewed by two apparently naked men, one considerably older than the other, fishing close inshore. From where he was he could see through the sparkling, lightly moving water. He saw nothing where the men were casting their net. However, on the other side he saw a dark cloud in the water. He called out to the fishermen.

"Have you caught anything?"

"Absolutely nothing," the older man shouted back.

"Try the other side," Yeshua suggested. "I can see a

dark cloud in the water there."

The two men argued vigorously. One obviously thought Yeshua was an arrogant fool, whereas the other, the older of the two, was prepared to give the landsman the benefit of the doubt. The older man appeared to win, and they cast their net on the other side, as Yeshua suggested. He saw them struggle to haul in a net now full of fish. In the end they did not bother, they simply sailed their boat up onto the beach, grounding it, and putting their clothes on, before getting out of the boat to haul the net in. The older man beckoned to Yeshua to come and help them. He did so, and the three of them finally got the heavy net on shore. The two fishermen were stunned at the size of their catch. The older man turned away and fell on his knees before Yeshua.

"I have never seen such a catch. We worked all night and morning without success. Are you some sort of god to be able to work such a miracle?"

"Get up man. You should only kneel before God. I am just a man, a carpenter, Yeshua Bar Yusuf, from Bethlehem, in Judaea. I've come up here to work, with some friends. I'm waiting for my family to join me. I need help. Will you two join me?"

"What do you want us to do?"

Yeshua laughed.

"You're good fishermen. Use your skills. I need to catch men! Will you help me?"

The older man laughed at the joke.

"I like your style Yeshua Bar Yusuf. Of course I'll help you."

Yeshua embraced the fisherman, who was at least ten years older than he was, greying, stocky and clumsy, but he suspected, hugely enthusiastic. The younger man was obviously a brother, younger than Yeshua. He suspected he was much slower and probably less able than his older brother. However, he believed the younger man would be the more reliable of the two, whereas Yeshua was not so sure of the older man.

"Welcome to the campaign," he began. "You have the advantage of me. You know my name. What are yours, and that of your partner?"

"I'm Simeon Bar Zebediah, and this is my younger brother Andreas. I own the boat. If you are going to travel around on your campaign, the boat will probably be your best form of transport. The Lake acts like a sort of transport hub, linking most of the towns of Galilee. The only real exception is the hill town of Nazareth, but no one goes there. The people are simply not worth visiting. We have a saying that nothing good comes out of Nazareth."

Yeshua smiled. He felt his campaign was under way.

"Thank you for joining me. Let's sell your fish and then I will take you to my home."

**

Two days later, Judah brought Mariam, Jochanan and Jacob, Yeshua's sons, to join them. Yeshua introduced his family to Thomas and Philip, and all four to Simeon and Andreas. The house was only big enough to hold Yeshua, his family and the two who had travelled with him from Qumr'an. Simeon was married, but he and his brother took Judah home with them. They became friends. The new campaign team had been formed.

Next morning, Yeshua got up early and climbed up into the hills above the town. He needed time to think. He had his campaign team. He had brought his family together behind him, and he had his transport. But what was he going to do about it? What should his philosophy be?

Jochanan had been an ascetic, who took a lifetime Nazirite vow. Yeshua realised that was not the way he wanted to go. He had never felt like renouncing wine or the other pleasures of life. He loved his wife and his children, and felt that God would not wish him to renounce such a natural feeling. His new followers were also married, with families.

He realised he wanted to bring hope. He needed to unite the people behind him before he set out to challenge the Authorities. He remembered his words in the desert about love, and wandered if this should be his key teaching.

Love God and love each other, he thought.

He believed that true love would always prove stronger than hate and fear, since love involved true knowledge of a person, and knowledge overcame fear, which was based on ignorance. You cannot hate a person if you really know them. So, therefore, that had to be his message – Love.

It seems stupid, his inner self said. *Is that all I have to say – Love one another! Can I love someone who is nailing me to a tree like that man I saw on my Bar Mitzvah? Had I been that man, would my love have saved me?*

The voice within him answered, *it all depends on what you mean by 'saved'.*

Yeshua was disturbed by distant voices drawing closer. He recognised the sound of his two sons and his companions from Qumr'an. Realising they had missed him and come in search of him, Yeshua sighed, abandoned his meditations, and climbed down the hill towards the voices. When they saw him, Jochanan and Jacob ran forward and, throwing their arms around him, almost smothered him. Yeshua suddenly remembered how young and vulnerable they were. He smiled at them.

"Well, my Sons of Thunder," his nick name for their somewhat emotional natures, as evidenced by what they had just done, "Did you really miss me so much?"

Neither boy spoke, but Thomas, walking more slowly up the hill with Philip, as befitted their greater age, spoke for the two boys.

"You shouldn't blame them, Yeshua. After all, you haven't seen them for over six months. They're only kids. You're their father. You must expect they would miss you. They were eager to greet you this morning, and you weren't there!"

Yeshua made an elaborate gesture to his sons, kneeling on the ground and begging forgiveness, but with a smile on his face.

Jochanan, the older of the two, solemnly accepted the apology, and then added with a grin and a wagged finger, in words he'd heard his mother say to him so often, "Don't you dare do that again, father."

The three older men laughed, although Thomas tried to maintain a straight face and the gravitas, which he felt the occasion demanded.

"You see, Yeshua. Even your sons know what you should and should not do! You should follow their wise advice."

Thomas spoilt the effect by laughing. However, Yeshua's previously sombre mood had been lightened by his sons' arrival, and, placing his hands on both their shoulders, accompanied by Thomas and Philip, he made his way back down to the house, where he could smell cooking fish and baking bread, both being prepared by his wife, Mariam, and the small group of local women she had managed to recruit since her arrival to assist with her enlarged family.

Later that morning the group travelled the short distance to Simeon's house. Here they found a scene of some disorder. Simeon's mother, a woman approaching her sixties, was ill. Simeon thought she had a fever. She cared for the whole household. Although Simeon and his wife lived with them, his mother and father still ruled the house. When she was ill, all the cooking and the normal routines of the house ground to a halt. None of the other women dared to appear to try to take her place.

Yeshua was not sure what to do in this situation, but felt that he should, at least, show concern. He went in to talk to the sick woman, trying to give her comfort. She obviously was running a high temperature, because she was sweating in the heat. Concerned about this, Yeshua sent for a bowl of water. He washed his hands, and found a clean cloth, which he dipped in the water. He rubbed this damp cloth over the woman's forehead, in order to cool her down. She began to respond immediately, and, as her temperature fell, she began to feel better. Eventually, she left her bed, against the advice of her eldest son, and concerned about the apparent lack of courtesy being offered her visitors, organised the women to prepare lunch for them.

The women, astonished at her swift recovery, praised God for the work he had done through Yeshua. It was not long before they were telling other women in the town about how Yeshua had cured Simeon's mother. Yeshua tried to stop them, since he was not entirely sure what had actually happened, and certainly did not think he had cured her by touching her, as the rumour began to say, but he could not stop the gossip, and, once started, it began to spread. Before long people were beginning to compare Yeshua's 'cure' with the miracles ascribed to the great prophets, Elijah and Elisha.

Things came to a head next Sabbath, when Yeshua took his group to the local Synagogue. He had a letter of introduction from the Rabbi of the Bethlehem Synagogue, at which he had been an elder, so he was made welcome and invited to read the Torah. A man, obviously mad, rushed forward.

"Who sent you?" he screamed dementedly. "I know who you are, Yeshua Bar Abraham. Have you come to destroy me, Son of the Father?"

Yeshua was alarmed. He did not want this sort of thing to be said or repeated. He was not sure whether the man knew the significance of his words, but was certain that some, at least, of the men present did know, and he wandered how they would react. He turned to the Rabbi for advice.

"Don't worry, Yeshua," the Rabbi said reassuringly, "he's a notorious madman. No one listens to him." Then he turned to the man. "Go away," he said angrily. "You know you're not allowed in here."

The man stayed put, shouting his challenge even louder. Yeshua left the shelter of the Bimah (the enclosed area in the middle of the Synagogue) and approached the man. He laid his hand on the man's head in an attempt to calm him.

"You are wrong," he said slowly and calmly. "I am Yeshua Bar Yusuf, the son of a carpenter from Bethlehem. I have not come here to harm you, but to set up a business. I do not claim any special powers and do not want to hurt you. Go in peace and do not be afraid."

Yeshua noticed that the man calmed down, possibly, he thought because he felt reassured by his touch and the calmness of his voice. The man smiled at the Rabbi, bowed his head in acknowledgement of his authority, and left the Synagogue. Yeshua completed the reading and the service came to an end. By then though, the story of how Yeshua had 'cured' the madman by a touch had begun to follow the story of his miraculous 'cure' of Simeon's mother around the town and neighbouring countryside. Yeshua's reputation was growing. However, it was not the reputation that he wanted. He began to find that he could not walk anywhere or stay anywhere without people coming up to him looking for a cure. He humoured some by touching them, and some improved – but he guessed the improvement was illusory or short lived. Most went away disappointed, either because he 'failed' or because he refused to 'heal' them. This did not stop the rumours spreading, however and Yeshua realised that he would have to get control of his mission, or have it decided for him. He decided to call a meeting of his followers to discuss the problem.

They met at his house: the former followers of Jochanan – Thomas, Philip and Judah; his sons – Jochanan and Jacob; the fishermen – Simeon and Andreas; and his wife – Mariam. They sat cross-legged on the floor of the room on the roof, forming a circle, sitting in their groups. Yeshua sat between his wife and his sons. He opened the meeting.

"You can see I have a problem. I don't think I have actually cured anyone, but these rumours are making me into some kind of quack doctor. The result is making it impossible for me to do anything at all."

Simeon fidgeted, moving his legs about and folding and unfolding his hands. He looked uncomfortable, and this drew Yeshua's attention.

Yeshua looked across at him.

"Do you wish to say something Simeon?"

"I started this, Lord, by telling you about my mother's illness. If you had not cured her we would still be anonymous."

Yeshua did not want to get into a blame game, certainly not with his oldest follower.

"No one is to blame for my action," he stressed.

"You did what any son would have done in those circumstances. I was the one who spoke to her and cooled her brow."

Thomas knew that he was the most experienced of the people present in doing God's work. He had also been trained at Qumr'an, and was present with Jochanan for most of his ministry. He felt he should take the lead. He stood up to emphasise his position and walked to the middle of the circle, turning slowly as he spoke, so he could face each person in turn.

"Most of you are unaware of the conversation Yeshua and his brother had with Philip and me on our way to Qumr'an. In a sense we addressed this problem then, and I feel that we could do worse than repeat the story here. It began with me offering a stone to Yeshua, whose brother said he was hungry. I told him to eat it, and he laughed. However, it could be argued that I was speaking for Satan and challenging him to prove himself by making stones into food. After all, the Messiah is expected to feed his people. Moses fed the Israelites in the Wilderness, so why not Yeshua?"

"I'll tell you why not," said Simeon truculently. "You need more than food to live a spiritual life, that's why!"

"Indeed," Thomas spoke like a teacher happy the message had been understood. He waved his hands in the air, making the shape of a mountain, as he turned to face Jochanan.

"We then imagined that Yeshua was sitting on top of a tall mountain, and here it was suggested that he should agree to buy the world by obeying Satan. Satan's way is the way of force, so, Jochanan, why should your father not follow it? Why shouldn't he recruit, arm and train an army and lead it against Pilate and his Jewish and Edomite minions?"

Jochanan leaped to his feet, walked across to stand

almost in Thomas's face, and waved his finger before Thomas's eyes.

"He can't do that, Thomas, because you can't obey the Devil. You can't do God's work, using the Devil's weapons."

"Very good, Jochanan. You're right."

Jochanan smiled at the praise and returned to sit down on the floor next to his brother.

Thomas turned towards Judah with a smile.

"Judah, my old friend, our last challenge to Yeshua was to stand on top of the Temple and jump off, calling on God to send His angels to catch him. Would this not get publicity? Don't you think people would flock to hear Yeshua after such a clear demonstration of his power?"

Judah leaned back against the wall, totally relaxed in this, to him, familiar Qumr'an format. He looked elegant as usual, and studied his neatly manicured nails before answering. He spoke slowly and clearly in his educated southern drawl.

"Thomas old friend, you're speaking out of the top of your head. You can't tell God what to do, and you know it!"

"You're wrong, Judah, as usual! You've forgotten Gideon and the other heroes of the Bible who demanded proofs that God was calling them."

"No I haven't Thomas. You should know me better than that! There is a clear difference between the two cases. Gideon wanted reassurance. In this situation Yeshua would be using God's power to promote his image with the public. The Bible tells us we can't do that.

"Incidentally, there is another, more practical reason, as Yeshua has just found out. If you carry out miracles and other wondrous actions, to attract attention, people will come to you, it's true, but for the wrong reason. They'll be too busy looking for miracles to listen to what you have to say."

"Thank you, everyone, for your contribution," Thomas said, bowing like a showman, before returning to his place. "I hope we have helped you Yeshua."

Yeshua had been following the dialogue with his eyes. He smiled as Thomas sat down.

"Thank you, Thomas, but I don't feel any the wiser! Does anyone have any new ideas?"

Jacob stood up, the youngest of the group, and stood where Thomas had stood. He tried to imitate Thomas, but whereas Thomas had exuded authority, Jacob merely seemed to be a child acting like an adult. He spoke earnestly, emphasising each point with his hands.

"You haven't done anything wrong, father. You have to do what seems right to you – and the consequences don't matter."

He stopped, his face having grown red. He stood in the centre wandering what to do next. Yeshua took pity on him.

"Sit down, son," he said kindly. "Thank you for your support."

Jacob returned to his place and sat down. Jochanan and he touched fists.

Mariam spoke hesitantly.

"I know women are supposed to be seen and not heard, husband, but you did allow me to join you for this discussion. Can I speak?"

"Of course Mariam," Yeshua said, turning to look at her. "What do you wish to say?"

"I think you ought to move away from here. Use Capernaum as a sort of headquarters, but travel around the country, visit the towns by the Lake and also those farther away, like Nazareth. In that way you can keep ahead of the rumours and concentrate on delivering your message."

Thomas agreed.

"Jochanan's biggest mistake was staying in one place. It meant that people had to go to him and also that he was easily picked up when the Authorities got their act together. Of course, the fact that he stayed in one place meant that he also had a much more limited impact. I think that Mariam's right. This will make a good base, but we do need to move around. I know that Nazareth is something of a joke in this area, but it is a good place to start our mission in the province. I suggest we go there, but we also need to leave someone here. What about your youngest brother Simeon? Would he bring his wife and children here?"

Simeon responded enthusiastically. They had all begun to realise that Simeon did everything whole-heartedly.

"It's a good idea. I will talk to my father, Zebediah, about it."

Philip urged caution. He copied Thomas by taking the middle of the floor and Judah by carefully emphasising every word.

"I agree we can start at Nazareth, but Nazareth is not a safe place at the moment. Many of their men folk were slaughtered or made slaves by Pilate's men after the recent revolt was put down. They know all too well the significance of the title Son of the Father. If the news of what the madman said has reached them, they may not react well when Yeshua calls them to fight for God and country. I would seriously suggest that the youngsters and Mariam stay here for their own safety until we return."

Yeshua agreed with this suggestion, over the vociferous objections of his wife and sons. They decided that they would leave for Nazareth after the following Sabbath. At this, the meeting closed.

Chapter 5

The Twelve

Nazareth, Galilee 30AD

They were right to be concerned about Nazareth. The visit was a disaster. It started well. The party of six left Capernaum when the Sabbath ended and they spent two days travelling into the hills. The land was very different here from Judaea. Judaea had been a few villages, surrounded by small areas of vegetation; green islands in a yellow and brown sea of sand and rock. Galilee was a green land; truly, as the Bible said, a land of milk and honey. Even the hills were different. In the south they had been bare, hostile and threatening; here they were gentle, covered with grass and bushes or trees, and reassuring. In the south they were bare and harsh, covered with prickly and inedible plants, and infested with dangerous animals. Here they were covered with grass and corn, or fed on by grazing cattle, goats or sheep. The villages were more frequent and bigger. However, most were also walled. They noticed many of the walls were new, and saw evidence of the fighting which had blighted this beautiful land since the Arabs invaded it to punish Herod's infidelity to his legal wife.

Nazareth, itself, was a typical hill town. It rested against a sheer drop on one side, and a gentle upward slope on the other. The approach to the town followed a path, which wound its way up that gentler slope. The town wall was of hasty construction, and the houses revealed the poverty of the inhabitants. Even the synagogue in the centre of the town seemed ramshackle compared to the marble used in the building at Capernaum. Yeshua and his party stayed with the local carpenter, in one of the better houses, using their common trade as an introduction. He offered to help the tradesman, while he was there, as a means of paying for their keep. He kept his word, and worked hard during the five days they stayed in the town. While he worked, the other five scouted around Nazareth, visiting the markets and the inns, talking to people, and trying to gage the local mood. They did not like what they heard.

Nazareth was a very conservative town. Whereas Capernaum had the cosmopolitan atmosphere of a port town, and traded with the Gentiles across the Lake, these people had no dealings with outsiders at all. The people of Capernaum were much nimbler in their minds and prepared to listen to, and accept, new ideas. The Nazarenes were quite the opposite. For them the Torah, in its most traditional and literal understanding, was the only Law and teaching that counted. They hated the Herodian dynasty and wanted to see an end to the Tetrarch. When part of his army mutinied and Judas the Galilean had come, claiming to be Messiah, they rose in his support. As much as a third of his army came from the town itself, and, in all, a half from the area around it. Of these 1500 men, only about 400 ever returned. The remainder were killed or sent to the Roman galleys by Tribune Marcus Antonius. They learned their lesson, as Pilate and Marcus intended. The Rabbi preached on the Sabbath after that disaster, urging them all to search their consciences and return to God. He told them they must have been unfaithful and sinned heavily to be punished so severely. Therefore, when Yeshua, as a southern visitor, was invited to read the Scripture and explain it, he faced suspicion.

Yeshua chose a part of Isaiah, which predicted the

coming of Messiah. He told them that the hour of deliverance was near. The reaction was instantaneous, hostile, and violent. Yeshua was interrupted by shouted objections, which became nosier and more threatening with every minute. Eventually, Yeshua's five followers became so concerned for his safety, they closed around Yeshua and forced their way through the crowd, escorting him out of the synagogue in their midst. The congregation took a little time to organise themselves before they gave chase. This gave the six men a chance to get out of the town safely. The Nazarenes followed them as far as the town gate, which they slammed shut behind the visitors, in an unmistakable message. Yeshua responded in kind. He shook the dust from his sandals, before turning away. He was only just in time. A large stone hurled from the town wall hit the ground only five feet behind him. Then, honour apparently satisfied, they let their visitors leave.

The six reached Capernaum safely two days later, to be greeted by a relieved Mariam and the two boys.

After their return from Nazareth, the group resumed their former programme, but, using Capernaum as a base, visiting the other villages nearby and also the other towns on the lakeside. They received a much better welcome here, where people were more receptive to change and also had not experienced the full fury of Roman retaliation. Yeshua's group slowly grew larger.

One afternoon, when they visited the new city of Tiberias, built by Herod Antipas as his capital, and named in honour of the Emperor, Yeshua paused to watch a customs officer at work on the quayside, estimating how much tax should be paid on each catch as it was unloaded. He was impressed by the man's calm efficiency and apparent honesty. He asked the others what they thought, and found they agreed with his judgement, although Simeon wandered how the religious leaders would react to Yeshua's having a tax official among his followers.

"You know, Yeshua," he said slowly, and with some hesitation, "the Religious Authorities judge a person by the sort of people they mix with. They believe tax gatherers are polluted because they work for Pagan Romans and, therefore, cannot be part of God's people. They also believe everyone connected with them shares their pollution."

"Many of them also believe people get ill because they have sinned, Simeon," said Yeshua with a smile. "It doesn't make them right!"

No one else argued, and so Yeshua walked over to the man, holding his hand out in greeting and smiling at him. The man, a big man, who could obviously look after himself, looked surprised. In his experience, no one smiled at him.

"I'm Yeshua from Capernaum," Yeshua began, taking his hand and shaking it, "these are my friends – Thomas, Philip, Judah, Simeon and Andreas, and my sons, Jochanan and Jacob. We are on a mission, and wandered whether you would join us."

The man looked startled. He put down his pen, gathered up the money he had collected into a bag, and closed his book. Then he looked up at Yeshua, standing, with his hands on the table. Yeshua stood in a similar way on the other side of the table, still smiling. The two men bent their heads towards each other. The man spoke, finally. He had an educated accent, and, Yeshua guessed, may have been a local man.

"It all depends what your 'mission' is," the man replied.

"It's not that different from what you're doing now," Yeshua said, the smile still on his face. "You're taking money from people who owe it to the Government and ensuring that the lawful Government

111

gets it. I want you to help take people who owe obedience to God and ensure that God receives that obedience."

"Sounds simple, the way you put it lad."

The man was about the same age as Simeon.

"It is, really, although some people can make it difficult," said Yeshua ruefully, remembering his Nazareth experience. "However, we work as a team, and can usually get over any local difficulty. And, of course, we have God on our side, and that can't be bad, can it?"

The man laughed at Yeshua's enthusiasm.

"Is he always like that?" he asked Thomas, who was standing beside Yeshua.

"As long as I've known him. This is one of his calmer days; he can get much more excited!"

The man smiled and turned away.

"When do I start?" he asked Yeshua.

"How much notice do you have to give?" Yeshua asked.

"Oh, I expect it will take about a week to wind up my affairs and hand over the records to my successor."

"That's fine. When you've done that, come to the house in Capernaum, just ask for Yeshua Bar Yusuf. Everyone there knows me and where I live." Yeshua paused. "By the way, what's your name?"

"My name?" the man responded, "It's Matthaus. I'll take you up on your offer and join you in about two weeks."

Yeshua smiled.

"My blessings upon you and your family, Matthaus. We will look forward to your joining us. Now, if you will excuse us, we have to go."

They moved away, leaving the quay behind, with its smell of fish, its noise and its bustle, and walked towards the Market. Their attempts to buy fish, meat and vegetables from the farmers and fishermen of the area were frustrated because the local people swarmed around them, once they realised who they were. Accepting defeat, they left the market, and, leaving the town, moved into the nearby hills, where they lit a campfire, prepared supper and then settled down to sleep.

Next morning, the group boarded Simeon's boat, and sailed across the Lake. The Lake was calm and the journey was quick, comfortable and uneventful. They crossed from the Jewish side of the Lake to an area occupied by descendents of Alexander the Great's Greek army. They landed near the town of Gerasa, a small walled settlement just inland of a steep cliff, which dominated a narrow beach, where they grounded. The area above the cliffs was used for grazing by a herd of pigs, watched over by two paid herdsmen.

The cliff contained a number of caves. Living in one of these was a semi-naked man, exiled there by the frightened townsmen, because he was a manic-depressive, who often threw fits, screaming when he felt frustrated. This happened when Yeshua and his followers walked up the cliff path. He rushed out, screaming. Yeshua calmed him down. However, the screaming frightened the pigs, which stampeded. They ran down the slight slope, which led to the cliff face, over the cliff, and into the lake, where they all drowned. The man recognized the authority carried by Yeshua, and sat at his feet, listening to what he had to say.

The herdsmen were terrified by the death of the pigs. They expected to be blamed by the owners. They ran away to tell the townsfolk what had happened. The townsfolk were angry and frightened for their livelihood. They sent a delegation to Yeshua, asking

113

him to leave their territories. He did not argue, and led his followers back down the path to the beach and the boat. The man from the cave begged Yeshua to let him come with them. Yeshua refused. He told him to stay in his community and act as God's messenger, telling them what God had done for him.

They sailed back across the Lake to Capernaum.

On arrival at the house, Thomas was surprised to see Thaddeus and Simeon the Zealot there. He knew they had been with Jochanan in prison, and asked why they were there.

"Jochanan's dead," Simeon replied starkly.

"When and how did this happen?" Judah asked.

"It's a long story," Simeon began, as the group crowded around the two men. "Herod came to trust Jochanan's judgement and often came to ask him for advice. Jochanan was pleased to give it, and Herod usually followed it. However, Herodias never forgave the prophet for his denunciation of her, and was simply biding her time, waiting for the right moment to strike."

"I always thought Jochanan made a mistake when he attacked Herodias in the way he did," Thomas commented. "Angry women never forget insults like that!"

"Indeed they don't!" Simeon agreed. "Well, everything came to a head on the night of Herod's last birthday. He threw a party, and got very drunk, together with his friends. Herodias sent their teenaged daughter, Salome, to dance for them, stripping off her clothes as she did so. Herod became very horny. In a drunken stupor he told her she could have anything she liked, even sharing power in the kingdom with him. Salome, prepared by her mother, ran to her, clutching her clothes. Herodias apparently sent her straight back, just as she was, to demand Jochanan's head on a golden tray. Shocked sober, Herod attempted to dissuade

Salome, but his friends, all as drunk as he was, shouted at him to do as he promised. Eventually, Herod gave way, and sent two soldiers down to Jochanan's cell.

"Jochanan accepted his fate calmly, was allowed by the soldiers to pray, and then knelt for the sword. One soldier cut his head off with a single stroke. Thirty minutes later, the two men returned with a golden dish, holding the head of the prophet in a crimson sea. The soldier handed it to a now fully clothed Salome, who took it to her mother."

There was silence after this description, broken by the other Simeon, who growled, "Bloody murderer!"

Thaddeus took up the story.

"We carried the prophet's headless body to Qumr'an. The Son of the Father had it buried within the monastery. Once the funeral was over he called us to meet him, and told us to come to join you here. I am to tell you that Yeshua is now the leader of the Cause – and he urges you to spread the word widely in the north."

Yeshua accepted this commission calmly. He had been expecting it for some time, and so the news did not come as a surprise. He told his companions that he was going to set up a new group of twelve.

"You will be my disciples and successors. In a sense, you will be like the twelve sons of Jacob, the founder of Israel. If I'm the new Jacob, the founder of the new Israel, then you are the heads of the new tribes. You will learn from me, and, later, continue my work."

Yeshua chose his twelve men from among his growing band of followers.

These were:

The former disciples of Jochanan – Thomas, Philip, Judah, Simeon the former rebel and Thaddeus;

The fishermen – Simeon (the oldest, biggest and clumsiest) and his brother Andreas (younger and smaller in every respect than his brother); His own sons – Jochanan and Jacob (the youngest);

Matthaus (the former Customs officer);

Judas and the Son of Ptolemy (often called Bartholomew). Judas had been an officer in the rebel army crushed by Marcus. He managed to escape the fiasco. Bartholomew was an Egyptian Jew, trained in traditional medicine, originally from Alexandria, who lived in Galilee. He was shorter and darker than the other Disciples.

The last two were from Capernaum.

The chosen disciples were aged from fifteen to forty, with most of them being in their twenties. None was highly educated, but none was uneducated either. Some were the sort of people that the Jewish religious leaders despised. Many were associated with violent opposition to Roman rule, while at least one was a collaborator. Nine were from the North, and one, Judah, was from Kerioth in Judaea. The other two were Yeshua's sons, who, of course, came from Bethlehem in Judaea. Judah had a clerkly air, and was made Treasurer of the group. Simeon the fisherman rapidly emerged as the spokesman of the group. He increasingly began to dominate their thoughts, words and activities.

Chapter 6

The Reaction

Capernaum, Galilee, 30 AD

Matthaus was as good as his word, and he joined the party after two weeks. He proved an effective member of the group. However, like Judah, disliked by some because he was a Judaean, he was treated with some suspicion by the rest at first because he was considered to be a Roman collaborator. Most of the others were directly or indirectly connected with the Resistance. The fishermen, however, became close friends with Matthaus, and, through them, he eventually gained acceptance from the rest.

Mariam announced that she was going to accompany them on their tours. She led a group of women. They were the wives or daughters of the men. The women cooked and cleaned for them. She said men were incapable of looking after themselves. They needed women to care for them. Yeshua accepted this arrangement, and so it was a mixed party of twenty men and women who set out to bring the news of the Kingdom of God to the rest of Galilee. Wherever they went, the crowds followed them.

The days faded into one another in all their memories. Some days stood out. One of them occurred quite early. They knew it as the day of the double miracle.

The group were in one of the Lakeside towns, when an agitated man interrupted their progress through the crowded market. The women were buying fish and vegetables for the evening meal. The man ran up to

Yeshua and stood in front of him, forcing him to stop.

"Come quickly Lord," he gasped. "My daughter's dying."

"What's wrong with your daughter?" Yeshua asked.

"She has a high fever and was unconscious when I left."

"I'm touched you came to ask me for help," Yeshua said warily, "but I'm not a doctor. Why don't you go to someone who knows how to cure her?"

"I've been to doctors, but they failed to help her. If only you will pray for her and bless her she will get better. I'm sure of it."

"Be careful Yeshua," Thomas said concernedly. "It could be a trap."

Yeshua looked at Thomas and smiled.

"I don't think so Thomas. The man looks too desperate to be lying."

Yeshua turned back to the man. He nodded encouragingly. "We will come with you. Take us to your home."

The man threw his arms around Yeshua, repeating, "Thank you Lord" several times, before he began to lead them away.

However, Yeshua stopped almost immediately and turned back, looking around the crowd. He called out, "Who touched me?"

Simeon the fisherman turned to face Yeshua, as an older man would face a younger one who was being silly.

"There are lots of people around us Yeshua. We can scarcely get through the crowds because of the crush. Lots of people have touched you in one way or another. It's a pointless question!"

"Simeon, do not presume to tell me things you don't know. The touch I felt was different. It had a desperate and deliberate quality to it. It wasn't a chance contact."

Yeshua continued to look around. His eyes chanced on an elderly woman who was standing close to him, head cast down and hands clasped in front. She looked desperate and guilty.

"Did you touch me, mother?" he asked gently.

She did not look at him, but knelt in front of him, head down.

"Yes, Lord," she confessed.

"Why?" he asked in the same gentle tone, laying his hand on her shoulder.

"I have been ill for years, Lord," she said, on the verge of tears, her voice trembling with fear and shame. "I have suffered a continuous haemorrhage which isolates me. I hoped that, by touching you, I would be cured."

Yeshua took her by her hands and raised her to her feet. They faced one another, holding hands. The man who had called for help was becoming impatient, plucking at his sleeve to pull him away, but Yeshua ignored this. He looked the woman directly in her eyes. She was older than Simeon the fisherman, perhaps as much as ten years older. Her hair was grey and untidy – evidence of her desperation.

"You realise, mother, that you should not touch a Jewish man or woman in your condition, don't you?" he said, still gently.

"I know, Lord. I'm sorry, Lord. But I was desperate. I knew you could help me. I feared that you might not, if you knew my condition."

Yeshua smiled at her.

"Illness should not stop you being a part of society. It is bad enough feeling unwell without also feeling isolated because of it."

He paused, still smiling.

"And how are you feeling now?"

119

"Much better. I feel well for the first time for twenty years."

Yeshua smiled. He kissed her on both cheeks.

"Then your action was justified. Go in peace. You have been cured by your own faith."

The woman let go of his hands and curtsied before him.

"Thank you, Lord."

She smiled, and disappeared into the crowd.

Yeshua turned away and looked at the man who had called him.

"All's well now. Let's go!"

Yeshua began to follow the man towards his home, followed by the disciples and the women, and then by the bolder members of the crowd.

The man's house was a large one, on the edge of the town. It took about an hour's walking to reach it. By that time, most of the crowd had returned to their businesses or their homes. Yeshua stopped near the house and asked the rest to leave.

"Go home. There will be nothing for you to see here, and, afterwards we are going to look for a place to stay for the night."

They left, and Yeshua was left with his team of nineteen and their guide. They approached the house, to find it surrounded by wailing women, mourning the dead girl.

Yeshua recognised them as professional mourners. They had no concern for the family of the child. They came to weep and cry on demand in return for payment. He ordered them all to leave, saying the child was only asleep. They laughed at him, thinking he was being stupid. The Man ordered them to go, saying he would not pay them if they remained. They went off to mourn another death – another job. It did not matter to them who had died, so long as they were properly paid.

Yeshua carried on to the house, with his team and the man. He ordered the group to remain outside. The father and Yeshua entered, to find the girl's mother and her siblings crying in the main room.

"Don't cry," he said gently. "Take me to the child."

Accompanied by the parents, he entered the child's room. He looked down at her. She lay still, very white. Her eyes were closed. She was about twelve years old. The whiteness of her face was emphasised by the blackness of her shoulder length hair, which lay tousled on her pillow. Her pillow was wet with her sweat. She was scarcely breathing. He knelt down beside her bed, and laid his ear to her mouth. After a moment he smiled.

"She's still breathing," Yeshua said. "She's not dead, she's unconscious."

Yeshua ruffled her hair and laid his hands on her forehead. He noted how wet her pillow was. He pulled back her blankets. He noted how wet her bedding was. Gently he replaced them. He turned to the parents.

"The fever has broken. Her temperature is falling. She will soon recover consciousness."

He turned back to the girl, studying her closely. He noticed her eyelids flutter. He gently laid his hand on her forehead.

"What's her name?" he asked the mother.

"Tabitha, Lord," she replied, looking hopeful for the first time.

Yeshua turned back to the girl. He knelt once more. He placed one hand back on her forehead while the other ruffled her hair gently. He spoke very quietly to her.

"Tabitha, it's all right. You're better now. You'll be able to go out and play with your friends tomorrow."

The girl opened her eyes and smiled at him. He smiled back at her.

"What's your name?" she whispered.

"I'm Yeshua," he replied quietly. "I'm a friend of your father's, and now I'm your friend too."

He stood up and turned to the mother. He spoke briskly to her.

"She's your daughter. Go and get her something to eat and drink, but don't let her get up too soon. Also, be sure to replace her bedding."

Tabitha's mother was crying with relief.

"Thank you Lord," she said between her tears. "I had lost hope."

"I have done nothing," Yeshua said. "Thank God and your husband, in that order. We have to go now, but we will pray for you all. Please don't suggest that I saved your daughter's life, let alone that I brought her back from the dead. I'm not the Prophet Elisha, and I do not want people coming to me, thinking I can do the impossible."

They wanted to leave quickly, but the girl's parents would not permit this. Tabitha's father pointed out that it was late and he had a duty of hospitality. They were reluctant to impose themselves on the family. Twenty extra mouths is a lot to feed! However, the women added their provisions and their labour to the girl's mother, and, together, they prepared an evening meal. Later, they camped in the ground around the house. Their presence also kept unwanted visitors away. Next day, they moved on.

**

About a month later, in an office in the Temple in Jerusalem, High Priest, Yusuf Caiaphas, was sitting with his father-in-law, the former High Priest, Annas, and two Sadducees, two of their relatives. This, effectively, was Caiaphas's cabinet. Together, they

122

decided what happened in Temple, City and beyond. They were the senior religious authorities in Palestine. Caiaphas sat behind a desk, the other three were in seats in a half circle in front of the table. Annas sat in the middle, the oldest of the four. All four were grey haired and richly dressed. Caiaphas reported on the Temple worship, and then continued, gravely.

"Gentlemen, I think we have to conclude that our efforts to destabilise Pilate have failed for the moment."

Zechariah, the older of the two Sadducees, looked up from the scroll he was studying.

"What do you mean High Priest? Has the revolt been crushed?"

"I understand that the Judaean was leading his men into the desert when Pilate intercepted and ambushed them. The rebels were scattered and the Judaean was crucified on the spot, together with whomever of his followers the Romans captured. Pilate is reported to have laughed at them as they hung there, urging them to be sure to accompany their leader into the after life. I was told he left them there to die. I expect the bodies are still hanging there now."

Caiaphas spoke matter of factly.

Annas looked at his son–in–law angrily.

"That is the Barbarian you allowed to depose me and appoint you in my place! That's the sort of man you have chosen to work with! Remember the saying that you can tell what a man is like by the company he keeps. What does that say about you, son-in-law?"

"I cannot be held responsible for Pilate's actions, father-in-law. Remember, though, we are trying to make the people react against him. He's doing quite a good job by himself! I will send people to recover and bury the bodies before they are eaten by wild animals."

Caiaphas looked across at Zechariah, sitting on the right.

"What are you studying so avidly, Brother Zechariah?"

"It's a report from the North – from Galilee, from one of my relatives at Tiberias. It is rather worrying."

"Please read it to the meeting."

"Certainly Lord Caiaphas."

Zechariah spread the scroll out. Caiaphas sat, chin in his cupped hands. The other two stared at Zechariah. Annas sat still, hands in lap, staring stonily. Amos, the second Sadducee, fiddled with his sleeves. Zechariah began to read.

"My brother. I am writing to you to acquaint you with news from Galilee. There is a new young prophet. He is apparently named Yeshua Bar Yusuf, from Bethlehem. He has settled in Capernaum, and surrounded himself with twelve men and a number of women. None of these are of any quality. He himself is a carpenter. He is untrained and unqualified to teach or preach. He mixes with lowlifes and other rubbish - women, tax collectors and outcasts of various kinds. No one of any importance is with him.

"His behaviour is of a kind with this. He regularly breaks the Sabbath Law and does not care about religious orthodoxy. He has attracted a strong following. Huge crowds follow him wherever he goes. Things got worse recently when he healed a woman with a haemorrhage, and then brought a girl back from the dead."

"He did what?"

Caiaphas looked up in shock.

"He brought a girl back from the dead," Zechariah repeated in a deadpan voice.

"That's impossible!" Annas exclaimed. "Are you sure you read it correctly Brother Zechariah?"

Zechariah handed Annas the scroll.

"Read it yourself Lord Annas," he said in obvious

annoyance.

Annas read the letter silently, while the rest watched him. He put the scroll down and sighed heavily.

"All right, Brother Zechariah. I'm sorry I doubted you. The letter says what you said it does. I'm sure there's a simple explanation of the apparent miracle – but that doesn't matter. It's the public perception that's so damaging."

Amos had been sitting silently, listening to the others. He looked up now, and made his only contribution to the meeting.

"I think, Lord Caiaphas, that we should investigate this so-called Prophet. We cannot allow him to rampage through the north unchecked. Send a couple of Pharisees north to watch him and report back to us. Then we can decide on a course of action."

"Why Pharisees?" Zechariah asked. "The letter was written to me. Why shouldn't you and I go to the North Brother Amos?"

"Because you two shouldn't get your hands dirty," Annas interjected with a smile. "Let the Pharisees do the dirty work. They seem to like mixing with the hoi polloi."

Caiaphas smiled enigmatically. He placed his hands firmly on his desk, and rose to his full height. He turned away from them, to look out of the window towards the Roman fortress. He turned back, still smiling, but more grimly.

"It's Pilate who's going to feel the full force of this, whatever it is," he said, "or Herod – or both of them. However, let's act responsibly and check this pseudo-prophet out. I will ask Brother Yusuf and Brother Moshe to go and inspect him."

They all agreed with this decision.

Caiaphas sat down again.

"Gentlemen, that concludes our meeting. I will

speak with Brother Moshe and Brother Yusuf and let you know their decision tomorrow."

The three men nodded, rose to their feet and left the room. Annas paused at the door, in case Caiaphas called him back. When Caiaphas ignored him, Annas left.

Once the men had left, Caiaphas pulled out a sheet of paper, and began to write.

"To Pontius Pilatus, Procurator of Judaea," he wrote, "Greetings. Please also give my greetings to the lady Julia, your wife.

"Please accept my congratulations on your successful repression of yet another attempted rebellion against His Imperial Majesty's rule.

"It has been reported to me that a new preacher has become active in the North – in the Tetrarch Herod Antipas' dominions. He is not authorised by us, but I fear that he could turn out to be a big danger to us all. I am sending two of my men north to investigate what is going on. I am not sure what the outcome will be, but I will report to you what I learn."

He read the brief letter through, before sanding it and signing it, "Caiaphas, High Priest". He sanded the signature, rolled the scroll up and sealed it. Then he rang a bell on his desk.

A Secretary entered.

"Saul, please arrange for a messenger to take this letter to the Procurator at Caesarea."

"Yes, Lord Caiaphas", the Secretary said, taking the scroll from his hands. "How urgent is it?"

"It must go today, Saul."

"Yes, Lord Caiaphas."

The Secretary left the office, carrying the scroll. Caiaphas sighed and looked up, as in prayer, before returning to his other duties.

**

In Galilee, Yeshua had a problem. He and his men had arrived at a small town on the Lakeside. A large crowd came down to the beach to hear him speak. Yeshua wanted to speak to them. However, he realised he could not do so in that place. He asked his disciples for suggestions. Simeon spoke for them all.

"Get into my boat, Yeshua. Andreas and I will take her out a few feet into the Lake and anchor her. You can speak to them from there. The rest of the lads can keep them from rushing into the water."

Yeshua saw the sense of this idea and clambered into the boat. (He was becoming used to getting in and out of boats.) The two men pushed the boat off the sand, and climbed in themselves. They used poles to move the boat away from the shore, and then dropped the anchor. The boat floated gently in the waves. Yeshua stood in the centre of the boat.

"I wish to welcome you all," he began. "Sit down on the sand or the grass and make yourselves comfortable. Give the children enough space."

Yeshua waited while the crowd settled, then he began to speak to them, using his hands to emphasise his points, and throwing his powerful voice, which bounced off the water, and was heard by the silent crowd with complete clarity.

"I'm an ordinary man. I trained as a carpenter, and haven't been to any rabbinic school. I don't know the legal and learned precedents and what I am supposed to make of the Torah. However, I do know what I believe, and what God wants. You have been taught to love your friends and hate your enemies. I tell you that you should love your enemies – make them into your friends. Then you will have no enemies.

"Our religious leaders tell us to restrict our love. God loves everyone – and so should you. You must not be too proud to see others as being part of God's Kingdom.

"Remember the story of the Pharisee and the Tax Collector in the Synagogue. The Pharisee told God He was lucky to have him, because he was so holy! He never sinned; not like the Tax Gatherer."

The crowd laughed. No one liked the self-righteous Pharisees.

"The Tax Gatherer beat his chest, stood at the door and begged God to forgive him his sins. Who do you think God heard?"

There was silence from the crowd. They did not like Tax Gatherers either.

"Have you nothing to say?" Yeshua paused.

He smiled.

"Then I'll ask one of my own companions. Matthaus – what do you think?"

"The Tax Gatherer, Lord," he grinned. "I know how much it cost him to say that."

"Thank you, Matthaus," Yeshua said gravely, but still smiling. "I thought you would say that! Professional solidarity! Of course it was the Tax Gatherer!" He raised his voice. "The Pharisee did not consider he had sinned, so God could not forgive him. The Tax Gatherer knew he had sinned, so he admitted it, and was forgiven. He is a member of God's kingdom, whereas the Pharisee isn't. So, if God accepts such a person, so should we."

Yeshua paused dramatically. He took a sip from his water bottle and wiped the sweat from his eyes. Then he continued.

"We should learn from this. Only the humble are acceptable to God. We must not be proud. All our gifts come from God – and we can accomplish nothing unless He permits it. Therefore, we cannot boast before God. We should not seek to judge one another either.

"Think of it this way. You can see a speck of dust in your brother's eye – but you've got a great log in your own. You cannot criticise your brother until you've removed the log can you?"

Again he got laughter.

"I thought not," Yeshua continued, smiling. "You can't even see properly, yet alone comment on someone else if you're like that. Yet that's what our rulers and so-called betters do all the time. They despise us and call us 'the People of the Land'. Yet they expect us to honour them and give them respect. Be careful. Respect them for their office, but not for their behaviour."

"That's all very well, Yeshua," a man called from the crowd. "But what are we expected to be like?"

"Simple," Yeshua replied. "You must be humble; peaceable; a person who trusts and loves God; a man who seeks peace between his neighbours; above all you must expect to be persecuted by those who consider themselves to be holier than you. If you are all these things, you belong to God's Kingdom."

There was a profound silence. Yeshua noticed that the sun was beginning to drop from the sky. The crowd noticed this as well and began to drift away. Yeshua sat down, and the two fishermen pulled the anchor up, and poled the boat to the beach. The rest of the disciples climbed on board, and Simeon and Andreas cast off, set sail, and steered the boat to another beach, a few miles to the east, where the women had prepared camp.

Mariam and the other wives welcomed the men back, and the whole party sat around the campfire, eating grilled fish, supplemented by local vegetables and fruit, washed down with red wine. Thomas and the other four former followers of Jochanan were delighted by the change.

"It's good working with you," Thomas grinned. "Jochanan never touched wine nor proper food."

"That won't make any difference to our enemies, Thomas," Yeshua replied, munching a piece of fish. "They believed that Jochanan was possessed by a demon. They will think I'm a drunkard! You can't win with them."

"Don't worry about them Yeshua," Simeon the fisherman said, drinking his wine, "If they don't like us; well, sod 'em I say!"

"I wish it were as simple as that," Yeshua said wryly. "However, let's enjoy tonight. Tomorrow is another day."

"Amen to that!" Judah said heartily, like Simeon, knocking back his wine.

*

In his Palace by the Dead Sea, Tetrarch Herod Antipas was sitting alone and feeling worried. He had believed he had stopped the erosion of his authority with the arrest and silencing of Jochanan. He still felt angry over the way Herodias had forced his hand, but that was in the past. However, the new reports he was receiving from Galilee were deeply worrying. This new prophet appeared much more dangerous than the old. It wasn't that he was attacking Herod directly. Far from it! He seemed to have learned from Jochanan's mistake. In fact, his attacks seemed directed at the High Priest and his cronies. Herod had no problems with that. He had no time for them. 'They're a crowd of hypocrites," he observed to his Chancellor. What really concerned Herod were the huge crowds, which seemed to follow Yeshua around. As he commented to Herodias one day, "He can turn them against us whenever he likes, and then we'll be in trouble."

Now he had a written report from his Governor in Tiberias, which showed just how potentially dangerous the situation was becoming. Herod wandered what to do. He had spoken to most of his advisors and there was no agreement between them. Eventually he decided to send someone to spy for him. He discussed the idea with Herodias, who pointed out that the Governor had written that Yeshua was accompanied by a group of women. She suggested sending one of her courtiers, named Salome, like her daughter, to join his group. He agreed, and Salome left them, with an escort, to travel to Capernaum.

He decided to inform the Procurator, and wrote to update him on the situation in Galilee, explaining that nothing that was happening in Galilee was being done with his authority. He assured him that he had sent a spy north to watch the situation.

Herod sighed heavily, clapped his hands, and, when his steward arrived, instructed him to convene his court and lay on the wine and the entertainment. Another evening of heavy drinking lay ahead. Herod persuaded himself that he was looking forward to it.

**

The Pharisees Yusuf and Moshe arrived in Capernaum and attached themselves to the crowds around Yeshua. They listened and watched, but saw little to concern them. Yeshua was extremely careful of what he said and did. They heard his veiled attacks on the Priestly caste, but noticed that they were much less strident than those that Jochanan had made. They saw no evidence of magic or misuse of power. They also saw no evidence that Yeshua was not observing the Sabbath. However, both men were patient, and waited for him to make a mistake.

Salome arrived from the south and was made welcome by Mariam, who accepted that she wanted to join the group. Salome gently probed the doings and beliefs of Yeshua and his men, finding, like Moshe and Yusuf that there was nothing to concern her, or the Tetrarch.

The first clash with the two Pharisees occurred later in that week. Yeshua was addressing a group in his house, when four men tore open the roof and lowered a man on a blanket to his feet. They all looked up and jumped back in alarm when the dust and plaster began to fall on their heads and clothes. They moved back out of the way. Yeshua walked over to the man who had arrived so dramatically.

"Why are you here?" he asked sternly.

"My friends brought me so you can cure me," the man answered, lying on his back and staring up at Yeshua.

He was a little shaken. He had not expected Yeshua to speak to him so sharply.

"What's your problem?" Yeshua stared down at him, his clenched hands by his sides.

"I'm lame. I am unable to walk."

"Is that recent, or long term?"

"I've been lame since I was a child."

"I see," said Yeshua quietly. "Have you prayed about this?"

"Many times," the man said bitterly, raising himself up on his elbows.

"Have you admitted your sins to God?" Yeshua asked gently.

The man felt more confident now.

"Of course, Lord," he replied quickly.

Yeshua stared at him. He studied the man's expression for some time without speaking. He wandered how genuine this man was. The man stared back; also silent. No one in the room spoke. The tension rose.

"Well then," Yeshua said at last, smiling, "God has forgiven your sins."

Moshe interrupted angrily.

"You can't forgive sins. Only God can do that. If you claim the right you're committing blasphemy."

"Am I?" Yeshua replied innocently. "Let's ignore the fact that I didn't forgive his sins – I said God had done so! You believe that God forgives those who confess their sins, don't you Pharisee?"

"Of course!" Moshe replied indignantly.

How dare Yeshua question his knowledge and beliefs, he thought.

"Well then, why is this man different?"

Yeshua turned away from the silent Moshe, who simply stared at him, and turned to the man.

"Since you know your sins are forgiven, why are you still lying there? Get up and go home."

The man slowly, almost reluctantly, stood up, aided by Jochanan and Jacob, who grasped him under the arms and pulled him up. Then he rolled up the blanket, and staggered out of the room, where his friends rejoined him.

Yeshua turned back to Moshe.

"Are you satisfied?" he asked.

"No," Moshe answered angrily. "Isn't it true that you also break the Sabbath laws?"

"I don't think so," Yeshua answered mildly. "The Sabbath is a special day for God, and a gift for man, but it is still a day when we are expected to be sensible. You know, don't you, that you can rescue a stranded cow on the Sabbath or a child who's fallen into a well?"

Moshe was silent, but Yusuf answered for him.

133

"You're right, Yeshua, but you're quoting emergency situations. Many of the accusations against you do not count as emergencies."

"Such as?" Yeshua challenged. "Give me chapter and verse."

"You are supposed to have allowed your disciples to pick grain from the fields on the Sabbath and rub off the chaff before eating them as they walked. That counts as reaping and grinding – both forbidden activities on the Sabbath."

One of the crowd groaned noisily. "Typical bloody Pharisee," he said angrily. "Nitpicking as usual, rather than facing up to reality."

Yeshua spoke firmly.

"I agree with him absolutely. You Pharisees do God no favours by such comments."

Moshe and Yusuf had seen and heard enough. They stalked out of the room.

Seeing the 'cured' man standing outside with his friends, Moshe snarled at them, "Don't stand there grinning. I will ensure that you are banned from the Temple and the Synagogues for this."

The grins turned to laughter. One of the men picked up some mud and threw it at Moshe, who ducked, but ducked into it. He wiped the mud off his face, and the two Pharisees pushed their way past the men, disappearing quickly into the town. When the former lame man's companions tried to follow them, they found that the Pharisees had disappeared.

Next day, after repairing the roof, the team began a tour of the area, focussing on the lands bordering the Lake. It was, as far as Yeshua was concerned, a crucial tour.

For me this is make or break. I've become a local celebrity, a sort of popular attraction – but nothing more. It's all as we foresaw back in Capernaum. Lots of people come to see me, to see if I can perform a miracle, although I don't feel I do anything other than make people feel better about them selves. Some even come to listen to me! However, very few seem to have accepted what I have told them and become my followers. This has got to change. This tour will have, somehow, to bring that change about – or we should all give up and go home.

Yeshua began the tour in some hope, but little expectation.

**

On the Mediterranean coast, at Caesarea, Pilate was reading for the fourth time the two letters he had received from the Tetrarch and the High Priest. He noted that there were no suggestions of treasonable actions. He was concerned, however, at the levels of popularity that Yeshua had attained.

"Such popularity can turn the head," he mused.

He knew that it had corrupted many minor Senators in the past. He suspected that the same might occur here, and wanted to keep tabs on the young prophet.

Remembering how he had failed with Jochanan, he decided that he would not send soldiers again. He wandered whom he could send, then remembered the two young slaves he had acquired in Jerusalem. They were Jewish, so they would blend in with Yeshua's followers. They were also brother and sister, so they could work together. He spoke to his wife, Julia, about his idea, and she reluctantly agreed. She had become very attached to the thirteen-year old girl.

He had the two slaves brought to him. They knelt before him, staring down at Pilate's feet. He sat behind his desk and spoke to them in a kindly manner.

"I know you both hate me; you have reason to. I'm

135

sure you hate Rome as well."

They were both silent. Pilate continued in the same manner as before.

"I am prepared to free you both, and even to release those of your family who are still imprisoned here, if you will do something for me."

The boy he had named Marcus looked up at the Procurator.

"What do you want, Master?"

"I want you to go to Galilee and join up with the prophet Yeshua in Capernaum. You are to keep an eye on his words and actions and inform me of anything that might be treasonous or dangerous to Rome's interests."

The girl his wife had given her own name to, Julia, became more interested.

"Are we allowed to say what we really think of you and Rome, Master?" she asked timidly.

"Of course! I expect you both to do so."

"And you will not punish us afterwards?" Marcus insisted doggedly.

"If you do as I ask, I will free you and you will be safe. If you don't, you will rejoin my household as slaves. That's my promise."

Armed with this promise, the two slaves agreed to do as Pilate asked, and, after clarifying how they would report back, set off for Capernaum. Pilate sat back in relief, and called his steward to bring him wine. Then he resumed working on his report to the Emperor, outlining what he had done to maintain the peace and crush rebellion in the province, and seeking the Emperor's approval to construct an aqueduct to carry water to Jerusalem, in view of the inadequate water supply in the capital.

Chapter 7

Who is he?

The shores of Lake Galilee, 31AD

The grand tour began two weeks later. By that time Salome was an active member of the support team and Pilate's two slaves had joined the company. Simeon the freedom fighter noticed them hanging about the group and spoke to them. They told him they were Jews, Roman slaves, who had escaped from Syria and made their way south.

"What do you want?" Simeon asked them.

"Safety and revenge," Marcus replied angrily.

"You will find both here," Simeon promised them.

Marcus joined the Twelve as a hanger on, while Julia joined the support team. Thus reinforced, and dogged by Moshe and Yusuf, the group moved out.

It proved an exciting journey.

It started just outside Capernaum, when a Roman officer appeared, supported by a rabbi. He stopped Yeshua as he and his group walked towards the beach to board their boat.

"Are you the Rabbi, Yeshua Bar Yusuf?" he asked cautiously.

"I am Yeshua Bar Yusuf, certainly," Yeshua replied cheerfully. "However, few would call me a Rabbi."

"I need your help."

"What do you want me to do?" Yeshua asked curiously.

He wandered why a Roman officer would come to a Jew for help.

"We can vouch for his friendship to our people," the

Rabbi said equally cheerfully. He smiled at Yeshua. "He has helped build our synagogue with his own money. If you can help him, please do so."

"I will do what I can," Yeshua promised.

(Yeshua recognised that the Roman was one of the increasing number of Greek and Roman intellectuals who, seeing the absurdity of worshipping stone statues, were beginning to show an interest in the Jewish faith.)

"I have a slave who is very ill," the officer explained. "I have been told you can cure him."

"Do you want me to come?" Yeshua asked.

"Certainly not!" the officer answered. "You cannot enter my house. You will be polluted. In any case it's not necessary. All I need is for you to speak and that's enough. I'm an army officer. I know all about authority and obedience."

Yeshua looked around in astonishment. He noticed the surprise on the faces of the Twelve and their companions.

"No Jew has ever spoken to me like that!" Yeshua exclaimed. "Go in peace, Centurion, your faith has saved your slave."

The Officer and the Rabbi thanked him, and left.

The party boarded two fishing boats and set off across the Lake. Their journey was peaceful, and their landing, uneventful. That night they camped in the countryside. Sitting around the fire, eating, they discussed their next move. Thomas opened the discussion

"Yeshua," he said. "I'm not sure it's a good idea to keep the women with us. The party is too large for one boat, and, of course, the cost of feeding everyone is much higher. I think it would be better if the women returned to Capernaum and we went on alone."

"I think you're wrong Thomas. Twenty people is not too many, and we need the women to cook for us,"

Simeon the fisherman responded.

(Yeshua noticed an informal rivalry was developing between Thomas and Simeon to be the major influence on their decisions.)

"I think you're being unnecessarily pessimistic, Simeon," Thomas replied. "We don't have to camp out every night. We have your boat and we can always travel backwards and forwards from our base in Capernaum."

"Are you sure that's feasible," Judah asked. "I'm not a sailor like Simeon and Andreas, but I have noticed that this lake seems prone to sudden storms."

"You're right Judah, the Lake can be unpredictable and dangerous," Simeon commented. "However, it would certainly make travel around the Lake quicker, and easier."

"My brother's right," Andreas added. "Imagine trying to walk all around the Lake!"

Mariam was not happy with the idea.

"I want to be with my husband," she said. "However, I suppose you're right, Thomas. It would be easier for you if we weren't there." She smiled, and added, "But I expect Yeshua and the boys back almost every night!"

The men laughed at this, and all looked at Yeshua, who had been listening quietly to the conversation, to make a decision.

Aware that they were all looking at him, he sat silently, staring at his hands in the darkness, lit by the flickering flames of the fire.

Would I be right to send the women away and depend on the Lake as a means of transport? It's extremely unpredictable, prone to sudden and dangerous storms. A fishing boat sank, with the loss of everyone on board only last month. On the other hand, a boat moves more quickly than we can walk. In addition it's possible to sail straight between two points, using the Lake like a road, whereas walking involves moving around the shore.

He looked up, brushed some dust from his face, and glanced around his group.

I love Mariam. We have been partners since we married and she so wants to be part of this mission. The boys need her. The other men need her too. She, and the women with her, help to keep them calm. We all need to keep calm under pressure.

He looked at each of the Twelve. He thought of calm, rational, capable Thomas, and his faithful friend and companion Philip, who were the first of his disciples, chosen for him by Jochanan. Then he looked at Judah, the man from Kerioth, the group Treasurer, another of Jochanan's men, and perhaps the most intelligent and reliable of his followers. Next came his two sons, his beloved Sons of Thunder, fierce, loyal and enthusiastic. Then his eyes moved to his first selections – big, enthusiastic, but impetuous, Simeon and his younger brother, Andreas, similar, but smaller in all respects. His eyes moved on to Matthaus, the former tax collector, big, quick thinking, and efficient. He looked at the two rebels – Simeon, tough and confident, an obvious soldier, and Thaddeus, similar, but darker. Last, but not least, he turned to Judas, the former officer from Herod's army, the tall quiet one, who said little, but thought deeply, and Bartholomew, the slim, short, dark man, probably of Egyptian background, knowledgeable in traditional medicine.

They all looked back at him expectantly.

"I accept Thomas's suggestion," he said finally. The women will go back to Capernaum tomorrow, and we shall go on to the Syrian side of the Lake, where we can escape the crowds and I can talk with you."

Next day, the plan was put into effect. After

breakfast, the two boats headed in opposite directions. The men headed east, whereas the women headed north. The second boat was provided and crewed by two of Yeshua's followers. The move by boat bought Yeshua and his followers twenty-four hours grace, during which he was able to talk to his followers, as they sat in a circle around a cooking fire. The two youngest disciples joined with Judas, who showed unexpected skills as a cook, to prepare an evening meal from fish and vegetables.

Matthaus opened the discussion. As they sat around the fire eating, he turned to Yeshua.

"Yeshua, would you mind if I asked you a question?" he asked diffidently.

"Of course you may ask questions, Matthaus!" Yeshua smiled. "What's troubling you?"

"Why do you use simple stories when you are teaching rather than the detailed authorities the rabbis use?"

Yeshua smiled.

"Matthaus, when you used to keep your accounts, would you have preferred to be told how much money a man had received and how much tax was due, or be given a complicated formula from which you would have to work it out?"

"I would like to think I would want the formula – but actually I would prefer the figures," Matthaus admitted, smiling back.

"That's why I use stories. The ordinary people can relate to them and understand them. There's no point teaching them something they can't understand."

"I don't always find your stories so clear," Andreas admitted ruefully. "It may be because I'm a fisherman, but what about that story of the farmer and the seeds."

"Do you mean the Sower and the Seeds?" Yeshua asked.

"Yes, that's it," Andreas said. "What was the point of all the different types of soil?"

"None at all," admitted Yeshua with a smile, "except that there are different kinds of soils and the seeds sown in them suffer different fates."

"So what did you mean?" Thomas asked.

"Think of it this way, Thomas. The farmer had a lot of seed. A lot of it was wasted, but what was successfully planted produced a bumper harvest. What do you make of it now?"

Andreas scratched his head.

"Are we the farmer?" he asked finally.

"Yes," Yeshua said, "Except that 'we' means all of us, me included. The seed is the work we do. The harvest is the result."

"So," Judah said meditatively, "all our work, despite the many failures will result in massive success."

"That's right," Yeshua smiled. "Don't get caught up in the details. Look at the general thrust."

Simeon the fisherman raised his hand, like a schoolboy. Yeshua smiled at him.

"You don't need to put your hand up Simeon," he said.

"I wandered about your wedding story," Simeon confessed.

"That's a simple one," Yeshua commented. "God called the Israelites when He gave the Covenant to Abraham and Moses. They have often failed Him. He is giving them one last chance. If they blow it again, He will look for others who will obey."

"And they are?" Bartholomew asked.

"Only God knows," Yeshua admitted. "I certainly don't, but, together, we may find out."

There was general laughter at this. The group broke up into private conversations, and then, eventually settled down for the night.

Next morning, they found a crowd had begun to assemble. It seemed that a large group had followed them around the Lake. Yeshua hastily gathered his group together and found a small hill a little way from the Lakeside. Here he sat down, surrounded by the Twelve, while the crowd began to assemble, seated on the ground, around them. They sat in family groups. Their brightly coloured clothing looked, from the distance, like clumps of flowers surrounded by the green of the grass. It was a chilly morning, cooled by an offshore breeze. Yeshua knew it would get hotter during the day, and sat under the shade of a palm tree. The crowd grew quite quickly, filling in the green spaces between the coloured clumps. Eventually, it numbered several thousand people. Yeshua waited until there were no more new arrivals. Then he began to teach them.

"It's good you've come," he began, smiling. "I know how desperate you are to hear God's Word. Next time I want peace and quiet, I'll climb to the top of Mount Hermon!"

The Crowd laughed. They knew Yeshua by now. They knew he liked to joke. People warmed to his down to earth style and his approachability. Jochanan had frightened them by his austerity. Yeshua was totally different. He was just an ordinary man like them. They settled down to listen.

"There was a farmer," Yeshua began, "who had two sons. One always did as he was told and worked hard, a bit like Simeon and his brother, Andreas, whereas the other tended to laze around, much like my friend Thomas."

Thomas objected to this, and those around laughed, responding to Yeshua's smile. (The two men had done this so often, that it had become almost a routine.)

"The second son eventually decided he had had

enough and asked his father to divide the property between them. Then he sold his half and went away, to live off the money. He went to join the Greeks, who helped him spend it, and then left him when there was no more money. After a few weeks working for a pig farmer, he decided to go home. After all, even the servants were better off there. When he got home his father made him welcome and threw a party, much to the disgust of his elder brother, who complained. The father was not happy about this and told him he should be as glad as he was to have his lost brother back."

Yeshua paused dramatically.

"God's like that," he continued with a smile. "He hates us to leave Him, and loves it when we confess our failures and return. That's what we all have to do. We all have to admit that we are sinners, ask for forgiveness, and God will take us back.

"Remember the Pharisee who told God he should be happy that He had him, and not the tax gatherer, who was hiding at the back of the Synagogue pleading with God to have mercy on him, because he had sinned. Believe me, it was the tax gatherer God forgave, not the Pharisee who did not think he had sinned."

Yusuf turned to Moshe.

"Have you noted down the attack on us?"

Moshe nodded.

"I have told you that the Kingdom is near," Yeshua continued. "Some of you have asked me what it's like and what you should do. It's like a mustard plant."

Yeshua held his left hand up, coiling his first finger behind his thumb to make a small circle.

"It's the smallest of seeds, but it grows to the biggest of trees."

He spread his arms out to their fullest extent.

"Every bird in the world can rest on its branches. In other words, there's room for everyone in the

Kingdom. So, what should you do?

"You should be like a person who discovered a hoard of gold in a field. Of course, he didn't tell the owner!" he said to general laughter. "He buried it again, and went to the bank to raise a loan. With the money, he bought the field for the lowest price possible, and then dug up the gold and made a huge profit. The owner, incidentally, was furious. That is how you should act, swiftly and decisively, because you do not know when it will come.

"Remember the customs at weddings. The bridesmaids are supposed to be ready with oil in their lamps to escort the bride and groom to the Reception. If they haven't prepared, they will be left behind. Or the King who was getting married and he found none of his guests wanted to come to the wedding. What did he do? He found other guests who would come.

"We all have to be careful. We have to be ready and willing to answer God's call when it comes."

One of crowd asked him, "How will we know when it's here?"

Yeshua replied, "That's a very good question. You all know the seasons by the date and the weather. You know when to plant and when to harvest. Read your Bible. The prophets made it clear what the signs will be. You cannot mistake them, and they are all around you at the moment. Believe me, the Kingdom is very near. It may even be here now. It will certainly come soon."

Moshe was angered by this, and called out, "Are you responsible for the Kingdom coming?"

Yeshua took the question seriously. "You're a Pharisee, Brother Moshe," he began, "one of the country's religious leaders. You claim to know the Law and explain it to others, breaking it up and putting a fence around it so we can't break it by accident. You've taken the gift of God, designed to make us free, and turned it into a form of tyranny. You've made us slaves of the Law. How can you ask a question like that? What do you think are the necessary conditions for the Kingdom to come?"

"People like you have to start obeying the Law properly and stop encouraging others to break it," Moshe shouted back.

"So, Moshe, you think I break the Law and encourage others to do the same! Presumably you have reported that to the so-called High Priest - the man the Roman Governor appointed to Aaron's sacred office, even though he's not of Aaron's line," Yeshua retorted angrily. "That's typical of you Pharisees. You believe that you are safely in the Kingdom and block the way to anyone else who wants to enter after you. You've claimed the Kingdom as your own. But you're wrong. The Kingdom does not belong to you, and you don't decide who will enter it. The Kingdom is God's, and He, and He alone, issues the invitations."

The crowd first laughed and then cheered at this riposte. Yusuf and Moshe, realising how hostile the crowd was towards them, were silent from then on, and left as soon as they could afterwards, trying not to seem to have been driven off by Yeshua.

The day wore on, with Yeshua continuing to tell stories to illustrate his points. He tried to drive home the urgency of the imminent coming of the Kingdom and its implications for them. He repeated his teaching on love and humility, as well as the need for honest admission of failure and the certainty that God would forgive a sinner who confessed and tried to do better.

"God is like a shepherd who had 100 sheep and lost one. He rounded up the 99, put them in a safe place, and then went off to search until he found the missing sheep and brought it back to the rest. We are like sheep.

God cares for us, and hates it when we stray. If we do so, He will look for us to bring us back.

"Alternatively, He's like a woman who lost a coin from her wedding necklace. She won't rest until she's found it and returned it to the necklace. Then she'll have a quiet celebration." Yeshua grinned. "Obviously it won't be too big a party – you don't spend a lot of money to celebrate finding a shilling!" The crowd laughed once again. (Once the Pharisees left, the atmosphere became very relaxed.)

Yeshua turned to comparing what the Rabbis said about the Law with what he thought.

"You know," he began, "that we are told to love our friends and hate our enemies. I think that's wrong. We should love our enemies too, and, by helping them, make them into friends.

"You know that we can only marry one person, and then only divorce if our partner commits adultery. I think you should worry if you are even thinking about another woman or man, or looking at them longingly.

"I have told you that we have to ask God to forgive us. However, be careful. There was a king who had a Minister who was corrupt and had stolen hundreds of pounds from the Treasury. The King discovered this and called him to face justice. He intended to throw him into prison. However, the guilty man confessed his crime, pleaded for mercy and forgiveness and promised to repay the stolen money if the King gave him time. After discussing and agreeing a repayment plan, the King let him go. However, the Minister was aware that his Secretary had borrowed money from him. Now he was calling in all his resources to repay his own debts, he demanded that the man repay his loan.

"The Secretary was unable to pay, and begged for time to do so. The desperate Minister was adamant, and had his Secretary imprisoned. News of this reached the

King, who was extremely angry, and called the Minister back. He pointed out that, having been forgiven himself, he should have forgiven his Secretary. Then he stripped him of his office and had the man thrown into prison. His family was sold into slavery and his property was auctioned, to help pay off the debt. You do not want that to happen to you do you?" Yeshua asked, sweeping the crowd with his eyes.

"No!" they shouted back in unison.

"Then remember the golden rule – Do to others as you would have them do to you. If you want your sins to be forgiven, forgive others when they sin against you. To help you remember this, make it part of your prayers.

"Pray something like this. 'Father in Heaven, may your name be blessed and may your Kingdom come soon. May your will be obeyed here, as it is in heaven. Give us the food we need to eat each day and forgive us when we sin, in the same way as we forgive those who sin against us. Spare us from the day of temptation and trial, and free us from Satan's power.' That's what God wants and it's what we all should want."

It was now mid afternoon and the sun was at its hottest. The crowd, still attentive, was plainly getting tired, and no one had eaten since morning. Thomas, ever practical, raised the question quietly with Yeshua.

"Everyone must be hungry and thirsty Lord," he said. "I think you should stop preaching and let them eat, and then send them home. Many of them have a long way to go."

"Do we have enough food to feed them?" Yeshua asked.

"Ask Judah," Thomas replied, "He's our Treasurer."

Yeshua called for Judah.

"Can we feed the crowd?" he asked.

Judah shook his head.

"I'm sorry, Yeshua," he said quietly. "There are over 5000 here. We don't have the resources to do that."

Yeshua smiled.

"I don't think it will come to that," he said.

Yeshua looked around, and saw a small boy sitting at the front of the crowd.

"Jochanan," he called to his son, "Bring me that boy – the one in the blue tunic."

Jochanan ran to the boy, helped him up and brought him to Yeshua, who smiled at him and asked him gently, "Did your mother pack you any lunch?"

"Yes Lord Yeshua," the boy replied, handing him a bag, which he wore on his waist, slung by a strap from his shoulders.

Yeshua opened the bag, finding five small loaves and two fish inside. He took them out and solemnly said Grace over them.

"Blessed be thou Lord who bringest forth fruit out of the earth."

He said this loudly, and with hands raised over the food in an unmistakable gesture of blessing. Then he broke one of the loaves and gave it to the boy. At this there was a murmur and a general movement among the crowd as they found their own food, and, taking their lead from Yeshua, broke their bread and shared with those who had none or very little, so that, at the end, everyone was satisfied. Then they left, one by one, until eventually only Yeshua and his team remained.

Judah took Yeshua aside quietly, as the others were tidying up the site.

"Do you know how this might be interpreted, Yeshua?" he asked seriously.

"Tell me Judah," Yeshua replied sharply. (Sometimes Judah's air of apparently knowing everything annoyed him.)

149

"Your enemies will claim that you're buying support and some of those who were here might think you're acting out the feast that is supposed to inaugurate the Kingdom."

"They may not be far wrong, Judah," Yeshua replied simply. "My enemies can and will say what they like. Neither you nor I can alter that. The crowds will also decide what they think happens. All we can do is the right, the caring and loving, thing, and hope for the best."

"I hope you're right Yeshua, but sometimes I feel you're too idealistic for your own safety."

"It's kind of you to be so concerned for me, Judah. But, are you sure that you're not equally concerned for your own safety?" Yeshua said this with a gentle smile, putting his arm around Judah's shoulder to soften the impact of his words. (Yeshua liked and trusted Judah.)

Judah paused for a moment, smiled, and added, "You know me too well Yeshua!"

Judah went to join the others tidying up. Yeshua turned away.

Judah may be right. Am I taking too many risks too soon, and just what are the Authorities thinking about me, and what are they planning? Should I continue, or should I slip away and return to obscurity and safety? Have I already gone too far for that?

Yeshua sighed, deeply, and went to join his team in removing the rest of the debris from the meal, before they all went down to the beach and boarded the boat, as the sun began to set.

They set sail as it became dark, intending to cross the Lake during the night and arrive at Capernaum next morning. Simeon and Andreas were confident they could handle the boat alone, and the rest found various places to settle down and sleep. Most slept in the centre of the boat. Yeshua found a cushion, and slept in the stern, where the sides of the boat rose higher than in the centre, providing him with shelter. Despite this, he still felt the spray on his face as he drifted off into a deep sleep.

Within a short while only the two sailors were awake. They had little to do, except watch the brilliant stars which glittered in the satin black sky and the white horses, which glistened on top of the equally black water, which rose and fell gently and regularly, acting like a lullaby. With nothing to do, except occasionally move the steering oar, the two brothers sat and talked.

"Why are we here?" Andreas began. "Our job is fishing, not acting as ferrymen! We have no income and no future doing this. So why are we doing it?"

"We responded to a call," Simeon answered. "Yeshua called us and we responded in good faith."

"But why?" Andreas persisted. "We threw up our livelihoods for someone we didn't know. I wouldn't have done that for any other person. So why did we do it for him?"

"There's something about him, Andreas, something special. I felt it, didn't you?"

"I suppose so," Andreas admitted grudgingly, "but it's not obvious, is it?"

"I felt it again today, Andreas, when he blessed that boy's food. You saw the reaction. It was almost a miracle the way the crowd responded – almost as though Yeshua fed them all from those loaves and fish, rather than just the boy. He seems to have that effect on people. Somehow he brings out the best in them."

They sat quietly, staring at the bottom of the boat. Simeon felt something, and looked up sharply, first at the sail and then at the water.

"There's going to be a blow, Andreas. Didn't you feel it?"

"I felt something, but you're much more experienced than me, Simeon. Do you want us to haul down the sail?"

"Not yet, it may be nothing. Anyway, Yeshua's here. I have a feeling that, however bad the storm, we'll be safe if he's here."

Andreas grunted and stretched. He used his hand to wipe the spray from his eyes.

"The sea is getting up,' he conceded. "It's strange you said that about Yeshua, Simeon. I too feel that there's some kind of hidden power there. You're right, he does seem to draw the best out of people and to discover faith where there was doubt and fear. How does he do it?"

"I wish I knew! Remember how he saw the fish when we didn't?"

"Yes, that was strange. You can sometimes do that from the shore though, Simeon."

"I know Andreas, but you have to know what you're looking for. Yeshua's not from these parts – he's from Judaea. There's no Lake there and no fish! So how did he know what to look for?"

"Perhaps he has special powers, Simeon, like the old Prophets."

"Is that it, Andreas, is Yeshua a prophet? Perhaps he's Elijah returned from the dead?"

"No, Simeon," Andreas replied seriously after a pause. "I think old Jochanan was Elijah."

"Then exactly who is Yeshua?" Simeon asked.

The question remained unanswered because the boat suddenly began to rock violently as the wind rose and the waves began to break around the boat. It began to rain. The two men stood up. They pulled the steering oar into the boat. They reached up and pulled in the sail. They struggled in the rapidly rising wind to tie the flapping fabric to the mast. Then they organised the

152

other ten, who had been awakened by the storm, to bail out the water from the boat, using their cupped hands or anything else they could find. It seemed to be a losing struggle. The boat was thrown about by the waves and wind, bucking like an out of control donkey. Thomas and Bartholomew were both seasick. Most of the others felt unwell. All worked together to fight the waves, while Simeon and Andreas tried to hold the boat steady with the steering oar. Everyone forgot Yeshua, who remained asleep in the stern. Eventually Thomas looked up from throwing water back over the side and asked, "Where's Yeshua?" They looked around and realised he was still asleep in the stern, getting soaked by the waves. Philip struggled against the wind and waves to reach him, and woke him up.

"Yeshua," he said in a voice of panic. "How can you sleep through this? Don't you care if we all drown?"

Yeshua stood up. He was surprised at how much things had changed since he had fallen asleep. The two fishermen were struggling with the steering oar. The rest appeared to be fighting a losing battle with the incoming water. He himself was soaked. He moved to the middle of the boat, among his obviously frightened and struggling disciples. He spoke to them sternly.

"Stop this! Where's your faith? You're with me, don't you realise nothing can harm you? Have you prayed? This storm is God's doing – not Satan's. He's testing you. Why have you not asked Him to stop the storm?"

Yeshua turned away from them. He raised his arms and turned his face to the skies. He stood, with the rain falling on his face and his hair flying in the wind, wearing clothes soaked black. Water washed about his feet. Spray covered his legs and body. He looked like Moses might have done at the crossing of the Red Sea.

"Father, tell the wind to stop and the sea to calm

down," he cried out.

Storms on inland lakes in mountainous areas can rise suddenly and fall just as suddenly. As Yeshua spoke the wind began to drop and the waves grew smaller. The inrush of water was reduced and the boat was restored to safety. The rain stopped. The men sat down, wet through and cold, but safe. Simeon and Andreas raised the sail again and the boat continued on its way.

Thaddeus, who had been the furthest away from Yeshua, and had not heard exactly what he said, believed that he had ordered the wind to stop. He turned to his friend, Simeon.

"Who is Yeshua?" he asked in awe. "Even the wind and waves obey him!"

"God knows Thaddeus," Simeon the Rebel replied, "I certainly don't!"

Chapter 8

Pressure

Capernaum, 31AD

The boat grounded on the beach at Capernaum as the sun rose. It was cold, still and quiet. Most of the townspeople were still asleep as the ten men, led by Yeshua and his two sons, made their way through the streets to their homes. They were all subdued and quiet after their experiences of the previous night. No one knew quite what to make of the sudden stilling of the storm after Yeshua spoke. They were not sure what had happened and one explanation was simply too extraordinary to be accepted. Although all felt confused, no one asked Yeshua what he believed had occurred.

Once home, Yeshua and the boys were greeted by a relieved Mariam. She had been worried, but was not sure why. Jacob told her the story of the storm, and she believed she had discovered the cause of her concern.

"You shouldn't worry, Mother," Jochanan said. "Father is doing God's work. Therefore God will always protect him and everyone with him; so we were never in any danger."

Mariam smiled at the strength of his faith and the vehemence of his assertion of it, so typical of her older son.

"I'm sure you're right, son."

She turned away from the two boys to face a tired Yeshua.

"Your brother, Jacob, arrived yesterday from Bethlehem. I found somewhere for him to sleep. He's waiting for you inside."

Yeshua thanked her, and hurried indoors.

Jacob stood up and embraced Yeshua. Stifling a yawn, Yeshua greeted his brother.

"Jacob, it's good to see you. What a surprise! Why are you here?"

"We've heard many things about you, and mother sent me to find out what's happening. I've also been back to Qumr'an at father's request. He also asked me to come up here to meet you. What's been going on?"

"It's all rather complicated at the moment, Jacob. People are flocking towards us, but for the wrong reasons. You remember what we said about miracles while we were in the desert?"

Jacob nodded.

"Despite my denials, the public think I am just a miracle worker. I have told those who come to me with a problem and go away feeling better to praise God and leave me out of it. No one takes any notice, and, as a result, the people think I'm only here to cure cripples and drive out demons. As a result, my teaching is being ignored, and I can't even get to the heart of the renewal message. Yes, on the surface I'm having spectacular success, but it's only on the surface, and it's for the wrong reasons."

"Do you think you can change this? If so, how will you do it?"

Yeshua sat down wearily, suddenly overwhelmed by tiredness, his body sagging against the wall. He sighed and scratched his head.

"To be honest, Jacob, I don't know the answer to either of your questions. I hope we can find a way – but I don't know how or when. My men and I have been working here for over six months, and have very little to show for it. All we seem to have done is to attract the attention of the various Authorities."

Jacob was concerned about this last statement.

"What do you mean Yeshua? In what way are they involved with you?"

"I have spies from the High Priest, especially two Pharisees, who have been dogging my footsteps. They're very high profile. I even know their names – Moshe and Yusuf. I suspect that Herod's men are also watching me, and possibly Pilate's as well, but I haven't spotted them. They're all watching me, waiting for me to make a mistake and then report to their masters. It puts us all under enormous pressure."

Jacob looked even more anxious.

"Are they watching your house?"

"Not that I'm aware of. However, I am certainly aware that I am being watched by the High Priest's men."

"Well," Jacob grinned, still standing and facing the seated Yeshua. "You and he are rivals, even if he doesn't realise it yet!"

Yeshua laughed, relaxing for the first time.

"He's going to get a shock when he does realise."

Yeshua's smile was replaced by a much grimmer expression.

"The problem I have is that I still don't know how and when I am going to challenge him."

Jacob sat down, next to his brother, in silent sympathy. Mariam brought in a wineskin and two goblets. The two men poured out wine and added water. They sipped quietly. Eventually, Jacob turned towards his brother.

"I may have an answer for you. Father told me to come here to advise you. He has received reports from Thomas and Judah, confirming what you have just said to me. He suggests that you should go away completely. Take your team, with the women, and go to Phoenicia and the outskirts of Syria. There you can work things out with the rest of your disciples undisturbed by the crowds. When you've sorted them out, you can all return to Galilee and try again. You may find the locals more responsive to your real message then."

"That's the advice of Abraham Bar Abbas – go to the Gentile areas. Is that it?"

"Yes, brother."

"And what about you?"

"He ordered me to return to Bethlehem after giving you this message."

"I suggest you do more," Yeshua said seriously. "Protect the family by disassociating yourselves from me. That will ensure that the Authorities leave you alone."

Jacob showed his surprise.

"You actually want us to denounce you?" he asked.

"I don't want you to, but I suggest that you should do something like it for the protection of the rest of the family."

"If we do that, Yeshua, it may make things more difficult for you."

"I know that, Jacob, but I think that's what you should do. The Romans, in particular, tend to assume that a whole family shares in the offence they claim an individual member has committed. As a result, they punish everyone in it, like they did the family of the boy who threw a stone at Pilate's men in Jerusalem a couple of years ago."

"I'm sure you're right," Jacob conceded grudgingly, "and we will do as you ask, reluctantly."

Yeshua stood up, shook his brother's hand and wished him luck.

"I really must sleep now," he added. "After the storm last night none of us slept much."

"I will be gone when you wake, Yeshua. However,

when you come south, we may have a chance to talk again."

"Indeed!" Yeshua responded. "Have a safe journey, brother."

Yeshua left his brother, to lie down and sleep. Later that day Jacob began the long journey home. They did not meet again until Yeshua returned to the south.

**

In Jerusalem, Caiaphas was seated at his desk in his office in the Temple. He was not happy. Messages continued to come in from the North. He heard that Yeshua was extremely critical of the Pharisees. As a Sadducee, Caiaphas was not unduly sad that his opponents were being savaged. However, he was concerned over two things. The first was the fact that the man, whom he considered to be a charlatan, was obviously extremely popular. He discussed this with his father-in-law. Annas was sanguine.

"Don't worry about it, Yusuf," he said. "The Galileans are fools. Look how they follow every Messianic claimant and end up as sword fodder for the Romans! Of course they follow the charlatan! That should not surprise us! Wait patiently. He will come south eventually. He has to. When he does he will be in our reach, and we will take him and stamp on him and his followers as though they are insects."

"He's also attacking you and me personally, father-in-law. He calls us Roman stooges and false High Priests. That is undermining my authority. One or two of the Council are already on his side."

"Who are they?" Annas asked.

"Nicodemus and Yusuf of Aramathea."

"You're sure of this?"

"Certainly."

159

"Do you want me to arrange for a knife in the back in a Jerusalem back street?"

Caiaphas was shocked by this casual reference to assassination by his father-in-law.

"Certainly not!" he replied vehemently. "I'm shocked you should even suggest it! I will deal with the two of them in my own way. At least I know who they are."

"As you wish, son-in-law," Annas replied drily. "When you change your mind, let me know."

Annas rose and left the office, closing the door without looking back. Caiaphas remained seated, head in hands, for a few minutes before sending for his Secretary. He wrote to his two spies, telling them he wanted detailed and accurate reports of the words and actions of their quarry. He sealed the letter and sent it off with his Secretary. The letter travelled north, but arrived too late. Moshe and Yusuf met it on their way south to report that Yeshua had vanished in the mists of the north.

**

In Caesarea, Pilate too had been receiving reports. He noted the rise in Yeshua's popularity, but also noted that he did not seem to be political at all. His two spies reported that his message was entirely religious. The man seemed to want to reform the Jewish faith. He decided that, so far, he needed to do nothing. Like Caiaphas, he wrote to his spies, expressing his gratitude for their reports, and urging them to continue their good work.

**

Herod in Macchaerus was also concerned. He felt he

was at the heart of what storm there was. Yeshua was rampaging throughout his dominions, and he was receiving only partial reports from Salome. (He was unaware that Salome had become a real follower of Yeshua.) He heard that the public was flocking to Yeshua, and this worried Herod. He knew Galilee was like a dry forest. He felt Yeshua could act as the spark that would set the whole country alight. He sent two men to Capernaum with instructions to order him to leave his lands. However, when they arrived they, too, found that Yeshua and his men had disappeared.

**

Yeshua and his team, both men and women, travelled directly north, through the valleys of Galilee, before crossing the mountains, which separated Herod's lands from the Mediterranean Sea, and the Phoenician cities of Tyre and Sidon. Here he was able to speak quietly to his disciples and teach them about his mission.

The crowds disappeared, but Yeshua still received visits from men and women who needed help. He was doubly reluctant to help these people because they were Gentiles. However, in this land where the great Elijah had once walked, he did make exceptions. One was a Phoenician woman.

She came up to him, carrying a small child.

"Are you the Yeshua all the Jews talk about?" she asked.

"I am Yeshua, certainly," he replied with a smile. "I'm not sure how many Jews talk about me!"

Yeshua paused, searching her with his eyes. Then he added kindly,

"What can I do for you?"

"My son is sick," she said simply. "Can you pray for

161

him?"

"I was sent to the Jews. They are God's children. I have not been sent to help the household dogs."

Yeshua softened the harshness of his words by his smile. The woman responded in kind.

"But Lord, the household dogs might eat the crumbs that drop from the table when the children are fed."

Yeshua laughed at this reply. He laid his hand on the child's head and prayed for him. He began to recover.

This caused Yeshua to wonder.

Why is it that the Jews are so different? The Centurion, a Roman pagan, did not doubt me. He did not even want me to come to his house. He believed his slave would be cured if he spoke to me. This Phoenician woman feels the same. She would not let me give her the brush off.

Yet my own people won't even listen to me! What else do I need to do to convince them? Am I wasting my time here?

Even my own disciples don't really understand me. Yes, I know the five who were with Jochanan know who I am; but what of the others? What do they think? What do I need to do to convince them?

There is nothing I can do other than remain patient. They have to find out the truth for themselves. It is more meaningful that way. I shall just have to continue as I have been doing.

The tour continued, as they re-crossed the mountains and passed into the lands ruled by Herod Philip, the brother of Herod Antipas. As they walked through the empty countryside, a man, whose arms were wrapped in dirty bandages, which had plainly not been changed for years, looking unkempt and dirty, with ragged clothes, approached Yeshua and knelt in front of him.

162

"Help me, Lord," he pleaded. "I have leprosy."

Yeshua felt angry. He stood over the man, hands behind his back, clenching and unclenching his fists. He spoke sternly to the man.

"Why are you here? You know the Law. If you have been cured you go to the priest for a certificate of cure."

"I know that," the man whined, shrinking visibly at the anger of Yeshua. "I want you to cure me first."

"How long have you had this affliction?" Yeshua asked, taking pity on the man's obvious desperation.

"I first saw the signs three years ago."

Yeshua looked at the dirty rags, which covered the man's arms.

"When did you last change these dressings?"

"I haven't. I've been afraid to look."

Yeshua paused, studying the man, noting his obvious distress and remembering that leprosy isolated a person from the community. It was the living death.

"Stand up man," he ordered.

The man stumbled to his feet and stood in front of Yeshua, who smiled encouragingly at him.

"Have you prayed about this?" he asked.

"Yes, Lord," the man replied. "Unceasingly."

"Do you believe that God can cure you?"

"Yes, Lord."

Yeshua placed his two hands, one on top of the other on the man's head and blessed him.

"Now take the bandages off."

The man with leprosy stood in front of Yeshua, too afraid to obey him. Yeshua turned to Bartholomew.

"Bartholomew, you've got medical knowledge. Change the man's bandages."

Bartholomew, reluctantly, took the man's left hand and began to unwrap the cloths, which covered his arm. The dirty fabric fell away, grey on the outside and yellow on the inside, to reveal a skin which was white, from lack of exposure to the sun, but otherwise unmarked. He did the same with the right arm, with the same result. Then he stepped back, showing the man's arms to Yeshua, who smiled.

"You see, there's nothing wrong with you! You were killing yourself with your fear. Go and show yourself to the priests and get a certificate of cure, so you can return to the community and lead a useful and productive life. Just don't say I cured you. Give the praise to God."

The man thanked Yeshua and left.

Simeon the Rebel was shocked. He turned and spoke to Yeshua.

"Why did you touch him, Yeshua? Weren't you afraid that you would catch his disease?"

"I don't think giving a man consolation and a blessing is likely to give me a disease. This man is also a child of God. It wasn't God who pushed him out of the community, it was frightened men, interpreting God's laws to protect themselves."

"You have to be careful, though, Yeshua," the ever practical Thomas commented, "He will tell it as though you cured him and that will make it all worse."

"I know, Thomas, I know," Yeshua said soothingly. "But what do you want me to do? I gave the man hope. He almost certainly didn't have Leprosy. But he was cut off from God and the community. I have restored him to both. It was the same with the woman who touched me. She was isolated. Matthaus will tell you that men who work for the Roman Government are treated in the same way. So are the poor. I am restoring their hope and bringing them together in God's kingdom."

Simeon the Rebel was walking beside Yeshua and Thomas. He interrupted their conversation.

"It's good what you've done, Yeshua, but what are you going to do with all these people? You've brought them together and given them hope – but hope in what? What are your plans and intentions? How do you intend to turn hope into action and fulfilment?"

Yeshua stopped walking and turned back towards Simeon, causing the rest of the group to stop as well and crowd around the leading three.

"Those are extremely good questions, Simeon. In fact they are questions I am asking myself. I wish I knew the answer. I do not know what I am going to do, yet. I am waiting for God, for the Son of the Father, or some other source to point me the way. So far it has not come. I am deeply troubled until it does. All I can do is continue to work with the poor and disinherited, denounce the cruelty and prejudice that creates this situation, and wait for God to tell me, one way or another, what I have to do."

The group stood silently, looking at each other. They all felt sympathy for their leader, but none knew what to say. Yeshua felt alone, even though his friends and family surrounded him. He realised that none of them understood his dilemma. Eventually, he turned away, and resumed the journey. The rest trailed behind him, silently.

Jochanan and Jacob and their mother, Mariam, left the trailing group and walked with Yeshua, giving him silent support. He realised they were there, looked round and smiled at them, but continued, walking in silent prayer, desperately seeking direction.

They reached the small town of Bethsaida. It was around midday. A beggar who called out for alms beside the road disturbed the silent group. Yeshua stopped, his thoughts disturbed. He asked the beggar what he wanted. The beggar laughed.

"My sight back of course, but, failing that, money, so I can buy food and drink."

Yeshua called Bartholomew, who looked at the man's eyes.

"I think we can do something about this," he told Yeshua.

Bartholomew collected soil, spat on it, and made a paste of the mud. Yeshua took it and put it on the man's eyes. He left it there for a while before removing it.

"Can you see now?" he asked.

"I can see something, but not clearly," the man replied.

Yeshua turned to Bartholomew.

"What now?"

"Do it again," Bartholomew said. "Sometimes it takes more than one application."

Yeshua repeated the action. This time the result was perfect.

"That's good," Yeshua said. "Now go away and live a productive life in your community."

They continued their journey north. They split into groups, talking quietly on the way. Thomas, Philip and Judah walked with Yeshua, in silent communion with him and his family.

Simeon and Andreas continued the discussion they had begun in the boat before the storm.

Matthaus had struck up an unlikely friendship with Simeon the Rebel and Thaddeus. The three were involved in an animated conversation about whom or what Yeshua actually was. Matthaus believed he was preparing to declare a revolt against Herod. Simeon thought he might be right, but did not feel the evidence was there to support the suggestion. Thaddeus thought he was acting more like one of the prophets, or even like a Rabbi. Matthaus told him he was wrong, because he was far too radical for that.

Bartholomew and Judas lagged behind the rest, arguing over the implications of the two most recent cures. Judas believed that Yeshua had declared war on the priests. Bartholomew was not so sure.

The group of women, who followed even further behind, were concerned mainly with the practicalities of that night's camp.

Yeshua and his immediate entourage ignored the conversations behind them. As the day wore on, a conviction began to grow in Yeshua's mind. He eventually made a decision, not as to his ultimate goal, but about his next step. He did not want to be forced into a decision by others, a danger of which he was well aware. He had heard of other religious reformers who had been trapped into fatal political action as a result of a combination of the ideas of supporters and the stubborn opposition of his opponents. However, he knew he would have to take the risk. He decided he would challenge his followers when he found a suitable place the next day.

Chapter 9

Decisions

Caesarea Philippi, Northern Israel, 31AD

Next day they came to another Greek city, far to the north. Behind the white marble buildings loomed the snow-topped peak of Mount Hermon, the highest mountain in the area. The town itself was open and modern, with colonnaded public buildings and statues, many of them naked or nearly so, of gods and goddesses. This was another Caesarea, Caesarea Philippi; the capital city of the Tetrarch Philip. The city was Greek in appearance and population. Such was the city to which Yeshua brought his followers for rest and reflection.

The party settled down and made camp on the banks of a local stream. The men cut wood for the fire or ensured that the donkeys they were using as pack animals were rubbed down, secured and fed, while some of the women washed clothes in the stream and spread them out on the grass to dry. The other women prepared, and, later, cooked the evening meal, assisted by the three teenaged males. While all this was going on, Yeshua went off alone. He sat, overlooking the stream; head in hands, sheltering behind a statue of the god Pan with his pipes.

Where do I go from here? This is a decisive moment. Are my followers ready?

Am I ready?

What am I ready for?

What am I trying to do?

How will I know if I am successful or a failure?

What is the reward for success? What is the cost of failure?

Yeshua asked the questions of the air.

Questions, there are always questions. There are more questions than answers.

The answers did not come. Yeshua was not sure where they would come from anyway.

Does God speak today? If He does, how does He speak? Will I recognise His voice? How will I differentiate God's voice and wishes from my own?

The questions continued to come but there were no answers. Yeshua listened to the silence, which was deep and profound. He sat and listened for what seemed a long time for the answers, which did not come.

Mariam saw Yeshua and walked over to him. She sat down beside him, in silent companionship. Yeshua felt her presence. He looked round and smiled at her. Eventually, the two stood up. Yeshua kissed her and the two returned to the rest, holding hands. They sat down, with the others, beside the fire, side by side. The other women served them food. They all ate and drank, and then relaxed around the fire.

Yeshua opened the conversation.

"What were you talking about on the way Judas?"

Judas looked embarrassed and did not answer.

"What about you Matthaus?"

Matthaus looked at Simeon the former rebel, who looked back at him. Both were also silent.

Yeshua looked away from Matthaus and Simeon to Andreas and the other Simeon.

"What about you two?"

Simeon was not one who was easily abashed. He answered bluntly.

"We were discussing what you are doing and who exactly you are Yeshua."

"I see," said Yeshua, "and what did you decide?"

Simeon was not prepared to answer that one. He stared at the ground between his feet. Yeshua turned to Simeon's brother.

"What about you, Andreas?"

He too was silent.

The remaining two, Thaddeus and Bartholomew were also silent.

Yeshua allowed the silence to linger.

It was Jochanan, impetuous as ever, who broke the silence.

"People are saying you perform lots of miracles, father."

"What do you mean, son?" Yeshua asked gently.

"Do you remember how you said that the woman who touched you had been healed by her faith?"

"Yes."

"I have heard people telling each other that you said power went out of you."

"And you corrected them?"

"Of course, but they just laughed at me."

Jacob joined in eagerly.

"That's not all, father! The same people claim that you raised the 12 year old girl from the dead."

"That's ridiculous!" Yeshua responded angrily. His eyes moved around the group, focussing on each member individually.

"Have any more of you heard the same rumours?"

Several of the group said they had heard the same thing.

Thomas added, "Others claim that you fed 5000 men, plus women and children with five loaves and two small fish. We all know that did not happen, but the more we attempt to stop the rumours, the more they grow."

Yeshua nodded.

"I have noticed the same," he agreed. "What do you think of this?"

"It was probably inevitable," Philip commented. "But, remember, the Authorities usually discount such rumours as exaggerated."

"However," Judah added cautiously, "In view of our ultimate aims, such rumours can be very damaging. You've been very careful, Yeshua not to attack the Authorities directly."

Simeon the fisherman interrupted.

"Except the Pharisees and the High Priest, Yeshua. You've been very critical of them."

"What do you think about the Romans and Herod?"

The voice was a young one, and not one of the Twelve. It came from outside of the inner circle around the fire. They looked around in surprise to see who asked the question. It was a teenaged boy, the one who had arrived with his sister. Yeshua called him to join the group by the fire.

"Who are you?" Yeshua asked.

"My name is Marcus. I was Pilate's slave, as was my sister, Julia. He freed us, and we came to join you. He blamed me for the attack on his men when he entered Jerusalem. He was right. I threw a stone at his soldiers because they were breaking our laws against idolatry by showing the symbols of their gods in our holy city. They arrested me, and Pilate made me his slave. He was not unkind to me or to my sister, but he did things to me I don't want to talk about, things that the Bible forbids men to do to other men."

He fell silent, and no one spoke. Everyone guessed what he meant, but no one dared ask him. Yeshua sought to reassure him.

"Did you cause Pilate's actions?"

"No."

"Did you cooperate with his actions?"

171

"Only when he forced me."

"So you did what you did with him under threat of punishment?"

"Yes. I was his slave, so what choice did I have?"

Yeshua stood up and walked over to him as he sat by the fire, his head in his hands, the picture of guilt and misery. He placed his hands on the boy's head and prayed a blessing over him. Then he placed his hands under the boy's chin and lifted his face up. Smiling at the boy, Yeshua said, "You were in no way responsible for what happened. The Procurator was in charge and you did as you were told. You had no choice. God was there and saw what happened. He will not blame you in any way. You have admitted your actions and shown remorse. God will forgive you – but do you forgive yourself?"

Yeshua stood in front of Marcus, his hands still holding the boy's face up. He noticed tears welling up in the boy's eyes, and gently pulled the boy to his feet. Once Marcus was standing, Yeshua released his hands, and cuddled Marcus' head to his chest, stroking his hair gently. He held Marcus for five minutes, until the boy had a chance to recover. Then he returned to his former position. Marcus sat down by the fire and stared at Yeshua, his gratitude showing in his eyes.

"In answer to your question, Marcus. The Romans were invited here by the King of Israel to fight the Greek King Antiochus. They overstayed their welcome and have no place among God's people. One day we will tell them so. We will invite them to leave, and, if they refuse, we will drive them out, like our ancestors did to Sennacherib and Antiochus."

"When will that day come, Yeshua?" Simeon the Rebel asked.

"I don't know Simeon," Yeshua replied. "However I am certain that the day will come eventually."

This dialogue ended in a long pause, as they absorbed the implications of Yeshua's words. No one had the courage to ask if he intended to be the one to ask the Romans to leave or, if they refused, to force them out. Yeshua did not offer any further comment on the issue.

Eventually, Yeshua turned to Judas.

"Judas, you've always proved to be a reliable witness. What are the ordinary people saying about me?"

"You've heard quite a lot already Yeshua," Judas began, swatting away the insects, which were beginning to annoy the group. "Most are drawing links between what they hear you say and what they've heard you've done, and the Prophets in the Bible, especially Elijah and Elisha."

"I see," Yeshua said slowly, also trying to flick away the annoying insects. "Is that all that people are saying?"

"No father," Jochanan said eagerly, "some think you're the prophet who has come to announce the coming of Messiah."

Not to be outdone, his younger brother added, just as eagerly, "And some think you're Jochanan the Prophet – the Baptiser – brought back to life."

"I've changed a lot then!" Yeshua said to general laughter. "I drink wine and eat normally with my team, and share jokes with them. I also dress properly and live in a house. Oh, and I've also shrunk a bit!"

There was even more laughter at this last comment.

"There have been greater changes, Yeshua," Thomas said seriously. "However, you're safe! Five of us saw you two together."

Yeshua smiled.

"I'm extremely grateful for that comment Thomas! I want to be Yeshua, not Jochanan reborn."

Another silence followed, longer this time. It was broken by Yeshua, who, looking down at the fire, spoke to no one in particular.

"Who do you think I am?"

There was a long silence, which Yeshua allowed to continue. Eventually, Simeon the fisherman answered.

"You are the Messiah, the leader and saviour we are expecting."

Yeshua looked around at his followers. No one looked surprised.

"Is that what you all think?" he asked.

There were nods all around the group. Only the five former disciples of Jochanan, who knew the truth, seemed unmoved. Yeshua turned back to Simeon.

"Simeon, you have acted like the leader you are. God has spoken to you and through you in a way I have not experienced for some time. I am going to give you the name Cephas, the rock. You are all going to have to be rocklike in the future. However, do not use the term 'Messiah' publicly please. There are too many expectations connected with it. You may yet see your Messiah stretched, naked, nailed to a tree, dying gradually before your eyes."

Simeon could not take this.

"You're wrong, Yeshua. The Messiah will kill our enemies. They will not kill him, by crucifixion or any other way."

Yeshua stood up and walked into the middle of the group, standing with his back to the fire. He turned around, meeting the eyes of each disciple in turn. He read in them agreement with Simeon's comment. Finally, he turned back towards Simeon, responding to his words.

"In many ways, Cephas, you are allowing Satan to speak through you. You see, you are thinking in human terms. For us human beings, success means that we have achieved what we want. In this case what we want is to liberate our land and re-establish God's rule here. However, the route to success is often through failure, and God's definition of success may be different from what we expect or hope. The cost of failure would be my agonising and humiliating death. It may also be the price of success. No one knows what the consequences of that would be, or even if that's what God wants. However, if we are obedient to God, and we must be, then we must leave the outcome to Him. You and I all have to accept God's decision, whatever the personal cost, to me, to you, to all of us. We cannot force God to do our will and must not try to do so. Do you understand that Cephas?"

Simeon nodded, shamefacedly. Yeshua noticed this and walked over to him. He raised him to his feet and embraced him.

"Cephas," he said. "You're an honest and forthright man. You say what the others are thinking. I will not forget what you said, and, in the future, others will remember it of you, when your mistakes are forgotten. You're a good man, and I love you."

"I love you too, Yeshua."

"I know you do," Yeshua said with a smile. "Let's both forget what we've just said to each other."

He looked around at the others, before adding, "None of us knows what God's timetable is, but I promise that some of you will still be alive when God's Kingdom comes."

He looked at his two sons, and at Marcus and Julia.

"I can't say which of you, but I am sure that some of you will see it. All of you, however, must be prepared to pay a terrible personal price for that Kingdom. For many of us, it could be carrying our crosses to the execution ground."

Yeshua's words first fuelled their sense of

excitement and then, as he intended, calmed it down.

Yeshua and Simeon sat down next to each other, and the group broke up into general conversation about their hopes, fears, and experiences. One by one they slipped into sleep and eventually silence fell on the small encampment.

In the general silence, Mariam rolled over and whispered to her husband.

"Yeshua," she said urgently, "I think you have made a serious mistake."

"What mistake is that my love?"

"You made Simeon the Leader. Jochanan and Jacob will not accept that, and neither will your brother, Jacob."

"I know that. I also have Thomas, Philip and Judah. They were with me before anyone else except Jacob."

"Then why did you do it Yeshua?"

"I didn't appoint him the Leader. That's not my role. I said he was a leader and renamed him because his faith is a model for the others."

"You may think that, Yeshua, but I don't think Simeon and the others saw it that way. I am sure you will have trouble over this."

"I will deal with it if it arises, don't worry love," Yeshua promised, before reaching out and embracing his wife. They both fell asleep shortly afterwards.

The group settled down in that area, where they enjoyed peace and quiet for several days, during which they rested and relaxed. The local population largely left them alone. A few people came out to see them, and some sat down to listen to Yeshua, who taught them in his normal way. The Disciples were grateful for the rest, and used the time to think and plan. The divisions foretold by Mariam began to surface, particularly in arguments between Simeon and Yeshua's sons. Eventually, Yeshua tired of the low level quarrelling, and ordered the camp to be broken up, and the group left the town, heading for the nearby Mountain.

Seven days after the conversation at Caesarea Philippi, Yeshua and his group were at the foot of Mount Hermon. He decided to take his two sons and the two fishermen with him. He ordered the rest of the group to encamp at the foot of the mountain until the five returned. He intended to climb up the mountain and spend time there in prayer and meditation with the quarrelling foursome. It was very warm at the foot of the mountain. They sweated as they climbed. Half way up, Yeshua called a halt so they could all take a breather.

Simeon, the oldest, was the most stressed by the climb. Jochanan was the most perplexed. In between his heavy breaths, he gasped to Yeshua.

"Father, why are we climbing this mountain?"

"So we can be nearer God, son," Yeshua said with a smile.

"I thought God was everywhere!" Simeon grunted.

"He is," Yeshua agreed, "But, remember, in the Bible He is particularly connected with mountains, and it is sometimes easier to concentrate up there than on the ground."

When they had rested, Yeshua led them further up the mountain. When they reached a ridge about three thousand feet up, they stopped and he gave them instructions.

"Sit down," he said, "and pray. Seek guidance for yourselves, and for me, from God."

The four sat in a circle on the bare rocks. Jochanan pulled out a water bottle from the pouch attached to his belt and passed it around. They all drank. Simeon thanked Jochanan and asked him what he thought he would do when the Liberation came. Jochanan said he hoped for a senior role in the Government. Simeon smiled and promised he would use his influence with Yeshua on Jochanan's behalf. Jochanan grunted at what he felt was Simeon's presumption. Jacob seemed about to protest, but Jochanan nudged him, to keep him silent. Jacob recognised the signal from his brother and did as he was asked. All four sat silently, staring at the ground, trying to still their sense of anticipation, and pray. They all failed. Slowly, they began to feel drowsy after their strenuous efforts.

Meanwhile, at the foot of the mountain, the rest of the group sought shelter from the sun under the trees. Thomas and Philip organised them into groups. They passed around water, and ensured that the donkeys were tethered and cared for properly. The women and other followers worked together to prepare the evening meal for when the five returned. Although the area was remote, news began to spread through the surrounding villages. A small crowd began to gather, led by the local Rabbi. His younger brother, a lawyer, who had arrived from Judaea, accompanied him. Seeing the small crowd, the five former followers of Jochanan, led by Thomas, persuaded them to sit down, and, explaining that Yeshua was on the mountain praying, began to teach them. They combined what they had heard Jochanan and Yeshua teach. Judas, Matthaus and Bartholomew joined them. In this way the long day began to wind away.

On the mountain, the four disciples had given up the effort, and had fallen asleep one by one. Yeshua continued to pray, seeking clear guidance as to his next step.

Simeon never knew whether he was sleeping and dreaming or awake and seeing reality. However, he was convinced that he saw Yeshua crowned in the light of the midday sun behind him. His face and clothes shone bright white. He saw, or thought he saw, the vague insubstantial figures of Moses and Elijah, the two pillars of the Jewish faith (Law and Prophecy), standing beside him. The three men appeared to be talking. As they did so, the vision became swamped in mist, as if a cloud enveloped them. Simeon was convinced he heard a voice saying to him, "This is my son, listen to him and believe what he tells you." The mist lifted and Simeon struggled to speak, as one does in dreams. Eventually he burst out, "Master, it's good we're here. Shall we make three shelters for you, Moses and Elijah, so you can be comfortable while you talk?"

His voice startled Yeshua, who turned around to see who had spoken, and also woke the other three. Yeshua was alone and the same as he always was. He walked over to them, where they were sitting, rubbing their eyes and obviously recovering from sleep. He was concerned that they were all right. He made a space and sat down among them.

"What did you see Cephas?" Yeshua asked.

"I saw you, shining white, talking with Moses and Elijah, and I heard a voice telling us to listen to you."

"What were we talking about?" Yeshua asked.

Simeon struggled to remember, rubbing his forehead vigorously and crinkling his forehead in the effort.

"I think you were talking about going to Jerusalem and liberating the people," he answered finally.

"Did you genuinely hear that Cephas, or is that what you hoped to hear?" Yeshua asked dubiously.

"I don't know, Yeshua," Simeon confessed. "However, that's what I think I heard."

"You may be right," Yeshua concluded. "Even if you dreamed what you saw, and that's the most likely answer, God may be sending me a message through you. We have to go to Jerusalem to challenge the

Authorities, and especially the so-called High Priest. The foundation is nearly laid, we must move on to the next stage."

"We're not ready to move south, father," Jochanan objected. "There are practical preparations to make."

"I agree, son," Yeshua answered. "We haven't quite finished up here, and I need to lay the groundwork down south. That's why we're going to leave here and return to Capernaum, before setting off for Jerusalem. I intend us to be there for Passover."

He paused, before continuing decisively.

"Come on, let's go down. There's nothing more to do here. Let's join the others, pack up, and prepare to go home."

They climbed wearily to their feet, and began to follow Yeshua down the mountain.

At the bottom, the meeting had begun to break up. Within the crowd there was a man with a boy, who, Thomas discovered, was the man's son. The man came forward, and spoke to Thomas.

"Can you cure my son?"

"What's wrong with him?" Thomas replied.

"He suffers from epilepsy."

"How serious are the attacks?" Philip asked.

"They can be very serious and are growing more frequent," the worried parent answered.

"We can try," Thomas said. "Bring your son here."

The man brought his son forward, and the crowd followed, curious to see what would happen. Thomas placed his hands on the boy's head and prayed as he had seen Yeshua do. Nothing happened. The remaining seven tried, also without success. The father stood, irresolute, wandering what to do next. The crowd stood around them, wandering what was going to happen. They felt slightly disappointed that nothing had apparently happened.

It was at this point that Yeshua returned with the other four. He summed up the situation at a glance.

"What's the problem Thomas?" he asked.

Thomas looked round with relief.

"This man has an epileptic son, Yeshua," he replied. "He asked us to heal him, but we failed."

"I see," said Yeshua slowly.

Yeshua turned to the father.

"So, your son has epilepsy?"

"Yes, Lord," the man, replied.

"Have you consulted the doctors and got the right treatment for him?"

"Yes, Lord."

"And it hasn't worked?"

"No Lord. In fact, the boy has got worse."

Yeshua felt impatient.

Will these demands for cures never go away? What can I do to deter such demands? Will they never understand that I have no magical power – that God, based on their faith, does everything?

"Do you have faith in God's power?' Yeshua asked.

"Yes and no," the man admitted. "I need help to strengthen my faith."

"Pray to God, then, while I lay my hands on your son and pray for him as well."

The boy stood before Yeshua, who placed his hands on his head, and prayed to God to remove the boy's illness. The boy was still for a moment, and then was seized by a severe fit, fell to the ground and writhed in apparent agony, before becoming still. Yeshua knelt down, felt his pulse and listened for his breathing, before raising him gently to his feet.

"He should be all right now," he told the anxious father. "Take him home and take care of him."

The father embraced his son, and then embraced Yeshua.

"Thank you Lord," he said, tears streaming down his face. "I will never forget your kindness."

Yeshua turned away, to hide his own emotions.

"Don't thank me, I have done nothing, thank God," he said, eventually. "Take your son home and let him rest."

After the man left, Yeshua turned to the crowd.

"Why are you here?" he asked.

"We came to listen to you," the Rabbi answered. "While you were away your followers spoke to us."

"That's good," Yeshua answered. "What did they say to you?"

"We should love our neighbours," the lawyer said. "Like the Commandments tell us."

"That's good too," Yeshua said. "I can't really add any more to that."

"Who is my neighbour?" the lawyer said. "There's been a lot of debate about this issue within Judaism. What's your opinion?"

Yeshua smiled.

"Sit down all of you, and I will tell you a story."

The crowd of visitors sat down in front of the disciples. Yeshua began to speak.

"There was a rich man, a merchant, who left Jerusalem to walk down the mountain road to Jericho. He was in a hurry and extremely foolish. He walked alone and unarmed. None of you would be so foolish, would you?" he asked with a smile.

The crowd shook their heads. Some smiled back. This was a familiar story and they guessed what was to follow.

"All went well at first. The rich man strode confidently down the road, leaving the City, and following the steep gradient downwards. About half way down, as the mountain road ran along the edge of a steep hill, robbers, who had been following him, unable to believe their luck, struck. Six of them leapt down onto the road, with drawn swords, three in front of the man and three behind him, so he could not escape.

'What do you want?' the man cried out, wetting himself in fear.

'All you have,' the leader said simply.

He reached forward and slashed at the man's belt with his sword. The belt split apart and the man's heavy purse dropped to the ground. One of the gang picked the purse up and gave it to the leader, while another fingered the man's silk gown.

'It's good quality cloth,' he said. 'Where did you buy it?'

Hoping to escape unharmed, the man replied, 'In Caesarea. It cost me a fortune.'

'So it's Roman silk?' the leader replied with a cruel smile.

'Let me help you find God,' he added mockingly.

'Amos, help the gentleman off with his Roman gown. Good Jews should not wear Pagan gowns.'

One of the robbers laughed, and began to tug the silk gown over the man's head. He tried to stop him, and the gown tore in the struggle. It was unavailing. All he did was to lose his sandals as well. So he stood, his corpulent body covered only by his loincloth, in front of an angry group of robbers, who took up sticks and beat him until he fell to the ground, covered with blood. The leader rolled the man's unconscious body into a ditch beside the track, and the group disappeared into the rocks, much wealthier for their endeavours.

"Time passed, and the birds who had been disturbed by the violence, settled down. Two vultures began to circle overhead, waiting for the man to die. The sun beat down on the track, and the morning moved to midday. In the distant haze a figure on foot appeared from the opposite direction. He was alone. Slowly he emerged from the haze. He was a priest on his way to perform his duty at the Temple. He saw the vultures and then saw the white body, plainly covered with blood, lying motionless by the edge of the road. He stopped, studied the body, looking for signs of life. Fearing possible pollution by touching a corpse, he did not approach the injured man, but walked on the other side of the road, and hurried away. As the day wore on, a Levite appeared, also on the same journey. He did the same, and also continued on his way."

The crowd were relaxed. They liked the anti clerical tone of the story, and knew that the next figure would be a Jewish layman who would help the victim. Yeshua was aware of this too, so he smiled and paused before continuing.

"As the afternoon drew on, a third figure appeared, armed with a sword and mounted on a donkey, riding towards Jericho. He was a tough and confident man, who knew the road. He passed the two clerics on their way to the city. Both ignored him pointedly, because he was a Samaritan."

Yeshua smiled broadly as he heard the crowd groan.

"He saw the man lying by the road, dismounted, and walked over to him, half drawing his sword. He studied the surroundings, listened to the birds singing, and relaxed, pushing his sword back in its scabbard. He knew robbers often hung around a victim, hoping to attract more victims. This had not happened here. The birds told him that. He turned the man over onto his back, checking his pulse and breathing. Once he was convinced the man was alive, he went to his pack, found some oil, cleaned the man's wounds, and tearing cloth from his clothes, bandaged the man's wounds. Then he lifted him and laid the man across the donkey.

He led him gently down the rest of the road to Jericho. Once there, he went to an inn he knew well, lodged there overnight with the injured man, and when he left, gave sufficient money to care for the man with the landlord, promising to pay any extra needed to ensure the man's health and safety, when he returned."

Yeshua turned to face the lawyer, smiling at him.

"You asked me a question; now I'll ask you one. Who was the man who was neighbour to the injured man?"

The Lawyer could not bring himself to say "The Samaritan", since, as a Jew, he hated Samaritans, and so he replied, "The man who helped him."

"Absolutely," Yeshua replied. "Go and copy him."

The Lawyer, furious at being told to copy a Samaritan, was silent, as Yeshua knew he would be, and the crowd, deciding the fun was over for the day dispersed.

As they walked away, the Rabbi chided his brother.

"You should have known better than to ask that stupid question, Jacob! It was obvious what he would say."

"I know, Jesse," the Lawyer replied. "However, I understand Caiaphas in Jerusalem is anxious to find out what this Yeshua is saying. He may be pleased to hear he's a Samaritan lover."

**

Two weeks later Yeshua and his group were standing on the beach near Bethsaida. It was midday, and the sun was shining hotly. The Lake reflected the sun in hundreds of small pools of white light, constantly shifting and changing as the waves moved the top of the water. They had returned the donkeys to the people from whom they hired them. Judah had paid the bills.

Most of the group had boarded Simeon's boat, which had been left there when they headed north, when a young Jewish lawyer approached Yeshua, his sons, and Thomas on the beach. He knelt before Yeshua.

"I want to join you," he said simply.

Yeshua looked down at him and felt touched. He placed his hands on the young man's head and blessed him.

"Do you know the Commandments?" he asked.

The young, richly dressed, lawyer, looked up with an eager face.

"I have kept them all since I was a child."

"Do you go to synagogue?"

"Every week."

"Do you tithe?"

"Regularly."

Yeshua drew the young man to his feet, embraced him, and then pushed him a little away from himself. He looked him up and down, noting the evidence of his wealth. He decided to test him.

"You lack only one thing," he said. "Sell your possessions and give your money to the poor. Then come down and join me, and my men, in Capernaum. You will be very welcome."

The young man turned away in obvious disappointment. He walked off, head down, not looking back. Yeshua turned to his companions, equally disappointed.

"Ah me," he sighed. "How difficult it is for rich people to trust God! I tell you," he said fiercely, "It's easier to negotiate a camel through the Eye of a Needle Gate in Jerusalem than for a rich man to enter the Kingdom."

Thomas expressed surprise.

"The Bible tells us that God rewards the Righteous with wealth. If even they can't enter His Kingdom,

Yeshua, who can?"

"It may seem impossible, Thomas, but God will find a way. Leave it to Him," Yeshua replied. "Now, let's get on board, and allow the others to sail home. We're all tired."

Next morning they arrived at Capernaum, and the group split up, to return to their homes. Yeshua and his family walked to their house. Two men were waiting outside. (Yeshua heard later that they had been there every day for several weeks, just waiting for Yeshua to return.)

One of the two, the bigger man, stopped Yeshua.

"Are you Yeshua Bar Yusuf?" he asked aggressively.

"I am," Yeshua replied. "Who are you?"

"My name is unimportant. I was sent here by the Tetrarch with a message for you."

"What does Herod want to say to me?" Yeshua asked mildly.

"Leave his lands, or face arrest, trial and possible death."

Yeshua smiled wearily.

"Are you Jewish?" he asked the man.

"Does it matter?" he replied truculently.

"Only insofar as you will understand my reply if you are Jewish."

"I come from a Jewish family."

"Do the names Ahab and Jezebel mean anything to you?"

"Of course!"

"Good," Yeshua smiled broadly. "Go and tell that fox that Yeshua asked whether he wanted to become the only Jewish king after Ahab to kill more than one prophet!"

"Is that all?"

"No. You can add a rider. Tell Herod that I am not

intending to stay much longer in his lands. I am intending to spend Passover in Jerusalem. If I have to die, it will be in the Capital, not up here. He can relax. I am no threat to him. Now, go. You've done your job, go and report to your Master and leave us in peace."

Chapter 10

Return

Capernaum, 32AD

A week after their return, Yeshua gathered his disciples together. He addressed them as a group.

"I am sending you out, in pairs, to carry our message throughout the rest of the country. I want you to travel light, stay where you are welcome, and work for your upkeep. Remember your training as Jewish boys. Practice your trade. If you're made welcome, stay in the town. If you're not made welcome, leave the town and shake off the dust on your sandals to witness against them. Travel fast and return here when you are finished. I want you all back here a month before Passover, so we can move on to Jerusalem."

He paused.

"Thomas?"

"Yes. Lord?"

"Take Philip, Judas and Thaddeus, and my sons, Jochanan and Jacob, and tour the area beyond the Jordan."

"Yes, Lord."

"Cephas?"

"Yes, Lord?"

"Take Andreas, Matthaus and Bartholomew, and tour Samaria and Judaea. Take young Marcus with you."

"Yes. Lord."

The two groups left the room, chatting together, and both left the following morning.

189

Judah and Simeon the Rebel remained behind, puzzled at being left out. Once the others had left, Yeshua turned to them.

"I have a special job for you two. Judah I want you to travel to Qumr'an, taking Simeon for support and protection. He's tough enough to frighten anyone, even you!"

All three men laughed.

"I wish you to talk to Abraham Bar Abbas and acquaint him with my mind."

"Which is?" Judah asked.

"I intend to travel to Jerusalem, during Passover, to challenge the High Priest to stand down in my favour, before challenging Pilate himself. I plan to make our base at Bethany with my aunts and uncle, and to ride into Jerusalem, thus establishing my claim to be the heir of David and the rightful king. I will follow that up by a visit to the Temple and a clearance of the Outer Court traders, thereby staking my claim to be High Priest.

"I will need you to buy or hire three things for me – a slave whip, a donkey and a house with an upper room in the City for our Passover meal and, ultimately, our base. All this should be done secretly.

"My aunts and uncle should be expecting us, and the rest of my family at Bethlehem should be aware of our plans and keep out of the way in case of failure."

"Are you aware of the possible consequences of what you plan, Yeshua? There can be no going back afterwards. Once you have entered the City in the way you have planned, your cards are all on the table. Then it's either a crown or a cross for you, and a cross is more likely. There are no other options, unless it's stoning."

"I know a cross is far more likely than a crown, Judah. However, there is no alternative. That's what was shown me on the Mountain and on the way back here."

Yeshua smiled.

"At least, if I'm hanging from a cross I won't have to walk anywhere else. My feet are killing me!"

"You'll tell us next that you'll get a good tan!" Simeon commented. "You seem to make a joke about everything."

"God gave us all a sense of humour Simeon. We should use His gift," Yeshua replied, smiling.

"Now, you need to set out. You've a long way to go, and I need you back here at the same time as the others. Please don't tell them what you're doing, even if they ask you. And, say nothing to them on your return either."

Judah and Simeon promised to keep silent, and left the house. They left Capernaum, early the following morning, before the departure of the other disciples and Marcus.

Yeshua and Mariam spent the next few weeks quietly in Capernaum, waiting for the return of their emissaries, from whom they received reports from time to time, and preparing mentally and physically for the trials ahead. Yeshua did some work in the workshop and preached, when asked, in the Synagogue. Otherwise he acted as though he had retired from public life, much to the disappointment of those who knew him in the town.

**

In his Palace by the Dead Sea, Herod Antipas and Herodias and their court drank their evenings away while they waited for their messengers to return. Being so far from the centres of Jewish civilisation, they felt free to do as they liked. What Herod, Herodias, and

Salome, Herodias' daughter, liked to do would have shocked the average Jewish citizen. Fortunately for them, the Jews suspected, but did not know, what the Tetrarch and his entourage did when they were alone.

Herod was usually the worse for wear each morning, and the day his messengers returned was no different.

The Tetrarch was seated on a chair, with a goblet of wine, on a terrace overlooking the Dead Sea far below, when his messengers were announced. They entered and abased themselves before the Tetrarch, using the words of the old Persian royal greeting.

"May the King live forever!"

(Among themselves, members of Herod's court always referred to Herod as 'king'.) Herod acknowledged the bow with a nod, indicating that the men should rise.

"Zedekiah and Amaziah," he said. "Why have you taken so long? It's been months since I sent you to the north."

"It's simple, Your Highness," Zedekiah answered for them both, "The man, Yeshua, had disappeared. We learned he and his followers had travelled north to your brother's lands and the land of the Phoenicians. We waited until they returned. Then we spoke to him."

"What did he say?"

"He asked us if you really wanted to be a second Ahab, Highness."

"He said that!" said an incredulous Herod. "What did he mean?"

"He specifically said that King Ahab was the only Jewish King to kill more than one prophet. He asked whether you wanted to join that select group, Highness."

"So this Yeshua chooses to threaten and defy me, the ruler of the land where he is living," Herod commented, appearing to be stunned. "Is that right?"

"Not entirely, highness," Zedekiah replied, flicking the sweat from his eyes. "He said he would die, if that was God's will, in Jerusalem; not in your lands."

"If he's travelling to Jerusalem, he's Pilate's problem or the High Priest's problem – and not mine."

Zedekiah and Amaziah agreed with this analysis and Herod expressed relief at this outcome. He thanked and dismissed his messengers, and continued his day as he had planed it. Later he discussed what he had heard with Herodias, who also smiled with relief.

"We know he's chickened out of criticising us directly," she commented. "We can afford to leave him alone. Don't interfere with him, husband. Leave him where he is until he leaves Capernaum."

**

In Jerusalem, Caiaphas received the report about the love of Yeshua for Samaritans much as one, today, would welcome a person who told you that you had won five pounds on the Lottery when you expected to win a million. He acknowledged the information was interesting as a means to blacken Yeshua's character, but not as evidence leading to his conviction or death.

**

Judah and Simeon arrived at Qumr'an and met with the dying Abraham. He heard their report, lying on his bed.

"I accept what Yeshua proposes. It is simple, clear and bold. It's right, but dangerous. Carry out the preparations Yeshua wants, but also warn his brother Jacob. Take money from the Movement Treasurer to buy a house, and for your other expenses."

He paused before continuing.

193

"I think the plan will fail, and Yeshua will die. In many ways, it's too early. However, Yeshua is right. He has no other way forward. Warn Jacob. He must be ready to take over the leadership as I always planned."

"I think that Yeshua wants either your grandson, Jochanan, or this fisherman, Simeon, to take over the leadership if he fails," Judah said.

"Neither is acceptable," Abraham whispered. "Jochanan is too young, and who is Simeon? Jacob is my choice. Tell Yeshua and Jacob so, from me. Tell them, too, that I am dying, and there will soon be a new Bar Abbas"

Judah bowed his head, accepted the instruction, and left the sick man's room, to begin the trip back across the desert to Bethlehem and Bethany. Two days out, he and Simeon were overtaken in the desert by a messenger with news of the death of Abraham and the election of his successor. Both men were surprised by the choice, which they realised would change things significantly for at least one of them. Judah considered returning to Qumr'an under the circumstances, but was persuaded by Simeon to finish his mission with Yeshua first.

**

Across the lands of central Palestine, the various teams of Disciples were spreading the message of Yeshua. They met with a generally good response, were able to pray for and bless the sick, much as Yeshua did, and preached Yeshua's message of Love and of the coming of the Kingdom. They found some evidence of the impact of Yeshua's work. Jochanan and his brother came across two men using Yeshua's name to exorcise demons. They ordered them to stop.

Marcus seized the opportunity of being near

Caesarea to send a written message to Pilate.

**

Judah and Simeon warned Jacob, the brother of Yeshua, about the death of his father and his father's words to him. They also passed on Yeshua's warning and advice. Jacob initially agreed to carry out Yeshua's instructions. However, Mariam, his mother, said she intended to travel to Bethany to be with her son during those final days. Jacob tried to discourage her, without success, and, eventually respected her wishes and gave up his arguments. He decided he would escort her, for her own safety. He realised Yeshua might be angry. However, he felt the advantage of a final conference with Yeshua before he began the decisive stage of his mission might be greater than the risks of disobeying his brother.

Judah and Simeon travelled on to Bethany, to make the necessary arrangements over accommodation and the hire of the donkey. Judah paid in advance for that. He warned Mariam to expect the arrival of Yeshua and his followers and told her that Yeshua's mother would probably also travel up from Bethlehem, possibly with her second son.

They spent several days in the City before finding an appropriate house for sale there. It had to be both large and fairly private. The negotiations took several days, and they did not leave until they had completed the sale and installed a caretaker in the building. Finally, before returning north, Judah bought a slave whip in the market in Jerusalem and left it with Mariam and Martha.

**

Pilate received the message from Marcus, while sitting

in his office in Caesarea. He opened it and read it. He smiled grimly at its warning that Yeshua was planning to come to Jerusalem at Passover, to depose Caiaphas and remove the Romans from Palestine. *We'll see young Yeshua*, Pilate thought. *Forewarned is forearmed.* He sat down, pulled out paper and ink and wrote out certificates of manumission for Marcus and his sister. He sealed them and sent them by a messenger with instructions to find Marcus and give the letters to him. Once this was done, he wrote to Trebonius, instructing him to put his troops on the alert.

**

One by one, the various teams returned to Capernaum. Yeshua received their reports and offered congratulations. He rebuked his two sons for their over-enthusiasm.

"If they use my name, they can't later turn against me," he explained.

He was pleased that Judah and Simeon had fully carried out his instructions, and sad at the death of his father, Abraham. Like Judah and Simeon, he was surprised at the name of Abraham's elected successor. He wandered what difference, if any, this would make to his mission.

When all was prepared, they moved out and began the long journey south.

The moment of decision was drawing close.

PART THREE

SEVEN DAYS IN APRIL

Caiaphas, who was high priest that year, said to them, "You know nothing at all! You do not understand that it is better for you to have one man die for the people than to have the whole nation destroyed.

Gospel according to St. John, chapter 11, verse 50.

Chapter 11

Challenge

Three men sat around a table in a small room in the Temple in Jerusalem. None were widely known outside their own circle. All were men about whom the Authorities were anxious to know much more.

The leader of the group was a priest in his thirties. In his other, more familiar role, he was a Pharisee, a junior member of the Council and Commander of the Temple Guard. The most remarkable thing about him was his unremarkabilty. If anyone met him, the person would quickly forget him, since there was nothing that would make the man's image stick in the memory. He was the original invisible man. To most people he was known as Judas Bar Micah. To the other two, he was known as Judas Bar Abbas.

To his left was another, slightly older, priest. He, too, was unremarkable. In a community where there were so many priests, he was just one more. His name was Hezekiah.

To Judas' right sat a man pretending to be a priest. His name, oddly, was Gaius. He was Jewish, like the others, but he was an ex slave, who had been freed by his master, a Roman local official called Gaius; hence his name. He was, like Hezekiah, in his forties. Unlike the other two, who had a bookish appearance, he looked like what he was, an ex gladiator, big, fit, and marked with scars.

Judas had an open scroll in his hands.

"I have called you because I received this letter from

Qumr'an by messenger yesterday. I spent last night decoding it. This is the message. 'Commander Judas,

'Greetings to you and your loyal lieutenants. We at Qumr'an value your services greatly. We wish you continued success in the Struggle.

'Know that Brother Abraham has passed away and the Brothers have elected a new Bar Abbas. His identity will be announced when it is safe to do so. We know you will support him as loyally as you previously supported Brother Abraham.

'We are writing to you at this time to inform you that our servant, Yeshua Bar Abraham, also known as, Yeshua Bar Yusuf, is coming to Jerusalem at Passover. He will challenge the illegal High Priest, Caiaphas, and the illegal Roman occupation. He is going to ride into the City and drive out the traders from the outer court of the Temple.

'We wish you to distract both the Roman garrison and the Temple Guards to give him a clear run. We leave the planning to you – just ensure it can't be traced to you or to Yeshua.

'Malachi.'

Judas looked at his colleagues.

"Who's Malachi?" Gaius asked.

"Malachi is the official secretary of Bar Abbas," Judas explained.

"What do you want us to do?" Hezekiah asked.

Judas put down the scroll and looked directly into the faces of his lieutenants.

"Hezekiah, yours will be the easier task. I want you to organise a riot in the Court of Israel just before this Yeshua enters the Outer Court. Screaming women will draw the Temple Guards away, but their presence will also deter aggressive action by the Guards. By the time they know what's happening, hysterical men and women running from the Outer Court will flood the gates. Then your rioters can fade away. With any luck none will be captured. But to be doubly sure, distance yourself from the affair and don't mention Yeshua Bar Yusuf to anyone."

"I understand, Judas."

Judas turned towards Gaius.

"Your task will be much harder, Gaius. But you've also got to distance Yeshua and us from the riot you organise. Choose your men carefully, because it's effectively a suicide mission. You will need up to a dozen men. Send them to the main Market. They should assassinate a tax collector or two and then scream anti-Roman slogans. Many in the crowds will join them. The Romans will attack them. Some will be killed, and others will be captured and later crucified. Tell your men to get out once the riot has started and before the Romans appear."

"I understand Judas. What about the timing?"

"About half an hour before Yeshua and his men pass through the gates of the city."

Judas paused, then turned to Hezekiah again.

"Hezekiah, you have contacts among the Herodian troops don't you?"

"Yes, Judas."

"It would be unhelpful if they were too keen to intervene against either riot."

Hezekiah smiled.

"I understand, Judas."

Judas smiled.

"I thought you would, Hezekiah."

He stood up, and the other two did the same. They left the room separately, leaving sufficient time between them to do so.

**

Yeshua Bar Yusuf and his group crossed the Jordan just below the place where the river left Lake Galilee and took the road south. Although this was not the direct route between Galilee and Jerusalem, Jews travelling from north to south frequently used it because it avoided the city of Samaria and the surrounding country. Relationships between the two communities had been bad ever since the return from Babylon five hundred years before, and Yeshua did not want a Samaritan complication on the eve of his intended challenge to Caiaphas and Pilate.

As they travelled south, Yeshua became aware that the bickering between members of his group, most especially between his sons and the two brothers, had increased. Both believed that they should have the most senior positions in his Government. He heard the continuing debate, and tried to ignore it. However, on the second afternoon, when they stopped to eat and drink, he was forced to take action.

Mariam brought his two sons to him.

"Husband," she began, "Jochanan and Jacob want to ask you something."

Yeshua groaned inwardly. He knew exactly what they wanted.

"Well sons," he said encouragingly. "What's this about?"

"Father, you're going to be a king, yes?" Jochanan began.

"In a manner of speaking, possibly. Why do you ask, Jochanan?"

"Jacob and I want to be your leading ministers, sitting on your right and left in your court."

This came out in a rush and a low voice, so that the others would not hear.

"It's not as simple as that Jochanan. The road ahead is very dangerous and may involve my suffering and possibly even dying. Can you share that?"

"Yes," they chorused eagerly.

Yeshua smiled sadly.

"I believe you, and am sure that you both will do so some day. However, I cannot promise you positions of power. Time and God alone will decide that."

Yeshua turned away from the two boys and called the rest of the group to him. He saw two small boys, about eight years old, begging by the side of the road. He called them over, blessed them, and told Judah to give them some money and, when it was ready, some food. Then, keeping the boys standing beside him, as he sat between them on the ground, with his arms around their waists, hugging them affectionately, he spoke angrily to the group.

"I know that you have all been arguing among yourselves over positions in what you expect will be my kingdom. Don't deceive yourselves. I am going to launch a challenge with a very uncertain outcome. However, if we win through, then my kingdom will be very different from those with which you are familiar. In the great Empires and Kingdoms of the world, the ruler is an absolute monarch and his ministers control everything that goes on. My kingdom will not be like that."

Yeshua pulled the two boys closer.

"You have to be like these children. You have to trust God and His wisdom and love each other. My ministers will not be rulers; they will be ministers. Ministers serve; and you will serve each other and the people. That's what I expect you to be – servants of each other. If that's what you are, you should not be arguing about positions of power and opportunities for wealth. Look instead for opportunities for service. Remember, I told you to love one another, as I love you. Let's have an end to this constant bickering.

203

Cephas, I told you that you were a leader. Show leadership. Jochanan, you're my son. Show what being my son means."

The disciples bowed their heads, ashamed to be rebuked in this way. Simeon and Jochanan nodded when Yeshua spoke directly to them. Yeshua felt relieved. He believed the crisis was over for the moment. He smiled at them, sadly.

"You are my friends. We are all in this together. You and I know that this journey may end in my death. It will not be an honourable death. Enemies will strip me naked and flog me, and then march me through the streets, before hanging me up on a cross, nailed to the cross bar to die publicly. Some of you may join me. I don't know. But let us, at least, be united. We have been a happy group, let us continue to be that."

Even if I can no longer share that happiness! Can one dance with joy at the foot of one's own cross? How long can I continue to hide my fears behind this mask?

Mariam came and collected the two children, sat them down and fed them before sending them off to their homes. The group ate at the same time, sitting in silence, subdued as they brooded over what Yeshua had said. Later, they packed up and moved off, crossing the Jordan again near the town of Jericho, before stopping and camping for the night.

As they sat in fields by the road, warming themselves in the cold April night, they heard rather than saw, a carriage, escorted by a troop of cavalry, coming from the river crossing, pass them on the road, leading towards Jericho. The Tetrarch and his wife were travelling to Jerusalem for the Festival.

**

At about the same time, far away to the west, Pilate

204

issued orders for the transfer of himself and his household to the Holy City.

**

At the centre of the world, in the Imperial Palace in Rome, the Emperor Tiberius wrote to his nephew, congratulating him on the firm steps he was taking in Judaea and the good order the province was showing. He promised him that, if he could contain the disturbances for a year or two longer, then the Governorship of Spain or Egypt would be his.

**

Next morning, Yeshua seemed strangely reluctant to move on from his camp and enter Jericho. The morning drew on, and the sun grew hotter. Thomas and Philip remembered, from their days with Jochanan, that it was always hot in the Jordan Valley. The members of the group became increasingly restive, but no one dared ask the reason for the delay. Yeshua, himself, said nothing, but sat by the road, deep in thought, pondering his future.

This is my last chance to retreat. I can go back to Capernaum or Bethlehem without loss of face, dissolve the group, and settle down to a quiet and creative life with my family, making a living as a carpenter. After all, that's what I was trained for. That's what I've always wanted to do. Why not do it? These men are only out for what they can get out of me. They are only concerned to get power and wealth. Even my sons don't understand what this is all about. They don't really care about my wishes or the cost of this mission for me. Why should I care about them?

You care because you cannot escape your destiny. You were born to this role. You have no choice. Having come so far, you cannot go back. Death will still find you – but it will be a knife in the back in a dark alley somewhere rather than as a public sacrifice for the people.

What is the point of living just for living, when I have failed in the main purpose of my life?

Your death would not necessarily be evidence of failure. So why not embrace it?

But I'm afraid. Crucifixion is a terrible death. Why should I die it?

Because God wants it!

But why does He want it? What good will it serve? I do not feel sure about the necessity for this sacrifice. I do not feel certain that God is with me. So why go on?

Because I have to! After all, I can still back out, even in Jerusalem. There is still time to change my mind.

Yeshua stood up abruptly and wearily, and began to walk towards the town without a word. His party followed, in groups, and in silence. Yeshua's suddenly sombre mood infected the whole party. The women were in the middle of the group, and the men had all equipped themselves with swords against the dangerous road ahead. Others trailed behind them. The numbers gradually grew, until they entered the town.

At this point, an additional two men quietly joined the party, unnoticed by anyone. They followed the party right through to Bethany, and were, eventually, assumed to be part of the forty men and women who had become followers of Yeshua's group. They said nothing to discourage this view.

A small man had climbed an olive tree beside the road to get a good view of the approaching procession. He called out as Yeshua passed below him, causing

Yeshua to stop. He looked up and saw the man. Despite his inner turmoil, Yeshua was amused by the sight and smiled for the first time that day.

"Come down," he called.

The man clambered down the tree trunk, causing general laughter by his clumsiness.

"What's your name?" Yeshua asked.

"Zacchaeus Lord," the man replied.

"What do you do, Zacchaeus?"

"I am a tax collector Lord."

Yeshua smiled and looked around at Matthaus.

"Another of your friends, I see Matthaus," he said.

"He's no friend of mine Yeshua," Matthaus protested.

"You had the same job," Yeshua pointed out playfully.

"I gave it up and refunded all the extra money I took," Matthaus said forcefully.

Yeshua, suddenly serious, turned around and faced the bewildered looking Zacchaeus.

"You see, Zacchaeus, your somewhat disreputable occupation does not suit even my disciple who once did your job. Are you prepared to give it up and refund all the people you have defrauded?"

"Yes, Lord," Zacchaeus said eagerly.

"Praise the LORD!" Yeshua exclaimed. "Today salvation has come to this son of Israel!" He paused before continuing. "I am afraid I have been very lazy today and we are far too late to continue up the Jerusalem Road. We are going to have to intrude on you. Can you cope?"

"Of course I can cope. It will be an honour," the reformed tax collector answered, sweeping them all off the road and towards a substantial house a few metres beyond the high road.

As usual, Yeshua's women helped the women of the

household prepare the meal for the extra mouths.

That night they ate in public, as befitted royalty or a wedding party. Many visitors watched the meal. One of them was a woman, well known locally as a prostitute. She came up to Yeshua, weeping and carrying a small alabaster vase. This priceless vase was full of specially refined oil. She smashed the vase, and poured the oil over Yeshua's head, wiping the residue away with her hair. Among the watchers were Moshe and Yusuf, who had returned in time to accompany them from Capernaum and continue to monitor Yeshua's activities.

"Why have you wasted this oil, woman?" Yusuf exploded. "You should have sold it and given the money to the poor."

The woman did not reply.

Moshe rebuked Yeshua.

"Why have you allowed this waste? You claim to be a prophet. Why do you allow women of this type near you?"

Yeshua was also angry. He had not wanted this demonstration, which could wreck his plans by alerting the authorities so they could arrest him before he even reached the City. It was so obviously the act of anointing a king. He remembered the story of Samuel and David, and guessed Moshe and Yusuf did as well. He noted they had tried to cover their duplicity by claiming that she should have sold the oil and donated the money to the poor. Yeshua decided to use their tactics against them, and divert attention from the possible royal function of anointing to another, more sinister, function.

"Leave her alone Yusuf. She has done a good thing for me. She has anointed my body in preparation for burial. You will always have the poor with you; but I am only here for a short time. You can't judge everything by its monetary value. You and your friend, as Pharisees, should know that. Some things mean more than money. One of those things is love, and another is forgiveness. She has performed an act of love for me, and she has earned forgiveness for her previously sinful life from God. You should praise her, not condemn her, if you also want to be forgiven."

Neither Moshe nor Yusuf answered, but neither did they go away. They stayed and watched, waiting for a mistake. Marcus and his sister Julia, confident in their newly restored freedom, walked up to the two Pharisees and advised them to leave.

"There is nothing for you here," Marcus said. "Even if there were, you're too obviously spies for anyone here to tell you anything or to say anything incriminating. Go back to the High Priest and make your report and leave us alone."

Yusuf laughed at the teenagers.

"Go and play with your toys children. Leave real life to adults."

Then the two Pharisees walked away.

The two strangers, who had joined the party earlier, noted this conversation. One of them followed the two Pharisees as they walked off, returning a few minutes later. The happy atmosphere of the meal was, however, ruined, and the general sense of gloom, which had hung over the party that morning, returned. The two strangers noticed the odd atmosphere and were very concerned. At the end of the meal, as the party was beginning to settle for the night, they called Judah over.

"You're Judah, the Man from Kerioth, aren't you?" the older of the two strangers asked.

"I am," Judah agreed warily. "Who are you, and what do you want?"

"I'm asking the questions," the man responded sharply. "Are you the envoy from Qumr'an?"

"How do you know about Qumr'an?" asked Judah suspiciously.

"I work for Judas Bar Abbas," the man responded. "My name's Enos."

"Who is the Bar Abbas?" Judah asked.

"It was Abraham. Now it's someone else. His name has been kept secret."

"Has Abraham finally died?" Judah asked innocently.

"Yes, very recently."

Judah relaxed.

"That's sad. I saw him a couple of months ago and knew it could not be long. What can I do for you?"

"What's going on here? I didn't expect to find such a gloomy atmosphere."

"Yeshua is on the brink of a make or break decision. He knows the reward of success, and the price of failure. Not surprisingly, he's nervous. Everything's planned, however, and he will follow though, even if reluctantly. Now, who exactly are you?" Judah asked, loosening the sword in his scabbard.

"Put your sword away," the man said hastily, using his hand to push the sword back. "I am Enos Bar Jeremiah. I have been sent by Judas Bar Abbas in Jerusalem to coordinate our diversions with your actions, to lure the Romans and Temple Guards away from you. I was worried since I expected more excitement and less fear."

"When you get to know Yeshua better you'll realise he doesn't do excitement," Judah said dryly. "Now, if you'll excuse me, it's been a long day and we have another long day tomorrow."

Judah left the two envoys, both of which looked a little more confident. They slept under the trees by the side of the road, and followed the party out of the town next day, staying close to the two Pharisees. By then the party had grown in numbers considerably, joined, as it was, by more followers of Yeshua, and also by other people travelling in that direction and linking up for security. In contrast with the previous morning, they left at first light.

**

Meanwhile, Pilate and his escort were on their way towards Jerusalem, hoping to arrive on Sunday morning.

**

The much larger group of hangers on, who walked behind them, followed Yeshua's group. This group included the two Qumr'an envoys and the Pharisees Moshe and Yusuf. Neither of the latter two was still with the party when it reached the end of the road.

As the enlarged party climbed up the track, Enos and his companion engaged the two Pharisees in conversation, causing the four to lag behind the rest of the party. Once they were on their own, the two men attacked Yusuf and Moshe, strangled them, and pushed their bodies off the track, and down the mountainside. Their bodies were recovered later, partially eaten by wild animals. No one else witnessed the incident, and no one later admitted any involvement in the two deaths.

Meanwhile, the size, obvious armament, and silent determination of the walking convoy deterred any would be robbers from attacking them. Yeshua and his team walked silently, each absorbed in his or her own thoughts and suffering from the heat and the altitude. Each man and woman was too busy trying to summon up the energy to take another step and wiping sweat from eyes and foreheads, to engage in conversation on any topic, either meaningful and controversial, or quiet and inconsequential.

In this way, as the day reached mid afternoon, they reached the end of the road. Yeshua turned away from Jerusalem and led most of his team to Bethany. However, he sent Judah, Simeon and Thaddeus on to Jerusalem to check out the situation there. Enos went with them, while his colleague stayed with the rest of the party.

The four men entered the city and walked to the Temple. At the Main Entrance, Judah and Enos spoke to one of the guards.

"Tell the Son of the Father that four men are here to see him."

The guard, carefully chosen by Enos, nodded and told them to wait. The three Disciples noted that the Outer Court was still used for trading in animals for sacrifice and changing the secular Roman coins, illegal in the Temple, for the Jewish ones used there. Judah walked over to one of the traders and watched the rate of exchange he was using. He quickly realised that the man was cheating his customer. He turned away as an anonymous looking priest approached them, accompanied by the guard, who spoke to them.

"This is Judas Bar Abbas."

He turned back to the priest.

"These are three Disciples of Yeshua Bar Yusuf and another man who is their guide, whom I think you know."

Bar Abbas nodded. He spoke to Judah, whom he knew was the most senior.

"Please come to my office, where we can talk in safety."

He led them into a side building, and they followed. They walked along a long corridor and down a flight of steps, before entering a small office where another two men were sitting at a small table. Judas found an additional four seats for the visitors. They made an enlarged circle around the central table. Judas provided them all with wine which he watered in correct Jewish style.

Judas opened the conversation.

"Judah, I know from visits to Qumr'an. I have seen you two as well, but don't know your names."

Judah introduced them.

"Both men were disciples of Jochanan, and were with him when he died. This is Thaddeus and the big man is Simeon, who was one of the Zealot resistance fighters and was an instructor at Qumr'an for some time."

The men nodded and each offered their hand to Judas when he was introduced.

"I'm glad to meet you," Judas said to the two men as he took their hands. "I was distressed to hear of the murder of Jochanan and am proud to meet the two men who were loyal and brave enough to stay with him to the end."

Simeon answered for them both.

"It's good to meet you. We know of the good work you do here. Jochanan always said that if Israel had one hundred men like you, we would be free of God's enemies."

"It's good to know our work is appreciated," Judas commented, sitting down and turning to face Judah and Enos.

"So, Judah, what can I do for you?" Judas continued, leaning on the table.

"We've come to see what's happening and consult on tomorrow's programme," Judah explained

"Fair enough," Judas said. "What do you expect to happen?"

"I expect we will leave Bethany at about midday and enter the city about one o'clock. Yeshua will ride on a donkey and we will make a carpet of palms and clothes to ride over. When we arrive at the Temple, Yeshua plans to use a whip and drive the traders out of the Courtyard."

"That's very helpful Judah," Judas said. "Our role is to cover you and buy you time by distracting the various guards. Gaius here," pointing to the burly ex gladiator, "has the task of distracting the Romans."

Gaius stood up to lecture them.

"I have chosen two Sicarii, professional knife men, backed by four Zealots. The six will go down to the Market Square, where, on an agreed signal, the Sicarii will assassinate as many tax collectors as they can reach, while the Zealots encourage the bystanders to shout 'Down with Rome' and begin a riot. They will then slip away and leave the crowd to fight the Roman soldiers. We know some will die – either then, or, later, on crosses. However, they will be martyrs for Jewish freedom, so we will be doing them a favour."

"Thank you Gaius," Judas said, turning to Hezekiah. "Hezekiah has the task of distracting the Temple Guards."

Hezekiah smiled, remaining seated.

"I have the easier role. I am going to organise a fight, followed by a riot, in the Court of Israel. The women's screams will distract the guards, and my men will slip away, leaving others to be picked up and flogged later."

"Gaius's riot will begin just before you enter the city and Hezekiah's just before you enter the Temple," Judas explained. "As for Herod's men, we have arranged a series of accidents that will delay them deploying in support either of the Temple Guards or the Romans."

"That all sounds very good to me," Judah commented. "I will get Yeshua and the others away before anyone can react. None of us, of course, knows of any connection between the two riots and the difficulties faced by Herod's troops and anything done by Yeshua Bar Yusuf and his followers."

"Of course," Judas added, "you also all realise this meeting has never happened, don't you?"

They all nodded.

"Fine," Judas concluded, "Now all of you please leave quietly and make your way out of the building separately."

Judah, accompanied by Thaddeus, Simeon and Enos, left the Temple and the city shortly afterwards, rejoining the others in Bethany, where the evening meal awaited them, as darkness fell.

**

At about the same time, Pilate's force made camp for the night, about twenty miles from the city, whose gates were, at that moment, being closed and locked for the night.

**

Yeshua was afflicted with doubt again the following morning. As the trumpets blared in Pilate's camp and the city gates opened, at Bethany little happened. Yeshua's disciples rose ready to depart, along with the hangers on. Judah had the donkey collected and brought round to Mariam and Martha's house, ready for their departure. The women prepared breakfast, and the party were fed, but nothing happened. Yeshua did not even appear. Judah asked about him.

Mariam replied, "Yeshua got up early, before the

sun rose, and went out to pray alone. He was fasting, so he'll have to eat before you leave for the city."

Armed with this information, Judah took the donkey back to its owner, saying that he would return later to collect it when they were ready. The owner smiled, and returned the animal to its stable, feeding it with oats.

Yeshua, meanwhile, had walked for half an hour to a small and secluded grove. Here he began to pray. He prayed that God might show him the way. Fear and doubt marched hand in hand. Yeshua could see the starting point but not how things might develop, and he very much feared what the finishing point might be.

He remembered Judah's words; *your only alternatives are a cross or a crown, and the cross is far more likely.*

He remembered, agreed, and was afraid. The image of a small boy standing near a cross with his father and mother came to him. It was easy, he reflected, for the others to urge him on. The Romans often struck at the leadership of a group, and allowed the rest to run away.

I struck the shepherd and the sheep scattered.

The words from the Bible came unbidden to Yeshua's mind. Would that be the outcome, he wandered. Would the Romans seize him and execute him, while his followers, including his sons abandoned him and ran away?

Trust me and obey me. Place yourself in my care. Follow my will and doubt no longer. I am in charge.

The words came unbidden into his mind. Yeshua did not doubt that they came from God. It was the reassurance, the message that he had been seeking for so long. He thanked God and rose to his feet. He looked around him for the first time. The birds were singing in the trees, and the sun indicated it was mid morning. Yeshua felt hungry, and he remembered he had not eaten since the previous evening.

With a much more certain step, he returned to Bethany, greeting his followers and disciples with a confident smile when he arrived. He saw Judah standing apart from the group, looking worried.

"Are all the arrangements in place Judah?" he asked.

"They are, Yeshua, if you're ready to implement the programme."

"I need to eat, then we will leave for the city. Do you have the whip and the donkey?"

"The donkey is available when I call for it and the whip is in my bag," Judah replied.

"Good, " Yeshua smiled. "I knew I could rely on you Judah. Have the donkey here in about half an hour."

Then he entered the house.

He reappeared forty-five minutes later, walking confidently and joking with his leading disciples, who were relieved to see him looking so cheerful. Judah, who had brought the donkey and laid cotton outer coats across its back, spoke to Enos.

"I told you it would be all right. He's been up and down on this ever since we left Capernaum. He hopes for success but fears the price of failure – and who wouldn't?"

Enos grunted a reply. However, Yeshua's previous uncertainty had communicated itself to him.

If the trumpet gives an uncertain call who will prepare for battle?

The Biblical quotation came unbidden to Enos' mind. Not for the first time he wandered if Abraham had made a wise choice.

Still, we're stuck with him and will have to make the best of it. Let's hope it serves.

With these thoughts, Enos joined his companion, and they prepared to follow Yeshua and the disciples towards Jerusalem.

Meanwhile, the rest of the group cut down large palm branches from trees beside the road, and carried them with them as they travelled. Some had cloaks and coats hanging from their arms. All wore the swords they had worn on the journey up from Jericho.

The group moved off about midday, and, about thirty minutes later saw the city spread out before them below the slopes of the Mount of Olives. Yeshua stopped the procession, and they crowded around him, as he dismounted from the donkey. They saw the Temple, full of people looking like ants, in its outer courts, while smoke rose from the Court of the Priests, the innermost of them, where animals were being offered in sacrifice. Looming above the Temple, they saw the redbrick fortress of the Antonia, and the glint of sun on the metal of the soldiers' helmets as they patrolled the ramparts. Further away, on the northern side of the city they could see the equally fortress like Herodian Palace, where the Tetrarch held court, with, again, the distant gleam of sun on metal. They did not see the column of troops Pilate had led from Caesarea entering the city ahead of them. Nor did they see Pilate and his cavalry dismount and lead their horses though the city gate, or the shields and eagles of the troops covered in fabric. Nor did they hear the sullen silence of the people who crowded the street and watched the occupying troops pass.

"Jerusalem, Jerusalem," Yeshua murmured. "The city that murders the prophets. How often have I longed to come to you, and how much do I fear the encounter! Are you ready to answer God's call?"

He turned away abruptly, remounted the donkey, and said to the rest, "Let's go. Let's get this over with, for good or ill."

As the group moved off, only Judah, who was looking for it, saw Enos and his companion leave the group and hurry ahead towards the city. Enos passed through the gate, shortly after the last Roman legionary had arrived in the barracks. His friend and companion waited in front of the gate.

The city was sullenly quiet, but also quietly seething. It was always like that approaching Passover. The Jews expected that God would use the great festival of the liberation from Egyptian slavery to free Israel again, so there was always great, but suppressed, excitement. The city was like a forest, wilting after months of heat and drought, waiting for someone to light a fire.

Six burly men entered the main market. They split into groups of two. The stallholders were doing a brisk trade, selling fruit and vegetables brought up from the country On one side of the market two tax officials were seated at tables dealing with a line of customers. Most of the customers complained at the amount the two men charged. Tax gatherers were expected to collect their salaries from their customers. Many charged steeply. These two were the worst in Jerusalem. Two of the newcomers joined the queues, but stood aside from them. The other four scattered around the stalls, apparently looking for the best bargains. Two bored bodyguards stood behind the two tax officials. They wore swords in scabbards hanging from their belts, but no body armour. They seemed to be trying to intimidate customers by their size alone.

At about the same time, in the temple, a dozen students, future members of the priesthood, strolled into the Court of Israel. They were engaged in an animated conversation, which never quite got resolved. Hezekiah, the bookish looking priest, entered the Court. He nodded to the students, and passed through. He crossed the Outer Court, where the traders were doing a brisk trade, and left by the Beautiful Gate. (This was the great gate which led out onto the wide ramp, which ran down from the platform on which the Temple was built, beside the great outer wall, with its huge cut stones, to the road, which led to the city gates.) Here Hezekiah sat on a rock at the side of the road, using a handkerchief to wipe his forehead, which was sweating in the sun, and awaiting the arrival of Yeshua's party.

All was ready.

In the Antonia fortress, Pontius Pilate was making his way to the Tribune's office. He had ordered his slaves to unpack for him and his wife, and received reports from the centurions that his men had settled in to the barracks. He was looking forward to meeting Tribune Lucius Trebonius again, receiving his report and updating himself on events in this unruly and unpredictable city. It was always a challenge to him, especially at festival time. Pilate did not understand the Jews, and knew he didn't. He hated the stifling atmosphere of the Jewish capital, stuck on the top of a hill, cramped and crowded and full of fanatics. It was worse than the slums of Rome, he thought. However, he realised it would be a formidable city to attack if it were defended by resolute defenders. He respected the city, but hated it, preferring the cooler and more open city of Caesarea, sitting by the Great Sea. The best he could hope for was a quiet week. He feared that it would be far from that. It was in this dark mood that Pilate walked slowly towards the Tribune's office.

Within the Temple, Caiaphas was in conference with his advisors. He, too, was in a sombre mood. That morning two bodies had been brought to the Temple. Caiaphas was initially shocked and angered that two dead bodies had been brought to the Temple, causing the risk of pollution. However, the individual who had brought the bodies from where they were found insisted that the High Priest identify them. He was shocked to see that they were the bodies of his two spies, Moshe and Yusuf. He asked how they had died and where they were found, before ordering that the bodies be taken to their homes and families prior to their burial. It was to report these deaths that he had convened the meeting.

"Gentlemen," Caiaphas began. "I have the sad duty to inform you that Brother Yusuf and Brother Moshe are dead."

The three men showed their shock on their faces. Annas spoke for them all.

"How and when did they die?" he asked.

"I understand, father-in-law, that they were accompanying the charlatan and his party up the road from Jericho. Their bodies were found at the bottom of the Pass. The two men appear to have fallen from the road and to have broken their necks."

"Do we know where Yeshua is now, Lord Caiaphas?" Zedekiah asked.

"No, Brother Zedekiah."

"So, son-in-law, we will just have to wait, as usual," Annas commented.

"I'm afraid so, father-in-law," Caiaphas agreed.

"Do you think that Yeshua's men murdered them?" Zedekiah asked.

Caiaphas considered the question.

"I don't think so," he conceded eventually. "I've learnt a lot about this man from reports sent me by Brothers Yusuf and Moshe. I don't think Yeshua would allow murder. He constantly criticised them, and me, but he has never argued for violence, or, at least, not yet."

"Do you think he's changing his methods?" Annas asked.

"I don't know," Caiaphas said eventually. "He may be changing, but I don't know. If he has changed, then we'll have to deal with him urgently."

"Indeed you will, son-in-law," Annas said seriously.

All four men stared at the floor silently. Finally, Caiaphas looked up, smiled, and turned to Annas.

"What arrangements have you made for the Passover sacrifices, father-in-law?"

An animated discussion on rotas and the provision of animals began and was continuing when the meeting was interrupted by an urgent message.

**

Yeshua and his disciples approached the city gate. As they did so, a man pushed in front of them, hurrying along the main street towards the market.

In the market Enos waited for the signal. When he saw his companion arrive, he nodded to the two Sicarii. They moved to the front of the two queues of customers waiting to pay taxes. The two men began to argue with the officials. They pushed the customers back. Suddenly, there was a flash of silver and two cries. The two tax collectors fell to the pavement. Blood poured from wounds to the chest. The two bodyguards tried to intervene. They moved forward, reaching for their swords. Before they could draw them, the two assassins were on them. The two Sicarii drew their knives across the bodyguards' throats, which began to spurt blood. The two bodyguards fell to the ground, clutching their throats, to die in pools of their own blood.

The crowd began to shout "Down with Rome." They gathered anything they could use as weapons and attacked four Roman soldiers, who appeared to investigate the incident. They were driven back. One soldier tripped and fell. He was hacked to death by the growing crowd, as he lay, helpless, on the ground. A messenger made his way hastily to the Fortress, to summon help. Shortly afterwards, a trumpet was heard, and the Tribune turned out the century on duty, which assembled in the courtyard.

Meanwhile, Yeshua entered the city, riding his donkey. His disciples and followers waved palms. They laid coats and cloaks on the road for the donkey to ride over. They chanted the psalms, which celebrated the arrival of the Chosen One. They passed through the streets, through crowds, which joined in the chanting and the excitement. A priest, standing in the crowd, objected.

"Stop them shouting," he called out. "They could spark off a riot."

Yeshua, flushed with excitement, answered, to cheers from the crowd, "If I silence them, the stones themselves will shout out."

The Priest left the crowd and hurried to the Temple. Yeshua, meanwhile, approached the ramp, which led up to the Beautiful Gate. He dismounted from the donkey, and handed over the reins to his sons and Marcus. He instructed them to lead the animal back to Bethany. Then, he took the whip from Judah, and entered the Outer Court.

**

The Roman troops drew their swords and formed a shield wall. They advanced on the market, driving the rioters before them. The mob fought back fiercely, injuring some of the soldiers. However, the six men, who had started the riot, were no longer there to lead them. Several men were killed and two, whom the Romans thought were leaders, were captured before the rioters were finally dispersed, slipping away into the side streets and abandoning the wrecked market, where broken stalls and scattered fruit and vegetables littered the ground. The troops withdrew with their captives to the Fortress.

In Herod's Palace, confusion reigned. Herod had hoped to use his troops to help crush the trouble he spotted in the market place and curry favour with Pilate. However, he was frustrated by one problem after another. First, the Duty Officer could not be found, and, when he was finally found, the troops took too long to assemble, properly armed, and the opportunity passed. A deeply frustrated and very angry Tetrarch ordered the Duty Officer to stand the men down.

**

As Yeshua entered the Outer Courtyard of the Temple, he heard screams from the next Courtyard, where fighting suddenly broke out among the group of students who had previously been arguing. Other men joined in, and the Temple Guards rushed to disperse the mob.

As they did so, Yeshua stepped into the Outer Court, seized the whip, and kicked over the first of the moneychangers' tables. Coins scattered everywhere, as Yeshua strode from table to table, shouting in anger, "This is supposed to be a house of God, not a den of thieves."

Many of the moneychangers picked up their purses and fled, before Yeshua could reach them. He turned his attention to the animal sellers, and soon the courtyard was full of broken cages and doves and pigeons fluttering away from confinement to an unexpected freedom. Yeshua's followers copied his example, as did men in the crowded courtyard.

Within a few minutes, the market was wrecked. Stalls lay on their sides intact or broken. Sacrificial animals that could not fly wandered loosely around the courtyard. Some escaped through the great gate. Men and women picked up the money dropped by the moneychangers as they fled. The screams from the Court of Israel were matched by screams from the Outer Court, as refugees fled from the one to the other, meeting refuges from the fighting inside trying to come out. The result was that the entrance between the two Courts became jammed and the scene of fighting between the fleeing crowds.

Meanwhile, the original twelve students had mysteriously disappeared from the Court of Women, and Yeshua and his remaining disciples, all fury spent, left the Temple.

Hezekiah and Gaius, missions accomplished, reported their success to Judas Bar Abbas. Enos and his friend returned to Bethany, to keep an eye on Yeshua's group.

In all, the incident lasted no more than ten minutes, but the Temple market was closed for the rest of the day, while the damage was cleared up, the loose animals were secured, and the people calmed down. Several people were trampled to death in the crush, which resulted from the fighting, and, the Guard made four arrests in the Court of Israel. Two men were arrested for theft in the Outer Court. All six were thrown into the dungeons below the Temple for interrogation.

**

News of the two simultaneous riots in the outer courts reached Caiaphas at his meeting. He was told that a fight had broken out in the Court of Israel, shortly

225

before Yeshua ran amuck in the Outer Court. The traders demanded an assurance of protection before they would return to work. Caiaphas asked about the second riot, but no one knew how it started. However, all four men noted that it had served to distract the Guards from Yeshua's actions. Had it not happened, the guards would have been able to intervene to stop Yeshua. Caiaphas felt that the coincidence was not accidental, but he could prove nothing. He issued instructions that Yeshua and his group should only be admitted to the Temple courts in future with an escort from the Guards, before ordering a meeting of the whole Council for the following evening to consider the Yeshua problem. Caiaphas summoned Judas Bar Micah and ordered the Captain of the Guard to conduct a full investigation. He asked Judas to prepare a report for that Council meeting. He also ordered that the Temple should remain open for the rest of the day as normal.

**

Pilate and Trebonius faced a much more serious problem. Two dead tax collectors, and their bodyguards, and one dead soldier, plus a number injured, two seriously. They had two prisoners, whom Pilate ordered to be interrogated under torture. Both Roman officers were concerned about this sudden apparently pointless outbreak, which they both felt boded ill for Passover Week. They were so concerned by the market riot that they missed the significance of Yeshua's demonstration. It was much later that day that Pilate was informed about the second demonstration, and he was not sure what to make of it, how serious it was, or whether there was a connection with the Market riot. The coincidence of timing was suspicious, and

226

Pilate was a man for whom suspicion was a challenge. He resolved to get a message to Marcus next day to find out the truth.

**

Herod, embarrassed by the failure of his forces to intervene in the crushing of the riots, called his officers to appear before him. He told them that he was shocked by their unmilitary behaviour and ordered them to sort the problems out. He warned them that he would expect a report by the end of the week and a straightening out of the chain of command. He expected his officers to select one or two of the worst offenders for exemplary punishment; public flogging before the whole garrison, next day. He also warned them he was going to organise extra training once the week was over.

**

Yeshua and his team, unaware of the chaos they had caused in the city, followed the three youngest and the donkey back to Bethany. As they did so, Yeshua spotted a fig tree by the road. The tree was in leaf but without fruit. It was far too early for figs to grow. Yeshua pointed to it and said to his followers,

"This is an image of this city. Everyone here thinks they know when God's Chosen One will come calling. Well, I'm here, but are the citizens of Jerusalem ready? Only time will tell."

On that note, they left the city and set out to return to Bethany.

Chapter 12

Arguments

Jerusalem and Bethany, April 32AD (Monday)

That night Yeshua was happy. He felt the day had gone well. The two demonstrations, both potentially risky, had gone off without a hitch. As they sat over the evening meal, he congratulated Judah for his brilliant organisation and thanked the three teenagers for bringing the donkey back safely. Judah smiled, aware that Yeshua, whom he knew was an idealist, was unaware of just how much had been done to make the day run smoothly, from the murder of the two spies to the riots in the market place and the Court of Israel in the Temple, which had distracted the Authorities from intervening.

As they ate, they discussed the next day's activities. Yeshua told them he planned to go into the Temple next day and seek to win support from the Jerusalem public.

"Then," he said, "we'll know where we stand."

After they had eaten, and before they slept, Yeshua announced that he intended to take a Nazirite vow until the situation was resolved.

"That means," he explained, "that I will not willingly touch alcohol or cut my hair or beard until the Kingdom comes."

This announcement raised the excitement among his followers to fever pitch. Yeshua was plainly expecting the Kingdom to come very quickly.

**

Caiaphas was in his home, in conversation with Annas.

"I've concluded," he said, as they sat at dinner, "that this Yeshua is more dangerous than we realised."

"So," Annas said slowly, "what exactly do you propose Yusuf?"

"We need to entrap him in his own words. If he dares come back after what he did, we'll send agents provocateurs to trip him up."

"Good idea, but you shouldn't be directly involved. Leave it to me."

"Thank you for the offer, father-in-law. I'll leave it to you."

"That's all right, Yusuf. We're family! Pilate thought he was being clever in removing me, and promoting you. I'm sure he didn't realise how closely we work together."

"Well, father-in-law, don't disabuse him. From what I've seen of him, he's not very bright."

"Be careful Yusuf," Annas cautioned, sipping his wine. "Pilate is not stupid. He may not understand us, or our culture and religion, and he certainly lacks sympathy with us. He's also typically Roman in that he chooses to use violence rather than diplomacy to solve a problem. However, he is very intelligent for a Roman and apparently has the ears of the Emperor. You can't afford to upset him."

"I will remember," Caiaphas promised.

"This week could be very difficult for all of us, Yusuf," Annas cautioned Caiaphas, "and you're going to have to keep close to both Pilate and Herod, however distasteful you may find it, if we are to survive the week and remain in power. Don't forget!"

"I promise, father-in-law. We both have too much riding on the High Priesthood. I will not offend Pilate, never fear. He's much too unpredictable to risk it."

Annas expressed satisfaction.

Shortly afterwards, he left, promising to meet his son-in-law the following day before the Council meeting.

**

In the Antonia, Pilate and Julia were entertaining visitors. Herod, after venting his anger about his troops' performance earlier in the day, had travelled the short distance from his Palace to the Fortress with Herodias, to meet the newly arrived Procurator, as had become his practice on these occasions.

It was a convivial evening. Pilate had a much easier relationship with the urbane Tetrarch, with whom he shared the experience of being foreigners ruling Jews, than he had with the prickly Caiaphas. The two couples shared a Roman banquet, using imported Roman luxuries and top quality Roman wine, which Herod and Herodias openly enjoyed. The men reclined on couches, Roman fashion, and their wives sat opposite them on upright chairs, as was proper. They talked freely about family, society and the latest fashions. Herodias, in particular, was anxious to be dressed in the latest Roman style. Julia offered to send her dressmaker over to Herodias next morning.

This led, perhaps inevitably, to a discussion about the difficulty of finding proper slaves for the household. Julia said she found some of the slaves she had acquired since coming to Judaea totally unsuitable. Herodias agreed. Herod asked about the fate of the men and women seized following the incident at Passover two years before. Pilate told him that he had freed his two personal slaves, for services rendered to him and the state, but that the others were still either in prison, serving as galley slaves, or working in Rome, following their sale in the market there.

"However," he added, "I am considering releasing the women and children we hold in Jerusalem as an act of mercy, to mark Passover, since the festival seems to mean so much to the Jews."

Herod agreed,

"That's a very good idea, Gaius," he commented enthusiastically. "The incident was scarcely their fault, and, if you've freed the main culprit, there's no point holding the women and children, except as hostages."

"I don't need hostages, Antipas," Pilate commented tartly. "My troops can crush any attempted rebellion, as you saw this afternoon."

Herod did not respond.

Shortly afterwards the women withdrew, enabling the two men to retreat to Pilate's study. Here Pilate sent for a new bottle of wine and two glasses, and the two men settled down to a serious discussion.

"Thank you for your advice about Annas, Antipas. I followed it, as you know, and have found Caiaphas to be more amenable than his father-in-law, as you suggested."

"I'm pleased about that, Gaius. However, don't trust Caiaphas too much," Herod urged. "The man is more of a politician than a priest. His words don't always mean what they seem to mean."

"I've noticed that," Pilate agreed, pouring them both wine, "But he does seem to know on which side his bread is buttered."

"I'm sure he does!" Herod said dryly. "So long as your position is secure he'll back you absolutely, Gaius. Always remember he needs our support more than we need his – the Jews hate him as much as they hate us."

Pilate interrupted.

"Why should they hate their High Priest, Antipas?

He's the only Jew among us three rulers. They should support him."

"You've always said that you don't understand the Jews Gaius," Herod replied slowly, sipping his wine, which he plainly enjoyed. "Among them everything depends on birth. The priests all descend from one tribe – called the tribe of Levi. Within that tribe, one family is more important than the others. You may have heard of Moses, the leader that led them out from Egypt?"

Pilate nodded.

"His brother, Aaron, was the first High Priest. All the High Priests are supposed to be descended from him. The last such High Priest was called John Hyrcanus. He was High Priest when Pompey came here. He was also the rightful king, since his ancestor, the liberator of the country from Antiochus IV, Judas Maccabeus, was also the rightful High Priest. My father, Herod, deposed John Hyrcanus, first as King, and then as High Priest, and later had him killed. Neither Annas nor Caiaphas are from that family, so the religious Jews consider them to be little better than usurpers."

"I see," said Pilate reflectively. "I never understood why the Divine Augustus spilt Herod's Kingdom up, rather than handing it on intact to one of you, which would have left it stronger. What happened?"

A look of pain crossed Herod's face. He gulped, swallowed a mouthful of wine, and began to speak.

"My father was always one to suspect plots against himself, even where there were none. He knew the Jews hated him because of his foreign birth, and never felt secure on the throne. The Divine Augustus kept my two oldest brothers in Rome, to train them and to act as hostages. They returned in the last few years of my father's life, when his natural suspicion was made worse by a painful disease, which ate away at his mind and body. He persuaded himself that his wife, Mariamme, and my two oldest brothers were plotting to kill him, and he ordered their execution. He died shortly afterwards, and the Divine Augustus, and, I suspect, his wife, the Divine Livia, didn't believe any of us three surviving sons capable of ruling the whole of Herod's kingdom. Therefore, they divided the kingdom between the three of us. The oldest of us was Archelaus. He was given Judaea and Samaria. I am the second oldest. I was given Galilee and Trans-Jordan. The youngest, Philip, was given the non-Jewish lands to the north, while the ten Greek cities to the east of Lake Galilee were allowed to govern themselves. None of us was given the title king; instead we were given the title ruler of a third – or Tetrarch."

"So, what happened to Archelaus?" Pilate asked.

"He was totally incompetent. Within eight years he faced rebellion, complaints about his misgovernment at Rome, and the risk of invasion. The Divine Augustus could not let that continue, and did not trust Philip or me to rule the area, unfairly, I think. He could have re-divided the Kingdom between us. Instead he annexed Judaea and Samaria to Rome, placing it under the overall charge of the province of Syria, but with an independent ruler, which is now you, Gaius. I have to admit that the experiment has been largely successful. However, this area will never be an easy one for anyone to rule; Jew or foreigner."

There was a period of silence as Pilate took this in. It was a comfortable silence, in which both men emptied their glasses.

Pilate topped up both glasses, and broke the silence.

"I share Pompey's confusion over Jewish religion. Why don't they have a god?"

"They do have a god," Herod explained. "If you read up about their religion, and I would recommend you to do so, you'll find it is very different from our religions. You'll find they have a set of ten laws, which are central to their faith. The first claims that their god is the only god, ridiculous as that idea seems to us, and the second forbids them to portray that god as a picture or a statue. I must say, I find sympathy with that view, as I'm sure you do. If gods exist, they have to be different from us – so how can we make statues of them as human beings or animals?"

"You have a point, Antipas," Pilate conceded, "and I will take your advice."

Pilate called a slave to bring more wine, before continuing the conversation.

"You talked to the Prophet Jochanan. What was he like?"

"He was very different to what I expected Gaius. I expected a wild mad man. I found a perfectly sane and sensible man, although he had what I would call a Messiah-obsession."

Pilate looked up sharply at the word 'Messiah'.

"I've often heard this word, 'Messiah'. What, or who, is Messiah?"

Herod paused for some time, thinking, and drinking slowly. He took a couple of figs from a bowl on the table and chewed them before answering. A slave entered the room with a new bottle of wine, opened it, and left. Pilate refilled their glasses, and began to sip from his own, as Herod spoke, slowly and carefully.

"There is a lot of debate among the Jews about Messiah. They all look back to a golden age about a thousand years ago when one of their military leaders seized an opportune time to drive out the Egyptians and carve out an empire that stretched from the Red Sea to the River Euphrates, including most of your province of Syria. His name was David. He had a son, Solomon, who became extremely rich and powerful because he had control of the trade routes and built up a series of alliances. He also built the first Temple in this city.

"It all fell apart when he died, but his dynasty ruled this area until the City fell to the Babylonian king, Nebuchadnezzar, four hundred years later. Many men think and hope that a man will emerge from this family who will lead the people in war, drive all of us out, and restore the ancient Empire.

"It's a pipe dream of course, but they all believe in it. From time to time, pretenders arise, claiming to be this Messiah. You've already dealt with two such."

Pilate nodded.

"That's very helpful, Antipas; thank you."

Pilate paused before continuing.

"Why did you order Jochanan's execution, Antipas?"

Herod looked pained.

"I wish you hadn't asked that Gaius!" he began. "However, since you have, the truth is that I was stupid. I got drunk at my birthday party. My daughter Salome danced the dance of the seven veils for my guests and me."

"That's a stripper's dance, isn't it?" Pilate asked.

"Yes, Gaius."

"Your daughter performed this for you and your guests in public?" Pilate asked incredulously.

"My step daughter," Herod corrected. "However, yes, she did. I can see your surprise. I was equally surprised at the time, even through my drunken haze. She knew what she was doing though, because her mother had ordered her to do it, was cool about it, and flaunted her body, beautiful as it is, in front of the men, all of whom egged her on."

"I'm sure they did," Pilate grinned. "I would have done the same! What did you do?"

"I offered her a reward, telling her to name her

price, up to half my kingdom."

"I'm sure that Tiberius would not have approved," Pilate commented, still grinning. "What did she ask for?"

"Jochanan's head on a golden plate."

"That shocked you, didn't it?"

"Indeed it did! I sobered up immediately. I realised that Herodias had set the girl up for it. She hated Jochanan because he called her 'an Edomite Whore', following our marriage. However, I felt that I was committed. I ordered the execution, and gave the girl her present, exactly as she asked. I'm sure the golden plate has some value."

Herod paused, reliving the event.

"I heard later that the golden plate was her own idea. Herodias did not specify the type of crockery to be used."

Both men were silent, as they contemplated what they saw as the uncertainty of life and the vengefulness of wronged women. They shared figs and nuts and continued to empty the wine bottle. Both men became more reflective as the wine took its toll. Pilate broke the silence again.

"I met this new prophet, Yeshua, once you know, Antipas," he said.

"I didn't know, Gaius. When?"

"Shortly after our first meeting. I was on my way back to Caesarea, when we came across a group of men trying to cross the road we were using. I stopped, spoke to their leader, who impressed me, and let them cross before continuing. They were on their way to see this Jochanan whose height you shortened by a head."

Pilate smiled at his own joke. Herod chuckled.

"I've never met him. What's he like?"

"I would say he's about six feet tall, broad in the chest and body – obviously a craftsman. His hands

236

show he's a worker – but he seemed too well dressed to be a farm worker."

"He was probably an artisan, Gaius," Herod interrupted. "Possibly a carpenter or tent maker. Every Jewish boy has to learn a trade. It's part of their education, a bit like you learning to be a magistrate."

"Thanks for that, Antipas. It explains something I didn't know."

Pilate paused, collecting his thoughts.

"He was in his mid 30s, I would guess. His black hair and beard were neatly maintained, and he seemed polite. I had the feeling that he smiled a lot. I also thought he was intelligent and a natural leader."

Herod winced.

"You have just described a very dangerous man," he concluded. "Perhaps the most dangerous man in the Province at the moment. You will probably, sadly, have to terminate his life as I terminated Jochanan's." Herod paused, before adding sadly,

"That seems to be our lot as rulers; to end the lives of others who are better than us and who threaten us by who they are, rather than what they do. My father did that; I've done it: and you'll have to do it. It's a sad consequence of being a ruler."

Pilate agreed, equally sadly. The two men then drank to the unfairness of being a ruler, before, the third bottle being empty, they stood up to find their wives and retire to their private apartments in Palace and Fortress for the night.

**

It was a cheerful and confident Yeshua, who, buoyed up by his successes the previous day, led the party out of Bethany, on foot, early next morning. The men

237

chatted happily to each other as they covered the two-hour journey to the City. The climb up to the Mount of Olives seemed less steep than the previous afternoon, and the day itself seemed brighter and kinder. Jochanan, walking beside Yeshua, pointed out an extensive garden of olive and fig trees and other plants and flowers, beside the road, near the summit.

"That's the Garden of Gethsemane," Yeshua told him. "I used to visit it when we lived at Bethlehem. It's peaceful, secluded, shady when it's hot, and a good place to pray. We may visit it later."

They passed on, and came to the solitary fig tree, which Yeshua had used as an illustration the day before. Thomas pointed out that it was wilting in the heat and drought.

"We're all wilting, Thomas," Yeshua replied. "We'll see today whether the sun has affected the people of Jerusalem as much as it has that tree."

They passed through the city gates, watched by two bored Roman soldiers who ignored them, since they appeared no different from the hundreds of men, women and children who surrounded them and also ignored them. It came as a shock to Yeshua and the thirty men who accompanied him that he appeared to be completely unknown to these people. It had all been so different in the north. However, the northerners were different. They were much more receptive to new ideas than these southerners seemed to be. For the first time that day, a doubt shadowed Yeshua's mind.

Have I got this all horribly wrong?

It passed like the shadow of a cloud on a sunny day. Yeshua brushed it aside.

They all shouted for me yesterday. Once they realise who I am, they will be like the Galileans. They're all Jews after all. They all want what I want. They all want their freedom. They will rally to my call once they hear it.

Once inside the city, in the cool of the narrow and crowded streets, Yeshua led his men towards the Temple. They climbed the ramp to the platform that led to the main gate, the Beautiful Gate, which was open for all to enter. The sun shone brightly down on the approach, but they were stopped before they could enter the gateway. An Officer of the Temple Guard approached them.

"Yeshua Bar Yusuf, Lord Caiaphas, the High Priest, has ordered that you and your men be denied entrance to the Temple unless you promise there will be no repeat of your antics of yesterday," the Officer said stiffly.

"I can assure you of that, Commander," Yeshua replied. "Yesterday served as a demonstration, a statement of intent, if you like. There is no need to repeat it, and I have no intention of doing so. You have my word on that."

"Personally, I accept it," the Officer replied formally. "However, the High Priest has also ordered that, if you do enter, you are to be escorted by four Temple Guards at all times. They will have the authority to arrest you if you attempt any repetition."

"I understand, Commander," Yeshua replied, equally formally. "I have given you my word, and accept your conditions. May we enter now?"

"There's one thing more," the Officer said. "Any weapons and any whips have to be left at the gate. You can collect them when you leave."

Yeshua smiled, raising his arms to allow a body search.

"We have no weapons or whips, Officer. You can search us if you like."

The Officer nodded, stony faced.

"There's no need to search you. I believe you and will take your word for it. You can enter, but please do not proceed beyond the Outer Court. After the riot yesterday, the Council is very concerned about the atmosphere in the Inner Courts, and fear that your presence might enflame it."

Judah listened to this conversation with mounting anger. Finally he could contain himself no longer, and turned to speak to the Officer.

"Zechariah Bar Simeon, I know you from when we played together as kids. I'm surprised you would try to stop a Jew from entering the Jewish Temple."

The Officer turned to face the interrupter in surprise. His expression changed to a smile when he recognised the speaker.

"Judah Bar Jonah!" he exclaimed. "It's good to see you. It's been too long. But, why are you with this lot?"

"I could ask the same about you, Zechariah," Judah commented dryly. "Why don't you trust Yeshua when he promises good behaviour? If you don't trust him, trust me. We don't need guards or restrictions. We all know the score. We won't do anything to risk a riot. You can trust me, even if you don't trust Yeshua!"

Zechariah paused, suddenly doubtful. He stared at the various members of the party, noting that none were armed, and many obviously were not soldiers or rebels. He stared at Judah and then at Yeshua, making his own mental assessment of them. Finally, he decided to take a risk.

"All right,' he said with a sigh. "No guards and no restrictions. You realise that I may lose my job or even my life if this goes wrong, don't you?"

"Of course I do, Zechariah, "Judah said soothingly, "and I will risk neither. We have promised and you can trust us."

"Very well," Zechariah said finally, "you can go

through."

They passed through the Gate, crossed over the busy Outer Court, where they noticed the traders were back in business, walked swiftly through the Court of Israel, and entered the Court reserved for Jewish men. Here Yeshua sat down in the shade of a colonnaded passageway, surrounded by his disciples and other followers, and began to attract a curious crowd of worshippers, one of whom drew Marcus away to one side.

"Marcus," the man said, "Pilate sent me to ask you an important question."

Marcus recognised the man as Lucius, another Jewish slave.

"What does the Procurator want Lucius" Marcus asked, pleased he no longer had to call Pilate 'Master'.

"The Master told me to thank you for the information you have sent him already."

"That's fine," Marcus said. "I'm only doing my job. However, when's Pilate going to keep his word to me? He promised he would free the other members of my family."

"He thought you would ask that," Lucius replied. "He told me to tell you he is issuing the order today. The women and children, who are imprisoned here, are going to be released for Passover."

"Good," Marcus replied curtly. "What else does he want to know?"

"Was Yeshua responsible in any way for the riots that happened in the city yesterday?"

"What riots?"

"There was one in the Temple and one in the Market Place. In the second riot, two tax officials, two bodyguards and a Legionary were killed and others were injured."

"Not to mention the Jewish citizens presumably,"

Marcus added dryly.

"Indeed!" Lucius agreed.

"The answer is 'in no way whatsoever'. Yeshua neither knew about, approved, or was even consulted about, either event. My guess is that both were the result of the normal heightened religious enthusiasm that happens here at this time of year."

"You're absolutely sure about this? You couldn't be mistaken?"

"Yes to the first question and no to the second." Marcus grinned. "Now, I suggest you go back to your Master, Pilate, and reassure him, and that I go back and listen to my Master, Yeshua."

Marcus suited the action to his words, and returned to the group around Yeshua, none of who had noticed his departure. Lucius looked around for a moment, before disappearing in the crowd near the gate.

As the crowd gathered around them, Yeshua began to talk. He told stories; such as he had done in Galilee, but found that they did not resonate so easily in Judaea. As he had suspected, Judaeans were much less nimble minded than his previous audiences. He moved on from there and became much more direct.

"Love one another," he said, "just as God loves you. Don't just love your friends; love everyone, including your enemies and opponents. If someone hurts you, forgive him or her and help him or her. In that way you make him or her your friend. If that doesn't work, and they remain hostile, still don't retaliate. Leave their punishment to God."

A young man, who sounded from his accent like a foreign Jew, called out.

"What if God fails to punish them?"

Yeshua looked up, trying to identify the speaker. Eventually, he spotted him, a teenager, no older than Jochanan.

"What's your name, son?" he asked.

"I'm called Saul," the youth replied.

"You're not from round here, are you?" Yeshua asked.

No," he replied. "I'm from Tarsus in Cilicia. I've come here to study."

"Well," Yeshua replied with a smile. "When you grow as old as me, Saul, you'll realise that God has His own time. It may seem He's doing nothing. But everything isn't always as it seems."

The boy smiled. A much older man, possibly the boy's teacher, Yeshua thought, stood beside the boy, leaning on a stick. From his dress, he was a Pharisee. He now spoke.

"You've earned the reputation of being a good teacher Yeshua. What do you make of this riddle? It's a favourite of the Sadducees. (They use it to argue against our belief in the resurrection of the dead.) A young woman married a much older man, but the man died before she could become pregnant. According to law, his younger brother married her, but he died too. There was some suspicion about this, since the two brothers were very rich."

He was interrupted by laughter. He paused until the laughter died down before continuing.

"She married the third brother, who also died childless. Despite the obvious danger the fourth brother also married her."

The man led the renewed laughter himself.

"He died, of course, as you would expect, and the woman married first the fifth, then the sixth and finally the last. None got her pregnant, and so she was no more married to the first than the last. So, who would care for her in the after life – since she married them all?"

"Lucky woman!" Yeshua retorted, to renewed

laughter.

He also paused to allow it to settle down, before adding,

"They've got it wrong. Marriage and child bearing are a consequence of our living here. All human life ends in death, so we have to reproduce – or life will end. In Heaven life is eternal, so there is no need for children and no need for marriage. You won't even have to eat, so why would a man need a woman?"

Yeshua asked this with a smile.

He waited for the laughter to subside before concluding,

"It's a false question, based on a misunderstanding. There is no marriage in Heaven. Everyone will be an angel, too busy worshipping God to think of anything else."

Another voice spoke. This man was also clearly identifiable as a Pharisee. He pushed his way into the middle of the crowd and stood aggressively in front of Yeshua.

"How do you justify what you did here yesterday? Whose authority do you have for your actions?"

"Which actions?" Yeshua asked sweetly. "Are you referring to my donkey ride into the city or my rearrangement of the Outer Court?"

"The riot in the Temple," the man snapped. "Don't pretend you don't know what I'm talking about!"

Yeshua looked at him silently. The man quailed before the look. Yeshua smiled.

"I will answer your question if you will answer one of mine first?"

"Fair enough," the man responded. "What's your question?"

"Where did Jochanan get the authority for what he did?"

The man looked confused. Yeshua knew he had got

him caught. If he answered that it was from God, the man realised Yeshua would ask why he had ignored Him. On the other hand, Yeshua knew the man dared not say anything else for fear of being lynched by the crowd, many of who had probably been baptised by Jochanan. Yeshua said nothing. He simply watched the man's mental struggle, aware that the uncommitted in the crowd were also watching him.

Finally the man spoke, so quietly it was almost a whisper.

"I don't know," he said simply.

"Then I won't answer your question either," Yeshua responded with a smile.

"However," he added seriously, "you would do well to think over your attitude to Jochanan. You criticised him because he was a Nazirite, neither drinking alcohol nor eating rich food. You said he was mad. On the other hand, up until now, I have been like a bridegroom at his wedding, drinking and eating and being happy – and you call me a drunkard and profligate. What will satisfy you?"

Many of the crowd growled their agreement, and the man withdrew hastily, retreating into the Priests' Court beyond.

Another cleric asked him about tithes. Yeshua told him a story.

"Yesterday, as I was leaving the Temple after rearranging the Outer Court....," he began with a smile.

Yeshua got another laugh as the crowd remembered the chaos he had caused and the sight of the unpopular moneychangers running for their lives. (Many had benefited from the chaos by picking up the scattered coins.)

"....I saw two people placing money in the Temple Charity Box. One was a rich man. I watched him as he calculated one tenth of his cash before placing exactly that amount in the box. Then I watched an old woman pass. She opened her purse and upended it over the box. A single coin fell out. I tell you God valued her gift more than the carefully calculated gift of the rich man, even though the Temple could do more with his money than hers. God does not see things as we see them. He values sacrificial giving, not careful calculation."

Some of the crowd left, and others joined. One had come separately from the rest. Yeshua later heard that he was one of Herod's men. He spoke next.

"Rabbi, what do you think about the tax we have to pay to Rome? Should we pay it or not?"

Now it was Yeshua's turn to be caught in a cleft stick. He knew he had to be careful. There was no Yes or No answer to this question, since 'No' involved charges of treason against Rome and 'Yes' involved charges of collaboration with Rome. Both were dangerous.

Yeshua put his hand in his purse and turned out some coins. He turned them over, pointing out that they were all Jewish coins. (No one was supposed to have Roman coins in this part of the Temple. That's why they had coin changers in the Outer Court.)

"Have you any Roman money?" he asked the man.

"Certainly," he said, producing a denarius.

Yeshua handled the coin gingerly, theatrically turning the coin over as though it was poisoned. He showed the side with the head of Tiberius on it first to the crowd and then to his questioner.

"Read the inscription." He ordered.

"Gaius Julius Tiberius Caesar Augustus," the man read.

"So," Yeshua answered, smiling. "The coin belongs to the Emperor. If he wants it back, let him have it!"

Once again, the crowd laughed. Yeshua let the

laughter die, before adding seriously, "Pay Caesar his due, but also pay your dues to God."

The Herodian courtier backed away. He realised he had been outwitted and had no reply to offer.

Yeshua then took the offensive, since there seemed to be no more questions.

"Listen to this story. A man built a vineyard. He did everything necessary to produce good quality grapes. He had the land tilled and banked, and also manured. He built a watchtower, and then looked for tenants. Once he had installed them and agreed the rent, he left them to it. However, once the rents were due, he found they refused to pay. He tried several times, without success, The tenants got worse and worse, beating and killing the messengers as the mood took them."

The crowd listened quietly. Many murmured agreement, since it was a common experience. Some saw a connection between the story of Israel and the story Yeshua was telling. They realised the tenants were their ancestors and the messengers were the Prophets.

"Eventually the owner became desperate. He sent his own son to collect the outstanding debts, expecting that the tenants would accept that he was now becoming serious and pay up. He could not have been more wrong! They thought he was an idiot.

'It's the heir,' they said. 'Let's kill him and the place will be ours.'

So that's what they did. The owner finally lost his patience, collected some friends, ex gladiators and the like, and came to visit. He took the tenants out and killed them and sold their families as slaves to collect the debt. Then, hoping everyone had understood the message, he let the vineyard out to different tenants who would pay the rent."

This story was greeted with silence, as everyone

tried to work out what Yeshua had been saying. The priests suspected it was directed against them, but had not grasped the meaning, and so did nothing when Yeshua stood up, followed by his party. He walked through his remaining audience, before turning back from behind the last row, to face them.

"Ponder this message from the Bible, 'The stone that the builders rejected has become the cornerstone of the new building'."

With that parting shot, he walked away, followed by his original party and one or two others. In all he was followed by no more than a couple of dozen new followers. Most of the rest of those who had listened to him had already left.

As they left the Temple, Thaddeus pointed to the huge cut stones that made up the base of the front of the building.

"Look at those huge stones," he said admiringly. "Have you ever seen anything like it?"

Yeshua looked grimly at the Temple and at Thaddeus.

"I warn you, Thaddeus, unless the people of this city understand that God is calling them, before long, scarcely one of these stones will be left standing on another. It's not for nothing that Jerusalem is called the city that kills the Prophets! I feel sure, too, that if the Romans are sufficiently provoked, they will destroy this city and everything and everyone within it."

The five former followers of Jochanan, looked meaningfully at one another after this reply, which cast gloom over the whole group, a gloom, which the journey back to Bethany did nothing to dissipate.

**

Pilate received Lucius in his office. He heard his report

in silence, noting that Trebonius had reported the same thing, arising from the questioning, under torture, of the two prisoners. He was still absorbing the possible implications of the Tribune's report.

Trebonius had spoken to him during the afternoon.

"The men said that they were in the market, shopping for food, when they saw two men attack and kill the tax collectors and their body guards," he said. "As they stood and watched, a number of men started shouting, 'Down with Rome', and began to attack some of our soldiers who were nearby, killing one and wounding the others. They joined in, but, when our other troops appeared and attacked them, they found those who had begun the riot and the two assassins had vanished. The rest you know, Excellency. There was no apparent connection with the minor incident at the city gate or the subsequent riots in the Temple."

Those had been the words of Tribune Trebonius. He had no reason to think that there was any falsehood in the account, which he now heard confirmed by Marcus, via Lucius. Pilate sighed and wrote the order for the temporary imprisonment of the two men, and for their crucifixion the following Friday. He decided to leave it that long, so as to prolong the uncertainty in the city. The result would either be no more trouble, or a single bigger crucifixion party on that day.

**

Yeshua and his enlarged party arrived back in Bethany. Here Mariam, Martha and the women who had accompanied Yeshua and his disciples from Galilee had prepared the evening meal. They ensured everyone was fed and supplied with wine. Yeshua, in fulfilment of his vow, only drank water. After the meal, Yeshua spoke with the few Judaeans who had followed him back from the City. He commissioned them to return to their homes and spread the word about him and his message. Following this, he dismissed them to return to their homes. Over the next few hours all but two left.

One of the two strangers introduced himself to Yeshua.

"My name is Nicodemus. I am a Pharisee, a member of the Council. He, ..." pointing to the other man "... is Yusuf of Aramathea. He is also a Councillor."

"You're both welcome," Yeshua said formally, offering his hand. "What can I do for you?"

"We have come to ask who you are and what you are doing?"

"I am Yeshua Bar Yusuf, the step son of the carpenter of Bethlehem. I am the descendent of John Hyrcanus and Aaron, and, through my mother, also of David. I am the lawful High Priest and rightful King. That's who I am.

"What am I doing? I am spreading a message of obedience to God and love of one another. I know that seems revolutionary to some people, but it's in the Bible!"

Nicodemus smiled.

"I'm sure that some will think that a very dangerous message! Few of my friends could claim to have kept it. I think I have done so."

He paused.

"So how do I convince God?"

"You need to be born again," Yeshua said.

"That's ridiculous, with respect, Yeshua. I'm too big to climb back into my mother's body!"

"Rebirth is not a physical process. It's a spiritual process, Brother Nicodemus. You have to abandon your old life and embrace a new one, pleasing to God.

That's all!"

Yeshua liked this honest Pharisee. He wanted to win him to his side.

"Your enemies claim you're trying to undermine and destroy the Jewish religion and state. Is that actually your intention?" Yusuf asked.

"No, Brother Yusuf. I intend to save the faith and rescue and restore the state. I am leading, if you like, a Reformation rather than a Revolution."

The two men thanked Yeshua gravely and left, promising to think about what he had said. They set off to walk through the darkness back to Jerusalem, so as to be back in time for the Council meeting set for next morning.

**

Caiaphas passed Annas as he left the Temple for his home. As he passed him, he spoke to his father-in-law.

"Yeshua Bar Yusuf is very dangerous. He has to be eliminated, whatever the risk."

Annas nodded.

"You've understood at last, Yusuf."

They passed each other without another word.

Chapter 13

Meetings

Caiaphas looked around from behind his table facing the massed ranks of the Sanhedrin, the Jewish Council. He watched as the members of the Council entered the room and sat down, talking to one another quietly or loudly depending on their particular characters. He noticed that, as usual, the Sadducees and Pharisees sat on separate sides. He looked out for people he knew. The elderly Gamaliel, the leader of the Pharisees and the one Pharisee Caiaphas respected, entered, leaning on his stick. He bowed to the High Priest, as he usually did before taking his seat at the front. The aristocratic and conservative Sadducees, led by Hosea, the ones Caiaphas was certain would support him, were quiet. The radical Pharisees, the ones Caiaphas was not sure of, were much more vocal. Caiaphas did the mental arithmetic. He knew the aristocrats would vote as a block, and suspected the radicals would split. He was certain that he would secure a majority. The last two to enter, he saw, were Yusuf of Aramathea and Nicodemus, the two he suspected supported Yeshua.

When he was convinced that everyone was present, Caiaphas nodded to his father-in-law, who acted as chairman, to open the meeting. Annas did so, gavelling the meeting to silence. He nodded to Caiaphas, who stood to address the Council.

"Gentlemen," he began, "I have summoned you to meet to discuss the events of the last few days and to make decisions about Yeshua Bar Yusuf."

He paused, to allow this to sink in, watching the faces. Some showed surprise. Some showed satisfaction. Others urgently whispered to one another. They all fell silent as Caiaphas continued.

"We have been following this man, Yeshua, for some time, ever since he emerged from obscurity in Capernaum (in Galilee), after the timely removal of Jochanan from the scene. I sent two Pharisees, Brother Moshe and Brother Yusuf, to monitor the man's words and actions, which they did, until they were found dead at the bottom of a pass through the hills from Jericho to the City. Their necks were broken, and their bodies showed evidence of bruising."

Caiaphas noticed the signs of shock among the Councillors. One, a Pharisee, known to be a friend of one of the two men, raised his hand. Caiaphas acknowledged him.

"Yes, Brother Malachi."

"Lord Caiaphas, you said Brother Moshe and Brother Yusuf were monitoring this Yeshua's activity. Were they doing this when they died?"

"I think so, Brother Malachi," Caiaphas answered. "Obviously I can't be certain, but I think they were still following the Group."

"Do we know anything for certain about the cause?" another Pharisee asked.

"Do you mean, was it an accident or was he murdered?" Caiaphas replied.

He sat down, since he felt the interruption might be a long one.

"That's exactly what I mean Lord Caiaphas."

"The answer, Brother Josiah is that I don't know. That doesn't mean that I haven't got an opinion."

"That's simply not good enough Lord Caiaphas!"

Gamaliel spoke vehemently.

"It's fine for you to have suspicions, but you cannot

ask us to act on them. Our laws are clear and designed to protect those who are accused of crimes, especially if a possible verdict is the death penalty. I know what you suspect, and I'm inclined to share your suspicions. If the two men were following Yeshua and his Group and had annoyed them enough, Yeshua, or someone acting for him, may have used the mountain road to stage an 'accident'. However, we have no evidence, unless of course you have two witnesses who saw the men being strangled, or having their necks broken and their bodies tossed into the ravine. If you have such witnesses, produce them and let us hear them. If not, continue your investigations and bring the suspected culprits before us, so we can hold a trial."

Caiaphas groaned inwardly. He looked around and saw that the Pharisees were united behind their leader, as they usually were. The Sadducees seemed to agree, and Annas summed up the feeling of the meeting.

"Son-in-law, " he began, turning to look at him. Caiaphas hated the way he used his relationship to put him in his place. "Brother Gamaliel is right as usual. Since you have no evidence upon which to base an accusation, you must look for it. We cannot proceed on the deaths of our two brothers until you have the evidence. Move on to the next issue."

Caiaphas stood up again.

"Thank you father-in-law," he said heavily. "Before they died, Brother Moshe and Brother Yusuf reported that this Yeshua committed three major crimes against our laws. They saw him working on the Sabbath, healing the sick and feeding his followers. They also reported that, on one occasion, he forgave a man his sins, which is the prerogative of God alone. Thirdly, he may have used the Divine name to raise a girl from the dead – which is either necromancy or sorcery; you can take your choice! Both crimes are capital crimes. Both

254

men wrote separate reports. I will make copies available for you to read. They meet the conditions necessary to establish a capital charge. What do you suggest?"

Gamaliel stood once more. Caiaphas sat down.

"Lord Caiaphas, you need to be very careful. You have two written accusations, but unfortunately we cannot question the two who produced them. The Law says we must be able to do that, to establish that both are saying the same thing. Unless we can do so, there is no case to answer. Of course, we may find others who will be able to substantiate what our two late Brothers wrote. However, as things stand, I'm sorry but you still do not have a case."

Gamaliel sat down, and Caiaphas could see that he was both legally correct and had the support of the Council. He decided to move on.

"Before turning to Sunday's events, I want us to consider what happened yesterday."

Hosea, the Sadducee leader, stood up. Caiaphas sat down to let him speak.

"Lord Caiaphas, you know I usually support you."

Caiaphas nodded.

"I was present for the whole of the dialogue that occurred yesterday, and I find little that Yeshua said that you can make the basis of a charge."

Caiaphas leaned forward, resting on his arms.

"Brother Hosea, I appreciate your record of support and that of your followers, but I am surprised that you failed to understand the point of that parable of his."

"Do you mean the Vineyard story, Lord Caiaphas?"

Caiaphas nodded.

"I heard him and understood that he was retelling the story of God's dealings with Israel, with the servants being the prophets and the tenants being the various kings of Israel and Judah."

Caiaphas nodded impatiently.

"Yes, yes, Brother Hosea," he said, showing his irritation. "We all know that! It scarcely needed saying. The point is what did he mean by 'the son'? The Bible does not say that God sent His son down – or even that God has a son to send."

Hosea remained standing, patiently listening to Caiaphas's comment. Annas motioned to him to continue.

"Lord Caiaphas, have you forgotten that the Bible refers to the Kings of Judah as God's sons? Could this Yeshua be making the same assumption?"

Gamaliel answered for Caiaphas.

"Brother Hosea, I think you may be right. It could be that Yeshua thinks he's the rightful King."

"In that case, Brother Gamaliel," Caiaphas responded eagerly. "He's accusing us of plotting his death."

"He wouldn't be far out, would he Lord Caiaphas? If he were here now, he would need no further evidence to convince him!"

Gamaliel smiled gently.

"But, Brother Gamaliel," Caiaphas said triumphantly, "He has claimed to be Messiah. That's enough to get him."

"Rubbish!" a Pharisee shouted.

Annas called for order and then invited the interrupter to speak. A young man stood up at the back, obviously one of the most junior Pharisees.

"What's your name, Brother?" Annas asked.

"Amos," the young Pharisee replied.

"Well, Brother Amos, what do you wish to say?"

"This Lord Annas. Last year Lord Caiaphas was told of a Judaean rebel who said he was Messiah. He didn't hand him over to the Romans – as, perhaps, he should have done. Instead, he gave him provisional recognition and gave him every chance to succeed. Why is this Yeshua any different?"

Before Caiaphas could respond, Yusuf of Aramathea stood up to speak. As one of the wealthiest members of the Council, he was always allowed to speak when he wished. Both Caiaphas and Amos gave way to him.

"Brother Amos is still very young. I am much older Lord Caiaphas, and I know the difference is even more marked than Brother Amos suggested. He is right in saying we normally give provisional recognition to Messianic claimants until they either succeed or fail, but, in the case of Judas the Judaean claimant, you went much further. You actually encouraged him, Lord Caiaphas! So, I repeat Brother Amos's question, why is this Yeshua so different?"

Annas had never forgiven Caiaphas for supplanting him. He turned to him with a triumphant smile.

"How do you answer, son-in-law?"

Caiaphas gritted his teeth. He smiled sweetly at Annas, thinking, *"I wish his body had been at the bottom of the Pass rather than Moshe's"*, before turning to face the two Pharisees.

"Brother Yusuf," he began, "I bow to your great wisdom and experience. You and Brother Gamaliel are lights to our humble gathering."

He paused, wandering whether his apparent compliment sounded as sarcastic as he hoped it did.

"You were right to spot the difference. It's a matter of politics and expedience. I believe that this Yeshua is the most dangerous man I have come across for many years. He represents a danger to all of us. We need to stop him. This meeting is to find a way."

"So you're not interested in an honest trial Lord Caiaphas," Nicodemus said, standing up. "Why don't

257

you simply rig the evidence if you're so determined to kill the man?"

Annas silenced the outcries, which followed this outburst.

"Brother Nicodemus, I must insist that you withdraw your remark. It's demeaning to the honour of the High Priest and this Council. You know that I, at least, would never tolerate such a miscarriage of justice."

"Really?" Nicodemus responded.

Interrupted by shouts of "Withdraw! Withdraw!" he continued.

"I'm glad to hear your reassurance, Lord Annas. I will, of course, withdraw the remark," he added with a smile, before sitting down again.

The opposition he had received from all sides of the Council shook Caiaphas. Above all, he was shocked by the accusation that he would rig evidence. He was not shocked that people thought that he did so. He was already considering doing it, and would have admitted it to anyone who asked, pleading reasons of state. He was shocked that anyone would say so quite so openly. He stood up warily.

"Let us move forward to the events of Sunday afternoon," he urged.

Caiaphas looked at a piece of paper in his hand, and began to read.

"This is a report from the Captain of the Guard.

'At about three o'clock on Sunday afternoon, Yeshua Bar Yusuf and his following entered the Temple. He walked over to one of the tables where the men who exchange Roman currency for our currency work, and toppled it over, cracking a whip and calling him a thief. The man picked up his money and ran away. Yeshua proceeded to the next table and did the same, after which his followers ran amuck, turning over every table they could find. Once they had started, other men and women, already there, joined in, releasing the animals and stealing the money that had fallen to the ground and been left behind. The whole incident lasted about ten minutes, but Yeshua's men all disappeared from the Temple before it was over.

'My men had been distracted by a simultaneous fight, which broke out between two groups of priest students in the Court of Israel. Others joined in. The women ran away screaming and this both attracted the guards to the fight and hampered their attempt to stop it.

'The traders fled from the Outer Court into the Court of Israel, meeting women trying to flee in the other direction. In the confusion, all of the original perpetrators of both incidents escaped.

'We arrested four of the fighters and two of the thieves. We hold them in the cells and have interrogated them. They stated that they had no advance notice of Yeshua's arrival and were not involved in his demonstration. The two thieves simply took advantage of the confusion to steal some of the Roman and Jewish coins which lay scattered about on the ground.'"

"Is that it Lord Caiaphas?" Gamaliel asked, standing and leaning on his stick.

"Yes, Brother Gamaliel," Caiaphas responded.

"So, let me summarize Lord Caiaphas. This Yeshua arrived in the Temple and organised a demonstration. We have to call it that because he did not repeat the act next day. We don't know why he did it, and nor do those who were innocently present in the Courtyard and got caught up in it. You plainly suspect the other incident was connected, but those involved have denied it, and you do not know who started it. Is that right, Lord Caiaphas?"

"You've summed up succinctly as usual Brother

259

Gamaliel," Caiaphas commented reluctantly.

Gamaliel turned to face the Council.

"I wish to make a suggestion and put it to you all for a vote."

Annas gave him leave.

"We have three issues here.

"The first two are straightforward:

Two men stole from the Temple. They have admitted it and the evidence was found on them. The Law is clear. They should have their right hands amputated;

"Four men were fighting in the Women's Court. This is a cause of disturbance to the main purpose of this building, which is the worship of God. This is a holy building; so such behaviour is out of place here. Again, they have admitted it and were caught in the act. The Law again is clear. Each man should receive forty lashes.

"Finally, we have the separate case of Yeshua Bar Yusuf. So far we do not have any convincing or conclusive evidence concerning his words or actions. We are all agreed that he may represent a serious danger to us all. I suggest that Lord Caiaphas and Lord Annas should conduct further investigations and come back to us with their conclusions."

"Do we have a vote?" Annas asked. "Brother Gamaliel has proposed that the two thieves lose their right hands. Do you agree?"

The vote was a unanimous approval.

"Do you also agree that the four convicted of fighting should receive forty lashes each?"

Again, the vote was unanimous.

"Finally, do you agree the High Priest and I should pursue investigations into Yeshua's case?"

"Agreed!" they all shouted.

"In that case, I adjourn this meeting until Thursday

morning, so the High Priest and I can report progress to you."

The meeting broke up. Annas and Caiaphas thanked Gamaliel for his advice and asked him for support in the preventative action he knew they would have to take.

"So long as it's legal," he answered. "If it is, Lord Caiaphas and Lord Annas, you will certainly receive it, and the support of my Party."

He left. Annas looked at his son-in-law, and smiled. "I think you need my help Lord High Priest," he said mockingly. "Leave it to me, I will find you your witnesses, never fear."

**

Yeshua was taking his time two miles away, at his Aunt's home in Bethany. He decided against returning to the city and Temple that day, but he did permit any of his disciples who wished to carry the message out to the nearby villages to do so.

Simeon and his brother, and Matthaus and Bartholomew travelled out on this mission. Marcus and his sister, Julia, accompanied Jochanan and Jacob on a visit to Bethlehem, twelve miles away to visit the boys' grandmother, as well as their uncles and aunts. They planned to stay in Bethlehem overnight and return the following day. The other six stayed in Bethany. Some of those who had travelled down with them from Galilee went into the City.

It was, therefore, a much-reduced party who sat down with Yeshua for lunch and shared in the discussion afterwards. Yeshua was accompanied by the former disciples of Jochanan, led by Thomas and Judah – the other Simeon, Philip and Thaddeus, and also by Judas. Together they reviewed what had happened the previous day. Thomas, as usual, acted as the leader of the discussion, and Yeshua, strangely withdrawn, listened.

"I think you dealt with the various issues very adroitly yesterday, Yeshua," Thomas began. "It was clear that the Authorities were trying to entrap you in some way."

"I agree," Judah added. "I was particularly worried by the tax question. Taxes are a very sensitive issue with both the local people and the Government. You handled the trap extremely well, but also made your position clear to anyone who knew the code."

Yeshua smiled, but Judas was puzzled.

"What code are you talking about Judah?"

"Paying God His dues is code for not giving the produce of the Holy Land to Caesar's agents," Judah explained.

"So Yeshua actually said 'Don't pay taxes,' did he?" Judas asked.

"Sort of," said Thomas, after a pause for Yeshua to answer, and actually answering when it became clear that Yeshua had no intention of doing so. "It could be read that way, but not necessarily. We could argue the opposite way in some circumstances."

"How would we do that?" Judas asked.

"We would argue that Caesar needs money and God needs obedience," Thomas explained.

Yeshua nodded and smiled.

"At least we avoided trouble over the demonstrations on Sunday," Philip observed. "I expected some comeback over that."

"There was," said Yeshua unexpectedly. "What did you think their question about authority was about?"

"You're right, of course," Philip conceded. "However, they didn't do anything, and we did win some support."

"Not enough support," Thomas said, pouring himself some more wine and offering wine to the others.

They all accepted a top up except Yeshua, who poured himself some water, looking intently at Thomas.

"Only a few came back with us, and they've now left. It's not like Galilee."

Galilee wasn't like Galilee either! True, lots of people came to see me, but how many stayed? Barely thirty travelled with us down from the north. I can't challenge the might of the High Priest and his Roman ally with just thirty men. But I have made that challenge, to both of them.

What do I do now? Do I slink away like a fox, with my tail between my legs, looking to hide somewhere until the storm is over, or do I try to bluff my way through, hoping enough will follow me to, at least, frighten Caiaphas to stand down?

Do I risk everything in order to try to change the situation? Dare I risk everything? I don't want to die, at least, not yet, and not that way! However, if I go on and fail, that's what will happen.

And what about these people – my friends of the last few years? Do they have to die too? Do they realize how bad things are? If they do, why are they sitting here discussing things so calmly? These are the elite, the most experienced of my Disciples. Can't they see it's all up?

Yeshua spoke calmly, sipping water, and breaking off pieces of bread to chew.

"I agree with Thomas. We are not making sufficient headway here. Unless things change, we are going to fail. We should consider what we should do next."

"Do you want to call it all off and return to Capernaum Yeshua?" Thomas asked. "It would be the prudent thing to do."

"It would also be an admission of defeat," Judah observed.

"However," he added, "if that's what you want to do, Yeshua. I will accept your decision and return to Qumr'an to inform them that the Mission is over. You might be advised, in fact we might all be advised, to go and stay at Qumr'an for a while as well until the troubles are over."

"What's Qumr'an, Judah?" Judas asked. "I've never heard of it."

"It's a village near the Dead Sea," Thomas answered apparently casually.

They all looked at Yeshua, waiting for his answer. Yeshua was slow to respond, still turning the options over in his mind.

Retreat to Qumr'an would be too abject an admission of failure. I set out open-eyed. My father entrusted this mission to me. God wants me to succeed, of that I'm sure. The trouble is I don't know what success is or how to reach it.

Look at them. They think I'm their General. In fact I'm as much a soldier dancing to the decisions of others as they are! Like them, I don't know what to do. Unlike them, I have to know what to do, or, at least, appear to know what to do.

I need more time. I also need to talk to Caiaphas – make him see reason.

"Judah," Yeshua said suddenly, with an air of authority.

"Yes Lord?"

Judah was surprised by the sudden change in tone and responded accordingly.

"I want you to go back to the City today. Leave in the next few minutes. Take Philip and Simeon with you. Go to the Temple and ask to speak to the High Priest."

"Do you mean High Priest Caiaphas, Yeshua?"

"Yes Judah. There's no other High Priest at present! I want you to arrange a meeting for us with him and, possibly, Annas, the former High Priest, sometime tomorrow. I'll trust you to arrange the place and time."

The five disciples were surprised by this decision. Thomas spoke for them all.

"What do you hope to achieve by this meeting Yeshua?"

"I hope, Thomas, to persuade Caiaphas to recognise the justice of my claims and stand down, so I can lead the people into the celebration of the Passover."

"It's a bold step, certainly Yeshua," Thomas observed. "You're hoping to use persuasion since we can't use force, is that it?"

"That's it, Thomas. We have no means of attempting force, so persuasion is our only chance."

"They won't do it, Yeshua," Judah said. "They may meet us and you, but neither man will stand down, and you'll just give them ammunition to use against us and you."

"That's human wisdom," Yeshua said quietly.

He rose from the table, leaning forward on both hands.

"You may well be right, Judah, but perhaps God has other plans. Only time will tell. Will you do as I ask?"

"Of course we will," Judah said, also rising, with the other two. "When and where do you want the meeting?"

"Tomorrow at the Mount of Olives. It's safer there, since we can see if anyone is trying anything. Remember, too, the Mount has a special connection with Messiah."

The three men nodded, donned their outer coats, took their water bottles and staffs and left to take the road to Jerusalem. Yeshua and the other three talked for a little more together before all three went for an afternoon siesta. When they left the room, the women came in and cleared the table, before thinking about that evening's meal.

**

Pilate and Julia, accompanied by some of their senior officers and an escort of cavalry, had travelled with Herod and Herodias, similarly escorted, to the Dead Sea. He had heard a lot about this lake since his arrival in the province two years before, but never seen it. Herod had heard of this desire, and, anxious to get out of Jerusalem, had offered, during his visit the previous evening, to take the Procurator there. Pilate, who also disliked the City, was happy to oblige, especially as he felt confident that Trebonius had a firm grip on things in Jerusalem, particularly after his swift suppression of the Sunday riot.

The party set out before it got too hot in the morning, and arrived in mid afternoon. As the soldiers made camp, and the cooks prepared the evening meal, Pilate, Herod, their wives and senior officers went down to the salt covered beach to examine the phenomenon.

"I've heard you can't sink in the water because it's too salty, Antipas. Is that true?" Pilate asked.

"Certainly, Gaius," Herod replied. "Do you want a demonstration?"

"That would be kind," Pilate replied.

Pilate turned and spoke to one of his officers, who saluted and hurried back to the camp.

"You can use one of my slaves," he continued. "I've sent Sextus to fetch one who needs a good shock."

Herod laughed. He tried to explain something about the Dead Sea.

"Nothing goes out of here," he explained. "It's the lowest part of the country, may be the lowest part of the world, and the river Jordan flows here from Galilee. The water goes nowhere, so the sun just makes it more and more salty. If you try to bath in it, you will have to wash the salt off your skin afterwards or it will quickly become white and sore."

"Interesting," Pilate mused. "Have you ever thought of mining the salt?"

"We do mine some of it. We trade it with Arabia, Parthia, and the rest of the Roman Empire. It supplements our grapes and figs. We get wines, silks and other delicacies in exchange."

"You export slaves as well," Pilate observed.

"True," Herod said, "but doesn't everyone do that?"

"Rome doesn't," Pilate replied with his mirthless smile. "We only import slaves."

Herod was silent. He recognised the consequences of Imperial power, and knew he could not make a remark about it that would not be dangerous. Silence and wisdom marched together in this case he thought.

He was spared the need for a response by the return of Sextus, accompanied by a middle aged male slave. Pilate ordered two of the officers to strip the protesting slave before picking him up by the arms and legs, carrying him to the water's edge, swinging him two or three times, and throwing him as far out into the water as they could. The slave could not swim and he screamed in fear as they swung him violently backwards and forwards. As he flew through the air, his arms and legs fluttered like useless wings. He fell into the water with a big splash, before reappearing on the surface of the water, where he floated like a stranded whale.

Pilate watched the struggling slave for a while, laughing in wander at the sight. Finally he turned to

Herod.

"Well, well, Antipas. You're absolutely right. I would never have believed it if I had not seen it."

Herod was shocked at Pilate's uncaring attitude to his slave. He noticed that he gave no orders for the slave's recovery.

"What would you have done if what I told you had been wrong and the slave had drowned Gaius?" Herod asked.

Pilate looked puzzled at this question. He wandered what Herod was expecting him to say. Finally he answered.

"I would have bought a new one, Antipas. It's not as though he was one of my men or my children. You can always buy another slave from the market. There are plenty for sale in Caesarea."

He turned to walk away. Herod and the rest, shocked at his callous reply, followed him.

"Aren't you going to recover your slave, Gaius?" Herod asked eventually.

"Certainly not, Antipas!" Pilate answered sharply. "What do you think I am, some sort of housemaid? He can get ashore by himself. He knows the way back."

With that they made their way back to the camp, eventually followed by the wet and bedraggled slave, who retrieved his clothes from where the soldiers left them. The following morning they returned to Jerusalem.

**

Jochanan, Jacob, Julia and Marcus arrived at Bethlehem at about the same time as Pilate and Herod were standing by the Dead Sea, watching the slave struggling in the water. They were made welcome by Yeshua's mother and brothers, and, after introducing

Marcus and Julia, the two brothers spent the evening telling them about their experiences over the previous eighteen months and their hopes for the next few days. None of the four noticed how concerned Yeshua's mother, Mariam, was at what they told her. They did notice that she made their uncle, Jacob, promise to escort them and her to Bethany next morning.

Meanwhile, the other Disciples were meeting mild interest but no enthusiasm in the villages around Bethany. Even the normally ebullient Simeon was subdued when they returned to Yeshua that evening. It was clear, even to him, that Yeshua's campaign was making little headway in the south. He reported to Yeshua and the two disciples who were with him, and noticed that they all looked sad, but unsurprised, at the report.

Simeon asked where Judah, the other Simeon and Philip were. Thomas answered.

"They were sent by Yeshua to go to Jerusalem, meet Caiaphas and arrange a meeting between Yeshua and Caiaphas tomorrow."

"Is that wise?" Simeon asked.

"It's Yeshua's decision," Thomas replied. "I advised against it, but it's what he wants, wise or not."

"As you say," Simeon agreed, sitting down wearily and waiting for the evening meal to be served, "Yeshua is our Leader. He commands; and we obey."

"Indeed," Thomas concluded, sitting down beside him, as the remaining members of the reduced party began to appear for the meal.

They waited for Yeshua, who eventually appeared, took his seat at the head of the table, took a loaf in his hand, broke it in two, said the grace "Blessed be thou Lord who bringest forth fruit out of the earth," and passed it to Simeon on his left and Thaddeus on his right. They each broke off a piece of bread, and passed the loaf on to the person beside them. Yeshua then held up the loving cup and blessed it in a similar way, before passing it to Thaddeus, who drank from it before passing it on. Yeshua shared the bread, but did not touch the wine. Mariam, Yeshua's aunt and their hostess, filled their glasses with wine and began to serve the evening meal.

**

Annas spent the afternoon with the six prisoners in the dungeon. He noted that all six were from Galilee. They looked up as he entered, hope in their eyes. That hope died when he spoke to them. They were chained hand and foot, and secured to the wall by chains attached to rings around their necks. They sat on the floor of the dungeon. Annas stood in the middle of the room, lit by the flickering light of the torches outside and the minimal light let into the cell through its small barred window three quarters of the way up the wall. The cell was damp and stank of both damp and its human occupants. Annas shuddered. He looked out of place with his neat grey beard and carefully managed hair, his long crimson robe with its long elegant sleeves, and his neat shoes. The men he had come to see were virtually naked, unshaven and dirty. All carried bruises from the beatings they had received under questioning.

"Well, gentlemen," Annas began.

(He believed in being polite when he wanted something.)

"The Council heard your cases this morning. I understand two of you were charged with theft. Is that right?"

Two men nodded.

"You are to have your right hands chopped off according to Law."

He noticed they both went white.

"You other four, the ones caught fighting are to receive forty lashes each."

They reacted in the same way.

"When are the sentences to be carried out?" one of the thieves asked.

"Friday; just before the Passover begins. You'll be freed after the Passover."

Annas spoke coldly, dispassionately.

"Can we appeal?" the other thief asked.

"No," Annas answered.

He paused to let this answer be absorbed, before continuing.

"However, if you help the Council, I will persuade the Council to show mercy towards you and let you all off with a warning."

"What do we have to do?" the first thief asked.

"Give evidence against Yeshua Bar Yusuf. There are six of you. I need two to tell the Council how he constantly broke the Sabbath laws. I need another two to tell the Council how he committed blasphemy by forgiving sins. I want the last two to show he was guilty of sorcery."

"How?" the second thief asked.

"I will give you your lines. I need you to learn them and repeat them when the Council's officers come down here to speak to you. Do it properly and you will be freed to celebrate Passover before returning to Galilee with your friends unharmed and, I hope, a lot wiser."

Annas waited while they held a silent dialogue, conducted by looks and nods. Eventually the apparent leader turned back to him.

"Tell us what to say."

Annas smiled and began to speak, giving each man

his story. The first two were told to tell how Yeshua healed people and allowed his men to cut and grind corn on the Sabbath. The second two were told to tell the story of how Yeshua told the man lowered through the ceiling on a stretcher that his sins were forgiven. The final two were told to describe how Yeshua had used the Holy Name to raise a girl from the dead.

One of them suggested he could also accuse Yeshua of threatening to use magic to destroy and rebuild the Temple.

When he was convinced that each man knew his lines, Annas concluded. "Be careful. Your stories have to match exactly, whatever questions you are asked. Fail in this and you lose either your hand or the skin off your back. You could also lose your lives if the Council suspects you of bearing false witness. Do you understand?"

They all nodded. Annas smiled.

"Very well gentlemen, I look forward to hearing the report from the officers. Goodbye. It's been good working with you."

With that, Annas turned away from them, opened the cell door, and left, leaving the guard to lock the door behind him. As he climbed up the stairs he smiled, confident he had done enough to ensure that Yeshua Bar Yusuf would be the next occupant of the cell. He made his way to the office of Caiaphas, intending to assure his son-in-law that he had everything under control, only to discover that the High Priest was deep in conversation with three strangers, one a Judaean, and two Galileans, judging from their accents, but all men he had never seen before.

**

272

Judah and the other two had considerable difficulty meeting Caiaphas. The guards on the gate simply laughed at their request to see the High Priest. Judah, however, was persistent, and, in the end, an exasperated guard had gone to fetch the officer on duty. When he arrived, Judah simply said, "Please tell the Lord Caiaphas that three of Yeshua Bar Yusuf's senior disciples wish to speak with him." It worked the trick. The officer told them to wait and disappeared into the Temple. He reappeared about half an hour later, and asked them to follow him. He led them down the Temple corridors to a small office. Here he opened the door and introduced them to the High Priest, who rose to his feet, greeted them, and offered them seats. A slave brought in wine for them.

Caiaphas sat, with his chin in his hands and his elbows on his desk, listening, as Judah introduced the disciples.

"I'm Judah, the Man from Kerioth. This is Philip. He's from Decapolis. And this is Simeon. He's from Tiberias, in Galilee. We have come to you from Yeshua Bar Yusuf."

"What does Yeshua want with me?"

"He has sent us to see if we can arrange a meeting between him and you," Judah told him.

"Why should I agree to this?" Caiaphas asked. "He's under investigation for alleged crimes against the state."

Philip interrupted the conversation between Judah and Caiaphas.

"Yeshua wishes to explain himself to you and answer your questions."

The door opened behind them. The three men looked round and saw Annas enter the room. He walked around them and moved behind the desk.

Caiaphas spoke quietly, without emphasis.

"I am perfectly happy to hear Yeshua's defence of his actions. If he asks to see me, as you have, I'll meet him and discuss the issues with him here in my office."

Judah smiled.

"Yeshua thought you would say that, Lord Caiaphas. He would not feel safe here. He has asked me to arrange a meeting on neutral ground some time tomorrow."

"What do you consider to be neutral ground?" Annas asked.

"I'm sorry," Judah answered. "I don't know who you are."

"No, I'm sorry," Caiaphas answered. " I should have introduced you. This is my father-in-law, the former High Priest, Annas." He turned to face his father-in-law. "These men are disciples of Yeshua Bar Yusuf. Their names are Judah, Simeon and Philip. They are here because Yeshua sent them to arrange a meeting with us."

Annas bowed his head in greeting. Then he repeated his question. Judah answered.

"I suggested to Yeshua that we meet on the Mount of Olives; you, Lord Annas, the Lord Caiaphas and perhaps two Temple Guards on one side and Yeshua and the three of us on the other."

There was silence as Caiaphas and Annas considered this proposal. Eventually Caiaphas spoke. He was calm, hiding his excitement at the mistake he thought Yeshua was making.

"I agree. I suggest we meet at midday tomorrow. The place and numbers will be as you suggest."

"I agree," Judah said. He stood up. "I think our business is over."

The other two stood, as did Annas and Caiaphas. They shook hands, and the three envoys departed, escorted to the gate by the officer who brought them in.

They arrived back in Bethany after dark.

Annas and Caiaphas remained behind in the office. Caiaphas asked how Annas had progressed in his investigation.

"I've used my imagination, Yusuf. I have two witnesses who will swear that Yeshua has systematically and deliberately broken the Sabbath laws, two who will swear that Yeshua used the Holy name to raise a child from the dead and also threatened to use magic to pull down and rebuild the Temple, and two who will swear that they heard him forgive sins."

"They couldn't, by any chance, be the six men we condemned earlier today could they father-in-law?"

Annas looked shocked.

"How could you suggest such a thing Lord Caiaphas?"

"Because I know you, Lord Annas," replied Caiaphas urbanely.

Annas smiled.

"You must decide for yourself son-in-law." He paused. "I think this meeting is a good idea. Let's allow it to go ahead. We won't try to arrest him. Instead, we will try to entrap him in his own words."

Caiaphas smiled back.

"At least we are agreed on this father-in-law. Yeshua is making a mistake. I say it's rude to disturb him. Later we will show him just how big a mistake he's making."

He refilled his and Annas' glasses, and raised his in a toast.

"To Yeshua. May he trap himself in his own words!"

"To Yeshua," Annas responded with a grin.

They clashed their glasses and drank the toast. Finally, leaving their empty glasses with the other three, to be

picked up and washed by the slaves, they closed the
door and left.

Chapter 14

Consequences

Bethany & Mount of Olives, April 32AD (Wednesday)

It was now Wednesday, three days before the Passover, which fell that year on the Sabbath. The house in Bethany was dark and still when Yeshua rose, kissed Mariam, dressed and walked into the dawn. The skyline was lightening as he walked east along the empty road. It was daylight by the time he reached his chosen destination, the small olive grove he found the day before. Birds were singing in the ever-brightening daylight and the fluffy white clouds were showing signs of disappearing. It was going to be a warm day. Yeshua left the road and turned into the grove, finding a clearing among the trees. He knelt on the ground, drawing his blue and white striped prayer shawl over his head.

Yeshua tried to pray, but he found the words would not come. The problem was that he no longer knew what to pray for.

It was so easy in Galilee. I knew, or thought I knew, what I was doing then. All I needed to pray for was strength and determination. I measured success by the size of the crowds and the growing understanding of my twelve disciples.

Now I'm not sure. I don't know what success is, or what God expects of me. Is it the same that those around me expect, or is it different? If it's different, who is right?

Can I obey God and disappoint my followers? If I disappoint them, do I have any right to expect them to follow where I lead them?

The thoughts came unbidden to Yeshua, as they did so often. He realised that he doubted more than he believed. He tried to seize control of his wandering mind. He thought back to the beginning, and found himself standing beside a small boy in the Temple.

"Mother, what is a bastard?" the boy was asking.

He listened again to his mother's explanation, but then left the boy, instead accompanying two grown men into an underground chamber in the desert.

Once again he heard his Father, the Bar Abbas, explaining how the Brothers were preparing for war to drive out the foreign oppressors and restore the legitimate Hasmonean kings and High Priests.

He reminded himself that he was the legitimate heir of Aaron and Judas Maccabaeus as well as of David. He tried to think of himself as the Priest-King of Israel, but found he could not do so.

Instead his mind raced through a whole series of pictures, as he recalled different episodes from his work in the north.

The voice of Simeon came back to him.

"You are the Messiah, the expected saviour of Israel," the fisherman said.

Yeshua called him Cephas, his rock, and this caused trouble with his own sons. He remembered how he tried to calm things down and teach them about true leadership by using a child as a model.

"True leadership is about service; not about power", he tried to tell them.

Yeshua knew they did not believe him or, what was worse, did not understand him.

'Via Dolorosa': (the road of tears).

The words came unexpectedly.

We have to love each other and serve each other. There is no greater love than dying for one's friends. Is

*that what you want me to do God? Do you want me to
die for my friends?*

Yeshua remembered his words about friends.

"Love your enemies and make them your friends."

*Is that it then God? Do you want me to die for my
enemies?*

The enormity of this idea reduced Yeshua's mind to
a shocked silence. He was horrified. It was too much
for him even to consider at that moment. He stood, his
mind reeling, and stumbled out of the grove. Pulling the
prayer shawl onto his shoulders, he ran from the little
wood in panic. The birds, disturbed by his sudden
movements, scattered and flew away, screaming.
Yeshua screamed too, inwardly.

*No God, I can't do that. You are asking too much of
me.*

Eventually he stopped running, standing still to
catch his breath and feeling sick. He realised that he
needed companionship. He needed to be with others to
exorcise the terrible thought that had come like a bolt
of lightening into his mind, scattering and destroying
all his previous ideas. He walked swiftly back towards
the village and the safety of his Aunt's house. He tried
to drive the thought from his mind, but it would not
leave.

*Love your enemies. Greater love has no man than
this that he dies for his enemies. Make your enemies
your friends. Die for them.*

Tears began to form in Yeshua's eyes. He thought
of his wife and sons, his mother and his brothers and
sister, his aunts and uncles. Did he really have to leave
them all to make God's enemies his friends?

The village drew near. His mind remained a
battlefield. The houses drew around him. Safety and
security drew closer. He opened the door. His aunts and
wife were inside. They were preparing breakfast.

Mariam, his wife, looked up as he entered. He saw the look of concern that crossed her face. She put down the plate she was carrying. She rushed over to him, and embraced him.

"What's wrong, darling?" She asked anxiously.

Yeshua wanted Mariam to hug him. He wanted to hide in her arms and drive the thought away, but he also did not want to frighten her. He smiled and kissed her.

"It's nothing, darling. Just some bad thoughts."

He lied to reassure her.

Mariam was not convinced. She led him away from the kitchen.

"Do you want to share them with me?" she asked tenderly.

"No, darling, I don't think there would be any point."

He paused, blinking back the tears, which came unwanted to his eyes, "Leave me. I'll be all right. Help the others with the breakfast. I need time to recover."

Mariam left him reluctantly, to return to the kitchen, while he went out into the courtyard at the back, where he found his sons bathing, using a bucket. He went to join them, hoping to wash away the evil thought with the water. He did not succeed. The thought remained with him all morning.

Love your enemies. Die for your enemies. Make them your friends.

It kept returning: unwanted and unasked, to torment him.

**

Pilate and Herod and their party also rose early, awakened by the trumpets of the Roman and Herodian troops calling Reveille. Once up and dressed, they shared a common breakfast with their men, before leaving to begin the daylong ride back to Jerusalem, and duty.

The city itself slumbered on, until night became full day, and the normal noise and smells of a city awaking from sleep took over. The Temple doors and the city gates were thrown open to business and the guards and crowds went about their normal occupations. Children shouted and played together. Men quarrelled and sometimes fought each other. Women cooked and argued. Angry men and women shouted at each other. A body was found in one of the back streets. A man with a knife had quarrelled too violently with another man. In the markets customers argued over the charges tax officials made. They first argued, then grumbled and finally paid. They and the tax collectors knew they had no choice. However, it was a ritual they both enjoyed. It was a normal day.

As usual during festival time all three sets of soldiers – Roman, Herodian and Temple Guards – started the day tense and alert, expecting trouble. However, as the day wore peaceably on they all began to relax, and what tension there had been at the beginning dissipated. All was well, as Pilate and Herod had anticipated when they took their trip to the Dead Sea.

When the Roman and Herodian party finally returned late in the afternoon, and clattered into their fortress palaces, they had a sense both of tiredness after the long journey and relief that the risk had been justified.

**

At Bethlehem, the day also began early. Once they had eaten, Jacob, Yeshua's brother, led his mother, Mariam, who rode a donkey, and his nephews, Jochanan and Jacob and their friends, Marcus and Julia, from the house to begin the return journey to Bethany. This twelve-mile journey across country took most of the day.

**

Yeshua and his chosen group of six left after breakfast. The six were Judah, Philip and Simeon (who were going to attend the discussion with Caiaphas and Annas), and Thomas, the other Simeon and Andreas (who were going to act as look outs in case the Priests were dishonest and broke the agreement over numbers). All six wore swords suspended from their belts. They reached the top of the Mount of Olives at about mid morning. Here they stopped and waited, looking over the city. Andreas remembered Yeshua's words about the Temple, which he had spoken on the Monday, as they left.

"On Monday, Yeshua, you told us that not one stone would remain on another. When will this happen?"

"I don't know when, Andreas," Yeshua replied, standing beside him and staring across at the building, which dominated the skyline. "However, it is as certain as anything can be that one day soon the city will erupt and seek to drive out the foreign oppressors. When that happens, unless the people are united and have God's support, those same foreign oppressors will come back and surround the city, like Nebuchadnezzar did, and, like him, will not leave until the city has been destroyed.

"The city and the Temple will be burnt to the ground and the people scattered. The land will be covered with crosses. Those who don't die on the crosses will be sold in the slave markets. Those who avoid either fate will be driven into the wilderness, to live or die as nature decides. Be sure that none of you get caught up in it."

"But surely you will stop it, won't you?" Simeon the fisherman said. "You are the Chosen One, so you will be the leader."

"If it were only as simple as that, Cephas," Yeshua said sadly. "I'm not sure I will be there. I'm not sure many of you will be either. It is a hard path we follow, one involving pain, suffering and death. If you want to be my disciple you must be prepared to carry a cross."

No one responded. No one knew what to say or even what he meant. They were afraid to ask. Instead, silence descended on the group, a silence that was oppressive, marked by fear.

Love your enemies. Die for your enemies. Make them your friends.

The words would not go away. Instead, they all stared towards the city along the empty road, waiting for the appearance of the High Priest and his escort.

**

Annas and Caiaphas left the Temple half way through the morning. Judas Bar Abbas, in his capacity as Commander of the Temple Guard, once he heard of the proposed meeting, ensured that the two Guards who accompanied the High Priest and former High Priest were men he could trust. Caiaphas was concerned over his own security, and Judas accepted he was right to be concerned. He agreed to follow up the party with an additional ten Temple Guards. These would halt some way off, near enough to intervene to protect Caiaphas and Annas if necessary, but not close enough to cause the meeting to be aborted.

The Roman Guards who greeted them as they

passed through the city gate knew Judas and saluted him. Judas returned the salute.

**

Simeon the fisherman was the first to see the priestly party and its follow up party leave the city. He alerted the others and they stood and watched as the party drew nearer. They noticed that the larger party of guards was some way behind the priestly party, and making no attempt to hide their presence. Simeon and Andreas were concerned about this and offered to go back to collect the rest of the Twelve. Judah and the other Simeon, both former soldiers, pointed out that the second party was making no attempt to conceal itself.

"They are there, as backup, to protect the High Priest in case we break our agreement," Judah concluded, with Simeon's agreement. "If it were otherwise, they would attempt to hide from us. They must know that we will be watching them. It's perfectly legitimate for them to do that. If I were the Commander of the Temple Guard, I would do the same."

Simeon agreed. "In any case, if they do try anything, we can quickly run into Gethsemane and they would have great difficulty finding us among the trees. There's no need to get anyone else here. We're not planning to fight them!"

Yeshua agreed with this assessment and ordered the three back up Disciples to enter Gethsemane and lie at the edge on the side nearest the road and nearest Jerusalem, to keep an eye on the Reserve force of Temple Guards.

"If they show signs of wishing to intervene, show yourselves and distract them. Draw them into the Garden after you. We will withdraw immediately, and you should make your way back to Bethany once you

284

have shaken them off. You're in charge, Cephas. Be careful. Be guided by Thomas. He has a calm head."

The three disciples disappeared among the trees beside the road, and the other four awaited the approaching Temple Party.

**

Caiaphas and Annas saw the four men awaiting them at the top of the Mount of Olives. They stopped and studied the terrain carefully, seeing no sign of anyone else. Caiaphas turned round and summoned Judas to join him.

"Everything seems to be above board, Commander," he commented.

Judas put his hand over his eyes and scanned the horizon ahead. He noticed the wood beside the road and heard the birds singing. He nodded.

"They may have one or two men in the wood watching us, in case we break faith with them. That's what I would do, anyway, in their shoes. However, I think they intend to keep the agreement. You can trust them Lord Caiaphas. I will keep the men back here, just beyond the edge of the wood, and watch the wood and the road. We can be up there in less than two minutes if we need to."

Caiaphas accepted this assessment.

"That's fine Commander. You're the expert. Carry on," he ordered.

Judas Bar Abbas saluted and walked back to his men. He ordered them to stand down, relax and watch the road and wood. They sat down on or beside the road, laid down their shields and spears, and began to eat and drink, throw dice and generally relax. On the hilltop, Yeshua and his Disciples noted this, and they relaxed as well. Caiaphas and Annas walked the remaining two or three hundred metres to the summit accompanied by their two Temple Guards. Yeshua stepped forward when they arrived and shook each man by the hand. The three men moved to one side of the road, where they sat down together to talk. The two Guards and three Disciples spread out to form a circle around the three and allow them to talk together uninterrupted.

Caiaphas opened the conversation.

"So you're Yeshua Bar Yusuf? You're not at all what I expected. I expected a rough, tough countryman, more adept with the sword than with the Bible. You're quite the opposite."

Yeshua bowed his head.

"Why, thank you, Lord Caiaphas! I did not expect to receive compliments from you!"

"My pleasure Yeshua," Caiaphas said, perhaps more abruptly than the words required. "However, you asked for this meeting, and, even though I also wish to speak to you, you have the right to start it."

"Not at all, Lord Caiaphas. It may be that what I have to say would come better at the end. What did you want to speak to me about?"

"Quite a lot, young man," the elderly Annas growled.

Yeshua looked at him in surprise. Caiaphas obviously deferred to him. Yeshua guessed he must be the former High Priest, Annas. He asked if this were so, and Annas confirmed his guess.

"What can I do for you Lord Annas?" Yeshua asked. "I did not expect to have the pleasure of meeting you as well as your son-in-law."

Annas nodded. He had no intention of repeating the pleasantry that Caiaphas had used. He did not feel that meeting this troublemaker was a pleasure. Rather, he saw it as a duty.

"I have read the reports from Brother Moshe and Brother Yusuf. They suggested that much of what you taught was normal Jewish teaching. What is your main message?"

"I remember those two," Yeshua said with a smile. "They were hopeless spies since they never took off their Pharisee uniforms. You should have sent someone else, like Herod and Pilate did. I never found out who their spies were. Where are they, incidentally? I've not seen them for nearly a week. I find I actually miss them!"

"They're dead," Annas said simply.

Yeshua was shocked and showed it.

"How and when?" he asked.

"We think they were murdered," Caiaphas interrupted. "To be honest, we thought you either arranged it or ordered it. Seeing your face, I'm not so sure now. Anyway, their bodies were found at the bottom of the pass that leads up the mountainside from Jericho to Jerusalem. Their necks were broken and their bodies battered, possibly by the fall. They were returned to us last Sunday morning."

"Let me assure you Lord Caiaphas. I neither ordered nor authorised their murder, if that's what happened to them. I did not even know about it. Had I known about any plan to hurt them, I would have forbidden it. As far as I know, my disciples and followers had no part in it. I rebuked Moshe and Yusuf for their attitudes it's true, but I quite liked them. They were so incompetent that I found them quite appealing! Please give my sympathies to their relatives and friends."

Annas drew Yeshua back to his initial question.

"What is your basic teaching?"

"Love one another. Serve one another. Love your enemies."

Die for your enemies.

"Make your enemies your friends."

"I can not object to that. I deal with our enemies, the Romans," Annas commented. "Is that all you teach?"

"Obviously not Lord Annas......," Yeshua said patiently, flicking the sweat out of his eyes. It was very hot sitting in the sun.

".........However, surely you do not want me to give you a whole sermon which you could just as easily give me? I feel sure that there is little difference between what you teach and what I teach."

Caiaphas interrupted.

"It's not so much what you teach Yeshua as what you do."

"What do you mean, Lord Caiaphas?"

"I hear that you not only break the Sabbath law yourself but also encourage others to do so."

"I don't think I've ever done either, Lord Caiaphas. I know how important that Law is."

"Do you agree that, if we all keep one Sabbath properly, God's Kingdom will come?"

"Of course, Lord Annas. However, what do you mean by the word properly?"

"Strictly according to the letter of the Law."

"The Law allows for human need to override the details of Sabbath observance, Lord Annas – whether that need is hunger, illness or rescuing a trapped child or animal."

"And that is what you claim you were doing?"

"Absolutely! Ask any of the people who were with me or attended my meetings in Galilee."

"I have already done that," Annas replied. "I got something of a different answer."

"Then," Yeshua said sweetly, "I suggest that your informants are mistaken or lying to you."

The three men fell silent as Caiaphas and Annas

took this reply in.

Yeshua broke the silence.

"Is that the only accusation against me?"

"No, Yeshua. It is suggested that you used sorcery to bring a child back from the dead," Caiaphas replied.

Yeshua laughed.

"Is that what you've been told, Lord Caiaphas?" Yeshua asked incredulously.

"That's what I've heard Yeshua," Caiaphas replied stiffly.

"I'm sorry I laughed, Lord Caiaphas, but I remember the incident well. The child was simply in a coma. She was far from dead. The family jumped to the wrong conclusion, that's all."

Annas groaned inwardly. He wandered whether he had got this all wrong.

"There's one other thing, which Brother Yusuf and Brother Moshe were especially concerned about," Caiaphas said. "Is it true that you forgave a man his sins?"

Yeshua was puzzled.

"I don't recall doing that at all," he replied. "Which incident did they refer to?"

"The man who was lowered through the roof."

"Oh that!" said a relieved Yeshua. "I did not forgive the man. I told him that God had forgiven him and that he should go home, which he did."

"Perhaps you were misheard," a disappointed Caiaphas concluded.

"I'm sure you were misinformed, Lord Caiaphas," Yeshua answered.

"Did you threaten to destroy the Temple and rebuild it using magic?" Annas asked.

Yeshua looked startled and then laughed.

"Who on earth came up with that one?" he asked. "Do you think I'm a preacher or a magician? Do I look like a magician?"

There was no answer. The conversation again petered out. The three men looked at each other. Yeshua waited to see if the two priests would raise any further question.

Eventually, Annas asked about his Parable of the Vineyard.

"Who was the son who was killed by the tenants of the vineyard?"

Love your enemies. Die for your enemies. Make your enemies into friends.

Again the words thudded in his brain.

"Yeshua," Annas asked. "Did you hear my question?"

"Yes Lord Annas. I'm sorry I was thinking about something else. You asked about my Vineyard Parable. The Son has not come yet. When he comes, who knows what will happen or what the consequence will be?"

"The early part was clearly a parable about God, the Prophets and the people of Israel. My son-in-law and I have no problem over that. But I am puzzled about the idea of God having a son. Do you mean son in the way the Kings called themselves God's sons?"

"Probably, Lord Annas. To be honest, I'm not really clear what I meant by the story. The words came to me as I told it."

"So we have to ask God for the explanation!" an exasperated Caiaphas commented.

"You could always try that," Yeshua agreed calmly, with a smile.

"We don't have anything else we need to ask you about," Caiaphas said after another long silence. He and Annas felt that their long walk had achieved nothing. They had nothing to go on, except Annas' bribed false witnesses.

"What do you wish to discuss with us?"

"Who do you think I am, Lord Caiaphas?" Yeshua asked.

"Yeshua, the Son of Yusuf, the carpenter from Bethlehem," Annas replied for them both.

"The self-appointed but untrained preacher," he added.

"I'm not Yeshua Bar Yusuf," Yeshua replied simply. "I could be Yeshua, the Son of the Father."

Judah noticed that the two Guardsmen suddenly stiffened. Annas looked surprised. Caiaphas looked confused.

"Who or what is the Son of the Father?" Caiaphas quietly asked his father-in-law.

"He's supposed to be the national leader of the Resistance. However, I think he's a myth." Annas spoke confidently to his son-in-law. "We used to hear a lot about this figure when a priest named Abraham Bar Jochanan suddenly disappeared into the desert. It was believed that the Jochanan he claimed as his father was the man we know as John Hyrcanus – the last Hasmonean Priest King."

"Do you mean that this Abraham should have been the High Priest, and not you or I or the other recent High Priests?" Caiaphas asked his father-in-law.

"That was the general idea, Yusuf. He was supposed to be in the desert of Judaea somewhere, but I have never believed in him."

"I am the son of Abraham," Yeshua said.

"We are all sons of Abraham," Caiaphas corrected with a smile.

"I mean, that I am the son of Abraham, the son of Jochanan, the son of Judas, the son of Aaron." Yeshua spoke very quietly. "I am also the descendent of David, the son of Jesse of Bethlehem."

These words fell like a huge stone from a Roman

catapult. Caiaphas and Annas looked shocked.

"What are you saying?" Caiaphas asked.

"I should be High Priest, not you, and King of Israel, not Herod."

"And you want us both to go?" Caiaphas continued, stunned.

"No, Lord Caiaphas. I want all three of you to go, Pilate included. I assume once I have reunited the High Priesthood and the Kingship in a legitimate Jewish Royal and Priestly Family, then I can renegotiate the treaty with Rome, so that she will withdraw her troops and officials from Judaea and Samaria."

"You're mad, Yeshua," Annas burst out. "You're mad and dangerous. You'll bring the whole house down and destroy us all."

"Hush, father-in-law," Caiaphas said, to Annas' obvious surprise. "It need not necessarily be disastrous." He turned to face Yeshua. "What if Rome refuses to go?"

"Then we'll drive her out by force."

Caiaphas waved down Annas who was about to object. Annas stared at his son-in-law, who gave him a broad wink, which went unnoticed by Yeshua and his three disciples. Then he turned back to Yeshua.

"We will go back and consider your request. I am prepared to see the rightness of your proposition. I will give you my response tomorrow night. Where can I find you?"

Judah stepped forward and stood beside Yeshua. He spoke before Yeshua could answer.

"We do not know where we will be then Lord Caiaphas, but I will come and collect your answer."

"I accept your proposal Judah. That is your name isn't it?"

"My name is Judah, the Man from Kerioth."

"Well, Judah, the Man from Kerioth, I look forward

to seeing you tomorrow evening."

Caiaphas stood up, and turned away from him to look at Annas. He raised a questioning eyebrow. Annas nodded and stood up. Caiaphas turned back to look at Yeshua, who had also got to his feet.

"I think we have finished here, Yeshua Bar Abraham. It has been good to meet you."

He offered his hand. Yeshua shook it. The two priests turned away, and, accompanied by their Guards, began to walk back towards the city. They joined up with the remaining Guards, who followed them, in closed order.

Yeshua, Judah, Simeon and Philip watched them go. Shortly afterwards the other three disciples - Thomas, Simeon and Andreas joined them. All seven began the walk back to Bethany.

Caiaphas and Annas returned to the Temple. They settled in Caiaphas' office and sent for Gamaliel, the Pharisee, and Hosea, the Sadducee, to join them. While they waited, Caiaphas and his father-in-law discussed, once again, the details of the planned organisation of the Passover sacrifices, a major logistical task.

Hosea came in first, and they welcomed him. He asked how the investigation had gone, and Annas promised to answer when Gamaliel arrived. He took longer, because he was older, and used a stick to aid his progress. Caiaphas, who treated Gamaliel with due deference, stood up and found him a chair. He helped him sit down.

Gamaliel opened the meeting.

"Lord Caiaphas why have you convened this meeting?"

"I have information for you about Yeshua Bar Yusuf, Brother Gamaliel."

"Why now? Why not give it to the Council as a whole?"

"I wanted to brief the two of you about what happened this morning, when Lord Annas and I met him and spoke with him."

"I see," said Gamaliel dubiously. "It sounds like yet another device to fix the Council meeting to me. What do you think about this Brother Hosea?"

"I share your doubts, Brother Gamaliel," Hosea said guardedly, "but let's give them a chance. Lord Annas you promised me that you would give me the results of your enquiries."

Annas cleared his throat, sipped some wine, and began to speak. He spoke quickly, hoping to obscure what he had done from two of the ablest members of the Council.

"I have found two men who will swear that Yeshua deliberately breaks the Sabbath Law and encourages others to do so. I have spoken to them both and they confirm one another's story that Yeshua heals the sick on the Sabbath and also encourages his men to reap and grind corn on that day. Two more will swear that he used the Divine Name to raise a small girl from the dead and threatened to destroy the Temple by magic. Two more will swear that he publicly personally forgave a man his sins."

"And, I assume, all three pairs of witnesses back each other?" Gamaliel asked, staring fixedly at Annas.

"Of course, Brother Gamaliel," said Annas soothingly. "Why do you doubt me?"

"Because I know you too well Lord Annas! We go back a long way together. I know all your tricks."

Gamaliel paused before continuing, detective-like.

"Let's see," he mused. "You have six witnesses. We sentenced six men yesterday for theft and fighting. It's a strange coincidence isn't it?"

"It is indeed, Brother Gamaliel," said Annas gravely. "It's a strange coincidence, but still a coincidence. Life is full of such coincidences."

Hosea smiled.

"Let me help my Brother, Lord Annas. Let me use the word 'convenient'."

"You can use whatever word you like, Brother. It's still a coincidence."

Gamaliel sighed.

"I've had enough of fencing, Lord Annas. What did you offer the six men for their evidence and did you, shall we say, 'assist' them with it?"

Caiaphas intervened, trying to save his father-in-law.

"I suggest we produce the witnesses before the Council meeting and let the Council judge."

Hosea had been sipping his wine. He put the glass down and looked up sharply.

"Lord Caiaphas, far be it from me to teach you the Law, but does not one of the great Moshe's Ten Commandments, which he received from the LORD God Himself, order 'Thou shalt not bear false witness'?"

Caiaphas nodded.

"So, if they're lying, you will make them sinners. Worse than this, since you intend to sentence Yeshua to death, then you will make them liable to death as well. Is that not so, Lord Caiaphas?"

Gamaliel sat up straight and hammered the words home word by word, emphasising each one, as he said it, with a thump of his fist on the table.

Caiaphas looked stunned.

Gamaliel pressed home his advantage,

"You said you met Yeshua this afternoon. Did you challenge him on these charges?"

Caiaphas nodded.

"What did he say?"

"He denied them all, explaining each away as a

mistake Brother Gamaliel."

"That is what I would have expected," Gamaliel continued.

"What do you think Brother Hosea?"

"I agree Brother Gamaliel. I don't think that the Council will be impressed. Do you have anything else Lord Caiaphas?"

Caiaphas paused. The other three looked at him as he sipped his wine, emptied the glass and refilled it, and those of the others, adding water. Finally he spoke, slowly and deliberately.

"Yeshua called for the meeting, and he did so in order to ask me to resign my position."

He ignored the surprised looks from the two Council members.

"He claims to be a direct descendent of Aaron and the Hasmonean Priest Kings, as well of the Davidic line. He also made a claim to be the de facto Son of the Father."

Gamaliel and Hosea looked puzzled. Hosea spoke for both of them.

"Did you say he claims to be a son of God – a priest king, like the Davidic and Hasmonean monarchies?"

"No," Annas explained. "He claimed to be the mythical head of the national resistance."

There was silence as the two visitors took this in. Eventually Gamaliel and Hosea exchanged glances. Gamaliel silently asked the question, and Hosea nodded. Gamaliel turned to face Annas and Caiaphas.

"What do you make of all this?" he asked.

Caiaphas spoke emphatically and urgently.

"I think he is a danger to us all. He spoke of replacing Herod and me with himself and then asking Pilate to go. He expects the Romans to evacuate Judaea and leave him as a client king. If they don't go, he said he would lead a national uprising."

"I don't see why you should be so concerned for your own position, Lord Caiaphas, that you consider your replacement by this man as a national disaster. It might be a good idea, and are you sure that Tiberius would not agree?"

"Brother Gamaliel, surely you can see that we provide a stabilising force, and our removal could bring the whole house down?"

"I can see that you might think that and also that you do well out of the position, both you and your father-in-law, Lord Caiaphas."

Gamaliel paused, then added,

"I'm not convinced, Lord Caiaphas, and, if I'm not convinced, certainly the Council won't be."

Gamaliel paused for thought before turning away from Caiaphas to face his Sadducee colleague.

"Brother Hosea, do you think the Council will accept written statements from the six witnesses?"

Hosea took his time to answer, rubbing his beard in a thoughtful manner. Eventually he spoke.

"They might, Brother Gamaliel, provided each statement was taken down by a different scribe, and the six witnesses are then discharged."

Hosea turned to face Annas.

"What did you promise them Lord Annas in return for their lying statements?"

"That the sentences on them would not be carried out."

"Then, Brother Gamaliel, we will have to release them."

"I agree, Brother Hosea."

Gamaliel turned to Annas.

"Will you arrange for the six to be released after their statements have been taken, Lord Annas?"

Annas bowed ironically to the two party leaders.

"Certainly Brother Gamaliel, if it pleases you. Will

the two of you then support us?"

"Provided the statements tally according to law," Gamaliel promised.

Gamaliel turned to the question of Yeshua's claims.

"I don't know what to make of Yeshua's claims. I suggest, Lord Caiaphas that you discuss them with the Procurator and find out how he sees them. He's out of the city at the moment. But, when he returns, I urge you to go and see him. Find out his reaction, and then call us back to meet you before you convene the full Council. I agree that a full scale rising would be disastrous, especially now, but I also feel that we should explore all the options before finally deciding what to do."

"I agree, Brother Gamaliel, but we don't have much time," Caiaphas observed.

"Why is that Lord Caiaphas?"

"Because I promised to give Yeshua my reply tomorrow night."

Gamaliel and Hosea stood and made to leave. At the door, Gamaliel turned back, leaning on his stick.

"Then you need to be quick, Lord Caiaphas!"

**

Yeshua and his group of six walked back towards Bethany. He seemed quite cheerful, and smiled as the two Simeons, Andreas and Philip drew ahead of him, apparently anxious to get back quickly. Yeshua walked more slowly; as did Thomas and Judah. They dropped behind. Once the gap had got beyond hearing, Yeshua became more serious and spoke to his two companions.

"I think that went as well as I could have expected."

"I'm not so sure, Yeshua," said the ever cautious Judah. "Be careful. You can't trust Caiaphas."

"If Caiaphas deceives us, Judah, you will be

exposed to risk," Yeshua said seriously. "You're the one going to get his answer. If he does betray us, then save yourself. You are far more important to Qumr'an and the Resistance than I am. Do what you have to do. I will do what I have to do."

Love my enemy, Die for my enemy. Make my enemy my friend.

"And Thomas?"

"Yes, Yeshua?" the surprised Thomas asked.

"If everything goes wrong, Thomas look after Judah. Forget me and forget the others. Will you promise me that?"

Yeshua spoke with an immense earnestness and intensity neither man had seen before. He stared intently at the disciple. Thomas nodded.

"Yes, Yeshua. You can rely on me. I will do as you ask and look to Judah's safety."

"One more thing Thomas," Yeshua added. "The others will argue about who will lead the group. I want you to keep out of it. Deter Jochanan and Jacob. Cephas will claim the leadership. Let him. In the end, Qumr'an has chosen my brother, Jacob, to succeed me. Support my brother."

"Yes Yeshua," Thomas answered.

"Good. We're agreed then. If all goes well, then fine! However, I agree with you Judah. I think things are far more likely to go wrong. If that happens, you will be burying my body. However, I am convinced that one day I will be vindicated, just as the prophet Job foretold of himself. Do you both understand?"

"Yes, Yeshua," they answered in chorus.

"Good. You both have your roles for the future and I know you will find them. I wish you both luck. Things will happen quickly from now on, and we may not have a chance to talk much together again. I know that, and wish to thank you both for your help and support. I could not have done what I have done without it."

Yeshua noticed the tears appear in both men's eyes. He felt them in his own. He turned away, struggling to get control.

"Come on," he said, finally. "Let's go home."

The three men followed the other four along the road, Yeshua in the middle, Thomas on the right and Judah on the left. They walked quietly, but determinedly, and slowly caught up their companions. As a result, they all reached Bethany together, shortly before the arrival of the party from Bethlehem.

**

It had been a long and tiring journey, especially for Mariam, who felt that she was too old for this sort of journey. She rode on a donkey, led by Jochanan, while her son and grandson, both named Jacob, walked on either side, and Marcus and Julia brought up the rear. The journey seemed much longer, and the sun seemed much hotter than they actually were. By midday, when the party had to stop and rest; they were all hot, dusty, sweating and tired. They fed the donkey, drank water and ate bread. After resting for half an hour, they moved on. They continued through the afternoon, struggling on in the heat and dust, stopping more and more frequently. They said little, but Mariam complained to her son and grandsons about how tired and uncomfortable she felt.

"It seems much further than when I walked this way to my cousin Elizabeth when I was sixteen and had just met Abraham," she commented ruefully.

They offered to go back, but she refused to allow it. In this way, tired, irritable and feeling hot and dirty, they came, eventually to the house at Bethany, shortly after the return of Yeshua and his six disciples from the Mount of Olives.

**

Pilate changed from military uniform to his tunic and toga, and settled down to relax with his wife, after eating a good meal and sharing a bottle of the best Valerian red wine. He felt exhausted after his long ride. He was looking forward to a relaxing evening, but was destined to be disappointed. Soon after it became dark, the duty officer knocked on his apartment door. Pilate called him in. The officer saluted and spoke.

"I'm sorry to disturb you, Your Excellency, but the High Priest has called to see you."

"Do you know what he wants?" Pilate asked.

"No, Your Excellency, but he insists it's urgent and that only you can deal with it."

Pilate sighed heavily, swore loudly, and stood, wrapped his toga around himself, and apologised to his wife. He then followed the officer out of the apartment, to return to his office. Once there, he called for wine, water, and glasses, and settled down to wait for his guest to be brought in.

Caiaphas arrived about ten minutes later, escorted by the duty officer, who formally introduced the High Priest. Pilate stood, extended his hand, shook that of the High Priest, and ushered him to a seat. He poured him wine, and Caiaphas added water, before Pilate poured wine for himself.

Once they were both settled, Pilate opened the conversation.

"This is a pleasant surprise, my Lord, what have I done to deserve it?"

Caiaphas plainly felt uncomfortable. He fidgeted as he spoke, and frequently reverted to sipping his wine.

"I have come to consult you, Your Excellency. I fear we have an urgent problem."

"Indeed, Lord Caiaphas," Pilate said smoothly. "And what problem is that?"

"Yeshua Bar Yusuf, or Bar Abraham, as he claims to be."

"You've mentioned this man before, Lord Caiaphas, and assured me of the danger he poses. You will remember that I told you that I didn't see much harm in him."

"I remember the conversation well, Your Excellency. However, things have changed since then."

Pilate looked surprised.

"I'm not aware of any major changes Lord Caiaphas. What has happened that has alarmed you so much?"

Caiaphas looked even more uncomfortable.

"My father-in-law and I met with Yeshua earlier today and questioned him. We put three religious charges to him, which he denied. We have witnesses to back these charges, but it's not very likely that they will stick. I felt that he might have been concerned with the murder of my two spies near Jericho. He plainly knew nothing about it."

"So, my dear Caiaphas, I was right all the time! You don't have a problem," Pilate replied with a smile.

"Unfortunately the discussion did not end there. Yeshua told us that he had connections with the National Resistance," Caiaphas explained.

Pilate smiled his humourless smile.

"That should not be a matter of concern to you Lord Caiaphas. I am well aware that the Temple is a centre of resistance to our rule. I am also aware that you personally have a rather murky relationship with Messianic pretenders."

Caiaphas choked on his wine, coughed and then

began to bluster.

"You've got it wrong Excellency. I've got nothing…"

Pilate cut him short.

"We both know the truth, Lord Caiaphas! Don't insult me by trying to maintain a lie. I'm not stupid, although I'm aware that you and your father-in-law think that all Romans are stupid. I have to work with you for the good of the country and the Empire. It does not mean that I also have to deceive myself about you and your motives. I have simply chosen to ignore them."

Caiaphas decided that silence was the wisest course. He let Pilate finish, before returning to his theme.

"As I said, Excellency. Yeshua revealed his claimed real identity and his intentions. He claims to be the descendent of the Hasmonean Priest Kings and of the royal house of David."

"And?" Pilate asked.

"And what, Your Excellency?"

"Why is that significant Lord Caiaphas?"

"He has challenged me to resign in his favour, Excellency."

"Has he indeed! I can see that's a problem for you, but why should I be worried? I have already shown you I know the double game you are playing. Why should this Yeshua be any worse?"

Caiaphas paused, wandering how to answer this. Eventually, after rubbing his hands across his brow, he spoke.

"He also wants to replace Herod Antipas as Tetrarch, Your Excellency."

"There's a logic in that too Lord Caiaphas," Pilate responded.

"So you're not worried, Your Excellency?"

"I can see that you should be worried, but you have

not mentioned Rome at all."

"He believes that he can renegotiate the treaty with Rome, and that the Emperor will withdraw all the Roman troops and officials from Judaea and Samaria."

Pilate grinned.

"He may be more right than he knows! The Divine Tiberius wants security here. If a loyal and popular Jewish client king secures peace and security: that's fine by us. The Divine Augustus was happy to allow King Herod to rule the country for us. The Divine Tiberius might allow King Yeshua to do the same."

Caiaphas refilled his glass, added water, and drank it to the bottom, joined by Pilate, who wandered what else the High Priest was after. Finally Caiaphas played what he thought was his master card.

"You realise that Yeshua wants people to stop paying the Roman loyalty tax, Excellency, don't you?"

"I haven't heard that, Lord Caiaphas. What's your evidence?"

"He told people in the Temple, in the hearing of our priests, that people should not pay the produce of the Holy Land to God's enemies."

"And you assume we are the enemies of your God, do you Lord Caiaphas? Is that not treason?" Pilate asked with a grim smile.

Caiaphas refused to be drawn.

"You will have to remove him from the scene, Your Excellency."

"He's more of a threat to you than us, why don't you kill him? You can order his death by stoning."

"The public will think it's a matter of personal rivalry."

"Well, isn't it, my Lord?" Pilate asked.

"It would destabilise the country and lead to civil war and probable revolt against Rome. Such a revolt would end in disaster," Caiaphas answered.

"You may well be right, however, since he has made no direct threat against Rome, I also cannot act, Lord Caiaphas."

"What do you suggest we do then, Your Excellency, wait until revolt breaks out? The Emperor would not thank you for that!"

Pilate paused, gulped audibly, looked at his wrists, reflecting that, if he failed, Tiberius might well send him a small knife and order him to open his veins, and finally replied.

"I will refer him to my friend the Tetrarch. At least most of Yeshua's work has been done in his lands. He can dispose of him quietly, like he did the former prophet Jochanan. If he declines, I will, of course, confirm your judicial decision by an executive order. However, understand this, it would have to be your judicial decision, not mine."

Caiaphas nodded his agreement, before Pilate and he stood, and shook hands, after which the duty officer showed Caiaphas out. Pilate watched the High Priest go, smiling grimly and shaking his head. He hoped that Herod would spare him the decision he knew he would otherwise have to make.

**

After their evening meal, Yeshua dismissed his disciples and other followers. Instead of leading their usual post meal discussion, he instructed them to pray together, have an early night, and be ready for a planning meeting in the morning.

After they had all gone, Yeshua sat with his mother and brother. He had had little time for other than a kiss and embrace for his mother and an embrace for his brother between their late and unexpected arrival and the evening meal. Now was a chance to catch up with each other.

He asked them about their journey, which he guessed was difficult, especially for his mother. Mariam grimaced, and Yeshua laughed. Words were not needed. He asked about affairs at home, and was assured that everyone was well and the business was doing well. Jacob told him that they had kept out of the limelight, as he and Abraham had wished. Yeshua expressed satisfaction.

"Your time may soon come, Jacob. We are reaching a crisis here. Tomorrow will be the decisive day. I'll tell you more in the morning."

Jacob nodded, but Mariam looked alarmed. She did not like this talk of 'crisis' or decision.

"What's going on, son? I haven't heard from you or seen you since the day you set out for the Jordan to see the Prophet."

"Haven't Judah, Jacob and my sons kept you up to date with developments, mother?" Yeshua asked in surprise.

"They have all given me reports, but it's not the same as hearing from you! Why have you kept away? You have neither written nor visited for over two years."

Mariam stared at her son accusingly. Yeshua wilted. He reflected that there is no fury like that of a mother who feels her son has ignored her.

"I've been very busy, mother," he answered lamely.

Mariam snorted in derision.

"Too busy to see me, you mean," she retorted. "But not too busy to see your wife."

"She has been part of the team, mother. You have the rest of the family to care about, and you're much too old to wander around the country like we have done, camping out at night and cooking over camp fires."

There was a period of silence as Mariam took this answer in. Then she smiled at her son, embraced him, and commented.

"I'm not as old as you think, young man! You never know, I might have enjoyed a few nights under the stars. Your father and I often walked out under the stars. That's how you were conceived. Unfortunately it was before I married Abraham – that's how you got your nickname and I got mine."

Yeshua was puzzled.

"Nickname, mother? What nickname?"

"You were called Yeshua the Bastard. I was called Mariam the Tiger Cat."

Yeshua winced at the memory.

He heard a small boy ask, *"Mother, what is a bastard?"*

After a moment, he added, "I'm sorry, mother. I'm sure you would have enjoyed a few days on tour with us."

Jacob added, laughing, "And she would have kept an eye on you brother."

They all laughed together.

Yeshua poured some wine for Jacob, to which he added water, before pouring water for himself. Mariam noticed this and asked him about it.

"I've taken a vow, mother. I'm not drinking alcohol until God's kingdom comes."

Mariam smiled.

"That could be a long wait, son," she commented.

"Not so long, mother," Yeshua replied. "I've spoken to the so-called High Priest, Caiaphas and challenged him to stand down in my favour. I am expecting his reply tomorrow night."

"He's your enemy, Yeshua," Jacob warned. "Don't trust him."

Yeshua repeated his mantra.

"Love your enemy."

Die for your enemy.

"Make your enemy your friend."

"The rewards for success are great," Yeshua insisted, "and I have received very little real support from the public here or in Galilee. Lots of people have come to see or hear me, it's true, but very few have committed themselves to following or obeying me."

"If the rewards for success are great, brother, the costs of failure for you are even greater – your life."

"I know, Jacob. I don't like it. I know the odds on success are very low, but I have no other alternative."

"You do have an alternative, son," Mariam burst out.

"Give up this crazy enterprise, this gigantic act of folly. Dismiss your followers. Send Abraham's men back to Qumr'an, and bring your wife and my grandsons back to Bethlehem. Be the respected carpenter of Bethlehem, and not another martyr for Israel. Israel has had more than its fair share of martyrs. Don't insist on adding to their number! Remember the man you saw crucified on your Bar Mitzvah. Do you want to be another victim?"

Yeshua promised to think about her words and give her an answer in the morning. With that, they separated, and the house became dark and silent.

Chapter 15

Final Meal

Jerusalem, April 32AD (Thursday)

Thursday morning dawned bright and cloudless, resonant with the prospect of a long sunny day. Yeshua rose at daybreak as usual, and walked briskly to his prayer wood. It was almost as though it was waiting for him, cool, shady, comfortable and familiar. He sat, listening to the call of the birds and the rustle of small animals in the undergrowth.

"God's in His heaven, and all's right with the world," Yeshua thought.

He realised that his doubts had been swept away with the previous day. He felt that he knew the outcome of his discussion with Caiaphas. Yeshua was no fool, and he knew enough of his enemy to know the likely outcome.

Love your enemies. Die for your enemies. Make them your friends.

Caiaphas was certainly his enemy.

However, it is not Caiaphas who will kill me but Pilate.

Today, Yeshua thought about Rome and Roman punishment. Hitherto he had ignored Gaius Publius Pontius Pilatus, Roman Procurator of Judaea and Samaria. Today Pilate was front and centre in his mind.

Pilate will order me to be stripped naked and chained to a post. I will be flogged to within an inch of my life, so that my body is a mass of blood. Then, bound, I will be forced to carry a heavy beam on my shoulders out of the city. It has to be heavy to take my

309

weight.

Yeshua used his knowledge as a carpenter to envisage just how heavy it would be. He imagined it resting on his naked shoulders, supported by his bound hands. He imagined the procession out through the noisy and crowded streets, his bare feet slipping on the cobbles, the weight bearing him down, encouraged by the whips of the guards. He imagined the pain in his lacerated back and the flies settling, drawn by the blood. He shivered, suddenly feeling cold.

In that way they will take me to the hill outside of the city. There they will take the beam off me, strip me, and force me to lie on the ground.

He remembered the man who was crucified when he was having his Bar Mitzvah. Yeshua put himself in that man's place and imagined himself lying, naked and exposed to the crowd, on his back, as a soldier knelt on his arm, holding it in place, for a second one to drive a nail through his wrist. Yeshua winced inwardly as he imagined the pain. He thought of this being repeated, and then of the soldiers pulling him along the ground, ripping his damaged back even further, and raising the bar up the length of the tree, until they reached the point where it slotted into place. He imagined the shoulder wrenching pain as his arms took the weight of his body, as he hung freely from the cross bar. He imagined the pain from his nailed wrists and vowed he would remain silent, however much he wanted to scream. Finally, he imagined the nail being driven through his ankles.

Then will come my full shame as I am exposed naked to the world until I die, like the man on my Bar Mitzvah. My body will become a loathsome thing, stinking of excrement and covered with flies, which will struggle to feast on my flesh and drink my blood.

I shall be like the bread and wine of the Grace.

That is what you have called me to do God. That is what I shall do for you.

Success for me will seem like failure to others. It will seem like a monstrous act of folly, which will deny my children a father; my wife a husband; my mother a son; my brothers and sisters a brother; and my followers hope.

I do not know why I am allowing it to be done to me. Will I be seen as a martyr for Israel, or as an idiot who committed suicide for a hopeless cause? Am I going to perform an act of supreme courage for an ultimate cause beyond my lifetime, or am I going to perform an act of supreme folly for no cause whatsoever? I don't know.

Others will decide.

But, Yeshua, Son of Abraham, Son of Judas Maccabaeus, Son of Aaron, and Son of David, that is what you are going to do for your God, and for your people.

It is what I am going to do for my enemies, my people's enemies and my God's enemies. I am going to die to make them into friends.

Yeshua stood up. He looked up, spread his arms out wide, and spoke to the sky.

"That's what I'm going to do for You, God, and for Your people, at Your command. However, it's still going to be hard."

He sighed heavily, and left the grove for what he guessed would be the last time. He walked back to the house with a firm step and a steady resolve. There were no longer any doubts. He was afraid; but he was also determined to face the future bravely.

Back at the house, there was a scene of bustle and noise, as the women prepared breakfast. The three Mariams - Mother, Aunt and Wife – greeted Yeshua as

311

he returned. Yeshua kissed each in turn. His mother looked at him steadily, studying his face and body movements. Then she turned away. Neither said anything, but she knew what he had decided, and he knew that she knew. Later, the other women saw tears in her eyes, and they knew too. Yeshua's wife embraced her mother-in-law, and shared her tears. Then both women blinked them back. Like their son and husband, if that was his destiny, they resolved to share it in whatever way they could.

In this way, breakfast was made ready for the whole party. It was to be a bigger breakfast than usual, since they were all aware that Yeshua's plans involved moving to Jerusalem to share an important meal that evening.

**

The inner courtyard of the punishment block within the Antonia Fortress rang with the clash of steel, as two naked men faced one another. They were armed with helmets, round shields and blunt swords, and egged on by four fully armed Roman soldiers. The two men had been released from their chains and ordered out of the dungeon as soon as it became light. Neither knew what to expect.

Since they had been arrested, following their moment of madness in the market place five days earlier, they had been stripped, tortured, raped and brutalised by their guard every night, flogged several times and forced to sign a confession. The clothes, taken from them after their arrest to facilitate their torture, had not been returned. As a result, they had spent the last five days, when not being tortured, raped or mocked, naked, surrounded by their own excrement and chained to the wall of their dungeon. In this state they were expected to eat and drink such food and water as the guards gave them. They knew it was not kosher. However, they also knew it was better not to protest. Protests only resulted in the protester being chained to the whipping post and flogged until their guards grew tired.

They noticed that the other three gave complete control over them to the fourth guard, whose name they learnt was Quintus. He appeared to be the senior jailor. If the others got involved at all, it was only to assist him. They also learnt that Quintus was a sadist who liked to flog a man before raping him, and he preferred it if the victim begged him to do it. They learnt it was better to play the game by his rules.

On Wednesday they had been told that they were due to be crucified on Friday morning, and they heard the sound of wood being cut and planed the previous afternoon, guessing it was destined for them.

Today, however, was a surprise. Quintus told them that they were going to perform for the Procurator and the garrison that evening. The winner would be nailed second, they were told. However, if they gave good entertainment, and fought well, they would be rewarded by being spared the scourge.

This was a training session, and the guards taught them some of the finer points of swordplay. They resolved to put on a good show that night, since they felt that, awful though crucifixion was, having your body torn apart for up to ten minutes by the heavy scourge and then having the additional pain of having the whole of your back open to the flies and the air, in addition to everything else, was something to avoid. The soldiers hated the scourging as well, but for different reasons. It was messy and resulted in hours of extra cleaning of equipment and uniforms, not to mention the area around the column, afterwards. The result was that the two pupils proved willing to learn and the four teachers were willing to teach them.

At the end of the session, both men were covered with sweat, and were allowed to wash down in buckets of cold water, before being given breakfast and chained up in a cleaned up cell. The soldiers were pleased as well, and showed their pleasure in the way they treated the two prisoners that morning. Quintus even smiled at them. He told them that they might well get a friend to join them during the night.

"There's rumours you're going to have a friend with you tomorrow," he said conspiratorially. "We've been told to get a third cross beam ready today, so you'll hear more woodwork being done. Rest assured that it's not for you. I can also promise you that you won't have to please me tonight. However, when the third prisoner arrives, you might pass on the wisdom of your experience to him if you have a chance! I intend that he should entertain me tonight."

He finished chaining them to the wall, stroking each man on the chin. Then he left them, locking the cell door. They both slumped against the wall, and slept, exhausted by the exercise they had performed that morning, and what Quintus had made them endure the night before.

**

At about the same time, Yeshua was issuing instructions to his group. He ordered Judah to take Mariam (his wife) and their two sons, as well as Marcus, and Julia, Thomas, and Salome, and make their way to the house Judah had bought to serve as their Jerusalem base. They were jointly to do what was necessary to prepare the meal for that night there. Thomas was to make his way back when all was clearly

314

on the way to being ready. He would collect the rest of the party and take them all to the house. Yeshua gave the rest a chance to relax and enjoy the morning, warning them to be back, ready to depart for the city, by two in the afternoon. He was in a decisive mood that morning, and no one saw fit to oppose him.

Yeshua's mother spoke to him later that morning. She said simply, "You've decided then, son?"

"Yes, mother," Yeshua replied. "I'm sorry."

"Don't be, Yeshua," she said sadly. "You must fulfil your destiny, just as your father, Abraham did. I've always known that. Just don't try to send me away."

"You know I could never do that, mother. However, I want you to do one thing for me."

"What is that, son? Ask it, and, if I can do it, I will do so."

"Look after my wife and sons, and keep my brothers out of trouble. One martyr in the family is enough!" Yeshua smiled sadly.

Mariam hugged her son and kissed him, she suspected for the last time. Through her tears she promised to do as he asked, adding, "I shall be with you until the end, son, whatever you say."

"I know, mother," Yeshua replied. "You wouldn't be my mother if you did anything else."

He smiled at her before turning to Jacob.

"Look after her, brother, and remember what I said to you."

"I will Yeshua," Jacob replied, tears forming in his eyes.

The two brothers embraced for a final time, and both embraced their weeping mother, before Yeshua slipped away from both of them, leaving Jacob comforting the already bereaved Mariam.

Yeshua went off to pray alone, seeking the inner strength necessary to face the terrors he suspected lay ahead, before returning to organise the departure of the rest of the group.

Mariam spent the morning being comforted by her two cousins and her brother-in-law, Lazarus, who was himself slowly dying from a degenerative disease about which no doctor could do anything.

**

Caiaphas met Gamaliel and Hosea as soon as all three arrived at the Temple. The meeting was short and was held in his office. A slave poured wine for each man, added water, and left. Without a word, Caiaphas handed the two men eight pieces of paper, containing the reports of Moshe and Yusuf, and the six witness statements. Hosea and Gamaliel read each paper without comment, passing them to one another. Caiaphas said nothing, drinking his wine and waiting. The two men returned the papers to Caiaphas. Gamaliel spoke for them both.

"The papers do all that is needful for the Council. Thank you for letting us read them Lord Caiaphas. Have you spoken to the Procurator?"

"Yes Brother Gamaliel."

"And..?"

"He has agreed to pass Yeshua Bar Yusuf on to Herod Antipas for quiet disposal in the way only he seems able to do."

"Do you believe that is sufficient guarantee, Lord Caiaphas? I don't think that the Tetrarch will go along with it. He already has the death of one so-called prophet on his hands. I very much doubt even he would want two!"

"I tend to agree, Brother Gamaliel. So I asked Pilate if he would assure me that he would deal with Yeshua if Herod didn't. I told him that he was opposed to the payment of the Roman tax. Pilate promised, but I do have a sneaking doubt. You never know with these Romans, sometimes their weakness for appearing to be just overcomes their common sense."

"So we need a fall back plan."

Hosea's sudden interruption was unexpected. Both men looked around at him. They had forgotten he was there.

"Do you have one, Lord Caiaphas?"

Caiaphas smiled.

"Of course, Brother Hosea. Do you think I'm as big a fool as our blundering Procurator? Of course I have a back up plan! We will ensure rumours of this Yeshua's arrest spread quickly in the city. You know the Jerusalem crowd; they can't resist a good show. They will turn up at the Governor's palace to see the fun. Pilate won't be able to resist parading his prisoners in the most humiliating way, in order to stress his power, humiliate the prisoners, and also humiliate us. He will expect the crowd to show sympathy for the prisoners, but he will be wrong. They will have tasted blood and, encouraged by my agents, will howl for crucifixion. Game over!"

Gamaliel and Hosea looked at each other. They were rivals in most things, but both felt contempt for Caiaphas and his father-in-law. However, they also realised that he was the ablest politician, as well as the most cunning, most devious and most dangerous, man, on the Council. Once again Gamaliel spoke for them both.

"Very well, High Priest. Neither of us will speak against you. We will not volunteer an opinion, but, if asked, will say we accept what you recommend. That does not mean that you will have an easy ride through the Council, but you already know that."

The three men stood up. Caiaphas shook both men's

hands.

"I fully understand, gentlemen, and thank you for your support. I will see you at the Council meeting at midday."

The two men left the room, and Caiaphas turned to study his other papers, waiting for the arrival of his father-in-law and the other officers of the Temple so he could pursue the routine business of the day.

**

Yeshua's advance party reached the house at about eleven o'clock. It was a reasonably sized town house, with an inner courtyard, entered through a strong, lockable gate. It had a dining room on the otherwise flat roof, reached by an outside staircase, leading up from the courtyard. The living quarters were under the upper room, opposite the entrance, and the cooking area on the left hand side of the courtyard. On the right hand side were buildings for animals and the household slaves. Judah had bought the property with money from the Essene Community. It was the ideal size for their use, and was in a quiet part of the city, among the houses of the richer citizens. Judah knew they would be undisturbed there.

Once they arrived, he organised the boys and Mariam organised the women. Thomas left them to begin the return trip to Bethany.

Julia was sent, with some of the other women, to the market to buy food. She seized the opportunity to slip away and approach the main entrance of the Antonia. She told the guards that she was a former slave of Pilate's wife, and was granted admission. Julia, Pilate's wife, welcomed her, having missed the young girl. She had agreed with her husband to let her go, but she was still upset when Pilate sent Julia away, and even more so, when he granted the girl her freedom. She asked Julia what she wanted.

"I know that Pilate listens to you. My lady," Julia said. "Plead with him to spare Yeshua's life. He's no threat to Rome; only to the Chief Priest, who hates Pilate and wants to destroy Yeshua."

Pilate's wife, who had her own reservations about the impending execution of the Jewish prophet, took Julia to meet her husband. He was busy, but made time for the two women. However, when Julia made her request, his face darkened.

"I have decided to free your mother, aunts, sisters and most of your brothers tomorrow, Julia, so they can celebrate Passover with you as free people. I have even decided to return your family home to you. I will see if I can free your father, uncles and brothers from the mines and galleys later."

"Thank you, Your Excellency," Julia said, surprised at Pilate's generosity.

"However, Julia, if you wish me to save this Jewish prophet instead, you need only ask. But you can't have both. Who do you and Marcus want me to free – your family or this Yeshua? If I free Yeshua, your family will go to the slave market in Rome. There they will be stripped, chained to posts, and displayed publicly for sale. Once sold, they may be treated like the animals that slaves are, and could be taken anywhere in the Empire. Your home will be sold. Your family will be split apart. Your father, uncles and older brothers will die as galley slaves or mining slaves. I will not intervene in their cases. That is the price of Yeshua's life and freedom, Julia. Are you prepared for your family to pay it?"

Julia cried.

"No!" she sobbed.

"I thought not," Pilate smiled, trying to appear kind,

but failing. "Come back here tomorrow afternoon, and your family will be waiting for you and Marcus to collect them and take them home."

Julia turned and fled.

"Do not bring her to me again," Pilate warned his wife.

She nodded and left the room.

**

As Julia ran from Pilate's office, Caiaphas entered the Council chamber, accompanied by Annas. The various statements had been copied out a number of times and circulated among the Council members as they arrived. Yusuf of Aramathea and Nicodemus were among the last. As usual, they sat at the back. The final two to arrive were Gamaliel, leaning on his stick, and the younger, Hosea. They took their customary positions at the front, and sat silently. The room fell silent as the High Priest entered.

Annas opened the meeting by asking if everyone had read the reports. Yusuf and Nicodemus were the only two not to have done so, and they had copies passed to them. They spent the next few minutes reading them.

One of the Pharisees asked whether sentence had been carried out on the six men condemned at the previous meeting.

"All six have been dealt with and released, so they can redeem their wretched lives by repenting and celebrating the Passover correctly," Annas reported.

No one asked for any further detail, and Annas was relieved. He did not like lying to the Council.

Another Pharisee asked whether the six witnesses were present. Caiaphas answered that they were not. Nicodemus picked up on this.

320

"Why are they not here, Lord Caiaphas? He asked suspiciously.

"All six are from Galilee and need to prepare for Passover. Having done their duty and made their reports, which confirm those presented by Brother Moshe and Brother Yusuf, it seemed churlish to detain them – churlish and unnecessary. Do you not agree Brother Gamaliel?"

Gamaliel nodded.

"I fear this Yeshua has broken the law and committed blasphemy Brother Nicodemus," Gamaliel added, "This compounds his behaviour on Sunday when he broke the peace of the Temple. The penalty for some of the offences is flogging – but for sorcery, it's death by stoning."

Yusuf of Aramathea put down the papers he had studied.

"Has Yeshua been questioned about this, and the alleged murder of Brother Moshe and Brother Yusuf?" he asked.

"I questioned him myself, with Lord Annas as witness, Brother Yusuf," Caiaphas replied.

"And what was his answer?" Yusuf continued.

"He denies any knowledge of the murders, and I believe him. He says the three accusations are misunderstandings and claims he's the rightful High Priest."

There were gasps of surprise at this final statement.

"What is his justification for that claim Lord Caiaphas?" a Sadducee asked. "Only Sadducees can be High Priests. This Yeshua is not one of us as far as I know."

"You're wrong Brother Zedekiah," Caiaphas replied. "The High Priest should be a descendent of Aaron. Yeshua claims descent from Aaron, David and John Hyrcanus."

"Rubbish!" another Sadducee shouted. "What are you going to do Lord Caiaphas?"

Caiaphas, who had been sitting on the dais, stood up and moved to the front, standing directly in front of the first row of seats. He placed his hands dramatically in his sleeves across his chest and drew himself up to his full height.

"As High Priest, I judge it to be expedient for one man to die for the nation," he pronounced solemnly.

Nicodemus laughed.

"Since when have you been the nation Lord Caiaphas? I can see it might be expedient for you for one man to die to preserve your position. But is that the same thing as being good for the nation?"

Yusuf of Aramathea agreed, but they were alone. When Gamaliel and Hosea pronounced judgement in support of Caiaphas, the fate of Yeshua was sealed.

"The only issue, Lord Caiaphas," Gamaliel concluded, "is who is going to kill him and how will it be done?"

"It is not expedient for us to execute him, Brother Gamaliel, as I explained to you earlier. It will look like a personal vendetta."

"Which it is," Nicodemus whispered to Yusuf, who nodded.

"So who is the lucky man?" Gamaliel added. "Pilate or Herod?"

"We are going to seize him tonight and pass him on to Pilate. However, Brother Gamaliel, I believe that Pilate is hoping that Herod will relieve us all of the problem."

"Don't bet on it, Lord Caiaphas," Hosea interrupted. "Herod's as crafty as a fox. He won't touch this with a steering oar. He burnt his fingers over Jochanan, remember?"

"In that case, Pilate will send him to Golgotha,"

Annas said from the chair.

"Why?" Nicodemus asked.

"Because he is a threat to stability and peace, and that is all Rome wants from here," Caiaphas answered. "In addition, I have persuaded Pilate that Yeshua has been preaching against the Loyalty Tax."

Annas rose to his feet.

"There has been enough debate. Does the Council agree that Yeshua Bar Yusuf is guilty of sorcery, breaking the temple peace, breaking the Sabbath laws and encouraging others to do so, and blasphemy?"

All but two shouted, "Yes".

"And do you agree that he deserves death?"

Again all but two shouted, "Yes".

"Finally, will you entrust execution of this sentence to the Lord Caiaphas and myself?"

The result was the same.

"In that case, I close this meeting."

Gamaliel objected. Annas was surprised and asked him to explain his reason.

"I have a second proposal to put to the meeting," He said firmly, standing in front of the meeting and leaning on his stick.

"What proposal do you wish to put to us, Brother Gamaliel?" Annas asked.

"I propose that our action stops with Yeshua, and does not include his family or his followers. Leave the fate of the movement to God. If we strike the shepherd, the sheep will be scattered. I think that will happen to this group."

Annas put this proposal to the meeting, and it was carried unanimously. He closed the meeting for the second time.

As the members began to make their way out, talking excitedly to one another, Annas turned to Caiaphas with a smile and said,

"My job's done! Now it's your turn."

Caiaphas smiled back.

"Thank you Lord Annas, and," seeing Gamaliel and Hosea about to leave, "Thank you Brother Gamaliel and Brother Hosea for your support."

Both men nodded grimly, before making their way out of the room.

Eventually, Caiaphas and Annas were left alone.

"Now I must go and break the good news to the Governor," Caiaphas said.

"Good luck, Yusuf," Annas replied, as he turned to leave.

**

Thomas arrived back at Bethany at about the same time that Annas finally closed the Council meeting. On his arrival, Yeshua sent messengers out through the village to collect his various followers, and Mariam's donkey. After about an hour, when all had gathered, the whole party left for the city, twenty men and women, with Mariam riding on a donkey led by Jacob. They were a subdued party, which set out for the city, with its members either silent or talking quietly and seriously together. They moved quickly and, within an hour, they were approaching the city gates.

**

As Yeshua's party approached the gates, Caiaphas was ushered into Pilate's office. The Procurator rose to his feet and courteously offered the High Priest a seat, before sitting himself and looking enquiringly at his visitor. Caiaphas leaned forward in his seat, and spoke urgently.

"The Sanhedrin has met and sentenced Yeshua Bar

324

Yusuf to death. We will arrest him tonight and bring him to you, bound and under escort, in the early hours. We do not consider his supporters or family to be a threat and do not intend to take any action against them."

"I see," Pilate answered. "I agree about the family and friends. Do you have the men you need to arrest this Yeshua?"

"I shall use the Temple Guard, supported by a group of specially armed priests. All I need from you is the city gates left open and men available to receive the prisoner once we bring him back. I do not want to hold him overnight, since that could complicate the process."

Pilate was curious.

"You want him dead, why worry about the complications of the process?"

"It's the time element. He has to be dead by six o'clock."

Pilate was puzzled and showed it.

"Why such a tight timetable?"

"The Passover and the Sabbath begins at six. It is forbidden to have a body hanging from a tree during a festival or over Sabbath by our Law. It follows that he must be dead by then. Therefore, the process must begin as soon as possible."

"Unless, of course, the Tetrarch takes him," Pilate pointed out. "He can pick his own place, time and method."

"Unless that," Caiaphas agreed.

Caiaphas stood up.

"Thank you for receiving me so quickly Your Excellency. However, I have to get on. I have a great deal to do and little time to do it in."

Pilate also stood.

"Thank you for keeping me informed, Lord

Caiaphas. I will have everything ready to receive your prisoner."

Caiaphas nodded and smiled. Pilate called for the duty officer, who escorted him out. He also asked the officer to call Quintus to his office. He sat down to wait, continuing to work on his papers. Tiberius had approved his idea of building an aqueduct to carry water from the pools outside of Jerusalem in to the city. Pilate had discussed the idea with Herod before commissioning a report on the project from his senior engineer. The initial report was given to Pilate just before he left Caesarea for Jerusalem. He opened the report and began to read it.

Half an hour later, there was a knock on the door. It opened. The guard showed a nervous looking Quintus in. Quintus saluted and stood to attention. Pilate looked up, put down the engineer's report, returned the salute lazily, and smiled.

"Ah, Senior Jailor Quintus. How are the two prisoners?"

"They're fine sir. They'll put on a good show tonight and a fine one tomorrow at Calvary."

"I'm pleased Quintus," Pilate responded with a smile, "I never expected anything else." He paused, before adding, "You are going to receive a third man overnight. His name is Yeshua Bar Yusuf. He's charged with treason against the Emperor. He will probably join the other two at Calvary. That is if we can't offload him on the Tetrarch. I want you to be waiting for him at the gate and take him into your charge. My guess is that it will probably be in the early hours of the morning."

"Normal process then Sir?" Quintus asked hopefully.

Pilate, who knew Quintus's penchant for handsome young male prisoners, nodded and smiled.

326

"Absolutely, Senior Jailor. I'm depending on it! I know what you do to your prisoners. I saw from the behaviour of Marcus, my Jewish slave, how guilty Jewish men feel if they have had sex with another man. I am counting on that to break this Yeshua's spirit before I question him. I need him to be cooperative when I speak to him in the morning."

"Don't worry, Sir. I'll ensure he has an interesting night," Quintus promised.

"You also need to arrange for the carpenters to get to work again, just in case."

"Yes sir!" Quintus said mechanically.

Pilate paused. Quintus saluted once more and made to go, but Pilate called him back.

"Do you still play the King Game with the prisoners Quintus? You know the one, where you choose the prisoner to be crucified last and dress him up as a king and pretend to salute him?"

Quintus turned back and grinned.

"Yes sir."

"That's what I thought," Pilate grinned in turn. "Play the game. Make this Yeshua the king......."

Pilate described how he wanted the scene to be created. Quintus's grin grew broader as he envisaged the scene Pilate had painted.

"We can do that sir," he promised.

"Once you've set it up, send a man to collect me. I plan to talk to this Yeshua once his spirit has been broken and he fully understands his position."

"Yes sir," Quintus responded.

"Very good, Senior Jailor Quintus. Carry on," Pilate said.

Quintus came to attention and saluted. Pilate saluted back. Quintus turned, opened the door, and marched out, closing the door behind him. Pilate sighed, and returned to studying the engineer's report.

**

Yeshua's party arrived at the house soon after Caiaphas left the Fortress. It was now mid afternoon. Mariam's donkey was stabled in the outhouse and Yeshua's followers were allocated rooms in the slaves' quarters, with four men sharing a room. The newly arrived women joined the women already cooking the meal. The disciples joined the rest of the Twelve in the upper room. A second table was prepared in the courtyard for the rest of the group.

**

Meanwhile, Caiaphas returned to the Temple and began to arrange the arresting party. He took a group of ten Temple Guards he thought he could trust, and added twenty volunteers from the priests, whom he armed. In all he selected a party of thirty men, and put them under the command of one of his friends. He instructed them to report to his house after dark, and ordered them to leave an officer and two guardsmen at the Temple gate to escort Judah to the house when he finally appeared. Then he left the Temple to return to his home.

**

Yeshua and his disciples sat down to eat at the same time as Pilate sat down to supper in the Antonia and the first of Caiaphas's men began to arrive at his house, where they, too, were provided with food and drink. Yeshua sat at the head of the table, with Judah on his left and Thomas on his right. Yeshua's two sons sat next to Judah and Simeon and his brother sat next to Thomas. The tables were arranged in the form of a big

U. On the left hand side, sat Philip, the other Simeon and Bartholomew, while Judas, Thaddeus and Matthaus sat opposite them. Marcus and Julia acted as servers. The overall mood was sombre.

Yeshua opened the meal with grace. He took a large loaf and split it in two, saying the words of the Grace.

"Blessed be God who brings forth fruit out of the earth."

He broke off a piece of bread and passed the two bigger pieces to left and right. Each disciple also broke off a piece of bread and passed the remainder on. When this process was finished, they all ate their portion at the same time.

Yeshua then raised the wine goblet and blessed it in the same way, passing it to Thomas without drinking it. Thomas drank some wine, then passed the goblet on, until it reached Matthaus. Marcus took the goblet and passed it to Bartholomew, who continued the process until it reached Judah, who passed the goblet back to Yeshua, who put it down untouched.

"This meal is symbolic. It represents the meal that will inaugurate God's Kingdom. That's why I have not shared the cup with you. My vow will continue until the Kingdom is here. My lips will not willingly touch alcohol until I see the Kingdom come."

Yeshua paused, before adding,

"That was my intention. However, I very much fear we are about to be betrayed......."

There were shocked gasps at this, which Yeshua ignored.

"...In that case, this bread and this wine may well come to represent my body and blood which may shortly be shed for the Cause. If I die, when you meet and do this in the future, remember me."

These sombre words caused consternation. Thomas and Judah alone seemed exempt from all this.

Jochanan leaned past Judah.

"Father, do you know who the betrayer is?" he asked eagerly.

"I suspect that I might know, son," Yeshua replied.

"Then tell us father, and we can take him out. If we know there's a traitor here we can save your life by taking his."

"It's not as simple as that, son", Yeshua explained patiently. "I appreciate your desire to help me, but you really can't."

Judah spoke quietly to Yeshua.

"Do you think it's really as bad as that?"

"I fear it is, Judah. Take care. You're far too important to the Movement to lose. They can, and will, replace me with my brother. You're much more difficult to replace, especially now."

Marcus and Julia served the first course, and the meal began to run its course, with the diners breaking off into small individual conversations. These began to become fractious. Simeon told Andreas that he expected to become the Number Two in the Kingdom. Jacob heard this and said loudly enough to be heard,

"It's not up to you Simeon. Jochanan and I are Yeshua's sons. We should be his heirs and his deputies."

Philip intervened.

"It's not up to any of us! The Movement will decide who rules and who advises. We should leave it to them."

Simeon the Fisherman objected.

"Yeshua appointed me to lead. Therefore no one else has the right to claim the leadership."

Jochanan intervened to support Jacob, and Andreas spoke in support of Simeon. Matthaus attempted to calm the growing argument. He appealed to Yeshua who appeared to be self-absorbed.

"Yeshua," he said, "can't you stop this growing disagreement?"

Yeshua did not respond. He appeared deep in thought.

Judah and Thomas tried to stop the argument, but it had grown a momentum of its own, and, eventually had engulfed all of the Disciples, other than the five connected with the Prophet Jochanan and Qumr'an. It was only when the voices began to rise that Yeshua appeared to wake up. He rose to his full height and shouted,

"Stop this folly! Stop it at once!"

They calmed down, like the wind and waves had once done. They fell silent and looked ashamed. Yeshua continued with sustained vehemence.

"You should all be ashamed of yourselves. We are supposed to be seeking God's Kingdom, not Yeshua's. Remember I told you that true leadership involves love and service. It is not a test of leadership to see how much you can force a person to do. Remember the ultimate expression of love is that you are prepared to give up your life for your friends."

Or even your enemies.

The argument subsided. However, Yeshua could see that they had not changed. He had merely suppressed the argument, not resolved it. He tried to move them on.

"Remember that I told you to take nothing with you when I sent you out on mission?"

They nodded.

"Tonight is different. You may have to fight for your lives and freedom. When we go out, everyone must wear a sword."

Each disciple reached down to his feet, and sat back up again, sword in hand. Each waved his sword. Yeshua grunted.

"That's fine. Remember, what ever happens tonight, you must make your way back here. I think they will leave you alone once they have seized me. Do not attack them. However, if they attack you, defend yourself. Otherwise, keep out of the way. Do not waste your lives trying to save me. God will help me."

Always assuming God chooses to do so.

The meal resumed a more normal course, conversation became more general and quieter, where the disciples more or less reprised the more memorable events of the previous two years. Each had different memories. The commonest were the calming of the great storm, the apparent raising from the dead of the small girl, and the apparently miraculous feeding of the multitude.

Yeshua let the conversation run on, while he remained in serious conversation with Judah and Thomas.

"Do you remember, you two, what I said to you on the way back yesterday?"

"You told us to take care and not take any unnecessary risks," Thomas answered.

"Absolutely," Yeshua said sadly. "We do not know what is going to happen – but we must trust that God is in control and does know."

"He has strange methods," Judah commented savagely, "and does not seem to care about our hopes, fears and feelings!"

"He's the King of the World!" Yeshua pointed out. "What king do you know who considers such things?"

Thomas and Judah did not reply. Yeshua waited for a few moments, before turning to look straight into Thomas' eyes.

"Thomas," he said sternly, "be especially careful to keep clear of trouble. Remember, your job is to look after Judah. If this all goes wrong, he will be compromised."

Eventually, at nine o'clock, the Party shared the second and final loving cup and set out on the road to Gethsemane.

**

At about the same time, Pilate entered the courtyard of the Fortress where he saw that the soldiers had created a mini arena. They had provided chairs for Pilate and Trebonius, who sat in the middle of one side of the circle, with the soldiers spread out on either side of them, using their shields to create a barrier. The Prison detail brought in the two prisoners, both naked and armed with just a helmet, a blunt sword and a round shield.

The two men were made to stand in front of Pilate and Trebonius, raise their right hands in the Roman Imperial Salute, and repeat the Latin phrase that always began gladiatorial contests in Rome.

"Ave Caesar, moritori te salutat."

(Hail Caesar, those about to die greet you.)

The soldiers clapped and cheered. The two men were then made to stand opposite one another and, at a signal from Pilate, began to fight.

The soldiers cheered the fighters, laying bets with each other. The two men fought with a clash of steel. They circled each other warily, moving in and out, attacking and blocking attacks. The younger of the two was the more active and seemed to be getting on top. Several times he pressed the older man up against the impromptu barrier created by the soldiers' shields. Each time, the older man managed to slip free.

The bodies of both men were glistening with sweat and both were plainly becoming tired, when the younger man made what he hoped would be the final attack. He drove the older man back and back. Eventually, they reached the barrier, and all seemed over as the older man was pushed back over the shields, with his back arched backwards into the faces of the soldiers behind, while the younger raised his sword for the final stroke. As he did so, in his eagerness to finish things off, the younger man over extended himself, giving the older man the opportunity he was looking for. He kicked the younger man in the groin, and, as he buckled in shock, the older man used his leg to pull his opponent down. The younger man hit the parade ground, dropped his sword and shield, and was winded. He looked up to find the other's sword at his throat.

Pilate clapped loudly, proclaimed the older man the winner and placed a laurel wreath on his head. He announced that they had been entertained so well that both men deserved a reward and that, therefore, they would both be spared scourging next day. The two men bowed to the Procurator and Garrison Commander, and were escorted back to their cell for their last night alive.

Chapter 16

Betrayal

Jerusalem, April 32AD (Thursday 9 pm)

It was cold and dark in the empty streets after the light and warmth of the Upper Room. The silent street seemed unfriendly to the thirteen men as they left the courtyard. Each disciple gripped the hilt of his sword. They passed silently out of the gate onto the street outside and began to walk towards the city gates.

Obsessed by their own thoughts, fears and hopes, none of the men noticed the youth, dressed only in a white sheet, draped like a toga around his slim body, and sandals, who began to follow them at a distance, making sure he was not noticed. Keeping the group in his sight, he made use of every shadow and every building to avoid the possibility of being seen by the men he was following.

Talking quietly together, the thirteen men approached the city wall, surprised to find the gates open and unguarded.

Thomas, walking with Judah, at the head of the group, alongside Yeshua, remarked on this to the Leader.

"The gates are open and unwatched at this time of night. That's odd, isn't it Yeshua?"

"I've certainly never known it to happen before," Judah commented.

Yeshua nodded his agreement.

"It's certainly odd. I wander what it means?"

"You can never tell with the Romans," Thomas concluded. "They're not like us and they don't think

335

like us!"

Yeshua and Judah agreed, and they led the party into the open country beyond the gate. The road lay ahead of them, straight as a sword, shining white in the light of the full moon, hanging like a silver ball in a satin black sky. The square stones stood out sharply as the minute gaps between them were accentuated by the dark shadows created by the moonlight into pencil thin black lines. On either side of the empty road, cypress trees pointed upwards like black fingers, blacker than the black sky. Behind the walkers, stretching to either side, the black mass of the city wall, broken by the square tops of its towers and the smaller squares of the battlements on its ramparts, crawled up and down the lines of the hills. To their left, as they departed, was the great square block of the Temple, massively dark and brooding in the distance. The towers of the Fortress and the Palaces formed further shadows on the skyline of the darkened city.

The party instinctively closed up for their protection, and began the uphill climb towards the Mount of Olives, an hour's walk away.

Their pursuer delayed his passage of the gates in order to widen the gap between himself and his quarry. He continued to follow the group, still making use of every available cover, to avoid being seen, although such an effort became more difficult in open country. After about half an hour, he noticed that two men separated from the group, and began to come back. Fearful that he had been seen, despite his precautions, the young man hurriedly left the road, and hid behind a tree a few yards from the track. Once the two men, who did not appear to see him, hurried past him, he continued his pursuit of the rest of the group, but keeping off the road.

At the end of the meal, Yeshua had asked each man to ensure they took a sword with them. There was great excitement, as each disciple buckled a sword belt around his waist. Unfortunately, most had revealed their inexperience by failing to clean or sharpen their weapons. Only five men had weapons, which were actually usable. One was Simeon the Fisherman, who had cleaned and sharpened his sword more for something to do than anything else. The other four were Thomas, the other Simeon, Judas, and Judah, all of who would no more wear a rusty or unsharpened sword than they would try to drink an empty goblet of wine.

The men were all subdued, following the arguments at the dinner and Yeshua's rebuke of them. They also felt confused by what some saw as Yeshua's negative attitude to the future, which few understood, and about which none had the courage to ask.

The conversation was muted and muttered. Yeshua could not hear what was being said, but he guessed that his followers were still planning his first Cabinet, despite his earlier rebuke. He decided to ignore them. They made their way steadily up the hill, still followed by their silent and unnoticed stalker. Half way up the hill, Yeshua stopped. His followers stopped a few paces behind him. He spoke in low tones to Judah and Thomas.

"We are going to wait at Gethsemane. Bring the answer to me there Judah."

"Yes, Yeshua," Judah replied.

"Remember what I told you, Judah," Yeshua said urgently. "Whatever happens, do what you need to do to protect yourself. Don't worry about me." He paused. "And Thomas?"

"Yes, Lord?"

"Do not enter the Temple or the High Priest's House with Judah. Wait outside until he comes out. If he leaves with a party, join it as a volunteer. Look after Judah. Stay with him, whatever happens. Don't worry about me."

They both nodded their agreement. Yeshua embraced them both and wished them luck. They wished him luck in return and turned away to return to Jerusalem, not noticing the distant figure, who suddenly disappeared from the road ahead of them.

Yeshua spoke to the rest of his party.

"We are going to wait among the trees in Gethsemane for Judah and Thomas to return. It could be dangerous. Be prepared for anything."

"Don't worry Yeshua," Simeon the Fisherman said reassuringly, reaching for his sword and placing his arm, almost proprietarily around his Lord. "We will all fight for you, and I will die for you."

Yeshua pushed Simeon's arm away.

"Will you really, Cephas? If things go wrong tonight most of you will run away and, as for you, you will be so afraid that you'll deny you even know me!"

"How could you say that, Yeshua? We will all stick by you, come Hell or High Water! Isn't that so lads?"

They all shouted, "Yes!"

"We'll see," Yeshua said grimly. "Let's move on."

Ten minutes later they reached the top of the Mount of Olives and entered the Grove beside it. The Garden of Gethsemane rose up to a peak, marked by a clearing among the trees, while the road wound around the edge of the garden. Yeshua ordered his disciples to rest and pray among the trees, while he ascended the peak, where he sat, with his back against a rock, in prayer and meditation.

The young man who had followed them from the Upper Room also entered the Grove, and made his way to the outside of the clearing, from where he could watch both Yeshua and the road from the city, but without being seen by either Yeshua or his disciples. He was naked beneath his hastily adorned sheet, which he wore, Roman fashion, like a toga. However, he was Jewish and not Roman, and the 'toga' was only loosely wrapped around his body. Despite his youth, he shivered in the cold April night air. He wondered why he was there, and why he had not resisted the temptation to follow Yeshua's group out of the city. He also wondered why he had not spent a little more time and dressed properly. He shivered. "I'm just a fool," he thought, "an April night fool."

**

Judah and Thomas did not waste time on conversation or speculation about the outcome of their mission. They burnt up the distance on the road back to the city. They were both surprised to find the gates still open and unwatched. Thomas was suspicious.

"I'm afraid, Judah, that Yeshua's suspicion was correct. Something's wrong here."

"I think you're right, Thomas. All my soldier's instincts are on edge."

They passed through the gates. As they approached the dark mass of the Temple, Judah instructed Thomas to fall behind him, and stay out of sight, but follow wherever he went, because he felt it would not be the Temple. Thomas nodded and fell back a few paces as they approached the ramp that led to the entrance. At the bottom of the ramp he stopped and slipped into the shadows, watching Judah walk slowly, but purposefully up the slope. At the top three men met Judah. Two were Temple Guards, armed with spears and shields and the third was obviously an officer, armed with a sword.

The officer stepped forward to greet him.

"I assume you are Judah, is that right?" he asked.

"I am Judah Ish Kerioth, on a mission from Yeshua Bar Yusuf to the High Priest, the Lord Caiaphas. I understand I am expected."

The Officer noted the sword at Judah's waist. He saluted Judah, responding to an instinct he did not understand. He ordered the two guards to accompany Judah.

He explained,

"The Lord Caiaphas is waiting for you at his house. These two men will accompany you there."

Judah nodded in reply, and followed the two men back down the ramp.

They passed the unseen Thomas, who followed a few paces behind, unnoticed by the two guards. The walk through the empty streets to the High Priest's house took about half an hour. It was conducted in silence. They reached the house and were admitted through the gate by the guards. One of them appeared to recognise Judah and gave him a half salute. Judah waved this down with a motion of his hand. Thomas slipped into the shadows and waited.

The two guards escorted Judah through a courtyard filled with armed men, some of whom he recognised. As at the gate, he used his hand to wave away signs of recognition. He knew at once what was going to happen.

He made no comment, but followed his escort to the office of Caiaphas, who was sitting waiting for him. He noticed that there were another four armed men in the room, two at least of whom he knew. He instinctively reached for his sword. He half drew it out. A spear was levelled at him, and he heard a sword scrape in its scabbard. Judah stared at Caiaphas. He knew some of the men behind him would fight to defend him if he called on them, as would others in the courtyard outside. He knew that he could easily kill the lying High Priest. However, he also knew it was too soon to throw the whole Temple and city into bloody confusion.

Judah relaxed and pushed his sword back into its scabbard, raising his left hand in the unmistakable gesture of surrender, but keeping his right hand on his sword hilt.

Caiaphas looked tense as Judah entered the room, and became frightened when he saw him reach for and half draw his sword and the look of hatred, which Judah gave him. Caiaphas leapt to his feet, knocking over his chair, which fell to the floor with a clatter, and stood with his back to the wall. He only relaxed when he saw Judah push his sword back in its scabbard. Judah's initial reaction, however, raised doubts in his mind. He was obviously more than a simple, but misguided, disciple of Yeshua. He was a military man. Caiaphas thought Judah was one of the most dangerous men he had ever met. He expressed his doubts as a question.

"Who and what are you, Judah?"

"I am Judah Ish Kerioth."

"No, Man of Kerioth," Caiaphas responded, "I asked you who and what you are, not where you come from."

"I'm the Man of Kerioth. I'm the man who spared your life you treacherous bastard. I'm more important than most, and less so than some. I've come to hear your answer, Lord Caiaphas, although you've already shown me what you are, a lying, treacherous bastard, unworthy of your high office, whose mind was probably made up before you met us. You should be grateful to me, because I can tell you that some of the men in here and many of those outside, who you think are your men, are actually mine and would fight for me against you and your murderers if I called on them to do so."

Caiaphas suddenly felt cold with fear. He looked around at the men in the room, wondering who supported him and who supported Judah. All of them were expressionless. He wondered whether that support would extend to Yeshua. He was afraid, but realised that he dare not show his fear. His heart was pounding, but he spoke boldly, almost defiantly.

"My answer is a choice, Man of Kerioth. Die here in defence of your leader, or lead my men to him. If you refuse to hand your leader over, you'll die the death waiting for him. If you accept my offer of your life for his, and lead these men, and those outside, to him, I will pay you the reward for handing over a wanted fugitive to justice."

"Thirty silver pieces; the price of a slave!" Judah commented. "That's not much of a price for what may come to be seen as one of the greatest betrayals in history, Lord Caiaphas! The Traitor is you, but I know everyone else will think it was me."

"It's the price of your life, and it's all that's offered, Judah, Man of Kerioth. Take it, and live with your shame privately, or leave it, and die on the cross in shame, publicly."

Judah remembered Yeshua's last words to him.

"Remember what I told you, Judah. Whatever happens, do what you need to do to protect yourself. Don't worry about me."

"Your threats do not move me, Lord Caiaphas. I do not fear you or what others may say about me or do to me. I am a man under orders, just like the other men in this room.

"Unfortunately for him, and fortunately for you,

Yeshua Bar Abraham is not the man you claim he is. You know that, of course, having met him. That makes your treachery even worse. However, he has given me specific orders, and, because of those orders and not because of your threats, I will do as you ask."

Caiaphas smiled an evil smile.

"I thought so, Judah, so-called Man of Kerioth. You could have haggled with me over the price. However, every man has a price and yours is very low!"

Judah ignored the insult and followed the guards, who were too afraid of him to attempt to take his sword, out of the room. They joined the men in the courtyard, who formed up behind him and his escort. Judah led them out though the gate, and Thomas joined the group, unnoticed in the throng, many of whom were unknown to the others. Thomas was accepted as just another volunteer, as Judah and Yeshua intended. The arrest party marched noisily through the empty streets, coming to the city gates, and passing through them. Judah realised that the men in the party knew the gates would be open, and understood belatedly why they were left open. They passed through the gates and trod the path previously followed by Yeshua's group along the silver road

**

In the Garden, the doubts had returned to Yeshua. His instincts for survival urged him to leave the grove and escape, to return to the obscurity of Bethlehem or Capernaum and the trade of a carpenter. His sense of destiny held him there. He was fully aware of the risks and knew what lay ahead of him if he was arrested, as he fully expected to be. He began to feel that his death might have a meaning. If that was the case, he thought, then he could not escape his fate and should not try to do so. However, it was hard for him to do this. He realised that he was on a suicide mission. His instincts as a human being and the Torah told him that this was wrong. However, he knew he was going to do it.

"Father," he prayed aloud, "what you want me to do is hard. I do not want to do it. Please take the cup from me, if it's possible. If not, then may your will be done."

At that moment, a figure in white burst from the undergrowth behind him.

"Lord Yeshua," the young man shouted, "escape!" There are armed men on the road, coming from the city, not far from here."

Yeshua stood up wearily. He knew the moment for choice was past. The time for action had come. He smiled at the boy who had tried to save him.

"Marcus, my son, thank you for trying to save me from my destiny. However, I am a servant of God and the Movement. I have my role to perform and you have your role."

Yeshua looked into the distance, through Marcus.

"One day you will write down my story, Marcus. One day, in the future, in a city far from here."

Yeshua paused.

"But for now, take your own advice. Escape from here. Go back to the house in the city or in Bethany and wait. You have done your bit for the moment."

Yeshua embraced Marcus, before pushing him away.

Smiling sadly, he added,

"I now have to do mine."

Yeshua turned away and moved down the hill towards his disciples and the men he saw advancing along the road. Marcus, after a moment's hesitation, followed him.

Chapter 17

The Garden

Gethsemane, April 32AD (Friday Midnight)

On arrival at the Mount of Olives, the Commander of the arrest party ordered his men to form a line and light the torches they were carrying. The moon had served them well on the road, but, under the dark shadows cast by the trees, darker in contrast with the bright silver light of the April moon, some other form of lighting was needed. The Commander kept Judah beside him, in order to ensure he did not slip off and warn their quarry.

Thomas stayed behind with a small group who remained on the road, in case any of Yeshua's men tried to escape that way. Thomas was determined to avoid being part of the arrest of Yeshua or any of his followers. He knew that Judah was inevitably compromised, but hoped to avoid a similar fate, in order to continue his role with the Group on behalf of Qumr'an.

Once the torches were lit, the arrest party began to move into the Garden of Gethsemane, ascending the hill and disappearing under the trees.

Yeshua saw all this from the top, and went down to join his Disciples. Most were sleeping. He woke them, chiding them for their failure to keep awake. He studied each man carefully, and realised that, with the exception of the two Simeons, none of them were in any condition to offer resistance.

"So, you couldn't even stay awake, despite all my warnings," Yeshua said sorrowfully. "If you cannot stay awake for me now, how will you stay awake for my return?"

No one understood this question and there was no time to ask. Simeon the fisherman mumbled an apology for them all.

Yeshua smiled sadly.

"You've often managed to stay awake during the long hours of the night fishing, Cephas. Never mind, your hour will come. I'm sure of that. When it does, remember this night and make your atonement. Let's go down to meet the treacherous bastards who have come to arrest me. Don't try to intervene. There are too many and you can't succeed. Don't be stupid. Escape while they are concerned with me. Make your way back to the house in Jerusalem and wait on events there. After Passover go back to Galilee. It may be that I will meet you there."

Yeshua led the men down the slope towards the lights moving in a ragged line of fire up towards them. Marcus followed just behind them. The lights flowed up the slope towards them, and the two parties came together half way up the slope. Judah stepped forward and embraced Yeshua. He whispered to him.

"The bastards betrayed us as you expected, Yeshua. Caiaphas gave me a choice between death and leading his men here. I did as you said, and brought them."

"Yours was the hard choice, Judah, and you made the right one, although you will pay dearly for it, just as I will. Remember, you are important to the Movement. Go back to Qumr'an and take up your new duties."

Judah nodded, and the two separated.

Yeshua walked towards the Commander of the Party, which he could see consisted of a few regular Temple Guards, who stood out because of their uniforms and discipline, supplemented by a mass of thugs, armed with anything they could lay their hands

346

on. He spoke to the Officer in command.

"Who are you looking for?"

"Yeshua Bar Yusuf," the Officer replied.

"So you think you need a crowd of thugs and ruffians to arrest me!" Yeshua spoke scornfully.

"Here I am, I'm not even armed! Take me."

The crowd were surprised and a little afraid by his calmness. They had all heard inflated stories of his magical powers, and half expected him to raise his hands and blast them away. They took two steps away from him.

Simeon, the fisherman, seeing their hesitation, drew his sword and charged the crowd, hacking off the ear of one of the men. The injured man screamed and placed his hand to his damaged ear, in an attempt to staunch the sudden flow of blood. Yeshua, angry at Simeon's disobedience, ordered him to stop, and come back. Simeon turned around, sheaved his sword, and then all ten disciples retreated into the surrounding trees.

Simeon made his way around the line of men, and descended to the edge of the road.

Marcus remained hidden in the nearby trees.

Angered by the attack on one of their number, and emboldened by the apparent flight of the disciples, the High Priest's men encircled Yeshua. Two men approached him from behind, seized his arms and pinioned them behind his back, while a third bound his wrists. A fourth, bold now Yeshua could not use his hands to cast a spell on him, came up and struck him across the face.

"So you're a prophet, you charlatan!" he snarled. "Do your work then - prophesy. What's my name?"

Yeshua smiled at him, pityingly.

Judah turned to the Officer in command.

"There's no need for that," he snapped. "Tell your

men to leave your prisoner alone. You and I both know what his fate is likely to be. Don't let them make it any worse."

The officer agreed, and ordered his men to take Yeshua away, but to treat him with respect.

He spoke to the man who had assaulted Yeshua.

"Since you have taken the right to administer justice on yourself, stay here with four of your colleagues and search the wood for the rest of them. I particularly want that bastard with the sword. Keep a couple of the professionals to give you back up."

Yeshua was hustled down to the road, where the party reassembled and began its march back to the city. The injured man was treated, and his bleeding head bandaged. Yeshua was placed under the control of two of the Temple Guards, and kept in the middle. No longer important, Judah slipped back to join Thomas, towards the rear, who muttered to him,

"So it's done!"

Judah described what had happened, grimly, adding,

"I suspect that Cephas may do something stupid, and we may have to rescue him before we leave."

Thomas nodded, and the two continued their journey in silence, anxious to avoid attracting attention from the thuggish element of the High Priest's force.

Simeon, meanwhile, quietly joined the rear of the party, unnoticed and unrecognised by the rest. In this way, the party made its way towards the city.

**

The search party left behind in the Garden spread out and began to search the trees beyond the arrest site.

One of the guards quickly spotted Marcus, conspicuous in his white sheet. He attempted to seize the boy, but only succeeded in grabbing the sheet.

Marcus slipped out of it, and ran away naked further into the trees.

The other Simeon took control of the remaining eight disciples. When he became aware that they were being hunted, he gathered them together and ordered them to lie in ambush beside one of the paths. The leader of the small group of hunters carelessly followed the path, and fell into their trap. Matthaus stepped out of the path to attract the man's attention. The man saw the disciple draw his sword. He drew his own sword and moved towards him, but did not get very far before he felt a presence behind him. An arm came across his chest, pinioning his arms. The sharp edge of a sword sliced across his throat. The last thing he felt, as his life began to drain from his severed throat was the hard push of a knee in his back, which sent his body crashing to the ground, where he twitched his life away.

Simeon took the man's sword and threw it to Matthaus.

"That will teach you not to attack a helpless prisoner," Simeon snarled at the dying man.

Before Simeon and Matthaus could go back into hiding, the two Temple Guards appeared. Seeing the two disciples, standing with drawn swords, and the body of the High Priest's man, still twisting in his death throes on the ground, they took up a defensive posture; their round shields on their arms and their spears pointing towards the two disciples.

Simeon laughed with relief.

"Well done Josiah," he said. "That's just the way it should be done. Just the way I trained you."

Simeon paused, suddenly doubtful.

"It is Josiah isn't it?"

One of the guards laughed.

"It's Simeon, isn't it?" he replied.

Simeon nodded. The guard turned to his companion.

"Benaiah, This is the bastard who trained me. He's the most black-hearted Sergeant you'll ever know. But, by God is he good! He's the best in the business."

He threw down his shield and spear and came over to embrace, first Simeon and then a puzzled Matthaus. Simeon explained to Matthaus.

"Many of the Temple Guards were trained at Qumr'an, and sent to the Temple, where they can legally bear arms. The Temple is our second major base. Josiah was one of the most promising of our recruits."

He turned to the guard.

"It's good to see you, but a sad reason."

"There's no time for talking," Josiah said. "There are four more thugs to deal with. Leave them to us. You get your men together."

He paused, called his friend over, and handed Simeon a white sheet.

"There's a naked kid around here somewhere. He's one of yours I think. Find him, and put this back on him. Tell him to dress properly if he's going out at night in future. Be ready for when we return."

"That'll have to be Marcus," Simeon replied. "I guess he slipped out of the house after we left and followed us, the stupid boy. We'll find him, and have him ready. Meet us back here."

The guards left and began a search of the Garden for the High Priest's men, while Simeon organised the remaining disciples into pairs in order to search for Marcus. Jochanan and Jacob found him after a brief search. They teased him for his nakedness, both then, and for a long time afterwards. They brought him back to Simeon, who made him cover himself with the sheet and recalled the rest of the Disciples.

The success of the guards was indicated by four cries in the darkness, as they cut down the four remaining thugs one after the other.

Guards and disciples rejoined each other at the ambush site. The guards carried four additional swords, which they gave to Simeon, who, in turn, gave one to Philip, one to Thaddeus, one to Andreas and one to Jochanan to replace their blunt and rusty blades.

"You're safe now," Josiah said. "All four are dead."

"We heard the cries," Simeon commented. "Did they give any trouble?"

"None at all," Benaiah said contemptuously. "They were amateurs, easily disposed off."

Simeon turned around. He looked for Marcus and introduced him to Josiah.

"This is Marcus, the boy you stripped."

Marcus looked embarrassed. Josiah studied the boy, noting how young he was. He smiled in a kindly manner.

"I'm glad you're all right, Marcus. Just be careful and dress properly if you're going out at night in future. You could catch cold."

Josiah and Simeon bent down over the dead body of the first thug, and stripped him. Simeon gave the man's dark coloured cloak to Marcus, and told him to wear it over his white sheet. A grateful Marcus did as he was told, and felt the warmth immediately.

"What do you propose to do now?" Josiah asked Simeon.

"To return to the City. That's what we were ordered to do. That's what we will do if at all possible."

"We will lead you," Josiah said. "The gates are open and unwatched tonight, but even if there are guards there now, they will assume we are the rest of the High Priest's party, returning after searching the Garden. Once inside, we will go to the High Priest's house and report that you escaped after killing five of his men, and you can go wherever you need to go."

Simeon agreed, and the combined party left the Garden. Silence fell over the Garden, except for the hooting of an owl and the rustle of the night animals. Only the five bodies, stripped of clothing, weapons, and any means of identification, spoke of the dramatic events that had so recently happened there.

Chapter 18

Friday Morning

Jerusalem, April 32AD (Friday 3 am)

The journey back to the city was a hurried one. The Commander was anxious to return quickly and hand his prisoner over for safekeeping. Speech was discouraged and the speed was swift. The only sounds were the clatter of swords and spears against shields, the thud of boots on Roman paving stones, the sound of heavy breathing, the whisper of the wind, and the call of the owls and nighthawks out hunting for prey.

The three disciples, each for different reasons, were grateful for the enforced silence. Judah, realising his cover was blown among the Judaean and, possibly, the Roman, authorities, as well as being totally compromised among the followers of Yeshua, was trying to contemplate a life running a community and training recruits in the Judaean wilderness. Thomas was wondering how to carry out his instructions from Yeshua to protect both Judah and Simeon, realising that it was impossible that those two would ever be able to work together again. Simeon was wondering how and why he had got himself into the situation he was in and how he could get out of it.

Yeshua was simply praying for strength to endure the pain of the tortures he knew were awaiting him, and trying to avoid falling when he received the occasional shoves in the back from his captors who felt he was walking too slowly.

They passed though the open gates, the clatter of their boots and equipment echoing in the confined space of the tunnel. The Commander spoke to two of the Temple Guards.

"Take the prisoner to the Antonia. Hand him over to the guards on duty, and tell them this is the man the Lord Caiaphas told Pilate he would send him. Then join us at the High Priest's House. Report to me there."

The guards saluted, and pushed Yeshua out of the line. They disappeared into the darkness of a side street as the rest of the party marched past them. Very few saw them leave the column. Once the column had passed, the two guards brought Yeshua back out and retraced their steps for a short distance, before heading towards the Temple. They passed around its base, across the vast courtyard in front of the Antonia known as the Place of Judgement, where the Procurator came out to stand on a raised platform to meet the people and announce decisions, to the main entrance of the fortress, between two round Roman battlemented towers.

Three soldiers stood at the entrance. Two were plainly guards, in full combat uniform. The third was also a soldier, who was wearing his gladius, the short Roman sword, but was otherwise simply wearing the red soldier's under tunic and kilt. It was he who came forward to receive the prisoner. He asked no questions and required no explanation. It was obvious to the Temple Guards that they were expected and their task was already known. Quintus, the third soldier, nodded to the two Temple Guards, took custody of Yeshua, and dismissed them. They nodded back, acknowledged the Roman guards on duty, and began their route back to the High Priest's house.

Quintus escorted the bound Yeshua to the fortress gates, which opened in front of them and closed behind them. They crossed a courtyard beyond, entered through another door, and climbed down an apparently

354

never-ending winding staircase. Quintus was careful to ensure that his prisoner, hampered as he was by having his wrists bound behind his back, did not fall. Yeshua noticed that flaring torches at regular intervals lighted the darkness.

Eventually, they came out into a large, open paved area, also lit by torches. Above, the stone ceiling was held up by stone columns, each of which had two rings hanging from chains, about a foot above average male head height. He also saw three other Roman soldiers, similarly dressed to the one escorting him. One spoke cheerfully to his escort.

"So that's the one we're expecting is it, Quintus?"

Quintus nodded.

"He's a bit different from the others," the man observed.

"He'll die just like the others," Quintus remarked, "and probably squeal like them too. It's not how they are when they come in. It's how they are when they go out!"

"Do you want any help with him?"

"I don't know," Quintus replied. He turned to his prisoner, speaking in Aramaic, which he had learnt from dealing with so many Jewish prisoners.. "You will be nice and cooperate, won't you my pet?"

Yeshua realised he had no choice. He nodded.

"That's good," Quintus said, untying Yeshua's wrists.

Yeshua rubbed the life back into them and then stood, irresolute, awaiting the next order. Quintus let him wait, watching as his prisoner restored the circulation in his wrists. Eventually he smiled.

"Are you comfortable now?" he asked kindly.

Yeshua nodded.

"Good," Quintus replied pleasantly. "Now strip naked and stand against that column with your hands above your head."

Yeshua looked startled and did not respond. Quintus picked up a whip and cracked it menacingly in the air.

"Let's take it a step at a time. Kick off your sandals."

Yeshua kicked his sandals towards Quintus, who bent down and picked them up. He threw them to one of his companions, who caught them.

"Now remove your outer coat and give it to Festus."

The coat was a long, open fronted cloth garment, such as all male Jews wore. It was brown, but seemed darker in the half-light of the torches. Yeshua removed it, folded it, and handed it to one of the guards.

Quintus smiled encouragingly.

"That's better! Now take off that tunic you're wearing and give it to me."

The white tunic was long, created from a single woven strip of linen. It reached down to Yeshua's ankles and covered his arms to his wrists. Yeshua bent down and pulled it up and over his head, before folding it neatly and passing it to Quintus, who smiled and bowed ironically.

"Thank you, kind sir! Now, place your hands on your head and stand facing me."

Yeshua stood; dressed only in a loincloth, which he knew, would shortly be taken from him, as Quintus studied his muscular, but lean and fit body. Yeshua was nearly six feet tall was well built, browned by months in the sun and toned by exercise and hard work. Quintus moved around him. He was two inches shorter than Yeshua and stouter. He drank in his image of Yeshua's body for five minutes, as Yeshua became increasingly uncomfortable at the man's expression. He felt his member growing hard under the scrutiny, and saw that Quintus had noticed it as well. Quintus began to grin and Yeshua suddenly realised to his horror, that

356

he was going to be raped, and that he had not prepared for rape in his mind at all.

"Stand with your back to the column and raise your hands above your head."

Yeshua moved back and felt the cold of the marble, oddly comfortable, against his back. He raised his arms and felt two hands, obviously from the other guards, grasp them and place them within the metal rings he had seen earlier. He heard two clicks and knew he was secured against the column and unable to resist anything that Quintus intended doing to him. He recognised that Quintus was the main man down here.

"Thanks lads," Quintus said. "I can take it from here."

The other soldiers wished him good night and left them alone.

Quintus stepped forward, so that his body touched that of Yeshua and began slowly to untie Yeshua's loincloth.

**

The remainder of the Priestly party made their way to the High Priest's house. Their mood had changed. Now the prisoner was beyond chance of help, they began to chant hymns and psalms of victory. Even the man injured by Simeon looked happier. In this way they came to the High Priest's house. All except Thomas went inside, and settled down around a fire in the main courtyard, where warm wine and food were waiting for them.

Thomas slipped away from the party unnoticed as it made its way through the streets, and followed at a short distance. He slipped into the darkness of the shadows caused by the houses opposite in the bright moonlight and watched the entrance of the High

Priest's house, waiting for Judah to reappear.

Simeon entered the courtyard and sat by the fire, warming his hands and sharing the food and wine, apparently oblivious to the risk.

The Commander of the party took Judah and went in to report to Caiaphas.

"The traitor and blasphemer, Yeshua Bar Yusuf, is now under Roman control, Lord Caiaphas. He made no resistance. One of his disciples tried to stop us. He injured Cleopas but the blasphemer stopped him."

"Is Cleopas alright?" Caiaphas asked anxiously.

"He lost an ear Lord Caiaphas," the Commander said matter of factly.

"I left seven men to scour the wood in an attempt to capture his assailant and others of the band if possible. You can expect them later."

"Did this man," pointing at Judah, "do his job properly?"

"Yes, Lord Caiaphas. I found no fault in him."

"Excellent," Caiaphas commented, turning towards Judah and picking up a purse full of coins.

"Thirty pieces of silver was, I think, the price of your treachery to your Master, Man of Kerioth."

Judah said and did nothing. Caiaphas threw the purse at him, and Judah caught it.

"Take it. You've earned it. I should express the Temple's gratitude, but instead I shall give you twenty-four hours to leave Jerusalem. If you are still in the city after the Sabbath, I shall inform Pilate that you are a leading member of the Rebel Movement. He has plenty of wood and can always make another cross."

"I understand you perfectly, High Priest," Judah replied. "I promise that you will not find me in this city for one minute longer than I need to be. I promise too, that next time we meet, I shall kill you."

Judah turned away, hand on sword, and walked out

of the room, not waiting to be dismissed. The Commander thought about trying to stop him, but thought better of it when he saw Judah's face. Caiaphas watched Judah leave without comment, turned back to his Commander, thanked him, and dismissed him, before retiring to his bedroom to sleep.

Judah returned to the Courtyard. He was only just in time, because one of the arresting party had come to stand beside Simeon. He spoke to him, and received a grunted reply. That was a mistake, because Simeon had an unmistakable Galilean accent. The man looked closely at him, and challenged him.

"You're one of them. I recognise your accent."

Simeon turned around angrily.

"Can't a man warm himself in this wretched place without being asked stupid questions? Of course I'm not one of them! Would I be so stupid as to come here if I was?"

"Yes you are," a second man, drawn by the exchange, said. "I saw you in the Garden. You're the man with the sword. The one they're out there looking for."

"Nonsense," Simeon said. "You've got the wrong man. I wasn't even there. I was in the street when you came back and followed you in here out of curiosity."

By now a crowd surrounded Simeon. A further man challenged him and he was denying it, when Judah returned. He summed the situation up in a glance. Pushing his way through the crowd, Judah reached Simeon's side. He drew his sword, and the crowd fell silent and moved back. Judah looked at them and remembered the words Yeshua had used at the conference with the High Priest and the effect they had.

"That's better!" he began. "None of you know me, but I am Judah, the new Bar Abbas."

He noticed the shock on a number of faces. This

359

was replaced by fear and most of the men who had surrounded Simeon began to edge away.

"You're right to move away," Judah continued. "You should know that this man is important to the Movement and I would not like to count the number of days left to any man who harms him. The Movement has long arms, as you all know, reaching even into this courtyard."

More moved away, until only the original two men were left.

The second man spoke.

"I am a cousin of the man this man injured, Judah Bar Abbas. By law I could demand to have his ear cut off. Instead I will accept compensation for the injury on his behalf."

"That's fair," Judah agreed.

He handed the purse over to him.

"Here's thirty silver pieces. Will they do?"

The man nodded, and Judah pulled Simeon away from the fire and propelled him out of the Courtyard.

"Are you mad?" he hissed, once they were safe. "What do you think you were doing here?"

"Looking for you. I intend to cut your traitorous heart out and throw it to the dogs, like Elijah did with Jezebel's head."

Judah smiled thinly.

"I know you and the others must think like that Simeon. However, it isn't what it seems. Yeshua used me to find out the answer to his challenge to Caiaphas to step down. We both knew Caiaphas might betray us. Yeshua told me to save myself if that happened - and that's exactly what happened. I had a choice of standing by him and dying or doing as they asked, which, incidentally is also what Yeshua asked me to do. I did as they asked. My choices were similar to yours. The choice you have just made to deny Yeshua was

360

only different in degree from mine."

Simeon turned away from him.

"So you say. Even Satan, when he appeared to Eve, looked fair and beautiful. To me you are, and will always be, a traitor, and the worst of traitors. Don't bother to follow me. You will find the door barred against you if you attempt to come to the house. Go and hang yourself. There's nothing left for you here."

Simeon stormed off into the night.

**

Yeshua was now naked and chained to the column, facing it, helpless to resist Quintus's probing hands. He explored every facet of his back, stroking his behind tenderly, and feeling around for his stiffening penis. He reached down for his whip and tenderly, almost caressingly, stroked his back with it several times. He turned Yeshua around to face him.

"My, my," he said in Aramaic. "You <u>are</u> a big boy, and you <u>do</u> like this don't you?"

Quintus looked up and stared at Yeshua's untidy beard and over-long hair, and tut-tutted.

"You've really not been taking care of yourself young Yeshua."

He went to the side and fetched a razor and a pair of scissors, before spending about thirty minutes shaving off Yeshua's beard and cutting his hair to shoulder length.

"That's much better," he murmured. "Have a drink, my darling."

He placed a goblet of red wine, which he had mixed with an aphrodisiac, to Yeshua's lips. Yeshua tried to refuse to drink the wine.

"I'm sorry," he said. "I took a vow."

Quintus did not answer; he simply lowered his right

hand, and punched Yeshua hard in the stomach twice. Yeshua gasped in surprise and pain. Quintus smiled and poured the wine down his throat. Yeshua drank unwillingly, but felt a lot better as the warmth flowed through his body.

Yeshua felt unable to resist Quintus when he raped him, despite the shock and pain of his entry, or the other things he did to him. He ignored the repeated whipping too, and, to his shame, accepted being fondled by the Jailor. The torture continued for most of the night, until Quintus tired of his new toy. Then he left Yeshua alone, still hanging from his chains for what remained of the night.

Yeshua tried to forget his condition and concentrate on God. He failed, as he could only think of his shame at his nakedness and the fact that he had allowed Quintus to rape him. He remembered his words to Marcus about Pilate.

It's easy to tell someone else that they are not responsible and that God knows it. Why is it so difficult for me to accept it?

He heard again his inner voice answer.

It's more difficult because it is you – but you have done nothing wrong. You trust God – then really trust Him. You will need to have faith in Him and yourself over the next few hours.

That's all very well – but I have nothing to hang on to – not even my clothes. Quintus has removed them, and he will not return them. I will be naked until I die. That is shameful.

Do not call shameful anything that God has created. He created you and gave you a body before you covered it with clothes. What else do you need? Trust God – He knows what you need. He will carry you through.

Yeshua felt calmer and eventually he dozed off,

still suspended against the pillar.

**

The second group returned from the Garden and entered the city over an hour after the first group. They too were very quiet. They separated just inside the entrance, and went their separate ways.

The disciples returned to the Upper Room and reported the disaster to the rest of the Party - Yeshua under arrest; Judah a traitor; and Thomas and Simeon missing. There was complete shock among those who had remained behind. Jacob took control of the situation. He halted the wailing among the women and ordered the gates to be shut and locked. No one was to leave until daylight, but two men were left on guard in case either of the two missing disciples returned. He ordered that Judah, if he dared to appear, should be turned away.

**

Josiah and his friend reported to the unit Commander.

"I regret, Sir, that five of the party, including the leader, were ambushed and killed by the rebels. Benaiah and I looked for the rebels. We saw no sign of them, so we assume they escaped. I suggest that you ask the High Priest to ask the Governor to look out for them."

"Thank you Josiah," the Commander replied grimly. "What's done is done. I suggest we just leave the rebels. Where are the bodies?"

"We found the bodies, naked and with all possessions and weapons removed. They are still there."

The Commander thanked them, and told them he would send a detachment to clear up and bury the bodies in the morning. Then he dismissed them, told them to get some food and wine before going off duty and getting some sleep.

**

Shortly afterwards, Simeon banged on the gate of the house with the Upper Room. A relieved Matthaus let him in. He reported that Yeshua had been handed over to the Romans and it was expected he would be crucified in the morning. This caused consternation among the group, who had hoped that, somehow, Yeshua would escape. There was a lot of discussion, recrimination and debate, but no conclusion was reached as to what could be done.

(There was nothing that could be done. How could thirty men face a Roman Legion?)

**

Thomas emerged from the darkness to join Judah. Judah recounted his conversations with Caiaphas and Simeon as they walked away from the High Priest's house towards the City wall. They passed through the open gates, and followed the base of the wall towards the north. They walked together, deep in thought, wordless, but swiftly, for several hours, following the line of the wall, looming blackly above them. Behind them the city and the temple slept. Eventually they came to the road, which lead east from the city, towards the Dead Sea, the Wilderness of Judaea and the settlement of Qumr'an. Judah looked around for a last look back at the city he loved, as the sun rose, glowing pink and beautiful in the rays of the early morning sun. He stood and stared for five full minutes, before brushing away a tear, sighing deeply, and turning away.

He never looked back as the city slipped slowly down the skyline behind them. It was to be many years before he returned.

**

As the sun began to rise on the departing figures of Judah and Thomas, Quintus shaved, dressed in his full armour, and went to report to Tribune Lucius Trebonius. He assured him that the new prisoner was safe below and that Pilate's orders had been carried out to the letter. Trebonius thanked him and said that he had never doubted that Quintus would do exactly what was expected of him.

Chapter 19

Failure

Jerusalem, April 32AD (Friday 6am)

Friday morning dawned bright and dry. It promised to be yet another hot and sunny day, the harbinger of a bright and sunny Festival weekend. There was no hint of the surprises the next three days would bring. Most of those waking up that morning in Jerusalem expected nothing more than the crush in the markets to buy the food needed for the festival and the other crush, in the Temple, for the sacrifices of the sheep needed for that afternoon. Men, women and children approached the day with a feeling of nervous excitement.

At the Antonia, Pilate, who did know that the day was unusual, rose, bathed and dressed early. His slaves served him breakfast, and he was in his office as the sun rose.

In one of his prisons, nearby, the surviving members of the family of Marcus and Julia were also early risers. They were awakened by their jailors, ordered to wash and dress, fed, and taken from their cells, under escort, to the Antonia, where they were held, isolated, in a room, awaiting the Procurator's attention. Everyone in the family was afraid. They saw nothing good in this sudden move, and expected to be sold to a slave trader and taken away; a fate with which they had often been threatened. Instead of this, they were ignored, and they feared to ask what was going to happen to them. The confused adults tried to comfort the frightened children.

Trebonius, having received the report from Quintus, made his way to Pilate's office. He saluted the

366

Governor, who had arrived, dressed in tunic and toga. Trebonius noticed the laurel wreath, which Pilate used to impress his authority on his subjects, lying on his desk, beside his usual wine bottle. He offered Trebonius a glass, and, on acceptance, poured wine for him. He received Trebonius's routine morning report, supplemented with the special report from Quintus, with satisfaction, saying that he would go down when he heard that everything was set up the way he wanted.

"Now, Lucius" Pilate said, leaning forward to make his point. "I want you to take an appropriate escort and go to the Palace of the Tetrarch Herod Antipas. Tell him that I wish to send him the prisoner Yeshua Bar Yusuf to deal with in an appropriate and discrete manner, much as he did in the case of Jochanan earlier. He has challenged Caiaphas's right to be High Priest, saying he should be High Priest himself, and so Caiaphas feels he cannot deal with his case. I do not really wish to involve myself with something that concerns the complexity of Jewish law, which is enough to drive any sensible person mad. Herod is the answer to all our problems. Tell him, if he agrees, I will argue the case for his being declared King before the Divine Tiberius."

Trebonius saluted and left the office.

$$**$$

In the torture chamber, Quintus and his companions had been busy. All three prisoners had been awakened, freed from their chains and given a light meal and water. Each had been ordered to wash each other. They were forbidden to talk. Once the four men thought they were presentable, Quintus fetched a stool and ordered Yeshua to sit on it. He found a red soldier's cloak and placed it over Yeshua's shoulders, securing it by the clasp, but taking the opportunity provided by making the cloak straight to stroke Yeshua's body once again. Quintus grinned at Yeshua.

"Do you still like this?" he asked.

Yeshua said nothing.

Another soldier brought a circlet made from thorns, which were arranged to form an imitation of the imperial crown, with its sun's rays. Quintus placed this on Yeshua's head, drawing some blood where the thorns pricked the skin. Despite his previous intentions, Yeshua winced as the thorns pricked his skin. He remembered Judah's words.

"You will either gain a crown or a cross – and the cross is more likely."

Well, Judah, I have the crown – rather different from the one we envisaged. Soon, now, I will also have the cross. Is there anything else I have to do for God?

Love your enemies. Die for your enemies. Make your enemies your friends.

The words came back to him.

Quintus is your enemy. Die for him. Make him your friend.

Yeshua looked into the eyes of Quintus as he forced the crown onto his brow. Quintus, unwillingly, looked back. They locked eyes. Quintus, to his surprise, saw only strength and determination in the eyes of Yeshua.

How can this be? Quintus thought. *The man's just a Jew. He should be guilt-ridden by what I made him do last night. How can he be so calm and sure about his fate? He will be dead soon, in horrible circumstances.*

Yeshua saw the doubt appear in Quintus' eyes. Yeshua said nothing, but he continued to hold the jailor's gaze, until, with an obvious effort, Quintus broke away. He turned his back on the prisoners and left the rest of the organisation of the tableau to his three colleagues.

The third and fourth jailors placed a large stone in one of Yeshua's hands, representing the imperial orb, and a long stick in the other, representing the imperial sceptre. The other two prisoners were shackled to Yeshua's wrists by short chains. Each man was made to stand, with a Roman helmet on his head, a blunt spear in his hand, and a blunt sword, in a scabbard, hanging from his waist. Otherwise, each man was naked. Once the four jailors were convinced that the tableau was perfect, Quintus went to fetch Pilate.

Pilate entered the dungeon about fifteen silent minutes later. He approached the tableau, right arm outstretched for the traditional December greeting. "Io Saturnalia!" in honour of the festival where slaves became masters for the day and masters became slaves. He followed this with an ironic bow and the words "Ave Maiesta!" (Hail Majesty) to Yeshua. The three prisoners, reluctant stars in this imperial drama, said nothing. Pilate called for a stool, and sat down opposite Yeshua. He spoke in a more friendly, almost solicitous, tone.

"You are Yeshua Bar Yusuf or possibly Yeshua Bar Abraham?"

"Yes, Excellency."

"I hope my men treated you well."

"I have no complaints, Excellency," Yeshua replied, after a short pause.

"We have met once before, I think," Pilate observed.

"Yes, Excellency," Yeshua replied. "On the road near Bethlehem, before all this began."

"That's what I remember too. I thought then that you were different. I have not been wrong. I'm not often wrong in my judgement of men."

Yeshua was silent. Pilate continued.

"You seem to have angered the High Priest, the Lord Caiaphas. He wants you dead, but he wants me to kill you. What have you done to anger him?"

"I told him I am the rightful High Priest and invited him to step down from his office in my favour," Yeshua replied.

"And are you the rightful High Priest?"

"I am a direct descendent of the High Priest Aaron, the brother of Moses."

Pilate paused at this. He smiled, before adding,

"I heard that you also believe that you should replace Philip and Antipas, and that Tiberius will allow you to become king of this sub province as well. On what basis do you think the Jews will accept you as both priest and king?"

"Three reasons Excellency. The first is that I'm Jewish, and the rest of you aren't. The second is that I am descended from my father from John Hyrcanus and the Hasmonean Priest Kings. The third is that I am also descended from my mother from the ancient royal family of David. No one has a better claim to the throne than I do, unless it is my brothers."

"And why do you think the Divine Tiberius will allow it?"

"Because it is cheaper, safer and more expedient for him than trying to retain Roman troops here, which the people hate."

"You may be right, Yeshua, but we will never know, because, sadly, one way or another, you are going to die today – as are you all" (looking at the other two).

Pilate smiled sadly.

"I have no choice in this. I have to preserve order. I have a feeling that all three of you are victims, tools of a much bigger organisation. I suspect that this stretches into the Temple, but I cannot prove it. If I could prove it, I would smash the priesthood, destroy the Temple, and crucify Caiaphas and his father-in-law instead of you. Unfortunately I can't prove it, and so it's you three who must die, as examples to the nation."

Pilate paused.

"Incidentally, did you call for the Jews not to pay the Temple Tax?"

"No, Excellency," Yeshua answered simply.

Pilate stood up.

"I'm very glad of that. I didn't think you had. Because of your answer, I won't seek your followers. Also, I won't order you to be scourged."

He smiled.

"The other two have already earned that favour."

Pilate turned to the four jailors.

"Leave them as they are and bring them out before the Judgement Seat if and when I give the order."

Pilate left and returned to his office.

**

Caiaphas left his house to make his way to the Temple soon after the last of his men left the dirty and disordered courtyard, littered with the debris of food, empty wineskins and the other evidence of large scale human occupation. He knew that it was going to be a very busy day. He needed to be on the spot all day until the evening sacrifices were made. He felt that he could rely on Pilate to do his duty. However, before long, people came to him to say that rumours were sweeping the city and people were beginning to gather outside the Judgement Seat. Caiaphas sent a number of junior priests to the Antonia, in order to orchestrate the crowds.

**

At the same time, Nicodemus, without his Phylactery

and fringe, went to the Palace to see Pilate. He spoke to the duty officer, explained whom he was, and was taken to the Procurator's office. Pilate offered him a seat and wine. He accepted the seat and refused the wine.

Pilate sipped his own wine, leaned on his desk, and asked what he could do for him.

"I want you to spare Yeshua Bar Yusuf's life, Excellency," Nicodemus said simply.

"Why should I do that Brother Nicodemus?" Pilate asked.

"Your very Roman concern for justice, Excellency," Nicodemus answered.

"So you don't accept that the charges brought against him have any foundation?"

"None whatsoever, Excellency!" Nicodemus said vehemently, using his hands to emphasise the point. "Caiaphas is afraid of losing his position and the income and power which it brings. He is not concerned about the nation. He's concerned about himself."

"That's true," Pilate conceded. "I agree that Caiaphas is playing both ends against the middle. I wish I could prove it, but I can't."

"We all need to work together in this situation, I agree, Excellency. Can you save Yeshua?"

Pilate did not answer immediately. Nicodemus had, unwittingly, hit on a weak spot, if it was a weak spot – Pilate's sense of justice. Eventually he responded.

"I know the man is an innocent victim of the machinations of others, Brother Nicodemus, and, as one trained in the Roman courts, I find it hard to go against the demands of justice. However, there is another issue here – that of public order. For that reason, I fear Yeshua has to be executed, Brother Nicodemus, but I promise you I will do what I can for him. Just be sure to be at Golgotha. Incidentally, you're not the only person, who has pleaded for him."

Pilate rose to his feet. Nicodemus did the same.

"You should come to me to ask for his body for burial as soon as he dies. Don't waste any time. I will give you formal written authority to take it. That's the best I can do. Ask the guard outside to call Centurion Julius to come here for instructions."

Nicodemus bowed to the Procurator, who came round his desk, and showed his visitor out of the office. A few minutes later, the Centurion arrived. He spent fifteen minutes with the Procurator and then left, a grim smile on his face, to organise an execution, a duty he hated.

**

Tribune Lucius Trebonius, escorted by four cavalrymen, rode to Herod's Palace on the northern side of the city. Three power centres dominated Jerusalem. The Temple and the Roman fortress dominated the North and West. Herod's Palace dominated the East. Only the southern part, the lower city, remained un-cowed. It was here that the poorest lived in small one-storied buildings in the narrow crowded streets. The streets between the power centres were wider than the others. It was along one of these that Trebonius rode. At the entrance to Herod's Palace, he dismounted and handed the reins of his horse to one of the soldiers. His men dismounted, tethered their horses, and waited in the courtyard.

Trebonius was escorted to the Tetrarch's office. Herod welcomed him cordially, and offered him a chair. Trebonius removed his helmet, revealing cropped grey hair. Herod offered him grapes and wine, both of which the Tribune took gratefully. After a gentlemanly exchange of greetings, Herod asked Trebonius what he could do for him.

"I have a message from His Excellency the Procurator, Your Highness," the soldier said.

Herod nodded.

"What does Gaius want?" he asked.

"He asks a favour of you and promises he will argue with the Emperor that you should be made a king if you agree," Trebonius replied.

Herod's brown eyes shone with excitement. Herodias was always asking him to seek the kingship. She wanted to be a Queen, not the wife of a Tetrarch.

"What favour does Gaius seek Tribune?"

"He wants you to take Yeshua Bar Yusuf from his custody and dispose of him in one of your desert fortresses."

Herod looked disappointed.

"What do you know of Jewish history and religion, Tribune?" Herod asked.

"Nothing, Your Highness."

Herod poured him another glass of wine and sat back in his chair in teaching mode.

"Eight hundred years ago, Israel was a small, but powerful kingdom. It was independent of the great empires of Assyria, Babylon and Egypt. A great and powerful king called Ahab ruled Israel. Ahab had made alliances with all the neighbours. The most important of these were the Phoenician cities of Tyre and Sidon. They founded Carthage, of which I'm sure you know."

Trebonius nodded. Every Roman knew about Carthage. He sipped his wine, wandering where this history lesson would lead.

Herod continued.

"Ahab married the daughter of the King of Tyre. Her name was Jezebel. She worshipped the local god, Baal. Ahab worshipped the Jewish God. She persuaded him to outlaw the worship of this God, and kill all of His prophets. They killed everyone except one, the most famous, Elijah. In the end Elijah was able to defeat her schemes, and the royal couple both met a sticky end. However, Ahab and Jezebel have the record of being the only Jewish king and queen to kill more than one prophet."

Trebonius smiled politely.

"Thank you for an interesting bit of history Your Highness. It was probably about the same time as my city was founded. I'm not sure how it relates to our present situation though."

Herod smiled and sipped his wine.

"A few months ago, Tribune Trebonius, I sent a message to Yeshua, ordering him to leave my dominions. He sent me a reply, reminding me of the story of Ahab and asking me if I wanted to be the second Jewish King to kill more than one prophet. He was referring to Jochanan whom I ordered to be beheaded. I'm not Jewish, of course, but I do not want that reputation. Yeshua hasn't attacked me directly either, unlike Jochanan."

"The High Priest is convinced that Yeshua intends to dethrone both you and him," Trebonius observed.

"I don't doubt it," Herod commented acidly. "The Lord Caiaphas can be very persuasive where his own interests are concerned. Personally I would not trust him further than I can throw him. If he wants Yeshua killed, and I can see why he might want him dead, he must do it himself."

Trebonius tried one final tack.

"I understand that the High Priest thinks Yeshua is planning a revolt against Rome, which could well destroy your own country."

Herod laughed.

"Trebonius, don't be so naive! Caiaphas and his

father in law have supported and even instigated most of the so-called Messiahs who Gaius and his predecessors have had to put down. The Temple is the centre of most of the conspiracies against Gaius and me. The only reason he's not supporting this one is because the revolt, if revolt it is, is aimed at Caiaphas himself!"

Trebonius finished his wine and stood up. He smiled at Herod and concluded,

"And not even the offer of a Royal title can persuade you?"

Herod smiled sadly, standing also to bid the soldier goodbye.

"No, Tribune. Although I admit that I am tempted, the price is too high. I will remain a lowly Tetrarch and resign myself to many more hours of haranguing by my wife on her sense of injustice! Give my greetings to Gaius and my regrets that I cannot help him in his dilemma, in which he has my fullest sympathy, since I have more experience of the results of killing prophets than any man alive in Israel.

"Perhaps I may be able to help next time.

"In the meantime, tell him I suggested that he should do one of three things. Either send Yeshua back to Caiaphas with a nice note saying, 'Thanks but no thanks', or he should find some punishment short of execution, like the galleys, or he should grit his teeth and sign the order for crucifixion and forget about it."

Trebonius thanked the Tetrarch, promised to convey his message to Pilate, and left. Herod escorted Trebonius to his horse, and watched as he and his escort mounted and clattered out of the courtyard. Then he turned back and called for his steward, to arrange the evening's Passover celebrations.

**

A meeting was just coming to an end at the house with the Upper Room. It had been a disjointed and dejected meeting of worried men and women. Simeon the fisherman was completely crushed by his failure to support Yeshua when he needed it and by the fact that he had been saved by the traitor Judah. No one knew where Thomas was, since no one could recall seeing him since he had left them with Judah to return to the city the night before. The assumption was that he was either dead or taken prisoner. The women were distraught, especially Yeshua's mother and wife. His sons were also very distressed.

Jacob, Yeshua's brother, took charge. There was no real discussion.

"You disciples are too well known to leave the house for any reason. Therefore, you must stay here. The gates must remain locked all day, and no outsider must be admitted unless I agree it. You, women, however, are not known. You can go to support Yeshua at Golgotha safely, I think."

"I will lead them," Mariam, Yeshua's wife, said.

"I am going too," Yeshua's mother insisted.

"I intend to go with my grandmother, to protect her, and say goodbye to my father" Jochanan added.

Jacob looked doubtful. Jochanan looked determined and defiant. Jacob gave way.

"That's fine. You both have the right to be there. My mother will need support, and you, as a teenager, will not be at risk. I will stay here with your brother, and, later go to the Temple to buy the Passover lamb, since no one there knows me."

Marcus interrupted.

"Julia and I have to go to the Antonia to collect our family when Pilate releases them."

"That's fine, Marcus. Of course you should do that. Pilate won't trouble either of you. Bring your family back here to observe Passover with us. While you're out, you can buy the food we need from the market. Some of the remaining women will help you. Incidentally, keep your ears open for any rumour. I would like to know what happened to Thomas."

Jacob looked around. No one had anything else to add, so he closed the meeting.

**

Trebonius returned to the Antonia, past the gathering crowd of curious onlookers. He dismissed his escort and sent his horse to be rubbed down and stabled, before making his way to Pilate to report.

Pilate looked up as he entered his office. Trebonius shook his head.

"I thought so," Pilate sighed, as he called for one of the Guards.

The Guard entered, saluted and listened as Pilate ordered him to go down to the prison and instruct the jailors to bring their three prisoners to the judgement seat. The Guard left.

Pilate turned his attention to his Tribune.

"Why?" he asked.

"Herod is afraid, Gaius. He has killed one prophet; he doesn't want to kill another. He was apologetic and appreciative, but not even the offer of a royal title could move him. He suggested that you should send the man back to Caiaphas."

"If I could send him to that Bastard, I would certainly do so," Pilate growled. "Did Herod suggest anything else Lucius?"

"Yes, Gaius. He said that, if you could not send

Yeshua back to Caiaphas, you should send him to the galleys or the mines, or, failing that, grit your teeth and send him to Golgotha."

"A masterly summary of my options, and he's right! It's Golgotha, I'm afraid. Did Herod say anything else?"

"Yes, he sent his sympathy. He said he understood your position probably better than anyone living today. He was sorry he could not help you, but promised he would make amends another time."

Pilate smiled.

"Antipas is as cunning as a fox, but loyal too. He's basically a good man and a friend of Rome. The Jews don't deserve to have him as their ruler. He'd make a good Consul if only he were a Roman."

They stood up. Pilate picked up the laurel wreath and placed it on his head.

"Come on Lucius let's get this over with."

Pontius Pilate and Lucius Trebonius walked together through the corridors, out through the doors, onto a wide raised marble patio, where a marble seat was set against the wall. The patio faced on to a wide plaza, where a crowd had gathered, held back by a line of troops. There was a buzz of conversation as the two Romans appeared. This turned to gasps of surprise as the three prisoners were produced, chained together by the wrists and dressed as a king with two guards, except that all were naked apart from the middle one, who wore a red cloak, which was secured around his neck but did not disguise his lack of clothing. He was carrying a stone in one hand and a stick in the other. He wore a circlet of thorns on his head. The other two wore Roman helmets, carried mock spears and wore swords. Pilate made them face the crowd and introduced them.

379

"This is King Yeshua and his faithful guards. I'm afraid they are somewhat impoverished, since they lack armour and Yeshua has forgotten his royal gown."

Pilate smiled at the crowd. They laughed back, as he hoped they would, at the ridiculous scene. Pilate turned to the prisoners.

"Guards, salute your King," he ordered.

They attempted to make the Roman salute, clenched fist across the chest, but, in doing so, the one on Yeshua's left yanked his arm sharply away. In his surprise, Yeshua dropped the heavy stone orb, which landed on his foot. He jumped back, bringing all three crashing down in a tangle of bodies. His crown fell off, he lost his sceptre and the two 'guards' dropped their spears and lost their helmets. This caused further laughter among the crowd. Pilate laughed too, as he had them hauled to their feet.

"Do you want to keep them or shall I send them to Golgotha?" he asked them.

"Send them to Golgotha!" they shouted back.

"What?" said an apparently surprised Pilate. "Shall I crucify your King and his attendants?"

"Caesar is our King!" they shouted back.

"That's fine," Pilate replied smiling. "That's the sort of loyalty Caesar likes to hear."

He paused.

"Golgotha it is then."

He turned to the jailors.

"Take them away and get them ready."

Quintus saluted and asked him,

"What about clothing sir?"

Pilate thought for a moment.

"Don't waste time looking for their outer clothes. Loincloths only. Otherwise, send them as they are. You'll only have to strip them at Golgotha, and they won't offend the sensitivities of the crowds because they'll be surrounded by troops on the way out."

Quintus saluted and the jailors led the prisoners away. Pilate and Trebonius left the Judgement Seat. The crowd, fun over, drifted away. Pilate wrote out three charges and sent them down, via a soldier, to the jailors.

On arrival in the courtyard, the manacles were struck off the prisoners. Each prisoner was given a loincloth and instructed to put it on. Quintus made a point of dealing with Yeshua personally. He removed the cloak with a grin, telling Yeshua that he was not going to hide his glories from the world.

"Thank you for last night, darling," he said assuming the tones of a lover.

Yeshua allowed Quintus to strip him, standing in silent dignity. Quintus was surprised. He expected Yeshua to react to his taunting of him. He stood back and stared at Yeshua.

"Have you nothing to say to me?" he asked.

"What do you want me to say?" Yeshua answered.

Quintus did not reply.

"You have your job to do," Yeshua continued, "and I have mine. Do your job Quintus. It's not your fault. Others are responsible. Don't be afraid."

Quintus was astonished. Of all the reactions he could have expected from a prisoner in this position, this was not one of them.

Who is this man? Why is he so calm? He knows what is going to happen to him? He knows what I did to him? Why does he not curse me? Show signs of fear and hatred? What does he really think of me?

Quintus took Yeshua's wrists more gently than he intended and tied them to the crossbeam. He ensured the beam was evenly balanced on Yeshua's shoulders. Almost reluctantly, he realised he cared what this prisoner thought about him – but he did not understand why.

I must be getting soft! Perhaps I'm too old for this game!

Almost in reaction, he shoved Yeshua into the line, before taking his place in front of him, holding the notice of the charge Pilate had written out for Yeshua.

The three prisoners were arranged in order of execution. Two jailors picked up the wooden cross pieces one by one and laid them across the prisoners' shoulders, ensuring the beams were balanced, and tying their wrists to each end. When all was in order, each jailor picked up one of the charges, now nailed to a wooden board at the end of a pole. They each stood in front of their respective prisoner. Quintus carried Yeshua's charge sheet. For the two men arrested during the riot, the charge simply read "Murderer". For Yeshua, it read "Yeshua the Nazirite: The Jewish King". Each was written in Latin, the official language of the Roman Empire, Greek, the lingua franca, and Aramaic, the local language. This was so everyone could read it.

The fourth jailor picked up the bucket of tools. This contained the ropes, nails, hammer and mallet they would need. The bucket was designed to hang from a strap, which was worn over a shoulder. He also picked up and carried a whip and a small ladder. He was to follow the prisoners.

The century arranged itself around them, in a move of silent efficiency. Six ranks of five were to precede them, and another six to follow them. The remaining twenty soldiers were arranged in two single files of ten soldiers, one file on either side of the three prisoners and their jailors. The centurion mounted his horse, took his place at the head of the column, and ordered the unit to move out. The slow procession to Golgotha began.

Chapter 20

Execution

Passover was to be memorable for Simon for all the wrong reasons. Like Simeon, he was a fisherman. Unlike Simeon, he was an off shore fisherman. He worked in the Mediterranean, off the coast of Libya. His hometown was the port city of Cyrene, which had been built by order of Alexander the Great and remodelled as a Roman town during the time of Mark Antony and Cleopatra.

He had left his home about a month earlier, and made his way by stages, across the Western Desert, to the city of Alexandria. He had spent a week in the city, marvelling at its great temples and libraries, its royal palaces, now used by Roman officials, the magnificent port and, supremely, the Pharos, the great lighthouse, one of the wanders of the world, whose light could be seen far out to sea at night, guiding mariners safely to the port. It stood, three stories high, on an island in the middle of the bay formed by the mighty Nile as it entered the Great Sea.

Simon thought he could have stayed in the city for ever, but time was against him, so he reluctantly left for the north, following the sea coast, and avoiding the notorious Sinai Desert, first east and then north as it curved towards Syria. He walked slowly, enjoying the sun and sea, able to buy fruit and bread as he travelled and sampling the local wine. He travelled as far as the former Philistine city of Gaza, snuggling whitely along the coast, before turning inland and heading east, through the green and then increasingly brown land of Judaea. Cities and towns gave place to hamlets and villages, as he headed towards the holy city.

His last stopover had been a village near Jerusalem, which he noticed seemed to be oddly disturbed, although he did not know why. He guessed it was the excitement of Passover. He had left early that morning, and now, he enjoyed the view of Jerusalem from the Mount of Olives. He stood and gazed in wander at the mighty Temple towering, so much bigger than he had imagined, over the northern end of the city, smoke already rising from the sacrificial fires. His eyes strayed along the powerful walls that skirted the many hills that made up the city. He noted the many gates and the people, antlike at that distance, travelling in and out of them. His eyes moved on, taking in the Palaces and the Great Fortress, which dotted the city, and the many smaller houses that sprawled in between the walls. There it was at last, the Holy City, white stone, reflecting the bright sun. Simon sighed in contentment and relief. He had made it in time. He began the walk down to the city, his pace quickening in his eagerness to walk its streets at last.

**

Centurion Julius led the procession out across the courtyard, and under the gate, into the street. The pace was slow, since the heavy crossbeams burdened the prisoners. The fourth jailor carried a whip, which he used to encourage a prisoner if he lagged. One slash across the back was usually enough he knew. He did not have to use it much on this occasion, since the biggest problem was prisoners slipping on the stones, as a prisoner's bare feet, sweaty in the heat, slipped and, unbalanced by the heavy wooden beam he was

384

carrying, the prisoner fell headlong. He then had to be pulled back to his feet. The beam had to be rebalanced, and the prisoner moved on. The whip did not help this process.

Quintus noticed how the two condemned men in front of him showed their anger at their fate. Realising that there was no point in trying to hide their feelings from their guards, they cursed and swore at the crowd and at the men who were escorting them. The soldiers ignored them and their jailors laughed at them, but any help offered to them when they fell was done in a harsh and aggressive manner. His prisoner, on the other hand, was different. He did not complain, kept his quiet dignity and acted as though he wanted to be where he was and in the state he was. When he fell, which he did twice, he gratefully accepted the help that Quintus gave him to get back on to his feet. All this confused Quintus.

I do not understand this man. He should hate me after what I made him suffer. Why does he not appear to hate me? It's as though I have acted as his friend. I am not his friend. I am his torturer and executioner. It is almost as though he loved me. But no one loves Quintus – not even Quintus!

Quintus began to realise that he was actually afraid of Yeshua. He was afraid that Yeshua actually did love him. He was not sure that he could cope with such knowledge.

**

Five horsemen, accompanying Herod, also on horseback, clattered down the road, towards the procession. Herod halted his escort, and drew it to one side, allowing the procession to pass. The officer in charge of the escort saluted Centurion Julius, who returned the salute, as he passed. Herod guessed the nature of the procession, and watched curiously as the first set of soldiers passed, followed by the three prisoners carrying their crosses. He read the charge sheets and was especially interested to note the third prisoner, whose hair seemed to have been recently shorn, and who appeared to have been shaven. He looked very un-Jewish. He looked more like a Greek slave. He knew who the man was, and realised, from reports he had previously received, that his appearance had been altered, forcibly he guessed. He wandered why.

He waited until the last file of soldiers had passed, and then resumed his journey, forcing his way through the crowd that had started to follow. "Ghouls," he thought. "Most of them deserve crucifying themselves."

The mounted group forced their way to the entrance to the Antonia, where the guards saluted and let them through the gate. Once inside Herod dismounted, handed his horse to one of his escort, and approached the officer of the day, who was standing on the steps leading to the offices and barracks, wandering whom this man was. The officer walked down to challenge the visitor, but it was the Tetrarch who spoke, busily and with authority.

"Please tell the Procurator that the Tetrarch Herod Antipas has come to see him."

The officer saluted, asked Herod to wait, and went into the building.

Five minutes later, Pilate appeared, smiling. He embraced Herod.

"Antipas," he said, "What a delightful surprise! I never expected to see you today I thought you would be too busy."

The two men walked up the steps together.

"You keep forgetting, Gaius. I'm not Jewish. I pay lip service to Jewish beliefs, like my father did, but I don't actually give any credence to them. I find the gods of Greece and Rome much less demanding."

Pilate laughed.

"You're right, Antipas. I do keep forgetting! I need a break. It's been a tough morning. Come and join me in my private quarters."

The two walked together, with the intimacy of old friends. Herod commented.

"I passed the execution party on its way out. I see you chose the Golgotha solution."

"Not entirely, Antipas. I've put in a few modifications, two of which you no doubt noticed."

"Do you mean the fact that the prisoners were not scourged and were virtually naked, Gaius?"

"Absolutely, Antipas. I have given other instructions too. Thanks for your excellent advice, but you forget a fourth alternative. You forget that I'm a Roman Senator. No Roman Senator ever forgets the crowd. We know, in Rome, ever since the Gracchi and Saturninus, and, most recently, the murder of the Divine Julius Caesar, just how powerful and dangerous the mob can be. That's why we keep them happy with grain from Sicily or Egypt and the Circus. Hence we talk about 'Panis et Ludi', bread and games. I got the Jewish crowd to send Yeshua to Golgotha."

"How did you do that?" Herod asked.

"I defused any possible anger by creating a comedy scene, using the prisoners. They laughed them to the scaffold."

Pilate described the scene at the Judgement Seat, and Herod chuckled in appreciation.

"Very clever, Gaius," he conceded. "I would never have thought of that."

"Thank you Antipas," Pilate grinned happily. "I will

take that as a compliment. Come in and greet Julia." He opened the door to his apartment. "Julia dear," he called out. "Come and greet Prince Herod who has come to spend some time with us."

**

Simon met the procession as he entered the gate. He stood to one side as it passed him. He watched the officer on his horse and the six files of five soldiers pass. Then the procession changed, as he saw two single lines of soldiers escorting three nearly naked men carrying crosses, each preceded by a soldier carrying a sign. The third fell, and he watched as two men tried to lift him up. They failed and one of the men made a sign to the soldiers on the outer line nearest him. The column stopped and a soldier came towards him, picking him out among the silent crowd along the street. The soldier grabbed Simon by the arm.

"You look strong enough," he began. "You're not local are you?" he added, noting Simon's dark skin.

"No," Simon replied. "I'm from Cyrene in Libya. That's in Africa," he added.

"I thought so," the soldier commented. "Come with me, I have a job for you."

Simon was led through the cordon, and found he was standing beside the man who had fallen. He was still lying on the road. He noticed that one of the soldiers had begun to untie the man from the wooden beam he had been carrying on his already bruised shoulders. The man, once freed from his burden, was pulled to his feet.

Freed from the weight of the crossbeam, Yeshua stood upright. He looked around him and felt the cool air on his body. Quintus tied Yeshua's hands together behind his back. Simon thought this was more of a formality than anything else, since the prisoner could scarcely escape from eighty heavily armed Roman legionaries.

Simon stood, as two of the guards lifted the heavy beam and arranged it as comfortably as possible, balanced on his shoulders. He hooked his arms around the beam, and followed the man with the poster, as the procession resumed its slow march to Golgotha.

The prisoner murmured, "Thank you" to him.

He muttered, "Don't mention it," in reply.

Before he was ordered to be silent, the prisoner added in a low voice, "After you leave me, go to the house of Zechariah in Hezekiah Street. It has a courtyard and an upper room. Tell them you carried the cross for Yeshua Bar Yusuf. They will invite you to share Passover with them."

Simon thanked him. They began to move off, behind the poster, which proclaimed Yeshua, "The Jewish King." Yeshua, freed of the crossbeam, became more aware of his surroundings. He heard the mixed voices of the crowd, hidden behind the ranks of soldiers guarding him. Some of them were shouting abuse at him or at the soldiers, and others were crying.

Later Simon heard Yeshua mutter quietly,

"Don't cry for me, people of Jerusalem. Cry for yourselves. If this is happening now when everything's peaceful, what do you think will happen later when there's war?"

Quintus, by now, was beginning to feel guilty about this prisoner.

I don't think this man has done anything to deserve this death. Yet he is going to it with the same calmness that I would go to a party. I don't think I have ever seen such courage. What did he mean by saying he had a job

389

to do? Is his death part of something bigger? Am I just a tool being manipulated by some higher power? Who is this man? Why do I care about his fate? I treated him badly – and he shows no hatred of me. I simply do not understand it.

I only obeyed Pilate's orders. Why do I feel guilty about doing it? I didn't get any enjoyment from it because he never looked frightened. So what am I?

This man is concerned about everyone else except himself. Is he concerned about me? Could I bear it if he was?

Quintus walked in silent self-loathing. He turned around at one point to check that Yeshua was all right. He saw the calm figure of his prisoner walking behind him, erect and seemingly free, apart from the rope that bound him. He looked in Yeshua's eyes and saw himself reflected in them. Quintus saw an evil sadistic torturer reflected back at himself – and he felt guilty – not just for what he had done to Yeshua, but for what he had done to so many other prisoners. He turned away, afraid, in case Yeshua saw through him, and, worse, forgave him. Quintus felt he would not be able to bear that.

Yeshua saw a man beginning to be wracked by guilt. He prayed for Quintus silently as he walked to his death at Quintus' hands.

**

The poster proclaiming the charge against Yeshua was noticed by other, less friendly, eyes. A priest hurried to the Temple to inform Caiaphas, who made his way hastily to the Fortress, where he encountered Pilate and Herod, who came out to meet him. This, however, was the only concession he received.

"What can I do for you Lord Caiaphas?" Pilate asked.

"I am concerned about the wording of the charge sheet Excellency," Caiaphas explained. "To write that he is King of the Jews is an insult to all Jews."

"Would you prefer it if His Excellency had written Yeshua the Nazirite: The rightful High Priest?" Herod asked. "After all, that's the real reason for your hostility to him, isn't it Lord Caiaphas?"

Caiaphas treated the suggestion with disdain. Pilate asked him icily, "What wording do you suggest Lord Caiaphas?"

"Write that he claims to be our king."

Pilate grinned nastily.

"I'm sorry Lord High Priest, I don't usually change the words of conviction notices. If you wanted to determine the charge, you should have carried out the execution, not pushed it on to me."

He looked at Herod and grinned. Herod grinned back. Caiaphas looked from one to the other and knew he was beaten.

"You may smile now but you will both pay one day," he thought bitterly.

Pilate continued,

"I suggest you get on, Lord Caiaphas; you have a busy day ahead of you."

The High Priest bowed, in acknowledgement of the dismissal, turned away from the two rulers, hiding his real feelings, and left.

Herod and Pilate turned back towards Pilate's apartments. Herod commented as they walked back,

"We will both need to be careful in future Gaius. Caiaphas is angry and an angry man is dangerous. I know people call me 'the fox', but Caiaphas is a snake. Snakes can be deadly."

Pilate opened the door to his apartment.

"Then we'll just have to be careful, watch where we put our feet, or draw his fangs, Antipas."

**

Meanwhile the procession moved on, followed by a growing crowd, among whom were three of the women from Yeshua's party, led by his wife, Mariam; his mother, Mariam, accompanied by Jochanan; and the two disguised Pharisees, Nicodemus and Yusuf of Aramathea.

**

Waiting at Golgotha were three more women, each with a wineskin full of wine. This wine had been mixed with a powerful narcotic. A man she would never after be able to identify approached one of the women. He was remarkable because he was so unremarkable.

"Go to the third prisoner. His name is Yeshua Bar Yusuf. He will try to refuse your wine. Tell him that Judas Bar Abbas orders him to drink it. Do you understand?"

She nodded.

"Repeat the message," he said urgently.

"Go to the third prisoner, tell him Judas Bar Abbas orders him to drink," she repeated.

"Good," he said. "Stick to the lines and make sure he drinks."

She nodded. He disappeared into the crowd.

**

The procession arrived at the foot of Golgotha. The soldiers spread out to form a ring around the foot of the hill, to keep the crowds back. Within the ring the three prisoners and their jailors stood. Quintus dismissed Simon with thanks. Simon wished Yeshua good luck, and passed through the line of troops, anxious to get away from this scene of future suffering and death. The jailors untied the three prisoners, taking the beams and laying them on the grass. Quintus untied Yeshua's hands. Yeshua looked at him with a gentle smile. Quintus turned away, feeling ashamed and unable to cope with Yeshua's strength.

The three women came forward, and offered their drugged wine, as was customary. The two rioters made no objection and drank deeply of the drugged wine. Yeshua tried to object, but, when the woman who served him whispered that Judas Bar Abbas instructed him to drink, he did so. He reflected that, in any case, his vow had already been violated by the actions of Quintus.

The women withdrew through the line of soldiers. The prisoners were ordered to strip and lie down on their backs. As Yeshua lay down, he murmured softly,

"Father, forgive them, because they don't know what they are doing."

Quintus heard these words and felt them like a sword going through his soul. The man he had tortured and was about to kill was praying for him. Quintus had served many years in the legions. He respected courage when he saw it, and he knew he saw it here. He felt he was beginning to respond to Yeshua's obvious love for everyone.

Does he love me? Do I love him? Is it too late for that? Can I love someone as I drive a nail through his wrist and hoist him up a cross?

The jailors waited for a few minutes, watching the drug take effect on each prisoner. When they judged that each was fully sedated, they gathered around the first man. The beam was pulled down to him and laid above his head. Two men lifted his left arm; one held his wrist down, and the other drove a nail through it. The same process was followed with the right hand. They moved on to the second man, and nailed him in the same way. Finally they did the same with Yeshua. Once all were nailed down, they gave them extra security by roping the arms of the three men to their crossbeams.

After this, working as a team, they dragged each man up the hill, and up an upright or a tree, already in the ground. They lifted each prisoner in the same way. One man placed the ladder against the back of the upright, and climbed it, ready to pull the crossbeam up the last few centimetres and nail it in place. Two men lifted the beam with its load, one holding each end. The fourth held the prisoner around the waist, lifted his body from the ground, and guided it as it rose up into the air. Once the bar was pulled up to its intended junction with the upright, they nailed and roped the cross beam in place. Afterwards, the first two prisoners' feet were secured to the bases of their crosses with a single nail in each case through both ankles.

The two rioters were crucified on either side of Yeshua. Yeshua's feet were tightly tied to the base of his cross. All three men hung about a few inches from the ground with their arms outspread. The two rioters were arranged so they half-faced each other.

Life had come full circle for Yeshua. He saw the man hanging from a cross on his Bar Mitzvah. Now he hung from a cross himself. The cross, which had first cast its long shadow over Yeshua on his Bar Mitzvah, had finally claimed him.

Julius ordered half his men to withdraw to the city. The excitement was over, and he no longer needed all his men. He ordered them to return after three hours to relieve those on duty. The executioners settled down at the foot of the crosses, playing dice. They played for the prisoners' clothes and possessions.

Quintus insisted on taking the tunic, which had belonged to Yeshua. He felt this was an important token of the feeling, the love that he realised Yeshua had for him. He had also given the tunic to him, albeit under duress. He did not want to give it to anyone else. In exchange for this, he stayed out of the game, instead wandering over to watch with sorrow the slow death of the man he finally accepted he had come to love. Later, after the game was over, the four men dug a deep pit to provide a burial place for the corpses of the three men on the crosses.

Yeshua's wife, Mariam, and some of the other women from his party quietly joined the crowd at Golgotha. They stood and watched in silence as the crowd mocked Yeshua and the Priests and their followers yelled at him to use his power to get off the cross.

Jochanan brought Yeshua's mother to join them. After standing, watching, with the women for some time, Mariam wanted to get closer to her son. Jochanan took her through the crowd to the Centurion, who was talking to some of the soldiers encircling the hill. He looked up as the two drew near. Two soldiers lowered their javelins to block their way, but Julius ordered them to let the two through.

"What do you want boy?" he asked Jochanan, not unkindly.

"I am Yeshua's son, and this is his mother, Mariam. May we go and stand by the cross to comfort him?" Jochanan asked.

Julius looked at the two, and at the crowd beyond them. It was not normal, but then, he reflected, there was not a lot that was normal about this execution.

"All right," he said at last. "I don't see that it will do any harm. Tell me when you've had enough."

He ordered the soldiers to let them through.

**

Herod eventually left Pilate, to return to his Palace. Pilate returned to his office, called the duty officer, and instructed him to bring the family of Marcus and Julia to him. They came to him, and stood in a line, nervously awaiting his judgement. Pilate smiled at them, and told them he was freeing them and returning their property as a Passover gift to their son and daughter, who had served him and the Emperor well.

"However, you have all been found guilty of treason against Rome. Therefore, I am keeping your youngest son as my slave and as a hostage for your good behaviour. I will keep him for three years. In that time he will be properly treated and educated like a young Roman. If you have all kept out of trouble I will return him to you after that time. I promise that I will also see if I can free your other male relatives at the same time."

They thanked the Procurator, consoled their youngest son, and left the Fortress. Outside they found Julia and Marcus waiting for them. They followed them to the House with the Upper Room, arriving there in the early afternoon. Shortly afterwards, Simon, the man from Cyrene, knocked on the gate. Jacob, who had returned from the Temple, heard his story and ordered that Simon should be admitted.

Pilate sent the young boy, destined to be his hostage, to Julius, his slave master, to be placed in his care. He told Julius the boy was to be treated as he would his own son, and ordered that the boy should not be branded as a slave.

**

The men on the cross slowly revived. Yeshua became aware of the heat, his sweating and aching body, the pain in his arms as they carried the unnatural weight of his body, and the flies, which settled on him, attracted by his sweat. He saw the same thing was happening to the other two men. He heard, as through a haze, the voices of the crowd taunting them. Some made references to his shrunken manhood, a direct consequence of crucifixion. Others jeered that he was a magician, but couldn't magic himself off the cross. The voices faded to a constant buzz, almost indistinguishable from the buzz of the crowd and the flies.

The other two spoke to him, but they, too, seemed distant in the haze of noise and pain. One man was more aggressive than the other. Yeshua thought it was the younger man. He promised the older man that he would sleep in Paradise with him that night. The world shrank to his own body, which began to show all the signs of fever, becoming both very hot and very cold in turn. He realised, to his shame, that he had lost control of his bowels, as he felt the warm liquid seeping out of his body and flowing down his legs. Yeshua tried to separate himself from his body. He concentrated on his breathing, which was becoming more and more difficult and more and more painful with every breath. He tried to think of events in his life, but found he could not do so. The sky grew dark, whether from his imagination or in reality, he did not know.

He cried out to God in his agony.

"My God, my God, why have you abandoned me?"

But it's not only God, it's everyone I know.

The only one who seems to care is the man who

raped and abused me last night. He is my enemy.

Love your enemy. Die for your enemy. Make your enemy your friend.

Is that what I have done? I'm dying. I know I'm dying.

Is this what God intends? Is this victory, or is it defeat?

If it's victory, how will I know? Do I have to wait, like Job, for the after life, to be assured of victory and vindication?

Will God send His angels to rescue me?

Will I see the Kingdom come?

Yeshua felt warm hands grasp his feet and legs, dirty as they were with dust and his own excrement. He looked down into the upturned, loving and concerned, faces of his mother and eldest son.

"I promised you I would be with you to the end, son," his mother whispered.

"Is this really the end, mother?" Yeshua asked quietly.

"For you, father, yes," said a weeping Jochanan. "For us, no. We have to go on without you, but carrying on your work."

"I know," Yeshua whispered, finding difficulty in breathing and talking. "Look after your mother and my mother for me, son."

"I will, father," Jochanan answered.

"Mother," Yeshua concluded. "Look after my sons and my wife. They will need you."

"Of course I will, son."

Yeshua looked up. He thought he saw a bright light appear through the darkness. He had seen the Kingdom coming! Satisfied that he had achieved his mission, he called out.

"I am thirsty, please give me a drink."

Julius gave Quintus a wineskin.

"Take it to the prisoner," he ordered.

Quintus desperately wanted to atone in some way for the way he had treated Yeshua. Julius' order gave him an opportunity. He ran to the foot of the cross, carrying the short ladder and the wineskin. He placed the ladder against the crossbeam, with the ladder ends against the crossbeam. He climbed up three steps, so his face was level with the suffering face of Yeshua. He saw the sweat and the agony lines on his forehead, as well as the scars from the thorns. Quintus wiped Yeshua's face tenderly with a cloth. He spoke to Yeshua.

"Forgive me, Lord, I didn't know what I was doing."

"You were my enemy, Quintus. I have forgiven you. Are you now my friend?"

"I am your friend, Yeshua," Quintus replied gently.

Quintus placed the tip of the wineskin in Yeshua's mouth. He lovingly eased the drugged liquid to sooth Yeshua's parched throat. Yeshua drank deeply.

"Thank you friend," Yeshua whispered.

Quintus climbed down the ladder. Yeshua raised his head, looked into the growing light, and, summoned up what remained of his strength.

"It is accomplished!" he cried.

His head then dropped forward, and he ceased to breath.

Chapter 21

Aftermath

Jerusalem, April 32AD (Friday night and Saturday)

When she saw what had happened to Yeshua, Mariam, his mother, burst into tears, and was helped away by an equally tearful Jochanan, and by Quintus. In the Temple, the bleating of lambs being led to the priests to be sacrificed marked the moment.

Julius walked over to the cross, looked up at Yeshua, gave him the Roman salute, and spoke loudly,

"Ave atque vale, Ieshua Patiens, Rex Iudaeorum. Tui interfecti te salutat." (Hail and farewell, Yeshua the Patient, King of the Jews. Your killers salute you.)

One of the soldiers added,

"He was only a Jew; but he died like a Roman, and like a Roman soldier too."

He also saluted.

Quintus wept openly.

Julius turned to the man in black standing near him.

"Go now, and go quickly," he said. "You've got very little time. Go to Pilate and get permission to take him down."

Yusuf of Aramathea ran from the execution site. He found Pilate in his office and was given a signed paper without comment. He returned within the hour.

Julius ordered that the soldiers disperse the few people who remained. Jochanan took his grandmother away, while the other women remained nearby, watching. Quintus helped Yusuf and Nicodemus remove the nails from Yeshua's wrists and take his body gently down. Yusuf took his feet and Nicodemus took his arms. Together they carried the body of Yeshua away, followed by Yeshua's wife, Mariam (who was also weeping) and Salome and another woman named Mariam, who were both supporting her. They carried Yeshua's body through a gate into a nearby garden, at the foot of a cliff. In a cave there, they laid the body on a stone slab at the back. Yeshua was laid on his back with his hands crossed over his stomach. His body was washed, and a white sheet was laid over it. Finally, the two men rolled a big stone across the front of the cave. They passed the women as they left.

"You can finish things off for us after Sabbath," Yusuf told them.

The women returned to the house in Hezekiah Street.

**

Judah and Thomas camped for the night and celebrated Passover without the food. Their thoughts turned to Yeshua.

"I wander how it all turned out," Judah said.

"We will find out in due course," Thomas replied. "But, I feel sure that something will turn up."

**

That evening Pilate received a report from Centurion Julius.

"I followed your instructions exactly, Your Excellency. Yeshua was persuaded to drink the drugged wine before crucifixion. Great care was taken not to damage any major artery during the nailing of the wrists. His ankles were tied, not nailed to the cross upright. As he

401

began to fail, we gave him the wine laced with Belladonna, the drug, which mimics death. Nicodemus was given enough notice to get him down. All was done according to your instruction. What the outcome will be, no one can tell."

"Thank you Julius," Pilate replied. "What happened to the other prisoners?"

"The older of the two men crucified with Yeshua saw what had happened. He begged us to help him die too. The younger abused him as a coward. The executioners looked at me. I nodded. One gave the dying man some of the drugged wine we previously gave to Yeshua. He collapsed on the cross and died shortly afterwards, after commending his soul to his god.

"After we had removed Yeshua from his cross and the oldest prisoner had died, I ordered the remaining onlookers to leave. Then I instructed the executioners to take a mallet and smash the legs of the remaining man, to hasten his death. The sound of the breaking bones echoed around the site. I thought they could probably hear it in the city. The shock of the smashing of the legs blasted through the younger man's body and smashed his heart. He cried out in pain and shock. He was dead within minutes.

"Once his death was confirmed, we took the two remaining bodies down and tumbled them into the burial pit, which we then filled with earth. Once our job was completed, we returned to the fortress."

"You have done all that you could do, Centurion. You have my thanks. Go and rest. Give your Century the day off tomorrow."

Julius saluted, thanked Pilate and left the office. Pilate gave an enigmatic smile, closed the office door, and walked to his apartment. On his arrival, he embraced his wife with more enthusiasm than usual.

That night, Quintus retired from the Army as the Passover began across the city.

**

Two men made their way to Caiaphas's house and reported the death of Yeshua and his burial by two unknown men in a private plot. Furious at what he saw as Pilate's chicanery and suspicious about his motives, worried in case Yeshua's followers were going to try to claim that Yeshua never died, and still smarting from his insulting treatment by Pilate and Herod earlier, Caiaphas ordered two men from the Temple Guard to guard the tomb once the Passover was over. As he said to his father-in-law later, "I would have preferred the Romans to have burnt the body publicly, or to have sent it to us for disposal, so we could be sure that there can be no question that the charlatan is dead and gone."

Throughout the city and country Jewish families were celebrating Passover.

Feeling angry but triumphant, Caiaphas and Annas joined together to celebrate Passover with their families. Even Herod went through the formalities.

**

Yeshua's disciples and family kept the Passover, observing the ceremonies, but without the joy. For the first time they used the grace as a memorial to Yeshua, as he had instructed them.

At the end of the meal, Jochanan and Mariam described the death of Yeshua. Jochanan said that he thought that there was something special about the feelings of Quintus for Yeshua.

Simon of Cyrene explained how he had helped Yeshua by carrying his cross.

The other women described how the two strangers in black had buried Yeshua and what the men had said to them as they left.

Jacob greeted the family of Julia and Marcus, and congratulated them on their release.

"At least," he said, "You have something to be happy about this Passover time. My brother did not die wholly in vain."

Jacob passed around the loving cup at the end of the festive meal, with the words,

"To my brother, Yeshua, the Son of Abraham and Yusuf, the Son of Judas Macabbaeus, the Son of David, the son of Aaron."

They shared the cup. Jacob repeated the traditional Passover Prayer, "Next year in Jerusalem".

Then they all rested.

**

Judah and Thomas continued their journey deep into the Judaean Wilderness. They camped overnight on the second night of their journey, and were disturbed, in the early morning by a movement in the earth. They woke up, on Sunday morning feeling strangely relieved, although they did not know why. Late in the afternoon they reached Qumr'an, and reported the whole sequence of events to the Community that evening.

Next morning Thomas began his journey back to Jerusalem, while Judah began his new duties as Bar Abbas, which were to last for many years, and resumed his former work training the Qumr'an recruits in theology and warfare. Thomas expected to be back in Jerusalem by Wednesday afternoon. He did not know what he would find there.

**

Next morning was the Sabbath. It was intended to be a day of rest. Pilate and Herod, however, had both had enough of Jerusalem. They had agreed at their meeting the previous day that they were both going to return home. They left at first light, although first light for Pilate's troops was earlier than first light for Herod's men, as Pilate pointed out as the men came together, on horseback, at the head of their troops, on either side of the Market Place. Pilate and Herod left their men and rode to meet each other. Both wore military uniform, surmounted by red cloaks, which flapped in the wind. They grasped each other's hand and Pilate greeted Herod with a relieved laugh.

"Your men find sunrise to be later than mine you old fox! Your men obviously have more fun at night then mine do!"

"Your men do too much soldiering for their own good," Herod laughed. "Have a safe trip to Caesarea, old friend."

"I hope you have an equally safe one to Macchaerus, old friend."

"I'm not going there, Gaius," Herod grinned. "I want to see some real life, so I'm going to visit my loyal subjects at Tiberias. I feel I need to be there to support my Governor, in case there is any negative reaction to Yeshua's death. He was very popular there."

Pilate nodded.

"I think you're wise, Antipas. If you need any help, tell me. I'll send Marcus Antonius back."

"Thank you for the offer Gaius. However, I'm sure they'll be no problems."

Herod paused and grinned, before adding, " See you at Pentecost."

They clasped hands for a second time, wheeled their horses round and led their cavalcades out of the city.

Pilate headed west and Herod headed north.

**

Watching the two pagan rulers of the city meet and leave was the third ruler, who had been called to the Temple. He was shocked to discover that an act of vandalism and sacrilege had occurred sometime during the night. He was taken to the inner sanctuary to be shown that the thick curtain that divided the closed inner half, which was open only to the High Priest, and then only on the Day of Atonement, from the outer half, which was open to the priests and where daily sacrifices were made, had been slashed in half, from top to bottom, with either a knife or a sword.

Enquiries established that the outrage had occurred sometime between late afternoon on Friday and first light on Saturday. Other enquiries established that an anonymous man had been seen near the sanctuary. He was remarkable because he was so unremarkable. No one could describe him. It was while thinking about this that he saw the two pagan rulers of the city meeting, laughing and separating, and remembered how they had ganged up against him the previous day.

"Never mind," he muttered darkly, "There will be another time."

**

Trebonius following the instructions of Pilate, issued Quintus with his retirement papers and paid him off. Equipped with these, and with the promise of a farm somewhere in Judaea or Samaria, Quintus walked the streets of Jerusalem, seeking out information about the family of Yeshua. All he learnt was that they lived in Bethlehem. Eventually, he left the city for Bethlehem, where, next morning, he made contact with the younger brothers and sister of Yeshua. They sent him on to Bethany, and, from Bethany, he eventually made his way back to Jerusalem and the Upper Room, where he finally made contact with the immediate followers of Yeshua. Once they were aware of who he was, and what Yeshua had said to him, they made him welcome and he became an early Gentile follower of what they called "the Way."

**

In the morning, as Pilate and Herod made their way homeward over the mountains of Judaea, the followers of Yeshua met to discuss what had happened to their leader and the consequences for them. Each was afraid of the outcome, fearing that the Authorities were on the lookout for them, although no one had seen any evidence of a search.

Simeon spoke first. He blamed Judah for the disaster, saying he was the traitor who led their enemies to Gethsemane.

"I also failed Yeshua," he admitted. "I failed him in the Garden by attacking the thugs who came to arrest him. I failed him, as he foretold, by denying him at the High Priest's house. I was afraid."

Here he paused, thinking, before adding,

"I saw the traitor Judah Ish Kerioth leave the High Priest's house. He was carrying a rope to hang himself with."

They all wanted to believe this and to pass the blame entirely on to Judah, since it exempted them from any responsibility. Each man knew he had failed Yeshua in one way or another. Judah made a convenient scapegoat. It was convenient, too, that he was Judaean, and most of the rest were from Galilee.

407

Andreas, supporting his brother, spoke about the group's money.

"There's money missing," he claimed. "I bet Judah stole it!"

They all agreed with this. Bartholomew suggested that could explain Judah's action.

"Perhaps he feared discovery," he suggested.

Jacob (the brother of Yeshua) and Philip, both of whom knew the truth about what Yeshua had instructed Judah to do, said nothing to deter this view. Later Jacob suggested to the surviving former disciples of Jochanan that betrayal; followed by a guilt-induced suicide, would be a good cover for the new Bar Abbas.

At the same time, they all feared that Thomas had been captured or killed. No one had seen him since Thursday night. Everyone missed Thomas's quiet and calm organising skills. It was only now that Thomas and Judah were both gone that they realised just how much they had depended on the two of them.

Jochanan spoke next.

"I am the eldest son of Yeshua. He entrusted his wife and mother to my care. I should be the leader of the group."

Simeon (Cephas) objected vehemently.

"No! Yeshua told me I was the leader. I'm also the oldest. You are too young to lead us."

The group split between the two candidates. Jacob (the son of Yeshua), Matthaus and Bartholomew supported Jochanan. The remaining followers of Jochanan the prophet – Simeon the rebel, Philip and Thaddeus, as well as Andreas supported Simeon. No agreement seemed possible and the argument became more and more acrimonious.

Jacob, the brother of Yeshua, wandered whether this was what Yeshua had been putting up with. He resolved he was not going to permit it to continue. He remembered Yeshua's words to him on this subject, and ordered them to stop the argument.

"It is my decision that Cephas should lead your group of twelve. It is clear that my brother intended that. Jochanan is too young, and no one knows where Thomas is. I, however, will be the leader of everyone, as Abraham Bar Abbas intended and my brother agreed as recently as Wednesday evening."

The proposal was agreed unanimously.

This debate took much of the morning and was interrupted by the afternoon meal. They rested in the evening and resumed their meeting when the Sabbath was over and Julia, as the youngest, lit the special Havdalah candle that marked the end of Sabbath.

The central issue in the second meeting was their own future plans. Some felt that Thomas was still alive and that they should wait for his return. Jacob the elder was not sure that this was a wise idea.

"I think you should all return to Capernaum, to get away from the reach of Caiaphas and his thugs," he said.

He had heard that both Herod and Pilate had left the city, and also that Herod had refused to have anything to do with Yeshua's death. There was a lot of debate about this, with the group again being evenly split. Jacob, however, made the decision for them once again.

"I will remain here with the Judaean recruits and keep the house open as Yeshua wanted. If Thomas returns during the week, as I suspect he might," he concluded. "I will send him on to Capernaum."

The women said they were going to visit the tomb in the morning to complete the burial rites for Yeshua before they left. Most of the disciples were opposed to this, but Mariam, Yeshua's wife was adamant, and the

409

sons and brother of Yeshua supported them. In the end they decided that Mariam would lead the two other women who had been at Golgotha and the Garden on Friday evening back to the Garden at first light, carrying the herbs, spices and bandages needed to complete the burial. When they returned, they would all set out for Bethany and, from there, to Capernaum.

**

The people, who had come into the city to celebrate the Passover, began to leave.

**

Annas visited his son-in-law and the two reviewed the events of that tumultuous weekend. Overall, they thought they had successfully averted a major crisis. However, Caiaphas was still seething over the wording of the Charge sheet, and Herod's slighting reference to him. He was concerned that the two secular rulers appeared to have struck up a personal friendship, which would translate into political cooperation. He saw himself as being marginalised.

Caiaphas was also concerned over the implications of the decision to allow the burial of Yeshua's body in private ground. He believed he had limited the risk by placing guards on the garden.

Both men were mystified and alarmed by the assault on the curtain in the Temple. Caiaphas reported to his father-in-law.

"I have asked Judas Bar Micah, the Commander of the Guard, to make enquiries into the identity of this mysterious stranger, and I have also given orders for two slaves to repair the curtain.

"When they have finished, they will be eliminated. I

want no rumour of this event to get out. It would be very damaging.

"If we can find the perpetrator, I will call on our friends the Sicarii to deal with him."

Annas nodded in approval.

"You're learning, Yusuf," he said.

**

The family of Julia and Marcus left the house in Hezekiah Street with their daughter, but not their son, who stayed with Yeshua's family and followers, who later included an uncle of his, a wealthy man named Barnabas, who had lands in Cyprus. The rest of the family returned to their home on the Main Street, which Pilate had ordered to be reopened, and resumed their previous life. However, they were to be seen frequently, in the months and years ahead, at the house in Hezekiah Street, which became the headquarters of the new Movement. After three years, their youngest son was returned to them, and, later, one of the men was returned from the Roman Navy. The other men had died.

**

Night fell and the city slowly fell asleep after a tumultuous and exciting weekend. Outside of the city, the naked body of Yeshua lay lifeless under its sheet, on the cold slab in the cave in the garden, lying in the cool darkness created by the great stone. Yeshua was still under armed guard, as he had been since early Friday morning, although the armed guard had shrunk to just two men at the gate of the garden, both of whom had fallen asleep through boredom, lulled by the calls

411

of the birds and the hooting of a night owl. A gentle wind whispered through the trees.

At three in the morning, the city was disturbed by an earth tremor.

The birds fell silent just before it happened. The earth movement caused the stone to roll away, topple and smash on the ground. The gate, beside which the men slept, swung open and began to creak backwards and forwards in the breeze. One of the guards dreamed that he saw a figure in white float down the path towards him, pass him, and go out through the open gate. The figure, dressed in a long white robe, with a white scarf about its head, looked back at the guard and smiled at him sadly. The guard saw the smile and the eyes in a blank, black, otherwise featureless, face.

He awoke and shook his companion awake. He told him what he thought he had seen. The other guard laughed at him and told him that he was dreaming. The first guard objected.

"He opened the gate and passed through it," he shouted, angry that he was not being believed.

It was then that they noticed that the gate was swinging backwards and forwards.

"Coincidence," the second guard argued. "The wind blew it open, that's all."

"I don't know," the first guard responded. "I don't like it. I think we should check the tomb."

They argued about this for a few minutes before agreeing to do so. They both lit a torch, to light the path through the trees. As they went, they disturbed the birds, which flew into the air, squawking loudly. The path through the trees ended in a clearing at the base of a low cliff, in which the cave lay. They came to the end of the trees, only to see that the grave was open, with the stone lying smashed on the ground, and the cave staring black against the dark grey of the cliff, at them.

An owl hooted on their left, a bad omen. A bat brushed past their faces, unseen but felt by them. The wind suddenly blew out their torches. It was all too much. In terror, the two men dropped their spears and shields and fled from the garden.

They did not return to Jerusalem or the Temple. Instead both fled back to their villages, and stayed there.

**

The three women were also disturbed by the earth tremor. They took it as an omen and got up early. They gathered together their equipment, and set out for the garden, as the sky grew lighter. They exited through the city gate as soon as it opened, and reached the open gate of the garden as the sun rose.

However, they were not the first to arrive at the tomb.

It was Sunday morning.

PART FOUR

EPILOGUE

And suddenly there was a great earthquake; for an angel of the Lord, descending from heaven, came and rolled back the stone, and sat on it.

Gospel according to St Matthew, chapter 28, verse 2.

Epilogue

65AD

More than thirty years has gone by since that momentous Passover weekend in Jerusalem. Many of those involved in Yeshua's crucifixion, including Mariam (Yeshua's mother), Judah (once Ish Kerioth and later Bar Abbas), and all the rulers - Pilate and his wife, Julia, Antipas and his wife, Herodias, his brother Philip, Caiaphas and his father-in-law, Annas, and the Emperor Tiberius - are dead.

A new Emperor, Nero, rules Rome, which at present is wracked by drought. A new Herod, Agrippa II, the grandson of King Herod's oldest son, holds sway in Galilee and Philip's former lands in the north and east of Palestine. He is also responsible for the Temple, including the appointment of the High Priest, whose name is Ananus. While Florus, whose corruption, brutality and simple incompetence have begun to unite Jews and Samaritans against Rome, is the new Procurator of Judaea and nearby Samaria. Judaea and Samaria are trembling on the verge of violent revolt against Rome. – for Nero a real headache, that will undoubtedly worsen when Rome shortly comes to experience a catastrophic fire.

Some of the disciples, including Simeon the former rebel, Judas and Yeshua's younger son, Jacob, are dead. The others no longer live in Jerusalem. Jochanan, the son of Yeshua, recognised as a temple priest, is living and working in Ephesus. Thomas, who returned to Jerusalem three days after the day that became known to Christians as Easter Sunday, is kept busy spreading the Gospel in India. As for Cephas,

417

comfortable in the knowledge that Greece and Turkey both now have many churches that celebrate Christianity, he has taken the new faith to Rome, where he has been joined by the man once known as Saul, but more familiar to us, perhaps, as Paul.

Jacob, the brother of Yeshua, is acting as an alternative High Priest, as well as the head of the Christian Church.

In the city of Alexandria, anti-Jewish riots are occurring. And it is here that Marcus, Pilate's former slave and spy, and later loyal follower of Yeshua, is now a Bishop. He is sat at his desk, studiously writing on a large role of papyrus: a man too engrossed in this labour of love to be much bothered by the arrival in the room of Elder Rufus - whose father, Simon, had carried the cross for Yeshua.

Rufus steps quietly behind Marcus' desk and peers over the bishop's shoulder, that he might see what he is writing today.

When the Sabbath was over, Mariam of Magdala, and Mariam the mother of Jochanan and Jacob, and Salome bought spices, so that they might go and anoint Yeshua's body. Very early on Sunday, when the sun had risen, they went to the tomb. They asked each other on the way to the garden,

"Who will roll away the stone for us from the mouth of the tomb?"

When they arrived, they saw that the stone, which was very large, lay shattered on the ground in front of the cave entrance. As they entered the tomb, they saw a young man, dressed in a white robe, sitting on the right hand side; and they were frightened. But he said to them,

"Don't be frightened; you're looking for Yeshua the Nazirite, who was crucified. He has been raised; he is not here. Look, there is the place they laid him. But go

and tell Cephas and the other disciples that he is going ahead of you to Galilee; there you will see him, just as he told you."

They went out and fled from the tomb, for they were terrified and confused; and they said nothing to anyone for they were afraid.

At this point, and with a contented sigh, if one touched with more than a little relief, Marcus lays his pen upon its rest: he has, at long last, completed his task, which, in time, will become better known as the Gospel according to St Mark.*

"You are surely not ending the book there Lord Bishop?" Has not the story has gone on far beyond that?" questions a puzzled Rufus.

Marcus smiles benignly. "You are right in what you say, Rufus of Cyrene. However, only God can complete this story, by sending Yeshua back, and none of us knows when He will do that."

"But we know that the women did eventually speak, and the riddles got solved,"

"Very true, but what they claim is a matter of belief, not of unchallenged fact. The facts are three women went to the tomb to complete the burial rites and found the body of Yeshua gone. A boy was sitting there who spoke to them, and they ran away because they were afraid. I personally can vouch for the truth of that.... I was that boy."

That revelation casually uttered, Marcus promptly rolls up the scroll to give into the care of Rufus. And, in handing it over, Yeshua's words in the Garden of Gethsemane come to Marcus' mind.

I have my role to play, and you will have yours,

---

* *The version shown above of chapter 16 verses 1 to 8 is in the NRSV translation, but slightly modified. See the note on the ending in the notes on John Mark, which follow.*

Marcus. Some day, in a city far from here, you will write my story.

"And now I have done so, Lord," he mutters, looking satisfyingly to Heaven.

"What did you say, my Lord Bishop?" asks Rufus, a little baffled.

"Nothing of importance, Rufus. Nothing of importance. I was just completing a conversation. I once had. Now let us get down to our daily duties. Take a seat. The latest information please about the Nag Hamadi Gnostics......."

As the morning lengthens, and the increasing bustling of Alexandria about its business invades the room, two clergymen hear it not, for they are in deep discussion.

Is it not said all men want to put the world to rights!

Note on John Mark

John Mark (called Marcus in the novel) was the writer of the first Christian Gospel. He was the nephew of Barnabas, the Companion of St Paul, and an important member of the Church in Antioch.

By tradition, he was the youth who ran away naked from the Garden of Gethsemane, and, some theologians have suggested, the boy in white in the tomb of Jesus when the women came to complete the burial.

According to Acts Mark travelled with Barnabas and Paul to Cyprus, where Barnabas had property on their First Missionary Journey, but turned back, ill (or homesick) when the other two crossed into Roman Asia. He caused a split between the other two men when Paul set out on his second journey and Barnabas wanted to take him with them. He travelled with Barnabas back to Cyprus, but, according to Paul's letters to Timothy and Titus, was later with Paul and Peter in Rome.

According to Eusebius, Mark was sent from there to Alexandria, which had become a centre of early Christian Gnosticism. It may be that his Gospel represents a first attempt by the Church to deal with this heresy, which downplayed the reality of the humanity of the Christ.

Shadow of the Cross is largely based on the Gospel of St Mark, which is one of the most influential books in the history of literature because it was a new concept when it was written. It shocked the leaders of the early Christian Church by its bluntness and the sharpness of its portrayal of a group of men and women about whom most of his contemporaries knew very little. The Gospel of Mark is interesting for what it did not include, as much as for what it did include.

There is no account of the life of Jesus before he

reached the age of 35. Jesus lived, according to most commentators, for 37 years. Mark's Gospel opens with the coming of John the Baptist. There is little attempt at a coherent account of his mission. Indeed, the Gospel moves at such apparently breathless haste, that all the events, except those of the last week, have been calculated as being possible to telescope into six months.

There is no interest in Jesus' personal life, even though this Jesus is the most human of the four Gospel accounts of the life of the Christ.

The account of his suffering and death covers 25% of the Gospel, and there is no account of the Resurrection appearances. Most modern theologians agree that Mark's last words were those in Chapter 16 verse 8: *They said nothing to anyone because they were afraid*.

Verses 9 to 20 appear to be a summary of the relevant passages in Luke and Matthew and seem to have been added later, to bring Mark into line with the other two Gospels. The last chapter suggests why Mark may have ended his Gospel as he did. (If you are interested, you will find the case argued in C. K. Barrett's commentary on Mark.)

The first Christian commentary on the New Testament comments, on the Gospel according to St Mark:

Mark wrote down, "although not in order, all that he remembered from Peter."

Afterword

Shadow of the Cross is a new story about Jesus of Nazareth. His life and teaching is central to European culture and the general cultural inheritance of the world. We all think we know whom he was, what he did, what happened to him, and why it happened, but we don't! I have used the unfamiliar Hebrew versions of the more familiar Biblical names to make the story easier to read on its own terms.

Shadow of the Cross is a novel. It is neither a statement of an alternative theology, nor is it intended to challenge orthodox beliefs. It is neither a different Gospel, nor an attempt to amend the traditions, doctrines and beliefs that have grown up around this most influential and enigmatic figure. Instead it is an exploration of what might have happened had things been different from the orthodox tradition, which you hear expounded every week in the churches. It is intended to entertain, but also has a message. It is up to you, the Reader, to discover it.

The starting point of the novel is the quotation about James, the brother of Jesus, from Eusebius, quoted at the start of the novel. The reference from Josephus quoted by Eusebius exists in another version, referred to by the Christian writer, Origen. This variant said that James was in the habit of offering sacrifices for the people of Israel in the Holy of Holies on the Day of Atonement. Origen claimed that Jewish extremists murdered him after one such sacrifice. Origen also, incidentally, claimed that John the Apostle was a senior member of the priesthood. If James was offering sacrifice for the people, then he was acting as High Priest, because only the High Priest could do it. If James was High Priest, then so also Jesus should have been, since the post was hereditary within the descendents of Aaron. That was the starting point of the novel.

At the end the reader is still left with a profound mystery, just as St Mark intended us to be. What did happen in that Garden outside the city wall of Jerusalem one early Sunday morning in April 32 AD?

Finally, I wish to thank the following people:

Ezechi, my eldest son, who suggested I wrote this novel and who read it for me;

Harry and Margaret, Leon, Elizabeth, David and my wife, **Joanna**, who have read it and made suggestions;

Kingsley Barrett, to whom this book is dedicated, and who started me on my road to Mark so many years ago, as my tutor, in Durham;

Elaine, my daughter, who designed the cover;

And **Daniel**, my editor and publisher, who has made the brave decision to publish it;

As well as all those who have consciously, or unconsciously helped or inspired me.

Without their help and encouragement, *Shadow of the Cross* would not have been written.